Fly by Wire

Fly by Wire

A Novel

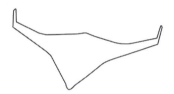

Ward Larsen

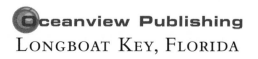

Oceanview Publishing

LONGBOAT KEY, FLORIDA

ISBN: 978-1-933515-86-1

Published in the United States of America by Oceanview Publishing,
Longboat Key, Florida
www.oceanviewpub.com

2 4 6 8 10 9 7 5 3 1

PRINTED IN THE UNITED STATES OF AMERICA

To Rose

Fly-by-wire \ 'flɪ-bɪ-ˌwɪ(ə)r \ adjective, (1968) : of, relating to, being, or utilizing a flight-control system in which controls are operated electrically rather than mechanically

—*Merriam-Webster's 11th Collegiate Dictionary*

Fly by Wire

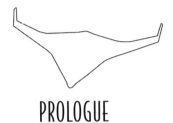

PROLOGUE

MARSEILLE, FRANCE

The room was cool and dark by design. Three dozen computer workstations sat ready, the hum of ventilation fans a constant backdrop. Most of the large circular screens were in a standby mode, vacant and black, but those in action glowed with flecks of green, tiny winged crosses that were accompanied by multicolored data tags. A handful of men and women sat watching, each hunched in a God's eye view of their respective domain. The air traffic control center, Marseille High Sector, was coming to the end of its night shift.

Dimly lit and without windows, the bunker had no natural circadian rhythm, no guidance from sunlight or darkness to govern the day's cycle. These customary markers were replaced by instruments of far greater precision — digital clocks. Mounted on walls and support columns, there were more than a dozen scattered throughout the room, glowing red numbers presented in twenty-four-hour format and synchronized to a painstaking accuracy. The clocks were situated, without fail, in pairs — one registering Zulu time, the universal standard of aviation, and the other, in a blatant act of Gallic defiance, Central European time. In France, it was 5:56 in the morning.

Serge Flourent was nearing the end of his shift. His coffee cup long empty, the air traffic controller struggled to keep his eyes open. Only five of the operating stations around him were occupied. In another hour, the morning rush would be well under way, no fewer than two dozen men and women issuing directives into their microphones, an incessant chatter of frequencies, call signs, and navigation fixes. In spite of the rough hours, Flourent preferred the solitude of the night shift.

His eyes fluttered as a new blip came to his screen. World Express Flight 801. The data strip told him the aircraft was a new CargoAir C-500, headed across the Atlantic to KIAH, Houston Intercontinental Airport. Another delivery from the factory, no doubt.

A female voice crackled into his headset, "Marseille, WorldEx 801 checking in, flight level three eight zero. *Bonjour!*"

Flourent grinned. English was the mandatory language for air traffic control everywhere, but at least the American pilot was trying to be civil.

"WorldEx 801, Marseille Control. *Bonjour.*" Flourent was in a generous mood. "WorldEx 801, you are cleared direct Sierra Hotel Alpha."

"WorldEx 801, roger. Cleared direct Shannon."

Flourent watched the blip on his screen change its vector ever so slightly as the pilot applied the shortcut. Everything again fell quiet. He looked up just in time to see the clock turn to the new hour. His relief would arrive for the hand-off briefing in fifteen minutes. Then Flourent could go home to his warm bed and his lukewarm girlfriend. These were the tired thoughts drifting through his head when he saw the first sign of trouble.

The altitude display for World Express 801 showed a descent of five hundred feet. *Careless Americans.*

"WorldEx 801, check altitude."

He waited patiently, but got no response. The number on Flourent's screen flashed red as it reached one thousand feet below the assigned cruising level.

"WorldEx 801, Marseille Control, over?"

Still no reply. Flourent watched incredulously as the big jet broke through thirty-five thousand feet — half a mile below where it was supposed to be. Thankfully, there was no traffic below. Ten miles to the east, a U.S. Air Force C-5 Galaxy was lumbering along at thirty-two thousand feet. Flourent would take no chances.

"Reach 961, turn right immediately to heading three five zero. Traffic!"

"Reach 961, roger. Heading three five zero."

At least his radios were working, Flourent thought. He watched the World Express jet dive through thirty thousand feet. The rate of descent was incredible and seemed to be increasing. Then he noticed the speed readout — it had fallen to less than a hundred knots. With a logic born of eighteen year's experience, Flourent reasoned that World Express 801 was making little horizontal headway because it was pointed nearly straight down.

"WorldEx 801, Marseille Control! Are you experiencing difficulty?"

Nothing.

"WorldEx 801, Marseille!" Flourent's voice carried an edge that drew the attention of his supervisor. The woman came over and looked at his scope.

"What is it, Serge?"

Flourent pointed to the flashing symbol. "World Express 801 does not respond to my calls. It's falling like a stone."

Twenty thousand feet. Subconsciously, Flourent adjusted his microphone. "World Express 8 — 0 — 1, this is Marseille. Do you read?"

His supervisor shouted to another controller three stations away, "Louis! You have a heavy jet breaking into your low altitude sector from above. Call up World Express 801 to your screen! Clear any other traffic!"

The low altitude controller acknowledged the order.

Flourent saw the altitude display break ten thousand feet. Then the flashing red numbers next to the jet's blip disappeared. His heart seemed to stop as he watched the only thing that remained — the primary return, a tiny white square floating tenuously across the black void of his display.

"We've lost his transponder," the supervisor said. She plugged her own headset into a jack at Flourent's station. "WorldEx 801, WorldEx 801, this is Marseille! Do you hear?"

Finally, a garbled reply, "Marseille . . . WorldEx 801 . . . Mayday! May —" Then a terrible pause.

"WorldEx 801," the supervisor said, "you are clear of all traffic. What is the nature of your difficulty?"

Again silence. Without altitude information, the two air traffic controllers could do little but watch the tiny white square that was World Express 801 and will it to not disappear. Seconds later, it did just that.

Flourent's heart skipped a beat. His supervisor tried one more time to raise the flight by radio. There was now a distinct difference in her tone — no longer urgency. Hope, perhaps. "WorldEx 801, Marseille. Do you read?"

The ensuing silence was thick and heavy, as if all sound had been pulled into some aural black hole.

"All right, Serge," the supervisor said, "activate the alert."

For the first time in his long tenure as a controller, Flourent positioned his cursor over a red icon in one corner of the display. Automatically, the disaster response began.

In fact, the alert proved redundant. Police and fire units took dozens of calls centered on the village of Solaize, just outside Lyon. The reports were of an explosion of some sort.

The first to the scene was a small village fire brigade. They found widely scattered blazes and enough wreckage to certify that they were indeed dealing with an air disaster. Seeing no chance for survivors, the man in charge decided to wait for help before tackling the inferno. There might be hazardous material involved, and the boys from Station 9 were better suited to handle that.

Looking at the other man in his truck, the lieutenant gestured downhill from the crash site toward an industrial quarter at the edge of town, along the Rhone River. He said, "It could have been worse, Claude. He might have hit over there."

THE GULF OF OMAN
TEN HOURS LATER

The gulf waters were relatively calm in the late afternoon, and light winds made for an easy landing as the Bell 429 settled onto a helipad at the stern of the megayacht *Sol y Mar*.

The ship was a Sparkman and Stevens custom, two hundred and nineteen feet of glistening paint, mahogany, and chrome. No expense had been spared in her construction, and in the three years since *Sol y Mar*'s christening, extensive upgrades had been made to her staterooms and salons, and the bridge had been updated to include the most advanced electronic gear for communications and navigation.

As had been the case all afternoon, an even dozen men were stationed around the ship at precise intervals. None would be mistaken for crewmembers — the uniforms they wore were not nautical, but more akin to special forces attire, to include the automatic weapons they displayed openly. Twenty miles out to sea, the only other ship presently in sight was a distant oil tanker, yet in these chaotic waters one could never tell when a show of force might be necessary to discourage the odd band of pirates.

The helicopter's skids planted firmly on the large *H*, and its thumping rotors changed pitch as the aircraft's weight transferred to *Sol y Mar*'s sturdy afterdeck. Moments later, a man in a flowing white robe stepped down, assisted at the elbow by one of the security men. It was the sixth and final delivery of its kind. The man, a Saudi, walked quickly across the helipad, his robe snapping and fluttering in the idling chopper's downwash.

He made his way to the main salon and found the others waiting — Dubai, Russia, Singapore, Abu Dhabi, and Switzerland. There were exactly six seats at the large conference table, and the Saudi settled into the only vacancy. Each place was set with a crystal carafe of water and a goblet. Nothing else was offered, no tray of fruit, no decanter of premium liquor. Unique to the day's hastily arranged meeting, there were also no servants hovering at the room's perimeter, no one to attend to the principals' whims and demands. All extraneous staff had long departed.

The rich cherry table was circular, reinforcing to all the nature of their arrangement. The men were here on equal footing, and while the Saudi was today recognized as "chairman," the title was little more than a parliamentary convenience. Determined by rotation — there was simply no other way — the main duty of the acting executive was to act as facilitator, arranging transportation and a venue for the gathering.

Without so much as a "good afternoon," the Saudi brought the meeting to order.

"Do we know why this has happened?" The question was open to all.

Russia said, "I have spoken with our operative in France. He has theories, but it may be some time before we have an answer. Fortunately, the same can be said for others—there *will* be an investigation."

Singapore, "The man has become worrisome. Is he still necessary?"

None spoke, and this lack of response was an answer in itself.

The Saudi addressed Switzerland. "Are the finances in order?"

"Ninety-five percent," a beefy man answered, not bothering to reference the ledger in front of him.

There was a distinct pause as each of the men performed a more personal calculation.

The Saudi said, "Very well. We have no choice but to advance our timetable." The other five nodded in concurrence. "I will notify Caliph by the usual means."

Singapore said, "Might I suggest—when he has finished his tasks, let us send him to France. We may have work for him there."

More nods. And with that, the meeting adjourned.

Twenty minutes later, all six of the meeting's participants were aboard two helicopters streaking westward over the Gulf of Oman's azure waters toward Muscat International Airport. There, they would disperse into six private jets and speed to six far-flung points on the globe.

As soon as the last helicopter had lifted off, the security crew lowered the runabout from *Sol y Mar*'s aft davits, a twenty-two foot Boston Whaler. When the last man was aboard, the helmsman gunned the twin outboard motors until the little craft was a hundred meters abeam its mother ship. There, the engines fell to idle and everyone turned their eyes to *Sol y Mar*. The commander pulled a small device from his shirt pocket and pressed a button. With a muffled thump and maelstrom of foam amidships, the glistening yacht buckled, her back broken.

Three minutes later she was gone.

CHAPTER ONE

FREDERICKSBURG, VIRGINIA

Jammer Davis had always made a lousy cup of coffee. He dumped the trails of this morning's effort into the kitchen sink and went to the foot of the stairs.

"Jenny!" he barked in his best drill sergeant voice. "Get a move on! School in thirty minutes!"

There was no reply. He heard music blaring. Davis stomped up the stairs, his boots anything but subtle. Nearing the top, he saw his daughter's bedroom door partially open. He stopped in his tracks. Jen was standing in front of the full-length mirror, twisted around, and checking out her own jean-clad rear end.

His mind blanked in ways it shouldn't have. In ways it never had. Davis wondered what the hell to do. Tell her she had a great butt? Tell her it didn't matter what kind of butt she had because no young man was going to get within a hundred yards of it? He decided to punt. Davis put his head down, and gave the banister a swift kick. He didn't look up until he came through her door.

Jen had straightened up, but there was a mortified look on her face. "Don't you ever knock, Daddy?" she huffed.

"Come on, sweetheart. Two minute warning."

"But my hair isn't ready. I can't find a scrunchy!"

"A what?"

"A scrunchy for my ponytail."

"Well — use something else."

"Like what?"

He threw his hands in the air. "How should I know? Try one of those plastic cable ties, the ones that zip up. They're in the garage."

She glared at him, then picked up a hairbrush and began yanking it through her shoulder-length auburn hair. At fifteen, she was changing every day. Jen was nearly a full-grown woman in stature, yet still awkward and frisky in that filly-like way. And she was beginning to look more and more like her mother.

She said, "It's those new housekeeping ladies. They clean too much."

"How can they clean too much?"

"They put stuff in the weirdest places. Can't you talk to them?"

"No. They speak Portuguese."

She put the brush down and picked up a tube of hair gel. "Do you know what they did?"

"We don't have time for—"

"The two books I'm reading for English were on the night stand next to my bed. The housekeepers put them in a stack and then pulled out the bookmarks—they laid them on top, as if that was more orderly or something!"

Davis saw it coming. She was a cresting wave headed for shore, just looking for a spot to crash.

"They pulled my bookmark out of *The Odyssey*. Do you know how hard it is to find your place in *The Odyssey*?" Her voice quivered, "Do you?"

"Yes—I mean, no. God dammit!"

"Daddy!" She threw the tube of hair gel at him, striking him in the knee.

Jammer Davis, all six foot four, two hundred forty pounds, stood helpless. He had no idea what to do. Jen collapsed on the bed, a sobbing heap of convulsions. He thought, *Nice going, Jammer. Now what?*

Davis went to the bed and sat next to his daughter. He heaved a sigh. This wasn't getting any easier. Her moods were like the weather. Sunny, breezy, gloomy—and always changing. He wondered how much was hormones and how much was the lingering effects of losing her mother. It had been nearly two years since the accident, but the tears still came almost every day.

Jen leaned into him, put her head on his shoulder. Years ago he might have whisked her up and taken her in his arms. But that couldn't happen anymore. Davis knew he had to just sit there and wait things out. As he did, he noticed the room. It looked different. The posters on the wall had changed — *High School Musical* was gone, replaced by a graffiti-strewn banner of something called Less Than Jake. A band, he figured. The old dolls and stuffed animals were gone too, probably stuffed in a closet. This bothered him. Not that she was discarding her childhood, piece by piece, but rather that she was doing it on her own. No, *Dad, can I give this stuff to Goodwill?* He wondered how long ago things had started working that way.

"Dad —" she sniffled, "I want you to stop the bad language."

"Bad language?" Davis tried to remember what the hell he'd said. "Baby, you hear worse than that a hundred times every day in school."

"No! Mom never allowed it in the house, and with her gone, it's up to me to keep you in line."

In a reflex probably born from some long-ago martial arts training, Davis took a deep, deep breath. "Your Mom was a strong woman, Jen. I'm glad you are too. I promise to mind my tongue."

Her head came up and she used the corner of a bed sheet to wipe her eyes. As she did, Davis noticed the framed picture on the nightstand next to her bed, the three of them with arms around shoulders, smiling on a ski slope. At least that hadn't been stuffed in a drawer.

He said, "And you have to promise not to throw any more hair care products at me."

She smiled. "Sorry."

He gave her a lopsided grin — the one that Diane had always said was roguish. The one that Jen said made him look like a big doofus. All a matter of perspective, he figured. "Okay. Let's get ready."

"But I still need something for my hair."

Davis got up and headed toward the door. "I'll go down to the kitchen and get you a twisty tie — you know, the ones we use for the garbage bags." Davis bolted for the stairs. Too slow. Just before he rounded the corner, a flying hairbrush smacked him in the hip. He heard the giggle, her mood having completed its one-eighty.

With no small amount of pride Davis thought, *That's my daughter.* Her hormones might be in a blender. But her aim was dead sure.

Ten minutes later, Jen was waiting in the car.

Davis was still in the kitchen poking buttons on the dishwasher, trying to get it out of the damned "potscrubber" cycle, when the phone rang. Davis wanted to ignore it. Should have ignored it. He picked up.

"Jammer here."

There was a pause at the other end of the line, then, "Hello, Frank."

Aside from the occasional phone solicitor or census taker — people he didn't want to talk to anyway — there was only one person in the world who called Davis by his given name. "Hello, Sparky."

Only one person in the world called Rita McCracken anything but Mrs. McCracken. Or Assistant Supervisor McCracken of the National Transportation Safety Board. Davis had given her the name on the spot when they'd first met, a not so subtle jibe at her fiery red hair. Davis often gave call signs to his friends, but in her case it was more like naming a hurricane. After first impressions had gone south, he'd kept at it just to torque her off. Not good form with the boss, but that's how Davis was. And probably why he'd never made it past the rank of major in the Air Force.

"Pack your bags," she said.

"Pack? Why?"

"Haven't you seen the news?"

"No, I'm a busy guy."

"Well, you just got busier. A World Express C-500 went down in France yesterday. I need you to go to Houston this afternoon for a seventy-two-hour on the captain."

Davis frowned. Much of the information gathered in aircraft accident investigations was a simple matter of reviewing records. Maintenance logbooks, flight plans, and air traffic control data were all documented, either electronically or on paper. But some of the most pertinent history was perishable — the short-term personal background of crewmembers. A seventy-two-hour look-back was standard procedure.

"You know my situation, Rita. I can't —"

"I know that you are on the 'go team,' Davis! Now pack your bags and get in here. I'll brief you myself." She hung up.

The horn honked in the garage.

Davis seethed. He had an urge to crack the phone across the counter. That would feel good. But then he'd just have to go out and buy a new one. He hurried into his room and slammed some clothes into a suitcase. As a member of the "go team" he was supposed to have his bag already packed, available on a moment's notice. One minute was all he needed. Davis traveled light.

The drive to school was quiet. Davis tried to think of a good way to break it to Jen that he had to go out of town for a couple of days. She interrupted his mission planning.

"You know, Dad, for a big-shot investigator you're not very observant."

"How's that?"

"We need gas."

He looked down at the gauge. One eighth. Davis never filled up until he had to. "Don't worry, baby. I keep up with these things."

"Go to Mel's. It's always five cents cheaper than that other place you use."

He considered explaining that a six-pack of his preferred beer at "that other place" was a buck less, which made for a wash. Now probably wasn't the time.

She said, "I'll be driving soon, you know."

"Don't remind me."

But he was reminded — a whole new set of worries, right around the pubescent corner. Jen was going to take driver's ed over the summer, learn to merge and parallel park, keep her hands at ten and two.

Right then, Davis decided he'd brake hard for any yellow traffic lights. Not step on the gas. Like she'd been watching him do for the last fifteen years.

"Your hair looks cool, Dad."

"Huh?"

"Your hair, it's getting longer. That tight military cut was getting pretty tired."

Davis looked in the rearview mirror. He needed a trim.

Jen said, "And we still have to work on your wardrobe."

He looked down. For twenty years it had been a uniform, something he'd never really minded. One less decision each day. Now that he was a civilian, Davis tried to keep things simple. He had on khaki pants and a brown polo shirt. He owned six polo shirts. Three were in a suitcase in the trunk. His leather shoes were old and comfortable, strung with the second pair of laces. A long time ago they'd been expensive. Davis didn't mind buying expensive stuff—not because he cared a whit about style, but because it usually wore well. Fewer shopping trips.

"Maybe some baggy gangsta pants and a Hawaiian-print shirt," she prodded.

He looked at her sourly, saw the grin. "You're yankin' my chain again."

"I'm the only one who can."

He nodded. "Yep."

Davis slowed as they came to the school drop-off loop. He still hadn't thought of an easy way to break it to Jen that he had to leave town. That being the case, he laced his voice in parental graveness and just said it. "Baby, I have to go away for a couple of days on business. You'll need to stay at Aunt Laura's. I'll set everything up."

Davis looked at his daughter, expecting concern or anxiety. She looked positively giddy. He tracked her gaze to the campus entrance.

"It's Bobby Taylor!" she gushed. "Red shirt."

A tall young boy leaned on a pole. The kid was rail thin and gawky, all elbows and knees and pointed shoulders. He was cutting up with his friends.

"Did you hear me?" he asked.

"What? Oh, yeah. You gotta go away." She leaned over and kissed him on the cheek. "Have a good time, Daddy."

"A good time? It's a crash investigation."

"Oh, right. Well, you'll figure it out, Daddy. You always do."

Davis watched his daughter get out of the car like she was arriving at the Academy Awards. "Aunt Laura will pick you up," he called out. The door closed in his face and Jen gave a finger wave behind her back. She strutted by the Taylor kid like a runway model.

If he looks at her butt, Davis thought, *I'll break his skinny neck.*

CHAPTER TWO

The Headquarters of the NTSB was centrally located, two blocks from the National Mall in L'Enfant Plaza. It was very nearly, and perhaps should have been, in the shadow of the FAA building, a far more imposing mountain of gray roughly a block away. The NTSB structure was demure by D.C. standards, a modernist undertaking rife with raw concrete and glass that blended to the point of invisibility among an ocean of the same. Unpretentious and anonymous. Which suited Davis just fine.

He crossed the lobby, his soft soles having minimal impact on an overpolished marble floor. Davis approached the elevator just as the door slid open. A pair of men had been waiting—perfectly Windsored ties, starch-stiffened collars, venti Starbucks lattes. They stepped inside and turned toward the opening, gave him an inquisitive look.

Davis shook his head. "No thanks, guys."

As soon as the door closed, Davis hit the adjacent stairwell and started out hard, taking three steps at a time. On the fifth floor he burst into the hallway and checked the numbers over the elevator. Just passing four. Davis grinned.

He turned into the office labeled ASSISTANT DIRECTOR MCCRACKEN. Davis passed the vacant receptionist's desk and walked straight into his boss's office without knocking.

It was a room Davis had never liked, the furniture more expensive and plush than a mid-level bureaucrat deserved. Rita McCracken, all five feet two of her, was standing behind her desk trimming perfectly green foliage from a leggy, anemic-looking indoor plant. Davis knew she fancied herself as something of a gardener, but he pictured her as one of those people whose time in the yard was all digging and cutting and pulling things up by the roots. More anger management than horticulture.

She dumped her clippings in the trash, stashed the clippers, and then planted herself in an oversized leather chair. When McCracken looked up, she didn't bother with a greeting. "What have you heard about the crash?" she asked.

"There was a short blurb on NPR as I drove in. Not much in the way of details."

She held out a collection of faxes. Davis took them and began skimming as he sat down. He'd been working under McCracken for two years now, ever since retiring from the Air Force and hiring on with the NTSB. They had never gotten along. She was a baseline feminist, a red-headed locomotive who didn't think much of ex-fighter pilots. And Davis didn't think much of fifty-something bureaucrats who'd never had their hand on a control stick, but were sure you could find the cause to any crash by organizing the right ad hoc committee.

"The lead page is a twenty-four-hour update," she said. "A C-500, near Lyon, France. It went straight down from thirty-eight thousand."

Davis scanned the cover document. There wasn't much. The aircraft in question was brand new, a factory delivery for World Express, one of the three big overnight package delivery companies.

She said, "The second page is a plot of the radar data. From the first sign of trouble to estimated impact, not much more than two minutes. This thing fell like a brick. The air traffic controllers heard one 'Mayday' on the way down, but that was it."

He looked over the data. Radar stuff was okay, but incomplete. It was essentially a series of snapshots — Davis had always likened it to those clay animation movies where the character movement was so awkward and choppy. The data flow had stopped abruptly as the aircraft dove through ten thousand feet. Which was odd. "Do you have any pictures?" he asked.

McCracken pulled an eight-by-ten from her desk. "This just came in, commercial satellite imagery. It won't tell you much."

Davis stared intently at the photograph. It was grainy, but right away told him a lot. A lot that didn't make sense.

"It hit in a farmer's field," McCracken declared.

Davis took his eyes off the photograph. "There were just two pilots on board? No mechanics or lawyers?"

"Lawyers? Why on earth would there be lawyers?"

"It was a delivery from the factory. Sometimes the airlines and manufacturers sign the papers airborne, once they're over international waters — big tax breaks."

"No. Two pilots. Both fatalities," she said matter-of-factly. "Their licenses and medicals are there."

Davis shuffled through and found two FAA pilot's licenses, two airman medical certificates. The faxes were simple reproductions of the original boilerplate documents, what the FAA spit out at a rate of 180,000 every year. Properly trimmed and with the right bond, the medical certificates could have passed as originals. It had always amazed him — you couldn't get into Sam's Club without a photo ID, yet to command an airliner with five hundred passengers or tons of hazardous cargo, all you needed were two documents any bozo could replicate on a home computer.

He studied it all. The captain was a guy named Earl Moore, Houston address. Forty-two years old, six foot one, one hundred ninety pounds. Airline transport pilot with five type ratings, including the C-500. First officer Melinda Hendricks, Dallas. Thirty-six, five foot five, weighing in at one twenty. ATP, typed on the Boeing 737 and C-500. Standard stuff.

"No evidence of a midair collision?" he asked.

"No. At that altitude any other aircraft would have been under positive air traffic control. The French tell us there was nothing else in the area."

Davis wasn't convinced. "Air traffic control can only see what's on their scopes. A military fighter with its transponder off, screwing around, going vertical. Stranger things have happened."

"Is that the kind of thing you did in the Air Force, Davis? Screw around in your jet?"

"You know me," he said with an easy glare. "Everything by the book."

McCracken frowned. "What do you know about the C-500?"

"CargoAir's had them in full-scale production for about three years now. Selling like crazy. Maybe a hundred in service."

"One hundred and fifty-six," McCracken corrected like a dog marking its territory. She loved her numbers. The woman was an engineer by training, basted with a few years of safety work at one of the big defense contractors. Davis had never quite figured how she'd gotten into a supervisory post in the Major Investigations Division of the NTSB. Politics, probably. But he never dwelled on stuff like that.

He said, "The C-500 is a great idea, a flying wing airplane specialized for cargo. Ever since FedEx proved there was money to be made in flying packages, all the cargo airlines have used bastardized versions of passenger airframes — long tubes with wings, the windows covered over. But the flying wing design, similar to the B-2 bomber, is a lot more aerodynamically efficient. It gives a roughly twenty percent advantage in fuel burn. And with jet fuel going for three bucks a gallon, the big cargo operators are tripping over themselves to get orders on the books."

"Exactly. So when one mysteriously falls out of the sky, people start watching. This is high profile. A lot of countries have an interest in the outcome of this investigation — Italy, Germany, Egypt, Dubai, China. It might be assembled in France, but that airplane is a global collection of components."

"I think some of our own aerospace companies are involved too," Davis added.

"Tell me about it. I've already had calls from three congressmen this morning concerned about jobs in their districts. With the C-500 being a launch airframe, CargoAir's corporate life could be at stake here."

Davis deadpanned, "The lives of a lot of pilots too." He never missed a chance to get in a dig that she wasn't an operator. Childish, really, but he kept it up.

McCracken ignored the taunt. "Your flight to Houston leaves

Reagan National in two hours. Michael has already made the arrangements," she said, referring to her assistant in the outer office.

Now there's a guy whose life has to be hell, Davis thought. He said, "So you want a standard seventy-two-hour profile on the pilots?"

McCracken stood and began to wander. She stopped in front of a painting, a big oil rendition of a battle-damaged B-17 bomber limping home across the English Channel. McCracken stared at it and contemplated, as if searching for insight that could be applied to the more contemporary air tragedy they now faced. It was probably the best spot in the room to appear thoughtful. There was a window on the opposite wall, but Davis had checked the view once, on a day when she'd kept him waiting. It was hardly inspirational — the roof of an adjacent building, and, if you looked straight down, three Dumpsters with open lids.

She said, "I talked to the World Express chief pilot this morning. The first officer on the flight had been at the factory for a week. She was kept in France after another delivery fell through. The French are working her profile. The captain," she paused, "had some issues."

"Issues?"

"He was going through a divorce."

Davis didn't like where this was headed. "Lots of people get divorced."

McCracken turned away from her painting. "And he went through alcohol rehab last year."

His eyes narrowed further, but he said nothing.

"Go to Houston and talk to his widow. Then you head straight to France."

"France? You've got to be kidding!"

"None of your smart-ass crap!" she shot back. "You are employed by the NTSB to investigate aircraft accidents. I'm sorry about what happened to your wife, Davis, but that was a long time ago. I have bent over backward to keep you local. Sooner or later this was bound to happen."

He fumed. "Why do I have to brief them in person? What's wrong with just writing up a report on my findings?"

"No."

"Why not?"

"Because the French have asked for an NTSB liaison. You will be part of the investigation team."

"*On the investigation?* That could take a year! Maybe more!"

"It won't be continuous—a few weeks there, a few weeks back home."

"No way! Find somebody else!"

McCracken moved behind her fancy desk and leaned forward on stubby, freckled arms. "You take this assignment, or I'll have your resignation."

Davis leaned across from the other side, giving the image of two rams butting heads. "You've got it! On your desk tomorrow morning!" He whirled and stormed toward the door.

"Davis!" she screeched. "Don't you walk out on—"

The door slammed, cutting off the rest. In the anteroom, Davis paused. He could hear Sparky screaming his name and spewing obscenities like some kind of verbal Roman candle. Michael the receptionist was at his desk now. Davis grinned at him.

Michael grinned right back.

By the time he hit the parking lot, Davis was feeling better. He'd done a lot of rash things in his time. Sometimes he regretted them. This one felt pretty good. With his military retirement he could get by without the paycheck. And he had enjoyed walking out on Sparky. Really enjoyed it.

Davis was unlocking his car when he heard a shout.

"Jammer! Wait!"

He turned to see Larry Green. Larry headed up the Office of Aviation Safety, one rung above Sparky in the organizational food chain. He was also one of Davis' old squadron commanders, a guy who'd made two stars before getting out of the Air Force and signing on with the NTSB. Green was running at a good clip, which came naturally—he was a marathon runner, one of those lean, wispy guys who could go all day. When he caught up to Davis he wasn't even breathing hard.

"Bad news travels fast," Davis said.

"Jammer, hear me out—"

"I can't work for that hellion, Larry."

"She needs your help."

"She needs her barnacles scraped!" Davis reached for the door handle.

"This is *not* about her, Jammer." Green stared with his trademark intensity. Davis knew him as an old-school commander, the kind of guy who would spend thirty minutes spitting profanity-laced nails at his squadron, then turn things over to the chaplain for a prayer. Even now, without the stars on his shoulders, he was a guy you listened to. Davis paused.

Green said, "An airplane went down. Two pilots are dead."

Davis gave no reply.

"Hell, Jammer. A new airplane type, just certified. Dealing with all the different countries and agencies that'll be involved. This one's gonna be a bitch. It might even be out of *your* league."

Davis put his hands on his hips. A challenge. That was good. Flattery wouldn't have done it. Intimidation? Not a chance. But Jammer Davis never turned down a challenge. A good commander like Green always knew which buttons to push.

"Larry, I can't shuttle back and forth to France for a year."

"I know. But Collins himself wants you on this one."

"Collins? The managing director of the NTSB asked for me?"

"By name."

Davis was skeptical. It must have showed.

"I talked to him about you, Jammer. I told him you're a guy who gets things done."

"No, I'm a guy who pisses people off—which sometimes gets things done."

Green kept pressing. "You speak French, right?"

"I'm a little rusty, but yeah."

"Look, give me two weeks. Go to Houston for the seventy-two-hour, take it to France and look things over. Then, if you want out, I'll get somebody else."

Davis crossed his arms, leaned back on his car. "Two weeks?"

"Not a day more — unless you agree."

"And you'll demote Sparky?"

Green didn't miss a beat. "She'll be cleaning toilets by lunchtime."

"Men's room?"

"Men's room."

Davis nodded. Almost smiled. Then he said reflectively, "You know, Larry, a lot of people seem to find me gruff, uncompromising. I've never figured out why."

His old boss shrugged. "Beats me, Jammer. I think you're a sweetheart."

CHAPTER THREE

DAMASCUS, SYRIA

At mid-afternoon, the streets of Damascus were busy. The air was laced with dust as throngs of black-clad women scurried to and from the markets. Businessmen and beggars plied their respective trades. Amid it all, children darted haphazardly between buildings, lean-to kiosks, and donkey carts, chasing a friend here, picking a pocket there.

No one bothered the two burly men who strode through the chaos. Their speed and posture indicated a purpose, and while no one could give their names, everyone knew who they worked for. The two were sweating heavily when they arrived at the Al-Koura Hotel—winter was a relative term here, and the simple exertion of a quick walk was enough to dampen even those accustomed to the conditions.

The men stopped at the front desk. Eyes hard and jaws set, they simply glared at the proprietor.

"Twelve," the man said meekly, already knowing why they were here. He held out a key.

The room was on the second floor and a key was not necessary. The door was unlocked. Barging into the squalid place, they found her on the bed, snoring and quite naked. The two men looked at one another in disgust. The woman before them was an unsightly vision. Grievously overweight, her pale, cratered folds sprawled wide, covering nearly the entire mattress.

"This," said one of the men, "is why God invented the burqua."

The other agreed. "Without it, such a woman could never hope to find a husband."

Together they went to the bed and, in the interest of everyone's dignity, one of the men drew a sheet over her bloated body. With considerable effort they rolled her until her face was displayed — a disappointment in equal measure to the rest of the woman. Flabby chin, pockmarked cheeks, hawkish nose, and a sallow, mottled complexion. Her black hair was bristly and coarse — a cut section might be used to scrub a filthy pot clean.

"Get up!" one of the men ordered. "You are late!"

The woman let out a snort that would have sounded more natral coming from a camel. Then she began to stir. "Wha —"

This one syllable rode on breath that was not only foul, but laced with alcohol — enough to make the nearest man turn his head in revulsion. Her eyes opened briefly, blankly. Then her head sagged back to the pillow.

"Wretched cow!" Frustrated, one of the men strode into the bathroom. The trash can was empty. He filled it with cold water from the tap, hauled it to the bedroom and took careful aim.

In the Old City of Damascus the streets were narrow, less busy. The cramped warren of mud-brick buildings was a maze that had evolved over the best part of two thousand years. Complicating things further, many of the most ancient structures within the ramparts of the Old City had been abandoned, simply left behind as a new generation gave up on tradition and migrated to outlying neighborhoods where reliable plumbing and uninterrupted power were a given. The result was predictably awkward — a snarled mix of timeless architecture, rubble stacks, and business as usual.

Nestled deep amid the confusion, in a labyrinthine network of mismatched buildings, a group of men sat on the floor of a dank teahouse. They formed a swerving line on a long rug, and sipped sweet tea as smoke spun in a blue haze over their heads, a noxious mix of harsh tobacco and hashish from rooms beyond.

The eight Arabs were encircled at the perimeter by a phalanx of servants and guards. They came from across the region, representatives not so much of countries, but rather tribes — different sects, slightly varied ethnicities. More to the point, each commanded an arsenal of committed warriors, men and women who were expert in the fine arts of rocket attack, ambush, and suicide bombing. Only a few generations back, their ancestors would have been skirmishing across the sands of Persia and Arabia. In the modern world, however, such ancient discord had to be put aside, superseded by the demands of a common faith — and a common, relentless enemy. Four of the room's occupants were on America's list of "Most Wanted" terrorists. The others, relative newcomers, hoped to attain the honor soon. It was a teahouse the Americans would love to have the coordinates of.

The organization was a loose one, none of the men having any particular authority. None allowing it. That being the case, the man in the middle, Abdullah al-Wajid, acted as spokesperson for the most ancient of reasons — he was the eldest. And he was none too happy when Fatima Adara was dragged in.

His men shepherded the great woman inside and deposited her on the floor, her bulk crushing a large pillow. She looked worse than usual, and for a moment al-Wajid thought Fatima might topple over. But then, with obvious determination, she righted herself. A large flowing robe hid her body, thankfully, but her face was uncovered. The olive eyes were lazy, two black pools of oil floating aimlessly over reddened sclera. Her hair was askew and matted on one side, exactly as it had come off the pillow, no doubt.

Al-Wajid forced a level of respect into his voice that was not truthful. "Thank you for coming."

Fatima blinked and her void expression seemed to focus. "Oh — sure."

"How is Caliph?"

"Caliph? Okay. He sends respect."

Clearly not through his deeds, al-Wajid thought.

Fatima licked her puffy lips. "You got anything to drink here?"

A surprised al-Wajid exchanged glances with the men at his sides. Left and right, he saw the same question percolate — did she mean alcohol? They had been watching Fatima since she'd arrived last night, earlier than scheduled. Instead of moving up the meeting, she had wandered off to a hotel, gotten drunk, and tried unsuccessfully to take the bellman to her room, no doubt to fornicate. Al-Wajid pushed away the repulsive thought and gestured to a servant near the door. The man quickly produced a tray with a pitcher of water and a glass. He delivered it to their guest. Fatima frowned, but poured a glass and began slurping like a horse at trough.

"Why has Caliph called this meeting?" asked the bearded man to al-Wajid's right. He spoke to Fatima slowly, enunciating each word with great precision as one might to a child. "Has something happened to change our plans?"

She coughed. Water dribbled over her chin and fell into her considerable lap. "Plans? Yeah, they change. We have to move everything ahead."

Again, the men swapped unhappy glances.

"To when?" al-Wajid asked.

"Right away."

There was murmuring throughout the room. Al-Wajid said, "You are sure about these instructions?"

"Sure? Yeah, I'm sure. Caliph, he makes me say everything until I know his words exactly."

This al-Wajid did not doubt.

One of the others said, "We have gone to great trouble to place Allah's warriors across the world. Why this change when we are already so near?"

Fatima shrugged, her mouth curling into an upside down U. "You know Caliph—he never tells me stuff like that." She cackled, "He's a real prick."

"Woman!" spat a gray-bearded man with a severely hawkish nose. "Do not demean your master!" The old bird was recognized as the most pious of those here, a strict Wahhabist who was always quick to thump his Koran. Fatima's lopsided grin stayed in place, and a fog of hesitation descended on the room.

Al-Wajid forged ahead, addressing his peers. "The time for questions has passed. For years we have been fighting the West in our backyard, killing their crusaders and striking against our own traitors and profiteers — those who have forsaken Allah in pursuit of American greed. But in doing so we also kill the innocent, tread upon one another." Nods of acceptance around the room. It was no small testament to Caliph's talents of persuasion that those here were an even mix of Sunnis and Shiites. "Caliph has given us a chance to take our fight to the enemy's ground, a chance to bring the West to its knees. He has united us like none before."

Another agreed, "And Caliph himself is blessed, having survived against America's most accomplished assassins. He is clearly one chosen by Allah."

There were no more reservations. All were in concurrence. All were eager to strike.

Fatima said, "Oh, and Caliph wants to know how soon you can do it."

"Everything is in place for the first phase," al-Wajid said. "Does the interval remain the same?"

"The wha — oh, the time in between. Yeah, sure."

"Very well. Tell Caliph the order will be given immediately, God willing."

Fatima emitted a throaty chuckle. "God willing. Caliph, he prays a lot, you know."

"He is a servant of the Prophet. A good example for us all," al-Wajid added pointedly.

"So I tell him everything will happen soon."

"Yes."

Fatima rose unsteadily, gave her bristly scalp a scratch, and meandered toward the door.

As soon as she was gone, one of the two men who had retrieved her appeared. "Shall we follow her to the airport?" he asked.

Al-Wajid shook his head. "No, do not bother. She somehow always finds her way." The man disappeared. Al-Wajid turned to the others.

"Why does Caliph keep such a messenger?" one asked.

Al-Wajid had often asked himself this same question. Two years earlier, the Americans had nearly killed Caliph. Afterward, he had gone into hiding, become more effective than ever. And Fatima Adara was now his only contact, his dubious messenger.

"She is an embarrassment," the same man said, "not even a be-liever."

"When a woman looks like that," another responded, "she should find religion. But then our leader is shrewd. Imagine — if any man should ever try to seduce her, Caliph will know he is a spy."

Muted chuckles came.

"Enough!" said the ever-serious al-Wajid. "For all her faults, she has been reliable. Our communications with Caliph have always been accurate, and the arrangement allows him to remain in the shadows, where the Americans cannot reach."

"I am left to wonder," a tall Shiite remarked, "why can all the at-tacks not take place at once? Why must we divide ourselves? After the first strike their security will certainly be —"

"No!" al-Wajid interjected. "The time for such questions has passed. We have all agreed to Caliph's plan, and he has never led us down any path without reason. Until we recover our lands from the westerners, we are a people cut in half. Only our faith will again make us whole."

More nods.

Al-Wajid declared an end to the meeting. When the men stood, they broke into small groups and embraced, the age-old tradition when clans formed an alliance. Yet on leaving, all were alone as they disappeared into the dusty haze of the Old City.

CHAPTER FOUR

HOUSTON, TEXAS

The flight from Dulles was on time, but Houston's traffic was a mess. Davis pulled in front of the house at three o'clock that afternoon.

Captain Earl Moore's widow lived in a relatively new two-story tract house in the suburb of Spring. Davis parked in the street and looked things over. The lawn was tightly trimmed, the bushes sculpted, and the street clean. Tidy. A shiny new BMW sat parked along the curb in front of his rental Hyundai. Davis walked up a neat paver-brick path to the front portico. There were more bricks here, Styrofoam racks of faux stone stuck to the side of the house with glue to give a timeless appearance. Like the place had been built a hundred years ago. Or like it might still be standing in another hundred.

Davis felt uneasy. The woman inside had certainly known about her husband's death for a full day now. Still, it seemed like he was bringing death to her door. He'd done two notifications during his time in the Air Force. It was lousy duty — pull up in a blue steely wearing your service dress uniform, shoulder to shoulder with the base chaplain. With a picture like that you didn't need to say much. The wives knew what it meant. Just like he had known two years ago when the highway patrolman with the dour face had come to his door — Diane was late, not answering her phone. You just knew.

He rang the bell and a bespectacled middle-aged man answered. He wore a suit and was well groomed. Fair hair, thin build, and pale. Very pale. The word that came to Davis' mind was "milquetoast." The fellow was putting some effort into his expression, trying for serious and skeptical. Davis still thought, "milquetoast." The BMW guy, he decided. A gatekeeper, but not family. A brother would have parked in the driveway.

"Yes?"

"Hello, sir. My name's Davis." He flashed his creds. "I'm with the NTSB, and I'd like to ask Karen Moore a few questions."

The guy took a long look at the ID, which was unusual. Most people only glanced. "She's had a pretty rough time. Can't it wait?"

"I'm afraid not. But it won't take long."

He hesitated.

Davis said, "And you are — ?"

"I'm Jason Lavender, her attorney."

Lavender, Davis thought. *Like the color of a flower.* He said, "Nice to meet you."

The guy deliberated, waffled, then said, "Just a minute." He disappeared into the house.

A lawyer wasn't what Davis needed right now. He'd always had a knack for sifting through data and debris, finding the secrets of what brought airplanes down. But delicate conversations with grieving widows, fencing with attorneys — not his game. That required tact and finesse. Soft words and gentle smiles. Like you might get from a crisis counselor or a parish priest. Jammer Davis had the god-given finesse of a wrecking ball. Which wasn't *always* a bad thing. Wrecking balls got results. Maybe not what you were after, but something always came down.

A woman came to the door. She was fortyish and looked a lot like the house — well-tended. She was fit, probably worked out a lot. Her short brown hair was nicely cut and styled with blonde highlights. Davis noticed her eyes, a cool blue with subtle makeup — makeup one day after her nearly ex-husband had died in a terrible crash. He also saw what wasn't there. No redness, no puffy bags. No crumpled tissue in her hand.

"Hello, miss. I'm Jammer Davis, an investigator with the NTSB."

He pushed out his ID again. Karen Moore didn't even look. "I realize this might not be a great time, but there are a few important questions I need to ask."

"No, it's not a good time." Her voice was winter.

"Eventually we'll want to talk more, once you're up to it, but there are a few things we need to get straight right away. Just basic stuff."

She nodded. "All right. Come in, Mr. Davis."

She led him to the living room. The lawyer was nowhere in sight, but had to be lurking within earshot. Right away, Davis spotted the I-love-me wall. All pilots had them, and former military guys had the biggest ones. Pictures of airplanes they'd flown, plaques of appreciation and commendation, maybe a chromed twenty-millimeter bullet they'd won in a strafing competition. In ten seconds, Davis' first five questions were answered — Earl Moore was a former Navy guy, flew F-18s in the fleet followed by a stint in training command. He put in maybe eight years, made lieutenant, then jumped to the airlines. These were the kinds of things Sparky should have told him — not just that the guy was a divorcing alcoholic.

"I was Air Force, myself," Davis said, meandering along the wall while Mrs. Moore took a seat on the couch. He saw an eight-by-ten picture of Earl Moore dancing on a stage in a Hawaiian shirt, clearly drunk, with a beer in one hand, a cigar in the other, and a no-kidding monkey on his shoulders. Davis smiled inwardly and thought, *My kind of guy.*

"I really never cared for those pictures," she said.

Davis nodded. "Yeah, my wife was never a big fan of mine either." He went to sit down, vaguely remembering some psychobabble crap he'd been taught about where to sit in relation to a distraught witness. Was it next to her? Or across? He couldn't remember. The couch looked more comfortable so that's where he parked.

She asked, "Can you tell me anything more about what happened?"

"No, sorry. I've only seen what's on the news."

She nodded. "I've just begun to make — arrangements. I've never done anything like this before."

"Do you have anyone helping?"

"Yes. His mother is still alive, and a brother is coming down from Chicago. Tell me, Mr. Davis, will there be an autopsy?"

"Yes." The real answer wasn't quite so easy, but Davis wasn't going to bring the condition of the body into play. "I'm here to do what we call a seventy-two-hour history. I need to know as much as possible about what your husband did in the days before the accident. Had he been eating right, taking any medications, getting his sleep?"

"Getting his sleep? He was a cargo pilot."

"Right," Davis said. He thought, *Widow–1, Jammer–0.* Of all the world's vampire shifts, none were worse than the one worked by cargo pilots. Go to work when everyone else was climbing into bed. Fly across a few time zones and land. Sit next to a coffeepot for an hour or two while packages are sorted, then fly again. More time zones. When you get to your layover city, take a shuttle to a hotel room while the horizon starts to glow in the east — reveille for the rest of civilization. Bacon and eggs for dinner, easy on the coffee. Then try to get some sleep so you can do it all again the next night. Just try.

Karen Moore said, "Look, Mr. Davis. I don't know if you're aware, but my husband and I had recently separated."

"Actually, yeah, I knew that. But not much more. Where was he living?"

"He had an apartment a few miles from here." She gave the address. Davis wrote it down. Then she pointed to the wall and said, "He never did get all his stuff out of here."

"I see. So was he living by himself?"

"No." A long pause, then, "Well, sometimes — I don't know."

"You mean there was a woman?"

The ice turned to venom. "I'd call her something else. She was there sometimes when I'd go to pick up Luke."

"Luke?"

"We have a son. He's twelve." She put on her battle tone, "And he's trying to deal with the death of his father. I don't want him involved in any of this, Mr. Davis."

"No, no need for that."

"So what else can I tell you? I saw Earl the day before he left for France. I picked up Luke at the apartment. They'd gone to a ballgame, I think."

"Just the two of them?"

"I didn't stalk him," she snipped.

"Okay." There was a long silence, and Davis sat uneasily on his next question. "Your husband was out on medical leave last year — alcohol. Had he been drinking lately?"

"How would I know?"

"You were married to him. I think you'd know."

She glared and fell silent. Then Karen Moore began to fidget, began to lightly wring her hands together. Davis heard papers shuffling in the next room — the lawyer in the kitchen. Still no answer. Instead, she said, "Excuse me, Mr. Davis. I'll be back in a moment." She stood, reflexively smoothing the front of her slacks, and walked more quickly than she should have into the kitchen.

Dammit. He had pushed too hard. It wasn't the first time. Davis had a knack for balling up interviews. He stood up, didn't smooth his Dockers. He'd never had these kinds of problems when he'd just flown airplanes for a living. Maybe when this investigation was done he could look around for a flying job. A cushy corporate gig might be nice. Fly a Learjet down to the Caymans, hang out with some Fortune 500 execs for a nice long weekend. It sounded good.

He heard Karen Moore talking in hushed tones to Lavender, heard more papers being shuffled. Davis strolled back to the wall and found another picture of Earl Moore — a team lineup, rowing crew in college. He was built for it, tall and beefy. Might have made a good rugby player — second row forward, Davis figured. Finally, Karen Moore came back. She returned to the couch, but this time her attorney stood behind her, hovering like a mortician at a funeral service that had overstayed its time slot.

"Yes," she said.

Davis was lost. "Yes what?"

"Yes, Earl had been drinking lately."

"Oh — I see." Davis didn't. "So you were with him at the time?"

"No, but like you said, I'd know. He was unhappy. That's always when he drank, when he was unhappy."

Davis was unhappy right now. He could really go for a beer. He didn't ask for one. "Unhappy? How?"

"He just seemed depressed. It could have been girlfriend trouble. Or perhaps he felt guilty about not seeing Luke very much."

"How much was that?"

The mouthpiece jumped in. "Earl Moore had been granted visitation one weekend a month and one week each summer."

Davis tried to imagine how he would react if a judge — or anyone — tried to tell him that he could only see Jenny a few days each month. Depressed? Unhappy? Homicidal was more like it. He knew what he had to ask next. "Mrs. Moore, why had the two of you split up?"

She said nothing, and her attorney filled the void again. "The grounds for divorce were irreconcilable differences. It was uncontested, nearly complete."

Davis ignored him, kept his eyes fixed on the widow. "That's not what I asked."

Silence from above and below. The interview was going south fast.

Lavender said, "I think we're done, Mr. Davis."

"Yeah, I guess so." He stood and meandered toward the door, then paused. He hoped they really wanted to get rid of him. "Oh, there is one thing," he said, his eyes on the widow.

"What?" she asked.

"Do you have a key to his apartment?" Strictly speaking, Davis doubted it was legal for him to search the place, but he didn't have time for any screwy court warrants.

"I think Luke might have a key," she said, turning to her attorney.

"Why don't you go check his room," Lavender suggested.

Davis thought, *Lousy lawyer.* He said, "Thanks."

With the widow Moore upstairs and Lavender guarding the couch, Davis strolled back to the wall. He stared at the picture of Earl Moore on stage. A drink, a cigar, and a monkey on his back. Loving life.

CHAPTER FIVE

In Davis' experience there were two kinds of flight surgeons. There was the one you visited twice a year that checked your eyes, took your blood pressure, and thumped your back. They got you in and out of the office quick, a rubber stamp. Then there was the kind you tracked down if you had a real medical issue. The kind of doctor you wanted on your side if you were fighting the feds to get your flight medical back.

As he sat in the waiting room, Davis studied the wall and decided that Dr. James Black was the latter type. There were two large, ornate diplomas — Dartmouth and Georgetown — and a bunch of smaller certificates for smaller achievements. FAA Aviation Medical Examiner, chairman of a professional association. The guy even had a law degree to boot. M.D., J.D. Now there was a scary concept, Davis thought. All the same, a good guy to have in your corner if you were up against the system. Dr. Black was probably on retainer for the World Express pilot's union, paid a healthy sum to wrestle a few tricky cases each year.

Office hours had ended for the day, but the doctor was still in and had agreed to an interview. Davis only waited five minutes, his personal record at any doctor's office. A receptionist led past a single exam room — not the usual row of holding pens — to a small, nicely appointed suite. Dr. Black was behind his desk and stood when Davis came in. He was middle-aged, medium height, medium build. He wore designer glasses and a lab coat with his name embroidered in black script. Black in black. The coat was pressed and clean. No blood, no wrinkles, no tongue depressor in the breast pocket. He didn't even bother with a physician's most basic accessory — a stethoscope hanging around his neck.

"Hello, I'm Jim Black."

Davis took a firm, professional handshake.

"Jammer Davis, NTSB."

The doctor cocked his head slightly. The "Jammer" part often threw people off.

"Thanks for seeing me on short notice."

"No problem. I was going to be in my office dictating for another hour. So you've come about Earl Moore?"

"Yes."

"Terrible, what happened. I suppose you know my reason for taking him as a patient?"

The doctor didn't mess around. Which was all right with Jammer Davis. "I know he took time off for alcohol rehab. You helped him get his medical back."

The doctor nodded. "Tell me, Mr. Davis, is this a formal interview?"

"I'm not a very formal guy, but yeah, I guess it has to be."

The flight surgeon shoved his hands deep into the pockets of his lab coat, and his expression took on an air of increased gravity. It was probably the same face that came when he was giving a patient bad news.

Davis tried to lighten the mood. "Look, Doc — I just need to get a few things straight before I go sticking my nose under charred lumps of metal. A brand-new airplane fell out of the sky, and it's important for us to find out why. Earl Moore had a recent medical history that's got to be looked at."

Black said, "You know about the alcohol. What about the divorce?"

"Yes. I just spent some time with his wife this afternoon."

"I've never met her."

"She's charming. Tell me, Doctor, when Moore had his ticket pulled last year — how did that come about?"

"It was pretty straightforward, as those things go. Moore's wife called his chief pilot, said he was drinking far too much. The chief pilot confronted Moore, who pretty much confessed."

"Confessed."

"Just said he'd been drinking heavily, volunteered for the rehab program."

"So an ex-Navy guy puts himself in drydock."

"Yes. It's a good program. For a first timer, very straightforward. Counseling, recurrent monitoring. Over ninety percent are back flying within a few months. And the recurrence rate is quite low."

Davis said, "I got the impression that Moore and his wife weren't getting along. Was there ever any suggestion of other problems — say, physical abuse, anything like that?"

"No. Nothing I know of."

"Were there other medical issues? Waivers for any conditions?"

"I think he had to wear glasses for far vision," Black said.

"Okay. So when did you see Moore last?"

"He dropped in last week."

"Dropped in? You mean he didn't have an appointment?"

"That's right."

Davis paused. A bright red flag fluttered in his cranium. Standard flight physicals were every six months — and always scheduled far in advance. "Was he having some kind of problem?"

"Well," the doctor hedged, "I'm not sure. He wanted to know what would happen to a pilot who got a DUI."

The red flag snapped stiff. "What did you tell him?"

"I said it would have to be reported to the FAA right away. And if *he* had gotten a DUI, given his background, his ticket would be pulled within twenty-four hours."

"So did he admit to it?"

"I asked. He said no."

There was a pause before Davis said, "And that was the end of it?"

"Yes."

"Forgive me, Doc, but it seems a little strange. A guy coming in unscheduled and asking something like that. Didn't you try to check it out? Maybe make a phone call or two?"

Black's tone was combative. "No. My patient told me he was clean. I'm not a detective."

Not much of a doctor either, Davis thought.

Black added, "And I can assure you that I was under no regulatory obligation to go digging."

Davis had no idea what the legalities were. The doctor probably did. Davis figured the Texas Bar Association would have been proud. Hippocrates pretty disappointed. "All right," he said. "I'll check with the Houston Police and Harris County Sheriff's Department."

"I think you should," the doctor agreed.

Perfect answer. Davis moved on. "Was he on any kind of medication that you know of—either prescription or over-the-counter?"

"Not to my knowledge."

The lawyer half was taking over, and Davis felt another interview ebbing. He was up against Dr. Jekyll and Mr. Hyde, except the monster was an expert in torts and civil procedure. Davis covered a few more formalities, then arranged to get copies of the patient records on Earl Moore. He thanked Black for his help, and headed to the elevator. For the second time today, he was an unhappy man.

He hoped to hell the toxicology run-up on the body of Earl Moore came out negative. He hoped to hell they could find enough of Earl Moore to *do* a toxicology run-up. But even if the skipper had been under the influence, it didn't explain much in Davis' mind. A drunk pilot might make mistakes, but it wasn't the kind of thing that would bring down a brand-new jet from six miles up.

Waiting for the elevator, Davis checked his cell phone. He saw a text message from Jen. OMG DADDY! BOBBY TAYLOR JUST ASKED ME TO SOPHOMORE DANCE A WEEK FROM FRIDAY! AUNT L SAYS I HAVE TO ASK YOU. PLEASE! PLEASE! PLEASE! KISSES, J.

The elevator opened. He snapped his phone shut and stepped in. There was another guy already there—thin, long hair, nurse's scrubs. Davis barely noticed. A vision of Bobby Taylor came to mind, his spindly little arms and legs. Davis needed to get home before next Friday. He wanted to shake Bobby Taylor's hand. Shake it with a real firm grip. A grip that would—

Ding!

The elevator reached another floor. He didn't know which one. The door opened and the other guy began backing out, eyeing him like he was a psycho. Davis had no idea why.

Five hours after arriving in Houston, Davis was on a Continental Boeing 777 headed for Paris. He heard a mechanical thump as the parking brake was released and felt the big machine begin its backward motion. He checked his watch. Thirty-eight seconds late. Davis had always had a sense for time. He could wake up in the middle of the night and guess right to within ten minutes. Always. But that wasn't good enough. Twenty years in the military taught a man the value of punctuality — bombs thirty seconds late were not bombs well spent. You could hurt a good guy. Not hurt a bad guy. Time was important in lots of things.

Nine minutes later, the big airplane accelerated down the runway. When it reached a speed that would have left an Indy car in the dust, the ground fell away. Davis yawned. He was sitting in first class, already sipping an orange juice. The NTSB would never have sprung for the upgrade, but during the boarding process he had recognized the captain as one of his old instructors from flight school. They chatted about their reckless youth, and before he knew it the skipper had bumped him up.

Once the big jet was at cruising altitude, the ship's resonance settled to a businesslike hum. It was an oddly serene coalescence — air vents hissing, massive engines droning, and a five hundred knot slipstream outside. Davis found it comforting, even relaxing.

A flight attendant came down the aisle carrying a stack of pillows — he knew if you called them "stewardesses" they'd look at you as if you were a dinosaur. Her dress, hair, and smile were all taut and professional. She handed over a pillow as gracefully as anyone could, and said, "Are you sure I can't get you a drink, sir?"

"No," he replied, swirling his juice cup, "this is fine."

"So you and the captain are old friends?"

He smiled. "We flew together a long time ago."

"You're not one of those pilots who hates flying in back, are you?"

"Doesn't bother me a bit."

"The first officer I'm dating doesn't like it. I guess it's a control thing," she said.

On hearing those words, Davis fumbled his thoughts. "Yeah, I guess," he managed.

The young woman smiled her pert company smile, went back to her deliveries.

A control thing. The words pinged between his ears. It was the last thing Diane had ever said to him, the ending volley of a silly spat they'd had, delivered as she was heading out the door. It was funny how memories worked. The good ones — and there were a lot when it came to Diane — were there if you went looking for them. But the bad came looking for you. They popped up in your dreams, whispered in your ear, drifted on a familiar scent. All it took was the slightest odd association. And there wasn't a damn thing you could do.

Davis pushed it all away, tried to settle in for the ten-hour crossing. He was familiar with riding in coach on long flights — you got to know the people around you. But here in first class it seemed different. There was more space. With a quick look around, Davis decided that might not be such a bad thing. An older woman across the aisle, dripping with diamonds and accessories, sat sipping champagne from a fluted glass. He had watched her slam down two before they'd even left the ground. One more, he figured, add in the cabin altitude, and she'd be out for the count.

In front of her, a middle-aged guy with slicked black hair kicked off his boat shoes and propped his bare feet on the table he'd be eating from in a few hours. Ahead of him was an angry-faced kid dressed like a rapper. He had a gold chain around his neck that would have anchored a trawler, and hanging from that was a gold bucket that reminded Davis of the things priests swung around to disperse incense. And he was already standing, even though the FASTEN SEAT BELT sign was on. He was an idiot.

Davis didn't like it up here. Didn't like being pampered. Jen would have loved it, though. He wished this assignment had come in the summer when he could have brought her. Davis felt for the cell phone in his pocket. They'd made him shut it off before getting airborne, which bothered him. He knew the thing would be useless while they crossed the pond, but it was his umbilical, his only link to Jen. Since Diane's death, his life had revolved completely around his daughter, a wobbling existence driven by the inertia of school dances, meet-your-teacher nights and swim meets. Not that he minded—it was a good whirlwind. And so blasting off to Europe seemed wrong. It was too damned far away.

The cabin lights went dim. Davis figured the flight attendants were trying to lull everyone to sleep. He looked out the window and saw a moonlit night sky. Soft white reflections played on a scalloped cloud deck below, a subtle image of the moon echoing upward from a smooth lake. It was a pretty night, the same kind of night Captain Earl Moore and First Officer Melinda Hendricks had certainly seen a thousand times.

Davis settled into his seat, pressed the recline button until he was almost lying flat. It was comfortable, and if a career in the military had taught him anything it was that you slept when you could.

As he began to drift off, he thought about what Dr. Black had told him. Did Earl Moore really have a run-in with the police last week? Maybe he'd gotten in trouble. Maybe he'd been pulled over after downing a couple of beers, *didn't* get a DUI, and went to Dr. Black to scare himself straight. It was a convenient theory—and probably not much more. Right now, there were a lot of possibilities.

Then Davis remembered the photo of the crash site he'd seen in Sparky's office. The debris had been strewn over a very large area, at least a mile. Which didn't fit. The airplane had fallen over six miles in two minutes. On a trajectory like that, it should have gone straight in and made a hole like a meteor crater. He'd seen it before. Deep impact, the densest parts burying themselves in fifty feet of earth. But that hadn't happened to World Express 801. It had been really moving, but the impact was low angle.

Once again, a lot of possibilities.

CHAPTER SIX

The black-clad figure was quick, skirting around the flood of a street-light and edging up to a chain-link fence.

The fence marked the property line of the sole manufacturing site of Colson Industries. By Texas standards, it was a modest operation, one acre of land with a single large building situated at the center. Around the outside of the place, stacked against corrugated sidewalls, was a sea of pipes, casings, scaffolding, and machinery. Some of the equipment was nicely organized, while other parts lay in haphazard piles, discarded in the course of day-to-day operations and waiting for the annual scrap heap collection. The whole collection suffered from varying degrees of oxidation, the depth of red and brown measuring the length of time each component had been surrendered to the elements.

At two in the morning, the workers had long gone home. The man in black had been watching for two weeks, and so he knew there was no night shift. He had expected a longer window for his surveillance, at least another week. But the orders from Damascus had come early — tonight would be the beginning.

The lone night watchman was a man in his sixties. His presence, according to Caliph, was not intended to repel invasion, but a mere ploy by the owners to gain more favorable insurance premiums. There was little of true value in the place — lathes, casting dies, heavy machinery. Colson Industries' very specialized product weighed in at over nine tons per unit, so no common thief was going to break down a door and drag one off.

The man in black moved, pulling along a heavy canvas bag. His name was Moustafa, and until recently he would have been described as an unemployed Palestinian accountant. Four years out of Hebron University, his prospects had turned increasingly bleak. It was one thing for a country to educate a million doctors, lawyers, and professionals. Quite another to create a society, an economy that could put them to good use. Unemployed and frustrated, Moustafa, like so many of his friends, had heard the calling and turned to his faith. Turned hard.

Moustafa was glad he had encountered no one on the streets because his English was miserable. Since arriving in America two weeks ago, he had remained secluded in a safe house run by a Saudi, a student at one of the local colleges. Moustafa had only ventured from the house late at night in order to study his two targets. Other than that, he prayed, read the Koran, and watched the decadence of American television. And yesterday he had made his martyr's video. This night, in fact, would not be his time of glory. If everything went as planned, he would survive. But Moustafa's appointment with destiny was near.

At a shadowed section of fence he brought his first tool to bear, a pair of heavy cable cutters. As he worked, Moustafa eyed the razor wire woven along the top of the barrier, twelve feet over his head. A dramatic selling point for the traders of security fence, he supposed, but quite useless. Like so much here, it was only for show. He made quick work of the fence, and once inside Moustafa pulled his heavy bag through the gap. He then pulled the silenced 9mm Beretta from his pocket. The gun felt awkward, unfamiliar in his hand. He was not an expert in handling weapons, yet Moustafa knew he did not need to be — the guard carried only a radio.

He pulled his heavy satchel to a spot outside the building's delivery entrance and left it there. Next to a pair of loading bays was a simple entry door. The guard had passed through earlier — he circled the grounds once or twice each night, always ending back at the front entrance where his podium, comfortable chair, and television were situated. *Americans and their television*, Moustafa thought.

The rear door was unlocked and Moustafa eased inside. As had been the case each night, certain lights inside the building were left on — not the full array, but enough to allow the guard to see clearly. Confirming that the man was not in sight, Moustafa pulled the heavy bag in behind him and closed the door. Leaving the bag, he began to move cautiously toward the front of the building. He saw machinery everywhere, a terrific assortment of metal pipes, hardware, and sheet metal. The smell of machine oil was thick. Moustafa did not know exactly how this place related to the strength of America. He could only trust in Caliph's vision. And in the blessed will of Allah.

The first thing that drew Moustafa's attention was not a sight, but a sound — the television. He heard thumping music and a woman's voice shouting strident commands. Moustafa raised his gun. As he rounded a huge wooden crate he saw the guard slumped in his chair. Moustafa's finger trembled on the trigger, but then, against the racket of the television, he heard the most amazing thing. Snoring. The guard was sound asleep. *Allah is indeed merciful.*

The man's back was to him, and as Moustafa closed in he saw the television. A group of women, wearing almost no clothing, were dancing in a line, gyrating to the beat of techno music. The women were very healthy, their tanned loins and large breasts straining against skintight coverings. A telephone number was posted at the bottom of the screen. For a moment, Moustafa found he was transfixed, staring at the crazy women. But then he tore his eyes free. Such a strange challenge, a strange temptation. He would not fall prey.

Moustafa stepped softly toward the guard. He slowly arced his arm upward and aimed at the center of the gray-haired mass only a meter away. *Phht.* The gun kicked back in Moustafa's hand. He saw the gray head shudder from the bullet's impact. Then the guard slumped and Moustafa saw a hole where the bullet had hit its mark. Blood and tissue had sprayed beyond, splattering across the glowing image of dancing whores. How appropriate. Moustafa raised his arm again. Caliph's instructions were clear — always make sure. *Phht.*

Finished with the guard, Moustafa noticed a small security monitor that alternated views of the place from different cameras. There was also a telephone on a pedestal and a few buttons that might have been alarms. This too had been addressed in his orders. Leave it. It was too complex to deal with properly. And if the next part was done well, none of it would be of any use. Caliph had considered everything. Which was why he had so frustrated the Americans. Why he had become a legend.

Moustafa retrieved his satchel and went to stand in the middle of the place. He took a few moments to study things in the half light of the cavernous building, sorting through by the guidelines he had been given. Then he went to work.

Moustafa identified two fifty-five gallon drums marked DIESEL, and another marked WASTE OIL. He found some empty cardboard boxes, a few pieces of upholstered furniture, and stacked these around the drums. He also found an assortment of small cans that contained — if the labels could be trusted — paints, solvents, acid, and machine oil. These went on top of the drums. He then found a hammer and used the claw end to breach each drum at the midpoint of height.

Fuel spilled out over the floor, the acrid stink tearing at Moustafa's nasal passages. He found a clean rag and held it over his nose and mouth. Next, he took the three packages from his satchel. He knew nothing of the formula that had been used, but Moustafa immediately recognized a smell similar to that of fireworks. The bundles were tightly wrapped in plastic, the simple fuses exposed. He placed them with care, one near each drum.

Moustafa stepped back and evaluated his work. As he did, his senses were keen for any disturbances outside. He heard nothing worrisome. As he reached into his pocket for one of the two butane lighters, sweat dripped into his eyes despite the cool air. He flicked the lighter and a flame sparked obediently to life. But then Moustafa snuffed it and cursed under his breath. He had nearly forgotten the last step.

He pocketed the lighter and looked straight up. In most buildings, dealing with the sprinklers might pose a problem — the spray heads were obvious enough, but pipes were often hidden, concealed above painted drywall or a lattice of Styrofoam ceiling panels. Here, however, in a factory setting, all Moustafa had to do was track the lines visually. He followed a series of painted metal pipes through joints and connections, searching for the main line. He felt like he was surveying some massive circulatory system, and in a sense he was — in the event of a fire, these were the arteries that would carry the building's emergency lifeblood.

It took only two minutes. A larger section of pipe led down along one wall and into the concrete slab. There, just above ground level, was a simple valve with a circular handle. It was even labeled for his convenience: EMERGENCY SPRINKLER SHUTOFF. *Like turning off a garden hose*, he thought. Moustafa turned the valve full clockwise until it stopped. He considered using the hammer to break the pipe above the valve, but Moustafa decided against it, reasoning that he didn't want the water already overhead in the system lines to flood down across the floor. It seemed logical enough.

He went back to the drums and flicked his lighter again. Moustafa worked quickly now, an effort to keep the explosions nearly simultaneous. He had been told this was not critical, but Moustafa took pride in his work. The six fuses, two for each package, were simplicity itself — a cigarette, and secured around it with plastic cable ties, four matches, the phosphorous tips grouped at mid-length. He had practiced at the apartment and found the configuration to be incredibly reliable, the cigarettes turning to ash at a rate that would give him between four and five minutes. In an idle moment, the accountant in him had calculated that each complete fuse had cost twenty-eight cents, most of this going to the American government as a tobacco tax. A delicious irony.

Moustafa lit the fuses in a flurry and ran out the same way he had entered — the back door and the hole in the fence. Once in the street, he slowed to a quick walk and did not pause to admire his work. Not yet. Two blocks away he heard the explosion. Still, he did not look back. Instructions. Get away immediately. Soon Moustafa would be needed for another task, his martyr's mission, and nothing could jeopardize this.

Only upon reaching his car, near a deserted warehouse four blocks away, did he venture a look back. Colson Industries, whatever it was, was out of business. Flames licked high above the roof, their pulsing orange glow reflected in the thick haze above. Moustafa felt pride in his success. But he also felt a tugging sorrow, apprehension. In a matter of days there would be another fire, similar he supposed. And that spectacle would represent his funeral pyre, his departure from this world.

Moustafa turned away, not wanting to watch. He would do his sacred duty. Allah would give him the strength. He began driving carefully toward the safe house. There, Moustafa would check his computer for any last instructions from Caliph. There, Moustafa would pray.

LONDON, ENGLAND

High in a Fleet Street skyscraper, two Barclays financial analysts were seated at adjacent desks. Each had two computer terminals, and the man and woman multitasked nimbly between their screens, deciphering information from one machine while the other spun through commands, then vice versa. As if this was not enough of an overload, stock tickers ran a sliding banner on the wall in front of them, all the major movers and indices represented.

The trading day was about to commence and, as was their custom, the man and woman scoured the Internet for traces of bad luck, disaster, or scandal, anything that could sway their specialized sector — energy. The problems usually came from the Middle East — pipeline attacks in Iraq, seaborne tanker politics in the Straits of Hormuz. Lately, Nigeria and Venezuela had been doing their share of damage, and pirates around the Horn of Africa had been acting up again. But this morning was quiet. No petro-tragedies, and little activity from Hong Kong, where the overnight volatility coefficients had been unusually low.

It was the young woman who spotted the first article, a quick blurb on the *Houston Chronicle*'s Web site. She said, "Colson Industries had a fire last night. Their primary furnace manufacturing operation has been decimated. It's going to be down for six to nine months."

The man, older and more experienced, did not even reply. He typed the name of a Russian corporation into his own computer. The results came immediately. "Bloody hell!" he said. "Petrov I.A. burned to the ground!"

The woman's voice took an edge. "There's one other manufacturer, right? Isn't it Dutch —"

"DSR," the man spat, having already typed the full name. The wait seemed interminable, but when the computer finally gave its answer, the man exhaled a deep, controlled sigh. "No, nothing there. DSR is fine."

The two looked at one another. If they had been corporate planners they might have viewed the events in strategic terms, a market opportunity worth targeting. If they had been policemen they might have been curious about the coincidence on a criminal level. As it was, the two financial analysts did their job. They got on the phone.

In the first thirty minutes after the London market's opening gavel, Barclays was on the leading edge of a small wave. Futures indices for gas oil, heating oil, and unleaded gasoline blendstock rose three percent. DSR traded up twelve.

Some people had trouble sleeping on airplanes. Davis could sleep anywhere. He had snoozed on a metal pallet in a C-130 transport, crashed on the deck of an Aegis class missile cruiser in the Red Sea, and slept like a baby in an ice cave during Arctic survival training. So when he got to France after a long night in a Boeing 777 first-class sleeper, he was fully rested.

His first stop was the airport restroom where he ran an electric razor over his face and splashed cold water on the back of his neck. He also donned a fresh polo shirt — dark green and dull, just how he liked it. Diane had bought him a pink shirt once, tried to tell him the color was something called "salmon." Jammer Davis knew pink when he saw it.

From Paris he caught the TGV, a high-speed train that would de-
liver him to Lyon in less than two hours. He took a window seat in
an empty row, settled back as the train began its smooth, quiet acceleration. Not like a Boeing, he reckoned, but quick all the same. In no
time, the urban center of Paris gave way to soft brown pastures. Trees
vacant of foliage and tawny hedges waited patiently for the coming of
spring. Davis watched the countryside roll by, a misty morning blur at
almost two hundred miles an hour.

He had spent three years in France as a teenager. His father, a sergeant in the army and a linguist, had been assigned embassy duty in
Paris, and so Davis had attended a high school for Foreign Service de-
pendents. He'd grown to like the country, enjoy the people. In the
course of it all he had picked up a new language — and a new sport.
Davis had played high school football in the States. In France he'd seen
the local kids playing something similar, only without the pads. Davis
liked the idea, and rugby had become his game.

The train flowed over the track easy and quick. Davis closed his
eyes, tried to let his mind go blank. It didn't work. The upcoming investigation was already there, cluttering his mental screen like hard
rain on a windshield. He had experience in both military and civilian
investigations. The military versions were close to the vest — clipped
press releases, no-nonsense colonels staring down cameras. But what
most people didn't see in the military boards was the infighting, the
flag-grade politics that went on behind the scene. Colonels and gen-
erals trying to pitch blame and catch credit. But at least the military
inquiries were quick. A month, two at the outside. Civilian accident
boards, like the one he was about to wrestle, could take a year or more.
And Davis, by nature, was not a patient man.

Aside from the time involved, there were other differences. Since
1947, the business of investigating civil aircraft accidents had been reg-
ulated by an agreement known as the Chicago Convention, or more
specifically, an obscure subsection called Annex 13. Among the more
important provisions was the tricky terrain of jurisdiction. Aircraft, by
nature, were transient beasts — they could crash in one country, be
registered in another, and owned by a party in a third. Annex 13 de-

clared that the "state of occurrence" governed the authority to investigate a crash, falling back on registration should an airplane go down in international waters. So it was, the investigation of World Express 801 would be administered by France. More specifically, the Bureau Enquêtes-Accidents, or BEA.

Davis would have preferred that World Express 801 had gone down elsewhere. England, Ireland. Or Lichtenstein, for that matter. France was peculiar, one of the few countries that always ran dual investigations — the traditional safety side that he would help guide, but also a parallel criminal version where prosecutors tried to make names for themselves, tried to tie someone to a post for cobblestone target practice. In the case of World Express 801, they might go after individuals who worked for the manufacturer, CargoAir; or the operator, World Express. Captain Earl Moore and First Officer Melinda Hendricks, posthumously, would at least be spared that indignity.

Davis dozed for the last hour of the trip. The TGV dropped him right at Lyon's Saint Exupéry International Airport. He exited through the rail terminal's high, fan-shaped arches. From there he could have walked to the investigation command center. Instead, Davis found a cab.

It was late morning when he arrived at the crash site.

CHAPTER SEVEN

SOLAIZE, FRANCE

The weather was hard winter, a gunmetal gray sky blurred by darker veils of rain in the distance. Light drizzle swirled on an arbitrary breeze that blustered back and forth, never seeming to settle on a direction. A French breeze, Davis mused.

He knew he wasn't going by the book. He should have checked in first at the investigation's headquarters. Signed off paperwork, gotten somebody's approval. But he always liked one initial look at a crash without distraction, without people pulling him by the elbow to places he didn't want to go.

The cab was at least a half mile from the crash site when an array of barricades and police cordoned off the road. A fleet of forklifts and sturdy flatbed trucks were parked nearby, lying in wait for the awkward task of moving the wreckage to a secure location. It was a difficult undertaking, as the pieces were often huge, some weighing tons. Through all the shifting and manhandling, evidence was invariably lost, damaged, and altered. There should have been a more delicate, clinical way to do it. There wasn't.

A helicopter was hovering beneath the overcast clouds. The craft was almost stationary, sideslipping now and again to give the men inside new lines of sight. The aerial photographers had likely been shooting since first light. There would be more photographers on the ground, and nothing on the site would be moved until every angle had been recorded, documented. Davis noticed a line of reporters and civilians standing at the best vantage point, the top of a nearby ridge.

They were all pointing and exchanging comments. Vulture's row. Something like it materialized at all aircraft crashes, onlookers drawn by the same morbid allure, Davis supposed, that made automobile wrecks so interesting.

He paid the cab and sent it away, figuring he wouldn't have any trouble getting a ride later — there had to be a constant flow of vehicles between the crash site and the center of operations. Following a rise in the road, Davis reached a perimeter that was marked with police tape. Probably four miles of it. Five men and two women, all wearing yellow vests marked POLICIER stood firm at the entry point. When they saw him coming, two of the men moved to stand in his path. That's how things worked when you were a wide six foot four.

One of the policemen held up an arm.

Davis came to a halt.

"This area is closed to the public," the gatekeeper said in French.

Davis pulled out his NTSB identification, said nothing.

The lead man eyed him critically, but stepped away to reference a clipboard. Next he got out his mobile phone. It took two minutes. When he spoke again it was in English. "Very well, monsieur. But you must soon find your proper credentials."

Davis nodded. "*Merci beaucoup.*"

He started walking again. Fifty steps later he crested the hill.

And there it was.

Davis stood still.

It always hit him this way. The first time he saw any accident site he could only stare. Even now, two days after the crash, a few thin currents of smoke drifted up from the charred earth, like the last wisps of steam escaping a once-boiling pot. Everywhere he looked, the colors and textures were those of death. Brown earth, slick and damp from the rain. Blackened, jagged clumps of wreckage strewn in a seemingly random pattern. He had seen the aerial photos, but from ground level the crash site looked different. It always did. The individual pieces of debris seemed incredibly still, an impression at odds with what the sum implied to the contrary — noise, fire, turmoil.

He shifted his gaze to the horizon. In the midwinter distance, dormant grass and leafless trees gave a dismal frame to the apocalyptic scene. A few broken clumps of mist hovered in the valleys, soft pools to cradle the chaos. Davis began walking again, steering toward the main debris field. A large downed tree was lying prone amid the wreckage, testament to the physical forces that had engaged in one cataclysmic moment. He navigated through a minefield of metal, composite, wire, glass, and fabric. Most was from World Express 801, but a few things had probably already been lying around. An old car tire, beer bottles, a discarded compact disc. That much more for the investigators to sift through.

It was the smell that hit him next, the stinging odor of jet fuel and soot grating on his respiratory tract. At least it wasn't mixed with that other smell, he thought. If there was any good news here, it was that the human element of the tragedy had been minimal. Two pilots. No passengers.

He stopped first at the largest section of wreckage — just like everyone would — and tried to place it. It was a central section, an arrangement of thick beams and bulkheads. Probably rectangular to begin with, it was now slightly askew. The attached skin and fittings were a mix — some clean with jagged edges, other parts drooping and charred where the heat had done its work. Davis scanned all around and saw it everywhere — fire. World Express 801 had probably been carrying a hundred tons of Jet A fuel. A lot of potential energy.

He began walking again. The ground was crisscrossed with deep ruts. These were not a direct result of the crash, Davis knew. Emergency vehicles always dominated the first few hours, and they did a lot of damage, running over debris, indiscriminately spraying water and fire retardant on the whole mess. Nobody could blame them. It was a tough job, and sometimes lives were at stake. But it only added to the forensic nightmare, made the investigator's job that much harder.

Davis stepped over a large metal tube that had one end ripped apart in three sections — it formed a perfect fleur-de-lis. He found a cockpit instrument panel, a twelve-inch square liquid-crystal display.

The glass screen was intact in its frame, black and empty, and a cable covered in melted insulation snaked out from the back. In years past, flight instruments were round dials with needles, "steam gauges" in the parlance. In those days, you could tell how fast an airplane was going when it hit by finding the indentation the airspeed pointer made on its glass cover plate. Now things were different. The actual instruments were void, black masks that hid whatever had existed at the moment of impact. The only way to tell was to mine chip sets, dig into memory cards, read bits of data. Clinical and secretive.

Davis drew to a stop and put his hands on his hips. He took one last look at the scene, taking a mental picture as he had done many times before. Not for the official record. It was just for his own sake.

By chance, airplanes could crash anywhere. By design, crash investigations were almost always based at airfields. The reasons were many. Airports were publicly owned, had communications gear, buildings to support meetings, trucks and tugs to haul things around. And they had hangars to hold wreckage. Sometimes there were only a few massive pieces involved. Sometimes there were millions. But a vacant hangar was always the way to go.

Davis hitched a ride with a photographer, an amiable Parisian who'd contracted himself out for air crash work to support his more artistic side — landscape black-and-whites. Like a good starving artist, he gave Davis his portfolio to study on the twenty-minute drive. The guy was actually good. As far as Jammer Davis could tell.

Davis got a good look at the Lyon airport as they drove. It was a fairly busy regional hub, maybe a dozen midsized jets nested at the passenger terminals. The terminal buildings had a modernist tilt, two grandiose main structures that reached for the sky. It was getting to be an architectural cliché, he thought. Give an airport designer a blank check, and you'd get no end of columns, arches, wings, and height.

The photographer drove around the airfield on a perimeter road, skirting the two north-south runways. He pulled into a quiet corner of the airport, a place that in the States might have been referred to as a "business park." There were groups of offices, workshops, and hangars. The photographer pointed to the correct building. Davis thanked the fellow and wished him luck. He really meant it, too.

It was labeled SOIXANTE-DEUX. Building Sixty-two. A boxy two-story support complex was attached to a larger hanger. Both seemed relatively new. Davis could just make out the faint impression of a name on the hangar's corrugated sidewall where the large letters of a sign had been removed. All that remained was a shadow where the paint had weathered unevenly — PRIMAIRE. The name stood there like some pale, ghostly apparition, serving as the headstone of yet another European budget airline gone into receivership. Now the place had found a new life. Any remains of the carcass of PRIMAIRE had been exhumed. Padlocks were snapped off, electricity restored, and the floors swept up. Building Sixty-two had been fully requisitioned and prepared for the cause of World Express 801.

At the main entrance a woman sat behind a table. She was shuffling papers, a bureaucratic bird featherbedding her nest with forms and messages. She was good at it, three neat piles. In, Out, Trash, Davis guessed. If she were a cashier, she'd be the type who put every bill in the tray face up, aligned the same way. He stopped right in front of her.

"*Bonjour. Je suis* Jammer Davis." He pronounced the J in his name hard, not wanting anybody to start calling him Zhammér.

The woman smiled officiously. "Yes, Mr. Davis. The investigator-in-charge has been expecting you."

She had gone right to English. Davis wondered if his French was that rusty. The woman checked his NTSB identification and said, "Follow me."

At the mouth of a hallway they passed a single rent-a-gendarme. He was sitting in a chair smoking a cigarette and reading *Le Monde*. Security, Davis reckoned. The first stop was a small office. The woman arranged Davis against a blank wall, then picked up a camera that was connected to a computer by a cable.

"Don't smile," she said.

"But I'm happy."

A disapproving frown.

Davis gave a subtle kink to his upper lip. All the pose needed was a number board hanging around his neck, maybe a height scale on the wall.

There was a click, and the woman started pressing buttons to feed his picture to the computer. As they waited for the finished product, she handed him a folder. Inside was a single page labeled, "Rules of Conduct for Investigators." Don't talk to the press without approval. Dress standards. A code of personal conduct. At the top of the page was a little cartoon policeman blowing a whistle. In case you didn't know what "rules" were, Davis supposed.

Minutes later, the woman handed over a smart photo ID with a lanyard. Davis hung it around his neck and fell back into formation. As they left the room he discreetly dropped the rulebook into a trash can.

They ended up in the hangar, a cavernous place with bright fluorescent lights that gave full detail and color to everything. The place was cold, and Davis wondered if it simply wasn't heated or if the heat had been turned off in some misguided effort to preserve evidence. An assortment of tugs, forklifts, and handcarts buzzed around in a frenzy, clearing the concrete floor so the remains of World Express 801 could be brought to its postmortem slab.

He followed his escort to the middle of the place where a group was gathered around someone giving a talk. The angles changed as Davis got closer, and he was surprised to see a large piece of wreckage. Usually debris was left in the field for the best part of a week, until every inch had been meticulously mapped and documented. This investigation was barely forty-eight hours old, so Davis decided that whoever was in charge was either very efficient or very rushed.

He settled into the fringe of the crowd. The wreckage was a large section of the cockpit, left front side. The captain's seat was still recognizable, though its back panel had been exposed to heat — the plastic was discolored and shot with a thousand tiny bubbles. It was a mystery how airplanes broke apart. Jagged metal and scorched wire bundles might surround a pristine section of seats or instruments, hardware that looked as fresh as the day it had come out of the factory. A photographer was at least snapping pictures from all angles, and a young woman was busy labeling parts and entering data into a laptop. Maybe they *were* just organized.

A man stood in front of the group talking and gesturing. He might have been lecturing a class of undergraduates. His frame was tall and angular, the face dominated by high cheekbones and a prominent nose. He had clear skin with few lines — mid-fifties, but not a guy who spent time outdoors. The gray hair on top was thin, but on the sides it was long and wavy and tousled. His outfit was a classic — tan cotton shirt and vest, pants with lots of pockets, and at the bottom a virgin set of hiking boots. Indiana Jones minus the hat, whip, and dust. His movement seemed stunted, locking in position now and again, and Davis realized he was posing for the photographer.

The man addressed the gathering in English, under a heavy French accent. One look at the crowd told Davis why. There were clearly a lot of nationalities here. But then, CargoAir was a worldwide consortium, a far-flung archipelago of suppliers and designers and subcontractors. The inquiry would have to reflect it. There would be a hundred interested parties — some helping, others getting in the way. For the most part, Davis would avoid them, because he wasn't here to make friends or build teams. He was here to solve a crash. And to do that, he preferred to work alone, a pelagic creature that swam where it liked and ignored the currents. There were always currents.

"You can see the captain's station is largely intact," the speaker said. His words flowed with a carefree ease derivative of two possible sources — competence or sublime overconfidence. "This indicates that the copilot's side of the aircraft was the first to impact. Of course, data will confirm this in time. But if proven, it will be a confirming indicator of which pilot was at the controls in the moments before impact." He paused, waiting for the obvious.

"Why is that?" someone asked obligingly.

"Empirical psychological studies have proven that in the last instant of any crash, be it aircraft or automobile, the operator will instinctively steer away from impact to save himself."

Empirical psychological studies? Davis cringed.

Another voice prodded, "Even if the outcome is hopeless?"

The speaker emphasized, "*Particularly* if the outcome is hopeless. So, with regard to the captain's thoughts, this section tells us —"

"Nothing," Davis interjected.

The speaker fell silent. A sea of heads turned.

Davis said, "When an airplane hits, tons of metal hit the ground and break up — it's chaos and it's random. Certain parts of the airframe, because of their inherent structural strength or frangible nature, tend to be the most intact. Wings, tail, landing gear. If a main body section this big survives, there's one of two reasons." Davis paused, but nobody asked. "You either have a low speed or low-angle impact."

The speaker reestablished control. "I don't think we have met, sir."

"Jammer Davis, NTSB."

"Ah, yes. Our American liaison. Thank you for your . . . opinion. As you are leading the human factors group, you will be happy to know that this is my specialty as well. I am a resident professor at Ecole Normale Supérieure in Paris, specializing in aviation psychology." The man paused, and Davis had the impression he was mulling coverage of the rest of his curriculum vitae. Instead, he edged through the crowd and held out a hand. "I am Dr. Thierry Bastien, investigator-in-charge of this inquiry."

Davis thought, *Christ, a shrink at the helm.* He said, "Nice to meet you."

The two shook hands. Then the Frenchman arced out an arm and said, "The others here are also involved in our investigation. We will be gathering for lunch soon. However, since all the working group leaders are present, perhaps an impromptu meeting would be in order."

"A meeting?"

"*Certainement!* Your information, Mr. Davis, the seventy-two-hour profile of the captain — it holds great interest for us all."

"Really? Why is that?"

Bastien did not answer. He only smiled politely, adjourned his lesson, and then asked for the key players to remain behind.

CHAPTER EIGHT

The meeting took place in a side room, a generic rectangular space that might have been a break room or an office in its previous life. There were a dozen scattered chairs and a white board was nailed to one wall. A square table sat empty in the middle, looking for all the world like it was waiting for a four-sided card game, and above that was a central light fixture. Someone had added a ceiling fan as an afterthought, and as it turned slowly its long blades clipped the incandescent glow to spin oblong shadows over a scuffed linoleum floor.

A young man came in with two pots of coffee. He set them on the table, along with a fancy assortment of china cups and saucers and silver spoons. Davis didn't hesitate. It was a nice blend, thick and smooth. He hoped it was a sign of things to come. If this had been an NTSB affair it would have been Folgers in a Styrofoam cup. Plastic lid and stir stick included.

Bastien had been buttonholed by a reporter in the hangar, and so the rest of the group began to mingle. Davis walked slowly through the room, nodding here, checking a credential badge there. He wasn't sure who or what he was looking for — he was just trolling, his eyes dragging a line. Then the hit came.

It was the company name on the badge that first drew his attention — CargoAir. Then the man. He was small with a compact build, almost certainly of Middle Eastern extraction. Egyptian or maybe Lebanese. His jet black hair was cropped short, showing the first few threads of gray at the sides. A bushy moustache hovered over his mouth like an awning. He stood away from the crowd, shoulders sagging and head bent down, like his entire body was subject to some great weight.

Davis went over and held out a hand. "Jammer Davis."

The dark eyes came alight, quick and intelligent, even though the rest of the man still lagged — it was like two bright searchlights reaching out from a deep fog.

"Hello, Mr. Davis. I am Dr. Ibrahim Jaber."

Davis shook a hand that disappeared in his own. "Good to meet you," he said.

"I understand you will be in charge of the Human Factors Group, Mr. Davis. You may find yourself a very busy man." Jaber's voice was every bit as dull and heavy as his body language.

"Yes, I think Monsieur Bastien will see to that. But I suspect we'll all be busy."

"Indeed," Jaber agreed. "You must have extraordinary expertise."

Davis cocked an inquisitive eyebrow. "What makes you think that?"

"You are the only foreigner on the formal investigation team."

"Really? So the other group leaders are all French?"

Jaber nodded and gave Davis a rundown on the room. He pointed out three men and a woman who were set to lead other groups. All were engaged in animated conversation, and many were clearly friends — not necessarily a good thing, Davis knew. Friends had trouble criticizing friends, and sometimes in an investigation you had to do exactly that. Six months from now, they might not be so close. They might be taking swings at one another.

Davis said, "Have they all done crash work?"

"Of course. Their backgrounds are a mix, as you would expect — government and corporate. But all are experienced investigators." Jaber was about to say something else, but the words were cut off by a retching cough.

"That sounds bad," Davis remarked.

"I've been a touch under the weather," Jaber replied. "It is nothing."

"So in what capacity are you here?"

"I will act as the chief CargoAir consultant, working closely with the Systems and Design Group." He made a sweeping gesture across the room. "Most of those you see here are like myself, technicians brought in to help understand what has happened."

"And the whole whirlwind is headed up by Monsieur Bastien," said Davis.

"Indeed. A very capable man."

Davis paused, then said, "Good. I like capable people." He sipped his coffee. "So tell me, Dr. Jaber, what is your usual job at CargoAir?"

Jaber also held coffee. His cup was full, like he hadn't touched it. "I am the chief project engineer for the C-500."

Davis' head tilted to one side and he pursed his lips. As if he was impressed. "So this is your baby."

The engineer's sharp gaze went awry. His English was good, but the metaphor had caused him to stumble. Then he smiled. "Yes, yes. I am the father."

Davis was trying to figure out why such a senior person would be present at this stage of the investigation. Usually a company would send a lower-level representative, someone whose diplomatic skills outweighed their use with a slide rule. The big technical guns only got their hands dirty when they had to. *If* they had to. His next thought was interrupted by a spoon tapping on a china cup. Bastien had arrived to call the impromptu meeting to order. There was a scraping of chairs as everyone maneuvered and sat. Twelve chairs, thirteen people. Davis was left standing like the kid who hadn't heard the music stop.

Bastien rose three quarters from his chair and held out an introductory arm. "Ladies and gentlemen, I would like you to meet our associate from the United States, Mr. . . . ." he hesitated, "Jammer Davis. We have been waiting for your report on Captain Moore, sir."

Davis set his coffee cup on the table and looked out at the faces —they were intense, maybe eager. A lot of anticipation. Had they been talking? Speculating? Of course they had. Gossip and innuendo would be rampant. Accident investigations were no different from church socials or office parties. The participants just stood around charred wreckage instead of a punch bowl. And in place of pay raises and sex, they talked about chafed wire bundles and metal fatigue.

"Yesterday, I began a seventy-two-hour look-back on the crew," Davis said. "The first officer was here in France for the week preceding the flight, so my efforts concentrated on the captain. I flew to Houston and interviewed both his wife and his flight surgeon." He decided to get the worst out of the way. "Earl Moore had his license pulled just over a year ago. Alcohol. He went through rehabilitation and got his medical back."

"And since then?" Bastien prodded.

Davis paused. "His flight surgeon thinks that Moore may have had a problem last week."

"A problem?" another voice asked. They were all looking at him like he was a suspect juggler — everyone waiting for the balls to drop.

"He may have had a run-in with the law. *Possibly* for an alcohol related offense. Let me stress that none of this is confirmed yet."

"Yes," Bastien said, as if the cosmos were aligning with great precision. "This would go with the rest."

"The rest of what?" Davis asked.

Bastien said, "We have interviewed several employees at the hotel where Moore was staying. The bartender there, a young woman, remembered Moore well. There is record of a significant bar tab on the night before our incident. I will provide you with a list of names and specifics, Mr. Davis, for your further pursuit."

Davis frowned. "Do we have anything from toxicology yet?" he asked.

"The body was . . ." the Frenchman hesitated, "in poor condition. But yes, forensic blood alcohol tests are ongoing."

"Blood alcohol tests," Davis repeated, his voice flat. He scanned the faces in the room, looking for suspicion. He saw none. "Am I the only one who finds this whole line of thought distracting?"

No replies.

"Even if Moore had alcohol in his system," Davis reasoned, "it's not the kind of thing that will make an airplane dive straight down from thirty-eight thousand feet. There are a lot of other things to consider. For example, carbon monoxide in the blood. If they lost pressurization, you'd have excess CO."

"Of course, yes, Mr. Davis," Bastien said with a shooing motion of his hand. "A full postmortem will be performed."

A voice in back asked, "What about Moore's personal life?"

Davis, still the only one standing, thrust his hands in his pockets. That way he wouldn't lunge for any throats. "He and his wife split up last year. Their divorce was nearly final."

"So —" someone else suggested, "the man was under some amount of stress."

"Stress?" Davis queried. "He used to land jets on aircraft carriers in the middle of the night."

"But that is different," Bastien argued.

"Is it?" Davis shot back.

There was a pointed silence, a pause that announced the imminent departure of civility.

Bastien ended the impasse. He redirected the discussion to more mundane matters, bland queries about medical licenses, Earl Moore's travel to France, and sleep cycles. Then he covered what the local team had discovered regarding the first officer's seventy-two-hour history. There wasn't much.

Davis made a conscious effort to ratchet down. The target was off his back for the moment, and while he wasn't happy about having been set up, he didn't need to alienate *everyone* in the first thirty minutes.

Bastien finally ended the ambush by saying, "Ladies and gentlemen, I suggest we break for lunch. It will provide a good chance for us to circulate these ideas, and perhaps get to know one another." He seemed to look to Davis for approval.

With all the control he could muster, Davis nodded and said, "Sure, Terry. Sounds like a plan."

Bastien cringed at the Anglicized stomping of his name. He said coolly, "Dr. Bastien, if you don't mind, sir. We try to keep things as professional as possible."

"Okay. But you can just call me Jammer."

Lunch was nice. Roast duck in wine sauce, poached oysters, and jambon persille. Presented with the usual selection of salads, cheese, breads, and pastries, it was offered in a buffet that stretched the length of a twenty-foot table. Included was a sampling of wine from the surrounding regions — Burgundy, Bordeaux, Champagne. Good food, casual atmosphere, alcohol at midday, and an investigator-in-charge still posing for photos as he pranced through it all. If there was an Apgar score for newborn investigations, Davis thought, this one would rate a flatline zero.

All the same, he knew now wasn't the time to start grumbling about a lack of urgency — or the high level of interest in Captain Earl Moore. Soon maybe, but not yet. Instead, Davis made an effort to work the room and meet as many of the investigative team as he could. He shook hands and tried to remember names. He was wearing his old Air Force-issue bomber jacket, and the side pocket filled up with business cards until he felt like a walking Rolodex. In one-on-one chats they seemed a reasonable bunch, more agreeable than in the "team-meeting" crossfire he'd just faced.

Aside from those he'd already met, there were dozens of new faces, representing the usual mix of government entities and corporate nameplates. Engineers, pilots, insurers, reinsurers, mouthpieces for individual companies. A lot of smart people, some wanting to get to the bottom of the crash, others only here to act as dummies for their corporate ventriloquists. It was quite the U.N. Davis must have heard a dozen different languages by the time he'd cracked the last crab leg on his plate. Of course, English would dominate the investigation, but most of that would be heavily accented. So when he heard a woman's voice with a straight Midwestern slant, Davis locked on.

She was standing by the bread basket, a trim thing with flaxen blonde hair pulled back hard in a ponytail — the way women did when they didn't have to worry about dark roots. From where he stood, she had a great profile. Wanting to be sure, he discreetly took a few steps to change his aspect and looked again. Still great. Probably just on the far side of thirty, she was dressed in dark slacks and a loose sweater, no attachments or baubles. Very basic. She was smiling, nice and patient, while an Oriental guy, Korean maybe, stood next to her butchering his consonants.

Davis edged over and heard, "America very big place. I study engineering there at jojotek."

The woman kept smiling, but her eyes were a blank.

Davis had spent a year in Korea. He said, "The Yellow Jackets."

The Korean's eyes lit. "Yes, yes!"

Davis turned to the woman. "Georgia Tech."

She smiled again. Probably meant it this time. "Of course."

"You go there?" The Korean asked Davis.

"No, no. I went straight into the seminary."

The man looked befuddled, and he eyed the collar of Davis' polo shirt. The top two buttons were undone. With the conversation suddenly at loggerheads, the man politely excused himself and went back to the buffet.

Her smile was definitely the real thing now. She said, "Thanks. He was nice, but—"

"A little hard to understand? Some guys can be like that."

She sipped orange juice from a glass. "You don't say."

"Jammer Davis," he said, holding out a hand.

Her handshake was good—not flimsy, but also not one of those girls-can-go-to-the-gym-too statements.

"Anna Sorensen."

There was that voice again. There was something about it. Rich, with a slightly nasal tone, the words clipped and precise. Davis turned his head to one side and read an identity badge that looked a lot like his. It was hanging from a lanyard, centered on her chest. "Anna V. Sorensen. S-o-r-e-n-s-e-n. Perfect!"

"What do you mean?"

"You've got eight letters after the *V*."

"So?"

"So I could call you V-8."

"A nickname?"

"In the Air Force we refer to them as call signs. You know, like Goose or Maverick."

"I saw the movie. Do you give one to everyone you meet?"

"Just the people whose names are a mouthful. Smith or Jones I could handle, but you can't expect me to call you Anna V. Sorensen for — well, for however long this investigation takes."

"You could just call me Anna."

He cocked his head, gave her a quizzical look. "But then again, V-8 isn't very original. I've heard it before. We'll come up with something else."

"*We* will, Mr. Davis?"

He smiled. "Just call me Jammer."

"And where did that name — sorry, call sign come from?"

"My first fighter assignment. When you get into dogfights there's an unwritten rule that you say as little as possible on the radio — another pilot might have something important to say, like, 'Break right dummy, you're about to get gunned!' As a new guy, I found the air-to-air tangles pretty intense. I tended to babble on the radios. Pretty soon the guys were giving me a hard time, told me I was 'jamming' the frequency."

"Jammer." Sorensen nodded like she got it. "I think Dr. Bastien might call you something else. You two didn't exactly get off on the right foot."

"He'll come around. Has to — I'm on the investigation team, the token foreigner."

Her eyes narrowed in mock suspicion. "And you're a pilot?"

"I am an operations human factors liaison."

"Uh-huh. Pilot."

He asked, "So what's your specialty?"

"I'm here representing a contractor."

Davis glanced at her ID again. "Honeywell. Avionics?"

"Yes."

Davis figured she might keep going, spout off some fancy qualifications. Nothing came. "Any other Yanks here?" he asked.

"I met a guy from Rockwell and somebody from the FAA." She

nodded across the room. "But these people are from all over the world."

"The C-500 is a global machine, so we'll get a global investigation. In the old days, a company just built an airplane and stamped their name on it. Now it's different. Avionics suites, landing gear assemblies, wings, entire fuselage sections. Designed and built all over the world. Computers coordinate the measurements and specs, then everything is shipped to one factory and snapped together like a big model airplane."

"Maybe they didn't use enough glue on this one."

He raised an eyebrow.

Sorensen smiled awkwardly. Her pale blue eyes then flicked over the room. "So given what you've seen so far, Jammer, what's your opinion?"

"I found the Burgundy a little brusque for this time of day, and the foie gras was definitely underdone."

One corner of her mouth curled up. "You don't have any ideas about what brought this airplane down?"

"I always have ideas. But there's a lot I haven't—"

"There you are!" a strident voice interrupted.

Davis looked up to see Bastien on final approach. He had a glass of red in one hand and gestured freely with the other. "I see you have found a fellow American. And a beautiful one at that."

Davis was quick with, "I'll look even better after a good shower."

Sorensen put her knuckles to her mouth, stifling a snicker.

Bastien forced a half smile. "You must come to the press briefing, Monsieur Davis."

"Press briefing?"

"It is next on the agenda, our second. There is a great deal of interest in this tragedy."

"There always is," Davis said. "What we need is a good scandal to drive it off the front page."

"*Précisément!*" Bastien said enthusiastically. "If only our president would have another of his affairs of the heart!"

Bastien was downright jovial. Davis wondered if it was the wine.

The NTSB would have frowned on alcohol in the middle of a work-day, but you couldn't keep the French from their wine. As a kid, back when the cockpit doors of airliners were simply left ajar on long flights, he remembered watching Air France pilots take wine with their in-flight meals. He wondered if they still did.

"But until something drives our work onto page two," Bastien looked over his shoulder and whispered theatrically, "we shall have to throw them something tasty."

The investigator-in-charge loped away.

Davis looked at Sorensen. "I wonder what he meant by that."

She shrugged and said, "I don't know. Should we go find out?"

"I think we'd better."

CHAPTER NINE

President Truett Townsend walked quickly through the West Wing corridor, his usual morning entourage in tight formation — three Secret Service agents, Chief of Staff Martin Spector, and two aides. Townsend was a tall man, and his long strides forced the others to nearly trot to keep up.

The president's energy level was already high, having been raised by his morning workout. He alternated each day — an hour of weight training or forty-five minutes on the treadmill. It kept him trim, but that wasn't why he did it. Townsend had come to find that his daily session in the White House gym was the only time when he could think without interruption, no one trying to slip him a memo or whisper in his ear. He'd made far more good decisions on the squat machine than in his regular bipartisan congressional meetings.

As he approached the West Wing conference room, Townsend slowed. A phalanx of Marines and Secret Service surrounded the entrance. Discreetly embedded in the frame of the entryway was a collection of security sensors. Townsend passed through and a distinct beep sounded. Without hesitation, he went back out to the hall, raised his arms, and one of the Secret Service men scanned the president of the United States with a hand wand as if he was a commoner at the airport. The offending contraband turned out to be a stainless steel cork-puller he'd inadvertently stuffed in his jacket pocket the night before.

"Sorry, guys. My bad."

"Not at all, Mr. President. You're clear."

It was a drill that none of Townsend's predecessors, nor their staff members, would ever have tolerated. But it had been one of this president's first directives. If he went through security, everybody did. The move brought some grumbling from his staff, but it had gained Townsend immediate standing with his security detail. As he'd put it to them, "If you guys can put your lives on the line for me, the least I can do is make your job easy."

Followed by Martin Spector, Townsend entered the conference room where the participants of the Daily Intelligence Briefing, or DIB, had already assembled. The director of national intelligence, heads of the FBI, CIA, and Homeland Security, and the chairman of the Joint Chiefs of Staff were all present. The vice president was abroad, fostering goodwill in the Far East.

As Townsend entered, JCS Chairman General Robert Banks came to rigid attention. The rest all stood and clasped their hands in front, the parallel civilian posture. This was another of Townsend's decrees. He didn't get any personal thrill from it, but there were always military officers at these meetings, and if they were going to show respect for the office of commander-in-chief, then so could everyone else.

The president took his seat at the head of a large conference table, his shoulders framed by a sagging American flag on one side and the presidential standard on the other. Townsend broke into a smile as he looked expectantly at the crowd. His face was not classically handsome, but more often described as having "character." His nose was a bit too large, close-cut hair mocked a receding hairline, and deep vertical furrows framed his mouth. There was an air of the West about Truett Townsend, a no-nonsense pioneer quality that had served him well during his campaign. He had proven wrong the adage that only candidates from big electoral states could reach the top. Amid a faltering economy and the federal budget nightmare, the electorate was in another of its "change" moods, and no one on the ticket was as far removed from D.C.'s chronic ills as the two-term senator from the frigid, bison-roamed wilds of Wyoming.

"Good morning, everyone," said the president. Even his voice came from the frontier — no silky orator's inflection, but a rich rumble of Rocky Mountain granite.

"Good morning, Mr. President," replied the chorus.

Everyone settled in and Townsend nodded to the DNI, Darlene Graham. "Go ahead, Darlene."

Graham was a tall, big-boned woman with long dark hair and a sultry voice — Townsend had always thought she'd have looked and sounded right at home leaning on a piano in a smoky nightclub. Graham had spent twenty years working her way up the intelligence community ladder, and she was guiding things confidently after eighteen months at the helm of the country's combined intelligence post.

She began her briefing. "We had a relatively quiet night, sir. There were a few skirmishes in the tribal areas of Pakistan — the government forces are cracking down again. We suspect it will last for a week or two, then things will die off. We have good Predator coverage on the area, just in case any of the cockroaches try to scatter into Afghanistan."

The president nodded his approval.

Graham went on, "There was a market bombing in Khandahar, a few IED attacks on remote roads — the usual chaos. Oh, and two defectors came over from the North Korean army. Not a big deal, but at least it's not the Middle East."

"Thank God," the FBI director said.

There were a few questions, which Graham fielded knowledgeably, and then a projection screen came to life at one end of the room. She began to manipulate a remote control. "Mr. President, you asked me yesterday for an in-depth briefing on the man who is quickly becoming our biggest thorn." A photograph of a very familiar face filled the screen, the same picture that was plastered on bounty posters all over Iraq. "We all know his face."

"Hell," General Banks said, "the way he posts photos all over his Web sites — it's like the guy's got a PR campaign."

Graham continued, "His given name is Abdul Taim. We all know him as Caliph. He grew up in Mosul. A dropout from university, he joined the resistance soon after our invasion of Iraq in 2003. He made his name initially as a sniper, with a reputation for engaging our own snipers. He had some success, I have to say."

"He'd have been no match in a fair fight," General Banks argued. "For a time our shooters were going in with an entourage, then getting left on their own in a hostile urban environment. The locals knew where our guys were and passed it along. If a sniper doesn't have concealment, he's not a sniper. He's a target."

"Point taken," the president said.

Graham continued, "Caliph acquired quite a reputation, and eventually a following. As you all know, about twenty months ago we launched a concerted effort to take him out. We actually received some timely, accurate intel on his whereabouts and a SEAL Team was sent in. Unfortunately, the size of the opposition force took us by surprise and there was a heavy firefight. Still, we thought we had him. One of the team members got an ID on Caliph, took a shot from medium range. Caliph went down, but there wasn't time to confirm the kill before our team had to pull back."

"I know that soldier personally," General Banks said. "He doesn't miss."

Graham said, "None of us here would doubt it, General. But in the weeks after this mission, incontrovertible evidence was received." A new photograph came to the screen, the terrorist lying in a hospital bed. His head was heavily bandaged, his eyes barely open. The mouth seemed to hold a smirk, and to one side was a Baghdad newspaper headlining his demise. "There were other Web postings and a number of firsthand accounts. Our analysts went over it all very carefully and determined that Caliph definitely survived."

"So we almost had him," the president lamented.

"Yes. And not only has he survived, but since that time Caliph has gone to ground."

"We try to squish a pest, and instead we create a legend," lamented Chief of Staff Spector.

"It would appear so," Graham admitted. "Unfortunately, his survival has only magnified his legend. More recent evidence suggests that Caliph has assumed a new role. No longer a trigger man, he has become a leader of sorts, an apparition who is rarely seen but controls an extensive network. We hear his name constantly when we interrogate detainees. By laying low, Caliph has become more potent than ever. He organizes the disorganized, takes loose bands of individuals and turns them into networks with common, coordinated strategies."

Spector asked, "And in your opinion, what are these strategies?"

Graham fingered the remote again. The next picture was of two buckets, both brimming with a gray, glutinous substance. "The photo you see was given to us by Dutch intelligence yesterday. Two days ago, on an anonymous tip, they raided an apartment outside Amsterdam. The tenant was a Yemeni national — at the onset of the raid, the guy blew himself up in a closet with some sort of improvised explosive. The police recovered what you see here. The exact chemistry is still being analyzed, but we think it involves aluminum and an oxidizer, maybe ammonium perchlorate."

"Which gives you what?" Spector asked.

"A high-temperature accelerant. Someone was trying to start a very hot fire."

The president said, "Do we know what this guy's plans were?"

"The Dutch are going over a computer as we speak, but so far they haven't found anything about a specific target. They did, however, find a martyr's video. It is quite clear that this fellow was one of Caliph's followers. He was only in the apartment for about two weeks, but given the level of preparation you see here," Graham gestured to the screen, "we think the strike was very near."

"Why the Netherlands?" General Banks asked.

"We don't know. But there are two other recent arrests that could be related — a Pakistani national who was detained in Indonesia, and an Iraqi picked up on immigration violations in Portugal. Both have been positively linked to Caliph's network, but neither has given any useful information. Chances are, they don't know much — they were just awaiting instructions."

"He's branching out," President Townsend said, "not restricting himself to the Middle East any more."

Graham replied, "It would appear so. Caliph is up to something. Perhaps something very big."

The president leaned back in his chair, laced his fingers behind his head. He wished aloud, "If we could only find the bastard."

The FBI director asked, "Do we know how he manages his network?"

Graham said, "Much is done by way of the Internet, Arabic Web sites with coded messages. But there are occasions when direct contact is necessary." She spun to point the remote and a video clip came to life on the screen. A large, shapeless woman lumbered through a busy corridor. Her gait was almost bovine, trundling from side to side as others walked around her. The image was grainy, probably taken by a security camera, and kept replaying in a loop that repeated every ten seconds. Judging by the background, she was in an airport or a train station.

"This is Fatima Adara. Some months ago, we identified her as Caliph's conduit—his messenger, if you will. She's not very discreet, turns up regularly all across the region. And Adara doesn't make any effort to slip into places quietly—she just uses her Iraqi passport."

"Has she ever been detained for questioning?" someone asked.

"We considered that, but thought it better to let her run in the hope that she would lead us to Caliph. We spot her occasionally. She's not very well trained."

Spector said, "Occasionally? This implies we're not monitoring her continuously."

Graham showed her first sign of discomfort. Her voice went down an octave. "We give Adara a rather long surveillance leash—as I said, hoping that she'll lead us to Caliph. We've lost track of her a few times. But she always turns up again."

General Banks gestured to the screen. "You lost track of *that*?"

Graham ignored the comment. "She was last seen in Jordan two weeks ago. However, one of our analysts recently made a startling connection. As you all know, we've been trying for some time to track flows of money from the sovereign wealth funds of certain oil-rich states. As petrodollars accumulate, the controllers of these funds are diversifying their holdings into a great number of businesses and investments. They are building companies, universities, even entire cities from scratch."

"Not such a bad idea, if you ask me," said Spector. "Sooner or later the oil wells are going to run dry."

"Yes," Graham agreed. "But we suspect that some of this largesse is being funneled to terrorist groups. And in the course of our watch, we found this —" Graham put one more photo on the screen.

"It's her!" the president said.

The image was high quality, and there was no mistaking Fatima Adara. She was sitting at a table at an outdoor café. With her was a middle-aged man — thin hair, pale skin, high Slavic cheekbones.

Someone blurted the obvious question. "Who is he?"

"His name," Graham said, "is Luca Medved. He was actually the target of the surveillance. It was taken two months ago in Marseille, France."

"She was in France?" Spector remarked.

"Yes. It's the first time we've spotted her outside the Middle East."

The president cut in. "So why were you watching this guy Medved? Is he some kind of terrorist?"

"Actually, anything but. I told you we were tracking companies created with oil wealth. Luca Medved is a Russian national. And, among other things, he is the current chairman of the board of CargoAir, the new aircraft manufacturer based in France."

"The chairman of CargoAir?" the president said, clearly taken aback. "He's got an association with Caliph?"

"That's not clear yet," Graham said. "We're trying to find out."

General Banks asked, "Wasn't it a CargoAir airplane that crashed recently?"

"Yes," Graham said, "one went down in France two days ago." She quickly headed off the next question. "Right away we considered a link between this crash and the cache of explosives found by the Dutch authorities. Our experts in that kind of thing don't see any connection — the evidence found in the Netherlands was not what anybody would use against an airliner. You'd never get it past airport security, even as cargo. And early evidence from the crash points away from any type of terrorist involvement."

President Townsend looked at his watch. He had the Indian prime minister in fifteen minutes. Central Asia was a whole new set of troubles — Tibet, Pakistan, free-trade agreements. "All right," he said, sensing Graham was at an end. "Suggestions?"

The CIA director said, "We have to put the word out all over the Middle East and Europe to find Fatima Adara."

The nods of agreement were unanimous.

Graham added, "And once we find her, we can't lose her."

Townsend took this as a measure of self-critique, one of the things he had grown to like about this DNI he'd inherited from the previous administration. "All right," the president said, "see to it."

"What about this link with CargoAir?" Spector asked. "Shouldn't we be watching it?"

President Townsend nodded thoughtfully and looked at Graham. He said, "Someone to take a look at the company? Maybe follow this crash investigation?"

Graham smiled, "I'll take care of it, Mr. President."

Townsend got up to leave. "All right everyone, carry on."

When he got to the hallway, Townsend's secretary handed him a piece of paper listing the names of the wife and children of the prime minister of India. The guy had seven kids. Townsend sighed and began to memorize.

Back in the conference room, DNI Graham edged over for a word with CIA Director Thomas Drexler. "And *are* we keeping an eye on this crash investigation, Thomas?"

The CIA man gave Graham a coy grin, like a magician anticipating the *oohs* and *aahs* that would come from his next trick. "I've already got a man on the job. He just doesn't know it yet."

CHAPTER TEN

Dr. Hans Sprecht sat calmly, his slight frame supported by a plush leather chair, his feet resting on an expensive cherry desk. He admired his surroundings. The fine wood trim was first class, not the imitation rubbish that had found its way into so many physicians' offices. The decorations and artwork were tasteful, no diplomas or tacky before-and-after photographs of successful facelifts. He leaned back. Yes, the chair was his favorite part. It not only did its job of keeping one upright, but the soft leather coddled and caressed. It was almost sexual.

He let out a heavy sigh. *If only it were mine.*

It was the kind of place he would have liked. By his own account, the kind of place he deserved. Unfortunately, lacking a license to practice medicine in Switzerland for at least the next twenty years, it would never come to be. His career had first gone adrift over a handful of superfluous prescriptions, an unfortunate misunderstanding that had swelled completely out of hand. Then, with the professional board circling overhead, one mistake had become his rocky coastline. The case involved a young man who had requested breast implants. In the preoperative conference, Sprecht had asked few questions, naturally assuming his patient to be a homosexual. The generosity of Sprecht's nature was lost on the man — who was, in fact, a hopeful bodybuilder — when he awakened to find himself sporting a new D-cup bustline.

The licensing board was swift. It took Sprecht's future. The bodybuilder's lawyers took the rest. In the period of professional limbo that followed, Sprecht had considered going elsewhere, practicing under the radar. South America, perhaps, or the Far East. Buy the right permits, pay the right fees. But just as visions of a boutique practice in Brazil or Thailand had begun to float regularly through his dreams, Dr. Hans Sprecht stumbled onto a very good living.

His first case had been a Russian mobster in desperate search of a "new look." The work was a great success, and six months later Sprecht connected with an Italian pedophile, a man wanted keenly by Interpol. The third, an ousted Balkan general, was one step ahead of a war crimes tribunal. All of his patients had two things in common — a need for extensive work, and the means to pay handsomely for discretion.

Yet it was the fourth procedure that had proven his most daring. The work itself had been straightforward, however the logistics had been a nightmare. Sprecht had demanded a premium for that job. A premium delivered. And that admirable performance, under supremely primitive conditions, had led to this new patient — an undertaking that would prove his most lucrative yet.

Sprecht looked around the room with a renewed sense of satisfaction. The plastic surgeon whose office he had quietly sublet was in Peru on a five-week mountain climbing expedition. The rest of the year, the man toiled here, injecting neurotoxins, vacuuming flab, embellishing bustlines. Sprecht, by comparison, only worked a few days each year, enjoying a highly profitable niche in his line of work. It was as though he had become a satellite to his profession — occasionally coming in close contact, then parting for long periods in an extreme orbit. Yet, as agreeable as it all was, Hans Sprecht was forced to deal with separate issues. Issues that the man climbing a mountain in Peru could never imagine.

He looked at the Swiza clock on the wall. It read one minute before four o'clock. Sprecht pulled his feet from the desk, took out a handkerchief, and wiped the dampness from his forehead. He tried to think about the massive advance that had yesterday been credited to his Cayman account — a sum that easily counterbalanced the indignity of yet another withdrawal from his moral slush fund.

The second hand hit twelve. Right on cue, he heard the outer door open, then close. A tumbler locked into place. Sprecht straightened in his seat. The patient came in, closed the inner office door, and looked carefully around the room without speaking. The two had met once before to make preliminary arrangements.

"It is good to see you again," Sprecht offered.

"This is where you will do the work?" The tone was level, without emotion.

"Yes," Sprecht replied cheerily, as if his greeting had not been wholly ignored. "The procedures will take place here, along with a recuperation period under my personal, full-time observance." He did not bother to mention that he would have an assistant during the surgery. There was really no choice, as certain procedures could never be performed by a single pair of hands. Sprecht, however, had no desire to face the questions that such an admission would bring. As with his other patients, he simply did not address the issue. His nurse would enter and exit the sterile area when the time was right. A wonderful thing, anesthesia.

"How long will my recovery take?"

In an ode to his efficiency, Sprecht directed his patient to a chair and, as he spoke, began measuring facial regions with a pair of calipers. "The amount of work you have requested is significant. I cannot imagine recovery in less than six days. More if you wish." The surgeon stepped back and recorded his results on a notepad. He normally would have taken pictures, but that, of course, was out of the question. "Remove your shirt, please."

The patient complied, and said, "You know how I want everything." There was no inflection at the end of these words, and so it was not a question.

Sprecht said, "Have no worries. I have extensive experience. Your more regionalized features, they will be softened. When I am done, the nose might appear Roman. The eyes — Spanish, perhaps."

As he pursued his examination, Sprecht felt the eyes tracking him, watching every move. He knew his best defense was to keep busy, tied to the rituals of his work. He went to a cabinet and found a section of rubber tubing and a hypodermic needle. Returning to his patient,

Sprecht wrapped the tube tightly around one arm as a prelude to drawing blood.

"Is that necessary?"

"Yes, absolutely," Sprecht said in his 'doctor's orders' monotone. "You will lose blood in the operation. I must have an accurate specimen to rule out complications." He performed the procedure quickly, efficiently. "You may get dressed now," Sprecht said. He moved back behind the desk, wanting some distance before again engaging the soon-to-be-Spanish eyes. "When will we begin?" he asked.

"The time is near, but I still require a certain degree of flexibility. Be ready in two days."

"Done. And you have decided to go ahead with everything we discussed? It is truly an extensive amount of work."

"Over the years many photographs have surfaced, doctor. My face is too well known in . . . in certain quarters. When you are done, I must bear no resemblance to my former self."

"We discussed this at our last consultation. You must understand that —"

"Doctor! Is there any doubt about your ability to perform the contract?"

Sprecht's thoughts stumbled. "I am only saying that you must temper your expectations. The scale of change you demand — know that I am a plastic surgeon, not God."

The patient's gaze fell hard and struck to Sprecht's very soul. The silence was discomforting, and at that moment Sprecht wished it was he who was climbing a mountain in Peru. The surgeon tried to hide his anxiety, yet knew he could not. Then the question came. The same question the others had always gotten around to.

"Do you know who I am, Doctor?"

As always, Sprecht considered a lie. As always, he knew it would be a mistake. "You found me with your connections. Not an easy thing, I hope. Yet I have connections as well. I must be every bit as careful as you, my friend, for in my line of work any misstep will be my last."

The patient was absolutely still.

"But to answer your question — yes. I know precisely who you are." Sprecht paused, averted his eyes momentarily. "You are the terrorist, Caliph." When he looked up again, Sprecht saw a thin curl at one corner of a mouth he would soon alter.

"You are indeed a clever man, Doctor. I only hope your work reflects it. Make no mistakes."

"Rest assured," the surgeon said. "When other doctors make errors, attorneys and insurers do battle. If I make a mistake —" Sprecht left it at that.

The press briefing room that had been fashioned in Building Sixty-two was a typical affair. Perhaps a hundred loose chairs were divided in six gently arcing rows, giving the appearance of a poor man's theater. Three cameras were situated at the very back so as to take in the crowd, a small trick used by news crews everywhere to make a venue look bigger, to enhance the importance of an event. Reporters were ushered toward the forward rows, while Davis, along with the other investigators and technical help, kept to the rear.

The room was dressed for a show. A short stage had been constructed at the front with a central podium, lending subliminal authority to the high-and-mighty professionals. Bastien was flanked by three experts on each side. They were not, as one might expect, the working group leaders, but rather a global collection of men and women who had been chosen, judging by the labels in front of them, for their impressive academic credentials. Five of the six had the title "Professor" in front of their name, along with their university association.

Bastien had rolled up the long sleeves of his nicely pressed shirt, giving the image of a busy man who was stealing a few precious moments for the press, taking time away from the somber task of picking up the pieces of World Express 801. His voice was carefully contoured, self-important and airy. Reservedly French.

"Thank you for coming, ladies and gentlemen. We are here to provide a brief update on our investigation into the tragic loss of World

Express Flight 801. Our work is well on course and, though it is very early, we have so far identified a number of issues that warrant further pursuit."

Bastien spread an arm theatrically across the stage. He had the whole point-and-pose act going on again. Davis heard the clicks, saw the flashes.

"As I said in our first briefing yesterday, we have brought in experts from around the world." Clearly not satisfied with yesterday, Bastien proceeded to give a rundown on each person's illustrious qualifications. The words flowed like quicksand.

Lost in a back row, Davis mumbled, "This is like some damned ivory tower academic conference."

"What?" came a reply. The woman from Honeywell had taken a seat next to him.

He asked in a hushed voice, "You don't have a Ph.D., do you?"

"No," she replied. "You?"

He gave her his best you-gotta-be-shittin-me grin. "Guys like this drive me crazy," he said. "They try to impress you with credentials and catchphrases."

"And guys like you?"

"I prefer the straight and true road of common sense. And if that fails, I go right to physical intimidation." He saw a smile from the corner of his eye.

Bastien prattled grandly, eloquently for the cameras, his head oscillating back and forth like a sprinkler giving full coverage. His only visual aid was a simple graph, a thing so embellished it bordered on the ridiculous. There were a dozen different colors and scripted artwork in the margins. Somebody had wasted a lot of time, Davis thought. The vertical axis, blue, was altitude. A chartreuse horizontal line represented time. The data points formed a line that dropped precipitously from left to right, like a stock market index that had fallen off a cliff. Bastien squandered ten minutes on the chart before reiterating that the investigation was in its very early stages. No conclusions could yet be drawn.

He ended in a flourish, and threw the floor open for questions.

A woman in the front row piped up, "Do you have *any* suggestion as to what caused this disaster?"

Davis rolled his eyes. It was always the first question. And the second, and the third. If the guy in charge was firm enough, the newshounds would move on, happy with whatever scraps they were given.

"To this point, we are pursuing no particular causal factor. However, there have been two anomalies identified." Bastien paused as the room fell still.

Jammer Davis fell still.

Bastien picked up, "The cockpit voice recorder and flight data recorder, or black boxes as you in the press so dramatically refer to them, both seem to have suffered interruptions during the incident."

The word "incident" did not escape Davis. "Accident" was more typical, but this implied randomness. An absence of fault.

"The cockpit voice recorder fell off line at the midpoint of the aircraft's severe dive. The reason for this has yet to be determined. The flight data recorder, which would have been supremely useful in our investigation, became inoperative just before the start of the final descent. We expect little useful data to be retrieved relating to the accident sequence. Of course, we are investigating the cause of this malfunction. Early evidence suggests that the data recorder may have been disabled at some point."

Davis stiffened in his seat.

A reporter near the front caught it too. "Disabled?" the woman said. "What do you mean by that? Did someone deliberately turn it off?"

Bastien replied, "The data recorder ceased functioning at an unusually critical moment, just before initiation of the aircraft's nearly vertical dive."

"How could this happen?" someone prodded.

"The data recorder does not have an on–off switch like most instruments on the aircraft. It can, however, be deactivated by pulling a circuit breaker on the electrical panel behind the captain's seat. Indeed, our initial examination of the wreckage has found this breaker to be in the open position."

Davis went rigid. He wondered why Bastien hadn't shared this news with *him*. He suddenly knew why everyone was so interested in his seventy-two-hour report on Earl Moore.

The reporter smelled blood in the water. "Are you saying that the captain might have turned it off? Why would a pilot do such a thing?"

Bastien said, "I should not speculate as to how this circuit breaker came to be deactivated." Then, after a momentary pause, he speculated. "Yet there is one precedent. SilkAir, December 1997."

Davis jumped to his feet. His chair scraped back hard over the floor and the noise drew everyone's attention, including that of Bastien. Davis canvassed the "experts" lined up on stage. None looked worried. None raised a finger to take exception. Had they known what was coming? Or were they just so many lemmings following the front man over a cliff?

Davis locked eyes with Bastien, the message written in stone on his face — *not another word*.

Bastien raised his chin defiantly, but then he guided the briefing to more routine topics. It didn't matter. Davis knew the damage was done. SilkAir. The press pool had no idea what it meant. Not yet. But give them ten minutes on the Internet, and they'd all have their headline.

Davis stormed out of the room and headed down the hallway, his long strides eating up ground. Halfway down the corridor he turned, burst through a door, and ended up in an outdoor courtyard. He came to a stop in front of a three-tiered fountain. Davis stood stockstill with his hands on his hips, staring intently but divided from his surroundings. He felt warmth at the collar of his polo shirt and tugged it away, hoping the cool air would lower his boiling point. He could not believe what the investigator-in-charge had just done.

Footsteps clacked over the cobblestone path behind him.

"Jammer?"

He turned and saw Sorensen.

"What was that all about?" she asked.

Davis turned back and stared at the fountain. Four cherubs were pissing in all directions. He said, "Bastien just told the world what caused the crash of World Express 801."

"What?"

"He accused Captain Earl Moore of committing suicide."

CHAPTER ELEVEN

"SilkAir Flight 185," Davis said, "December 1997."

They had found a bench on one side of the courtyard. Stone steps, wet and mildewed, connected to the main path. Cigarette butts littered the ground around the bench, and a nearby trash can was full of old newspapers and take-out coffee cups rimmed with lipstick. Sorensen sat very still, listening intently.

"It was a Boeing 737, just over a hundred people on board. Without warning, it fell straight out of a blue sky and crashed into the Musi River in Sumatra. You've never heard of it?"

"No," she said, then added, "that was a little before my time in the business."

"It was overseas, the kind of thing that usually starts out on page eight in our newspapers. After two days, it probably disappeared completely. The investigation took three years. In the end, the Indonesian authorities claimed the evidence was inconclusive—no cause could be determined. But our own NTSB was very involved from the beginning."

"And they thought differently?"

Davis nodded. "They had a strong case. Just before the airplane went into its dive, the voice and data recorders stopped streaming data. Evidence suggested that at least one recorder had been disabled by pulling a circuit breaker."

"Exactly what Bastien just said happened here."

"Yes. But in the SilkAir case, the captain of the flight did have some serious issues. He'd recently been disciplined by management. He was in a big financial hole and had just bought a life insurance policy." Davis paused. "And years before, during his time in the Indonesian Air Force, he had lost four squadron buddies in an accident — all on one day. The very same calendar day that SilkAir 185 went down."

She said, "So that crash really *was* suicide?"

He leaned forward and put his elbows on his knees. "Very possibly. But who can say for sure? Who can look into a dead man's soul?"

"Could this accident be the same?"

Davis thought about what he'd seen in the field, what he'd seen in Earl Moore's apartment. "Right now there are a hundred possible causes," he said, his evasion clear.

"But why would Bastien even bring this up?"

"A very good question."

"It sounds so . . ." Sorensen struggled for the word, "I don't know — alarmist."

"Alarmist? Hell, everyone involved in this investigation is alarmist. They all want to find the secret to the crash — but only as long as it points blame away from their own organization and toward somebody else. This whole thing is a bunch of goddamn government and corporate Boy Scouts trying to earn their whistle-blower badges." Davis paused, dug his heel into a loose stone and pried it from the mud. "Blaming a dead pilot is the easy way out. To some degree it happens in every investigation, but you're usually talking about bad decisions, maybe carelessness."

"And sometimes it's true," she suggested.

"Yes, sometimes it is." He jerked a thumb hard toward the main building. "But what was implied in there, an intentional act — that's way out of bounds for this stage of an inquiry. Not to mention the *way* Bastien did it. There is one inviolate rule for investigators. Whatever you say, you say it in private. Especially if you're the guy running the show. You don't just toss a grenade in the outhouse like that and run."

Sorensen looked away. She said, "That's a great visual, Jammer."

Finally starting to cool, he shrugged. "I'm a visual guy."

"So what now?"

As Davis turned the same question, he looked up at a darkening sky, hard gray against the fading day. In the official terminology of aviation weather reports, it would have been given the code X — sky obscured. It meant there was no ceiling, no definable level where the clear air ended and the clouds began. In strict reporting terms, it was central to that weather observation no pilot ever wanted to see. Weather, ceiling 0, obscured, visibility 0, fog. WOXOF. When you saw that, you weren't going anywhere.

Davis checked his watch. There was less than an hour of daylight left. He looked at her and said, "Now? Now we get to work."

PORT ARTHUR, TEXAS

Moustafa sat very still in the driver's seat of his rented car.

No more than a hundred meters in front of him was a huge industrial complex. Unlike his haphazard destruction of the place owned by Colson Industries, this target would be addressed very specifically. Of course, he did not really think of it as a target. For Moustafa it was a destination. His final point of passage from this world.

It was 1:57 in the morning, or at least that was what the green lights on the dashboard displayed. The numbers glowed incredibly bright, one of so many gadgets on this massive car. Moustafa had asked for the largest rental available, and the American clerk had not disappointed, offering up a behemoth. How fitting, he thought.

He tried not to look at the car's clock, knowing it better to use the wristwatch he had so carefully synchronized before leaving the safe house. It was quite impossible. The green numbers were surreal, almost like his own personal line of communication with Allah.

1:58.

Moustafa took a deep breath to calm his nerves. This was not an easy thing. The others at the safe house had told him he would feel a sense of calm, an overwhelming tranquility as he undertook his fate. Of course, none of them had fulfilled their own destinies. Then Moustafa remembered the words of Caliph, received only yesterday in a personal e-mail — *Every faith has its soldiers. The victorious are those with the greatest conviction.*

He picked out an aim point on the fence, stared at his objective just beyond. There were no guards in sight. Moustafa knew there were typically twelve on duty. If this was Cairo, he might have been tempted to bribe one or two ahead of time, try to arrange their absence. But Caliph had warned against this. Things were different here. And if all went as planned, the guards would be helpless anyway.

He turned his thoughts to his family, envisioned how proud his mother would be. She would weep, of course, but she would understand. Moustafa's mother and sister would watch his video, and on seeing it pray for Allah's mercy, pray for His guidance. They would be alone now, but Caliph had promised to care for them. Caliph had given his solemn word.

1:59.

He started the car and gripped the steering wheel firmly. Moustafa felt a tear run down his cheek, but he wiped it away with a sleeve. *I weep for joy*, he told himself, *I weep for the glory I will now bestow upon Allah*. This gave him strength. His grip on the wheel might have cracked it.

2:00.

Moustafa stomped on the accelerator and the big car lunged forward. Building speed rapidly, it hit the curb and careened upward. Moustafa was thrown out of his seat, his head striking the ceiling, as two tons of metal ricocheted airborne and smashed through the perimeter fence. There was a terrible grating noise, metal on metal, as the car lurched out of control and slid sideways. With a jolting crunch, everything came to a stop.

Moustafa moved his hands, moved his feet to scramble out the door. His balance suffered under the heavy backpack and he stumbled to the ground. For a moment he lost his bearings — the car had kicked up a massive cloud of dust, something he had not anticipated. But then Moustafa spotted his target looming high, fifty meters away. It was an ordinary thing, a rectangular iron box the size of a small delivery truck. Bathed in the yellow sulfur glow, it seemed insignificant against the towering array of stacks and pipes and holding tanks. Yet Moustafa knew the importance it held.

He scrambled to his feet and ran, felt glory surging through his body. Someone in the distance shouted. It meant nothing. With only meters to go, Moustafa's destiny was all but complete.

He heard the noise first, a thumping pulse like a massive heartbeat — which it very nearly was. Next he felt the heat, radiating strong and constant, increasing as he closed in. An arm's length away, Moustafa stopped, turned and positioned his backpack firmly against the rectangular side. The heat was very strong now, and searing waves blistered his exposed skin. Moustafa welcomed the pain, imagining it to be the warmth of heaven, the embrace of an eternal sun. His hands fumbled to find the trigger taped to his chest.

"Allah Ahkbar!"

The primary explosion had the desired effect. A shaped charge blew a tremendous hole in the containment wall and superheated crude oil burst in all directions. Heating elements fractured, and another blast fueled by natural gas sent shrapnel into adjacent pipelines and equipment. This secondary blast was even more spectacular than the first, as separated butane, naphtha, and jet fuel exploded, the only limitation being the speed at which air could rush inward from the perimeter to feed the conflagration. Nearby holding tanks were breeched and a slurry of volatile chemicals erupted into the chaos, adding a toxic element to compound the disaster.

In the control room at one corner of the facility, the three engineers tasked to operate the place faced an array of warnings. They barely noticed, having already been distracted by the initial explosion that peppered the walls of their small building with fiery debris. This was all the warning they needed. The men set off their alarms and ran.

Inside fifteen minutes, over an acre of the RNP Number 2 oil refinery in Port Arthur, Texas, was glowing like a massive torch.

CHAPTER TWELVE

It was called L'Hotel Continental Lyon. A mile from Building Sixty-two, it had been virtually taken over by the investigation's contingent. Davis thought it was a nice enough place, comfortable but not self-absorbed with the likes of high thread-count Egyptian sheets or matching terrycloth bathrobes. His room was on the third floor, with a tree-scraping view of the Lyon airport in the distance.

His first real night's sleep had gone well, his body now fully adapted to the time shift. Davis hit the restaurant for breakfast at eight. He occupied half a table for two, ordered eggs, toast, and coffee. Service was fast, and he polished off the meal before tipping the coffeepot. It was good stuff, better than what he brewed at home. Not that that was saying much. Halfway through the first cup, he spotted Sorensen.

She was smartly dressed in slacks and a long-sleeved shirt. She looked fresh, well rested. But then, women like Sorensen always did. She was attractive — not like a fashion model, but in a more basic sense. Sorensen could wake up first thing in the morning, run a quick hand through her hair, and she'd be nice to look at.

She smiled on making eye contact, and Davis nodded her over.

"Buy a girl a drink?" she asked, pointing to the spare coffee cup.

"You bet, Honeywell. Have a seat." Davis did the honors.

"Honeywell? Is that my new call sign?"

"I like it."

She let it go, and asked, "Did you sleep well?"

"Always do."

"That's the sign of a clear conscience."

"Or no conscience at all."

Sorensen smiled a morning smile, bright and cheerful. The waiter came and she ordered fruit and a pastry. As soon as he was gone, she went to her handbag and pulled out a rolled-up newspaper. She set it on the table and pointed to the headline.

Davis ignored the print, found himself looking at her finger. It was long and slender. No fake nails or stylish colors. Just a basic manicure, maybe a coat of clear. A woman who kept herself up, but didn't have time for the works.

She said, "Have you read this article?"

"No, but let me guess — *Suicide suspected in air crash.*"

"That's pretty much it. Bastien has to prove it now, doesn't he?"

"Not much choice."

"And what about you? Are you going to try and disprove it?"

He paused for a long moment. "I will be a pattern of all patience."

Her gaze grew pensive. "That's Shakespeare. *King Lear.*"

"Is it? Damn. Thought I had it first." The phone in his pocket vibrated. Davis said, "Excuse me."

He saw a text message Jen had sent last night — for some reason it was just now reaching him. She was still fired up about the dance, convinced that to miss it would be ruinous, a social disaster of cataclysmic proportions. He pecked out a response: WILL TALK TONIGHT AFTER SCHOOL. Davis snapped the phone shut and shook his head, exasperation seeping out. "Women," he fussed.

"Daughter driving you crazy?"

Davis paused, looked at her closely. "Yeah." He topped off his cup, taking his time. "Tell me, Honeywell, have you been out to the crash site yet?"

"No. Have you?"

"Yesterday. It's always the first thing I do."

"Why is that?"

He considered it. "Like I told you, I'm a visual guy. I like to see the big picture."

"And did the big picture tell you anything?"

"It told me lots of things. For starters, nothing is missing."

"I beg your pardon?"

"Jammer's first rule of accident investigation — look for things that should be there, but aren't."

"Such as?"

"My first investigation was a T-37. A training airplane. It went down out in the middle of nowhere in New Mexico, one pilot dead. My partner and I found the wreckage easy enough, and on the first look we noticed something strange — the two main landing gear were gone."

"Gone?"

"Completely missing — no wheels. By the scars on the ground you could tell which way he'd come from, so we hiked back in that direction. Half a mile later we came to a mesa, one of those big oval plateaus with a flat top. We still didn't see anything, so we went around it, and at the base of the far side we see a pair of main landing gear, nice as can be."

"How did they get there?"

"That's what I wondered, so we climbed to the top of the mesa — which wasn't easy. And do you know what we found?"

Sorensen shook her head.

"Skid marks."

"Skid marks?"

"Lots of them. You see, the top of this mesa was very flat, and apparently it had become sport among the local instructors to drop in during training flights and do touch-and-go's. Until one guy came in too low. He sheared off the landing gear, and that took out his hydraulics. From there, he lost control of the jet. Too low to eject."

"So this guy was just out messing around? I can't believe a pilot would do something so dangerous."

Davis eyed her. He fell silent and his gaze turned hard.

"What is it?" she asked.

Davis did not reply. Very deliberately, he picked up the spoon Sorensen had just used to stir her coffee, held it over the table, and slowly bent the stem to a ninety-degree angle.

Her words came in the measured cadence of forced calm. "What are you doing, Jammer?" The good humor that had framed her was gone, lost under his attack on the flatware.

"Tension or torsion?" he asked.

"I beg your pardon?"

"Did this metal fail in tension or torsion? Anybody with rudimentary training in crash investigation would know."

Sorensen drew a deep breath, looked down intensely at the table — if she'd been drinking tea, he might have thought she was trying to read the leaves in her cup. Davis dropped the deformed spoon on the table. It clattered when it hit, and a few other patrons looked their way.

"What gave it away?" she asked.

"A few minutes ago, when I took that message. You asked me if my daughter was driving me crazy."

"And —"

"And I never said I had a daughter." He held up the wedding band he still wore. "You should have deduced I was talking about my wife. But then — you already know my wife is dead."

The silence was extended. No more pert expression or snappy comebacks. "Jammer, look —"

He raised an index finger to cut her off, then deliberately moved his hands to grip the cloth at the sides of the table — as if at any moment he might turn the whole thing over. His voice fell low and ominous. "Who the hell are you?"

Sorensen bit her bottom lip. "I'm sorry," she said. "I should have been upfront with you."

"Upfront about what?"

Her next words were quiet, yet distinct. As if she didn't want to say it twice. "I work for the CIA."

"*CIA?* As in Central Intelligence Agency?"

She nodded once. "Jammer, we need your help."

CHAPTER THIRTEEN

"And here I thought I was doing great with you," Davis said, his eyes boring into her. "What the hell does the CIA need me for?"

"It's a long story. I—"

"Wait a minute!" he interrupted. "Larry Green, my boss back at the NTSB, said the director had requested me by name for this assignment. Did the CIA *put* me on this investigation?"

There was no shake of the head, no quizzical expression. "Honestly, I don't know anything about that. I was only told that you might be able to help. I know you're a top-notch investigator, Jammer. You speak French. And you were a career military officer."

"Which means what? That I'll follow orders? If that's what you think, your file on me isn't very complete. I'm a known troublemaker. My performance reports from the Air Force are riddled with words like 'headstrong' and 'uncompromising.' I don't like bullshit. Right now I'm trying to think of one good reason why I shouldn't dump this whole carnival and go home!"

Sorensen kept to her hushed tone. "I'm here to monitor the investigation, but I need help. I'm walking into a minefield and I need you to guide me through."

"How? By stepping on them? Since when do spooks get involved in aircraft accidents?" Davis considered the question himself. Then it hit him. "Wait a minute. Are you suggesting that a terrorist act brought this airplane down?"

"We have no direct evidence of that," she said. "But the agency has been watching CargoAir for some time."

"CargoAir? Why?"

Sorensen explained that the CIA had been monitoring CargoAir for months. The big consortium had a heavy dose of financing and ownership from countries not completely trusted by America. Then she produced a photograph from her handbag and laid it on the white tablecloth. Clearly she'd been anticipating this little confessional. The image was of a man and woman sitting at a café table.

"You probably don't know either of these people," she said.

Davis looked at the picture, shook his head.

"The guy's name is Luca Medved, he's a Russian national. And he's also the chairman of the board of CargoAir."

"Okay, I'll bite. Who's she?"

"Her name is Fatima Adara."

"Never heard of her."

"Not many people have. But we've definitely linked her to the most wanted man in the Western world — the terrorist known as Caliph."

"Caliph?"

"You've heard of him?"

"Sure, everybody has. But isn't he in Iraq?"

"He started there. But lately we've been finding his fingerprints all over the world." Sorensen was getting back in stride, confidence returning to her voice.

Davis looked closer at the photograph. Grainy as it was, he could tell the woman wasn't much of a looker.

Sorensen said, "Fatima Adara is his messenger, the only one as far as we can tell."

"So what does this have to do with me, with this investigation? You can't think CargoAir is tied up with Caliph."

"We don't like what we've been finding out about CargoAir. The company has been around for five years, yet the organization and financing are very unusual. Most of its backing comes from oil-rich states, and the management team has been pretty darn elusive for a publicly traded corporation. In certain ways, it almost functions like a shell company."

Davis argued, "Rumor has it they make a pretty good airplane. It's been certified by the FAA and Europe's EASA, no easy hurdle. Over a hundred C-500s are flying, and this crash is the first real problem."

"Yes, but we see it as an opportunity."

"An opportunity for what?"

"To get inside the company, get a good look. This crash forces their hand — CargoAir will have to let the investigators in, let them see everything."

Davis sat back in his chair. "So this isn't about finding a cause for the crash of World Express 801. It's about spying on CargoAir, looking for links to Caliph. You think the company might be funneling money to suspicious local groups or carrying a few of the wrong people on the payroll. Maybe they're even providing material help to terrorist cells. Operating with suppliers in so many countries, they must send and receive a lot of hardware. Lots of crates and boxes, stuff that probably gets minimal inspection."

She nodded. "You're a quick study, Jammer. We don't know the exact form, but yes, something like that."

Davis locked his gaze appraisingly on a woman he had liked ten minutes ago. She cocked her head and a wave of blonde hair slid over one shoulder. Her eyes were blue, open and clear. Too clear for such jaded work. And they pleaded for help. Davis looked hard for something else. Guile, flecks of dishonesty. It just wasn't there.

"Jammer, the CIA is scouring Europe and the Middle East for this guy. We're stretched thin, and I'm in way over my head here."

"Somehow I doubt that."

She implored, "We could work together on this."

"That's one more person than I'm used to dealing with."

Sorensen seemed to make a decision. Her tenor changed to one of pure business. "All right. I wasn't truthful with you. I'm sorry, Jammer. You go your own way. But I have to ask one favor."

Davis raised an eyebrow, inviting her to continue.

"I'll never get through this if I don't have some credibility, some idea of what to do. I need to know the basics. Meet me at the accident site and show me what to look for, explain how this investigation is going to run."

He deadpanned, "So you want a — crash course?"

"Yes," she volleyed back, no trace of humor.

He looked at his watch. "All right. It's eight twenty. Meet me at the site this afternoon. One o'clock sharp."

"Deal," she said.

"Oh — and *I* want something from you."

She hesitated. "All right. If I can."

"I met a guy yesterday, Dr. Ibrahim Jaber. He's the lead engineer at CargoAir, in charge of the C-500 program. I want to know all about him."

"What makes you think I can —"

"*You,*" he said, cutting her off, "are the CIA. That's what you guys do, right? Find out about people?"

Sorensen frowned.

He said, "Besides, Jaber is a big wheel at CargoAir. If you people are really targeting that company, chances are you have a lot on him already."

"You think he's involved?"

"I don't know. I just want to know who I'm dealing with — besides Langley. Once I know the teams, then I'll choose sides."

"Just like on the playground."

Davis didn't answer, and they stared at one another. Sorensen's displeasure shone through. Davis had been here less than twenty-four hours and he was already catching spears. Which put him about a day ahead of schedule.

It was Sorensen who broke it off. She drained her cup, threw a few bills on the table, and walked off in a huff. She moved fast, like she had things to do. Phone calls to make. Davis knew she was pissed, and in a way he was glad. He didn't like people who just rolled over and took what came in life. She was saying, *If you won't help me, then to hell with you. I'll do it on my own.*

He watched her leave. Her slacks had a nice fit around her hips and waist, and she got the same looks every slim, pretty blonde got when she walked through a public room. Davis forced his eyes elsewhere.

They went naturally to a television mounted over the bar on the far side of the room. The volume had been muted, but the flat screen flickered with life. This, he knew, was an essential human impulse, a proven quirk of the species. Bright lights, movement — that's where the eye was naturally drawn. Light, color, and motion were integral to the design of aircraft flight decks. Green lights were good. Amber lights not good. Red lights bad. Flashing red lights — real bad. In the last few moments of his life, Earl Moore had probably been looking at a Christmas tree. At least, Davis hoped that was the case.

A scrolling red banner ran beneath the news commentator on TV. Breaking news. Davis thought, *Isn't all news breaking? That's why it's —* he dropped the line of thought. On the television screen he saw an industrial area on fire, a nighttime shot taken from what had to be a helicopter's perspective. Dancing orange flames licked at pipes and machinery, and smoke intermittently blotted out the lights of emergency vehicles. He wondered briefly what it was all about, but then decided he had enough fires of his own to put out.

Davis signed his check and headed for the field.

When Sorensen got back to her room, she threw her purse on the bed and booted up her computer. She sat behind the tiny hotel desk and tapped her nails impatiently on imitation hardwood. She was still ticked.

When the screen came up, Sorensen fed in her password and checked her mail. It was a secure system, a satellite feed — she'd had to move the desk near a window to get a good uplink. It wasn't the picture most people had when they thought about spy work, shoving around furniture to get good uplinks, but this was reality. There was still an occasional smoky room, a dark alley now and again. But the most useful information almost always came from file downloads, not fat men in white suits.

She found one message from Langley. It was wordy, full of dubious speculation, but had one recurrent theme — find Caliph. She read through once and filed it away. Her nails were still tapping. He had really gotten to her. She'd expected certain things about Jammer Davis. Some of them had held. Others felt wrong. Sorensen called up the saved file labeled FRANK DAVIS.

She had read it once yesterday, and figured she'd known what to expect. Her favorite part was where they listed "Jammer" as an alias. Davis had gone into the Marine Corps right after high school, served one stint, then taken an appointment to the United States Air Force Academy. After graduating, he'd spent sixteen years on active duty flying fighters. He'd retired at the rank of major, then hired on with the NTSB.

On paper, he was straightforward, even a cliché. She reread the part where Davis had gotten into trouble during his last Air Force assignment — he'd punched a hole in the officer's club wall with his fist. The first time she'd read it, Sorensen remembered thinking, *And that's all I need to know about Jammer Davis*. Now she wondered.

At the end of the file was a section labeled PERSONAL. His wife had died in a car crash almost two years ago. One daughter. And Jammer Davis played rugby. No surprise there. He was built for it. *Who digs this stuff up?* she wondered. Sorensen stared at the word PERSONAL and decided it was rubbish. You couldn't get to know somebody this way. She had gone in expecting a Neanderthal, but come out with something else. Something she couldn't quite peg.

There was a picture in the file, an official portrait from somebody's archives. Again, the real thing was different. It was a classically handsome face in structure, square and angular, but rich with life's trials. Tousled brown hair, slightly crooked nose, a smattering of small scars — a face that would look right at home with a butterfly bandage or two. The voice had been deep and loud, made for barking orders at Academy underclassmen. But it wasn't dim or brutish. There was an intelligence about Davis — an intelligence he'd be happy to bash you over the head with.

Sorensen's fingers moved up from the desk and momentarily stroked the keyboard. The machine's thought bubble asked, ARE YOU SURE YOU WANT TO DELETE THIS FILE? She moved the cursor over the

YES option, paused for just a moment. Then she tapped down.

The machine whirred faintly as it digested her command. Sorensen navigated elsewhere and typed in her request:

NEED ALL AVAILABLE INFORMATION
ON EGYPTIAN NATIONAL DR. IBRAHIM
JABER — EMPLOYED AS EXECUTIVE WITH
CARGOAIR CORPORATION — HIGHEST
PRIORITY

CHAPTER FOURTEEN

The White House Situation Room was living up to its moniker. There was indeed a situation.

The president had been awakened at two-thirty in the morning, as soon as word of the third refinery disaster registered at the FBI's Strategic Information and Operations Center, the country's one-stop repository for bad news. Given that the attacks came within minutes of one another, the tsunami hit shortly thereafter.

Twenty-one attacks, clearly synchronized, had occurred on oil refineries across America. Details were still filtering in, but the newest reports were little more than battle damage assessments — casualty counts, fire containment estimates, and bulletins detailing a handful of small-scale evacuations that had been ordered for hazardous material contamination.

The atmosphere in the Situation Room was chaotic. The National Security Council had been called into emergency session. Staffers came and went in a constant flow, delivering spectacular details of the attacks. The reactions in the room were a predictable mix — shock, outrage, calls for defensive action. The offense would come later. High on one wall, an array of televisions showed the major news networks. The volumes were muted, but each screen blazed with rotating video clips of smoking wreckage. CNN had a running casualty graph. The present score: twenty-one dead, forty injured. The televisions, in fact, were for more than visual affirmation of the scope of the strikes — if anything further happened, this was where the national command structure would likely see it first.

President Truett Townsend was trying to make sense of a Department of Homeland Security report in front of him. It was a load of bureaucratic gibberish explaining the legal ramifications of raising the
national threat level. The noise in the room was deafening, and he had
difficulty concentrating.

"Mr. President —"

Townsend looked up to see his chief of staff, Martin Spector.
"Martin, this is chaos."

"I realize that, sir, but this *is* the first crisis of our administration.
In light of that, your address to the nation is critical. I have the first
draft of your speech." He slid a six-page document in front of
Townsend. "You're scheduled to come on at eight a.m. eastern. That's
just over an hour from now. You'll have to edit —"

"Not now!" Townsend shoved the draft aside. He looked up to see
no fewer than thirty people. Half were yelling into cell phones, and the
rest were arguing. This was not going well. He'd had all he could take.
Townsend stood and yelled at the top of his lungs, *"Enough!"*

It did the job.

The room went silent and everyone fell still — Townsend thought
they looked like a bunch of kids playing freeze tag. He pointed distinctly to the ones he wanted. "Martin. DNI. CIA. Chairman of the
Joint Chiefs. Homeland Security. Everybody else, out!"

The room parted, rearranged before him, and Truett Townsend
took his seat at the head of the conference table. His five advisors followed suit without asking. It didn't show often, but Truett Townsend
had a temper, and nobody wanted to be on the wrong side of it.

"All right, everyone," the president said slowly, consciously trying
to lighten his tone, "let's establish our priorities. Homeland Security,
give me your best overview. How were these attacks undertaken?"

A beleaguered director of Homeland Security said, "It seems to
have been a painfully simple operation, sir. Some of these refineries
had a respectable level of physical security — motion sensors, vehicle
barriers, low-light cameras. I expect we'll find that most of the security operation centers recognized the perimeter breach. Unfortunately,
we are talking about tremendous facilities. The response times simply

weren't fast enough. For the suicide bombers, once they'd breached a simple chain-link fence, all they were looking at was a hundred-yard dash with all the explosives they could carry. Twenty, thirty seconds. Maybe a minute at a few of the biggest targets."

General Banks said, "This doesn't surprise me one bit. The more we rely on laser guided bombs, satellites, and unmanned aerial vehicles, the more our enemies rely on simple bullets, suicide attacks, and messages delivered by hand. Pretty soon they'll be using a match and a length of fuse cord like goddamn Wile E. Coyote."

"And the problem," Darlene Graham fretted, "is that it'll work. At least for a time."

Townsend said, "Let's move on. Has the immediate threat ended?"

Homeland Security again, "We think so, Mr. President. All the attacks occurred within a window of no more than ten minutes. Chances are, they were supposed to be simultaneous. The news wires have reported subsequent explosions, but these are likely secondary — at least half of the facilities struck are still battling uncontrolled fires. There's been the usual spree of copycat bomb threats, reports of suspicious packages and vehicles. So far it's all turned out to be spurious."

"All right," said the president, "then let's assume the threat has ended for today. What can we do going forward?"

Homeland Security said, "Our emergency response plan has been put into effect. The command center is fully staffed, coordinating with the first responders."

Townsend gently pushed the six-page speech back toward his chief of staff. "All right, ladies and gentlemen. In a short time, I am going to talk to the American people. I will speak from my heart, tell them we've been attacked, but that the situation is under control. I'll briefly cover our response plan and make myself personally accountable for the nation's recovery. Having said that —" Truett Townsend paused for effect, "there is one very important question to be answered." The president let his words hang.

General Banks piped in, "It has to be Caliph, Mr. President. Our intelligence told us something was coming."

Graham added, "We've been able to track three of the rental cars so far. All were contracted to men with Arabic names, two of them here on student visas. We'll get more soon, but Caliph's fingerprints are all over this."

Townsend looked to each of his advisors in turn. One by one, they nodded in agreement. He was convinced. "All right. We are going to make this guy the new Osama Bin Laden. That means you all need to clear the decks at your respective organizations. We have one mission." Townsend smacked his palm hard on the table. "Find this bastard!"

The president got up and began to leave, but as he passed his director of national intelligence, he tapped her on the shoulder and motioned for her to follow with a crook of his finger. When they hit the hallway he began to talk.

"Darlene, I want a briefing this afternoon."

"On what, sir?"

"Oil. Refineries. These were not blind, random attacks. Caliph had something very specific in mind. I need to know how this will affect our country. What other threats do we face? What could be next? You find me the biggest egghead out there, somebody who knows oil inside and out. I want to know exactly what's going on here."

Darlene Graham nodded confidently. "I know just the guy."

CHAPTER FIFTEEN

He spotted Sorensen at the controlled entry point. She was standing between a pair of orange barricades, signing an entry log. The rain had been on and off. Right now it was on. Not the fat drops of summer, but a cool, caressing midwinter drizzle, the air and water seeming to combine as a kind of intermediate element.

Sorensen was dressed appropriately — jeans and well-worn running shoes acting as foundation for a gray raincoat. The coat was a little on the stylish side, but had a hood hanging loose at the back. It would do the job. Her hair was pulled back in a ponytail again. Davis liked ponytails — there was something youthful and bouncy about them, but more to the point, he knew it was a style women preferred when they were in the mind-set of exercise or manual labor. Sorensen had come ready to work.

When she looked up and saw him, there was the trace of a smile. Just a trace. He found himself wondering if it was real or contrived. Now that he knew she was CIA, Davis would doubt everything. Every adamant word, every skeptical frown, every careless shrug. He tried not to get too wrapped around the thought.

"Hi," he said.

"Hello, Jammer." Her tone was flat. The smile gone. Still pissed. "So have you had a productive morning?" she asked.

"The usual." He pointed to her shoes, New Balance cross-trainers. "Good choice. It's pretty muddy out here."

"I figured as much. Let's get to work."

"Fair enough."

Davis led the way. They slogged toward the debris field using a rut some heavy vehicle had left behind as a path. Ahead, he watched a man wearing a blue BEA windbreaker blaze a new trail across fresh ground. It was a nuance Davis had picked up on before, in the course of other investigations. If this crash had involved a passenger jet, with hundreds of fatalities, the field would be hallowed ground, given the same gentle deference as a cemetery. On the other hand, if it had been a military fighter crash where the pilot had ejected safely, the place would be trod over like an automobile junkyard. As it was, with two pilots dead, this accident fell into a middle ground. Everyone would show respect, but a year from now there would be no somber memorial service, no stone marker surrounded by flowers. It would just be another field.

From the corner of his eye, Davis watched Sorensen take everything in.

He said, "So has the CIA found Caliph yet?"

"No. But did you hear about the bombings?"

"Bombings?" He shook his head. "No. I saw some smoke and fire on TV as I left the hotel, but I've been out here all morning."

"Over twenty strikes back in the States. Oil refineries."

"Oil refineries?" He paused. "And you guys think it was Caliph?"

"That's the consensus. My boss says there's a real full-court press to find him now."

"And we have to do our part?" Davis eyed her for a moment, saw no reaction. He started off again, skirting around a freshly sheared tree stump. "So tell me, where *is* your boss? Back at Langley?"

"Yes."

"Nice arrangement, isn't it? Mine's in D.C." He gave this some thought. "Although, I'm not even sure who my boss is right now. I fired my last one."

"Why does that not surprise me?"

"I like being independent."

"Me too."

Davis pulled her to a stop, put his hands on his hips. "You really want to get into this, Honeywell? Alone?"

"I'll do what I have to do."

Davis nodded and thought, *Good answer.* He said, "Okay, we'll start here. This is simple detective work. And Monsieur Bastien's theories aside, the culprits aren't generally deranged people. It involves weather, poor maintenance, faulty design, bad decisions." He arced out a hand toward the crash site, the debris field only fifty meters away. "Remember, I'm a visual guy. Our wreckage pattern here is long, at least fifteen hundred meters."

"Almost a mile," she remarked.

Davis pointed to a deep scar in the earth at one end. "That's the primary impact point. She hit there, then broke up. Probably a million pieces now. Hopefully the big chunks will tell us what happened so that we won't have to dig out every little fragment."

"How do you know where to start? Surely you've got some theories about what happened — now that you've had a good look."

"I had theories before I saw any of this." Davis began walking again. "The radar data was interrupted, but it gave me a good place to start. This airplane was at 38,000 feet, and without warning it pitched over and went nearly straight down. There's only a few things that will cause that to happen."

"Speaking as a frequent flyer, I'm happy to hear it."

He couldn't contain a slight grin. "First, you have to consider structural failure. It's a relatively new design, so maybe the engineers screwed up somewhere — very rare, but certification and testing these days rely a great deal on computer models and wind tunnel testing. Harmonic vibrations at certain speeds, weak points in the pressure hull. It's possible that something slipped through the simulation and flight test program. But the thing is, if an airplane has some kind of catastrophic failure at altitude, there's generally one telltale sign."

"Something missing!"

"Good, Honeywell. You've been paying attention. If she came apart at 38,000 feet, we'd find the suspect piece thirty miles from here embedded in some poor farmer's bean patch." He kept moving. "This morning I partnered up with some people from the structures and design group. We used engineering diagrams, pictures of factory parts —we can't find anything missing. All the primary flight control surfaces are accounted for. And since this airplane is a flying wing design, there aren't the usual secondary controls—no flaps or slats. As a passenger, those are the panels you see moving on the front and back of the wings during takeoff and landing."

"So no structural failure."

"We'll rule it out for now. And no midair collision. If that was the case, we'd not only have found missing parts, but there would have been some extra pieces from a different kind of airplane."

"Okay. What about the engines? Could they have quit?"

"A reasonable question." Davis led to a pile of metal the size of a delivery truck. Sorensen didn't recognize it until she saw it from a better angle.

"That's an engine?"

"That's an engine."

Huge fan blades the size of surfboards were still attached to a central core. The metal duct around the fan was crumpled and dirt had sprayed everywhere—it looked like some huge mixer that had been turned loose on the wet earth.

She said, "It's pretty torn up."

"Check the fan blades. What do you notice?"

Sorensen cocked her head sideways as she examined the circular array. "Every one is bent, near the outer tips."

"Exactly. Uniform rotational damage tells us that this engine was running at impact. The powerplant guys will eventually calculate a precise speed, but the point is that it was turning. The other three engines show the same kind of damage. And aside from that, even if all the engines had quit, say from a contaminated fuel supply, this airplane would have turned into a glider. Take away all power, and a C-500 will still fly a hundred miles from that altitude."

"Okay," Sorensen said, "so no structural failure and the engines were fine. What else?"

Davis said, "As a pilot, there's one thing that came straight to mind when I saw the severe descent profile — fire. If Earl Moore had been facing a fire up there, he'd have wanted to get on the deck fast. *Really fast.*"

"That fits the rapid descent."

"Yes, but —" Davis moved to a new section of wreckage and found what he wanted under a twisted cargo deck floor panel. He bent down and put a forearm across one knee. Sorensen followed suit, and he pointed to a lump of molten metal. It was shaped like a mound of wet sand that had dripped into a pile.

"That was from a fire!" she said excitedly.

"Yes. But it doesn't help us." He tossed his head in a looping motion. "You'll find these all over the place. For any fire you need three things."

"Fuel, oxygen, and ignition."

"Right. Now when this thing hit the ground, about thirty thousand gallons of Jet A fuel — which is basically kerosene — sprayed everywhere. Lots of ignition too. There's fire damage all around this field, but as far as I can tell, it was all postcrash."

"It's such a mess — how can you know that?"

Davis stood straight. "In-flight fires have one telltale feature. They begin burning inside a pressure vessel and, at some point, will typically breach and get exposed to the wind stream. That's an extremely high-oxygen environment, acts like a blowtorch." He pointed again to the molten lump. "This fire was probably about fifteen hundred degrees Fahrenheit, give or take. In-flight fires get twice as hot. Over three thousand degrees. Metals burn differently in that kind of heat. Also, if there was a fire in flight, we'd see liquid metal sprayed in a splashing pattern along with a soot stain somewhere on the aircraft's outer skin."

Sorensen nodded.

"On the ground," he continued, "molten metal pools, soot goes up. That's the only kind of fire evidence I've seen this morning. And I've been looking."

"Okay, I get the idea. Check off all these things that *didn't* bring the aircraft down. But any idea what did?"

"This is day one, Honeywell. These investigations can take years."

The rain had stopped, but a look at the sky, charcoal gray curtains all around, suggested it would be a brief reprieve. Sorensen stood straight and took a deep breath.

"This is surreal," she said.

Davis gave no reply, but watched her as she surveyed the disaster. Sorensen squinted, and Davis registered gentle, thin creases at the corners of her eyes. She was the kind of woman who would age well. But then, he had always thought the same about Diane.

Sorensen shifted her gaze, caught him looking in a way that had nothing to do with soot or fires.

"So will you do it, Jammer?"

"What?"

"Help us?"

He found himself wishing she'd used the singular pronoun. "Us" implied helping the CIA—just the kind of big, faceless Washington bureaucracy that drove him crazy. Davis didn't answer. He simply turned away and began to walk.

CHAPTER SIXTEEN

Sorensen was in tight formation as they stepped carefully through a tapestry of jagged metal and twisted wires. A woman nearby was using a handheld GPS to lay down markers for a reference grid. She glanced up as they passed and everyone nodded cordially.

"There's one more thing I want to show you," Davis said.

He stopped at the piece he was after. It was ten-feet long, two-feet wide, tapered slightly at one end. The materials involved were a combination — metal framework acting as the base for a composite surface. Two actuator rods poked out, bent and sheared off.

"What is it?" she asked.

"It's called an elevon, a primary flight control. Your standard airplane has a different arrangement, but again, the C-500 is a flying wing design. It doesn't have a vertical tail."

"So this controls the airplane aerodynamically?"

"Right. A number of these surfaces along the trailing edge of the body control both the pitch axis, for up and down, and the roll axis for turning. Now — look at this part." He showed her where the trailing section was warped. "I won't bore you with the details, but this surface was damaged in flight. I can tell by the way it failed — it's deformed in a very uniform, consistent way. I found another elevon that shows the same unnatural twist."

She bent down and ran her fingertips over the bowed edge. "So what does that mean?"

"One very significant thing. This is what happens when a flight control surface is under extreme load. Gs were being put on the airplane — I suspect right before impact."

"Gs?"

"Sorry, pilot talk. Gs refers to acceleration. It can be in any of the three axes, but in airplanes we're usually talking about pitch, what you feel in the seat of your pants."

"So in this case, the pilot was trying to pull up?"

"Exactly. In the seconds before this thing hit, one of the two pilots was pulling back desperately on the control stick." Davis stood straight and pointed out over the long, extended debris field. "And hitting at such a low angle — I'd say they came damn close to making it."

Sorensen stood and took it all in.

The sun came out momentarily, and the steady breeze continued its sweep over the accident scene. It seemed almost like a cleansing, a reminder from above that the destruction here was no more than a temporary blight. In time, everything would revert to its natural state, green grass and blue sky.

Davis said, "You see, Honeywell, it's easy to get lost in the bits and pieces, the metal fatigue and fuel lines. But, without getting too philosophical, you have to remember that there *was* a human element to this crash. There always is."

Sorensen nodded thoughtfully. She pulled down the hood of her jacket and let it fall over her back. A few rebellious strands of blonde fluttered in the breeze. One wisp came over her eyes, and Davis watched her wipe it aside with the back of a wrist. It was a curiously feminine gesture, designed no doubt to avoid fingertips that had to be black with soil and soot.

"Yes," Davis found himself saying.

"Yes what?"

"Yes, I'll help you."

The briefing in the Situation Room took place promptly at eleven. The entire National Security Council was in attendance, minus the vice president who was returning from Bangkok in light of the crisis, but still ten hours away.

The day's intelligence and news reports had not added much to what was already known at this morning's emergency session. Twenty-one refineries hit, massive collateral damage, one primary suspect behind it all. Every news anchor in the country was backed by a photo image of Caliph. The crisis had bumped global warming, health care policy, and tensions in Pakistan right off the media map — nobody cared about any of that when they couldn't fill up their gas tanks to get to work or drive the kids to T-ball practice.

After a few formalities, Darlene Graham gave them her man.

"Ladies and gentlemen, I'd like to introduce Dr. Herman Coyle. Dr. Coyle is formerly a professor of Petroleum Engineering at the University of Texas, and now serves as chairman of the OMNI think tank. He is an internationally recognized expert on energy security, and has published a number of papers regarding vulnerabilities and weak points in the design of our country's energy infrastructure. Dr. Coyle —"

Graham yielded the podium to a man who was a good six inches shorter. Coyle was slightly built and wore wire-framed glasses. A text-book receding hairline split two tangles of dark gray hair that sprouted wildly on the sides, giving the appearance of twin bird's nests above his ears. As Truett Townsend studied Coyle, he was encouraged. Here was a man about to brief the president of the United States who hadn't even bothered to stop at a hallway mirror and run a hand through his hair.

"Good morning, everyone," Coyle said. If he was nervous about a rushed briefing to the national command structure, he didn't show it. Coyle began without notes in a voice that was clear and confident — not bravado, but rather the simple strength of a man who knew what he was talking about. "Director Graham has asked me to give my thoughts regarding what occurred last night. As she implied, I am something of an expert on such matters. In truth, of course, if I was really so insightful I would have seen these attacks coming in their exact form and insisted on countermeasures."

The president said, "I can assure you, Dr. Coyle, there will be more than enough blame to go around."

"Yes, I suppose so. To begin, let's admit that most Americans have a limited knowledge of refined fuels. You all know that high octane is better than low, and at some point you've spilled a few drops on your shoes at the pump. But there is great complexity to this industry, and inherent to that, great risk."

DNI Graham broke in. "Dr. Coyle wrote a report outlining specific threats to our refineries."

"I think I read it," the president said. "One scenario had to do with an acid cloud."

"Yes," Coyle picked up. "We uncovered the blueprint of a plot some time ago that involved attacks against domestic oil refineries. The scenario went something like this — pressurized anhydrous fluoride tanks were targeted. If these could be breached, the result would be a cloud of vaporized hydrofluoric acid, highly toxic and traveling on the wind."

General Banks said, "So is this what we're up against, Dr. Coyle? I heard at least one report of a toxic cloud outside a California refinery."

"I think I can say quite definitively, no. There have been two, perhaps three reports of some kind of toxic vapor, but these are almost certainly secondary effects. Oil refineries are a chemist's playground of hazardous substances. The smallest breach can easily lead to fire, and the smallest fire can quickly become a superheated catastrophe. Once a chain of destruction has been initiated, collateral damage will be widespread and indiscriminant."

Graham said, "I thought refineries were getting away from the more hazardous chemicals for that very reason."

"Precisely. In the case of anhydrous hydrogen fluoride, most no longer use it, and the remaining facilities concentrate security measures around these holding tanks. What we saw last night was not an 'acid cloud' attack. It was something else."

President Townsend shifted in his seat. If this guy had any other reports sitting on shelves gathering dust, he was going to read them soon.

"First of all, the refineries targeted were not our largest. Most would be considered mid-range in terms of capacity — a hundred fifty thousand to two hundred fifty thousand barrels a day. It stands to reason that these facilities were chosen because their level of security was less stringent than what would be found at larger sites. Once inside, the attackers appear to have gone after the crude heaters. A good choice, really," he admitted, his grudging admiration obvious.

"What's a crude heater?" someone asked.

"It's just what you'd think — a large furnace that heats the primary feed of crude oil."

The president sensed bad news coming but felt compelled to ask, "How important are these heaters?"

"To realize their significance, one has to understand the basic industrial process. Refining petroleum involves distillation, much as a Tennessee moonshiner uses heat to separate his white lighting from the remains. Crude oil is first heated to begin the refining process. As the temperature rises, the flow is routed into distillation columns, the tall cylindrical stacks most of you are familiar with. At progressive stages in this heating process, different compounds — that is, different types of fuel — are fractioned and recovered. In the end, the remains undergo what is called 'cracking,' which involves using various catalysts to increase yield — it's the kind of thing only petroleum engineers care about. But the salient point is that these primary heaters are the workhorses of the entire refinery. Without them, the operation shuts down. And replacing these units amid acres of toxic rubble will take considerable time."

"How long?" the president asked.

Coyle rubbed his temple, giving Townsend the impression of a man who had been calculating all morning. "The level of damage will take a few days to accurately assess. And it will vary considerably from one plant to another. But to get all capacity back on line — I estimate at least six months."

"Jesus!" General Banks said. "Where was the security?"

Coyle said, "You have to understand, General, refineries today are highly automated. I toured an average facility last week — a hundred thirty-eight thousand barrels a day. It was a twenty-four-seven operation run by six engineers from a control room. At night, there might

be a few dozen others on the property, mostly wrench-turners and a
limited number of contract security men. The level of training for
guards at these facilities is a mixed bag — some companies take it very
seriously, others less so. Regulatory oversight is minimal."

The room sighed collectively, and President Townsend recognized
one piece of legislation that would find its way to the Hill this week.

"Last night's disaster could have been worse," Coyle argued. "Many
of the largest facilities along the Gulf Coast were spared."

Townsend asked, "So there won't be any serious disruption to our
gasoline supply?"

Here Coyle paused. His head went down and he seemed to study
the base of the podium for a moment. Something in the question had
disrupted his form. When he spoke again, his pace and demeanor were
markedly different. He was now lecturing, a parent scolding a wayward
child.

"This, Mr. President, is the tune I have been playing to deaf ears
for years. Mind you, it is only the theory of one academic, but hear me
out." Coyle left the podium and began meandering back and forth, his
hands now moving freely for emphasis. "Our country has been the
dominant economic and political force in this world since the end of
World War II. It is my contention that this is a direct result of our system of transportation. The roads allow a flow of goods and materials
that no economy on earth — even the most advanced European
democracies — can match. America invented and embraced the mass-
produced car, and our way of life, both at work and leisure, now re-
volves around it. But this great advantage we have made for ourselves
will, I fear, soon become our Achilles heel."

Coyle finally stopped for help. He pulled a notepad from his jacket
pocket and flipped it open. "As I now speak, we have likely lost between eighteen and twenty percent of our domestic refined gasoline
output. The price of a gallon of gas will likely rise by fifty percent
within two weeks — for those who have access. Regional shortfalls
are inevitable, and gas will be unavailable for short periods in the hard-
est hit areas. *With* immediate action, I project a midyear decrease in

domestic GNP of between three and four percent on an annual basis. A moderate recession given no other complications."

A chorus of muted expletives tarnished the air. Then silence.

President Townsend eyed Coyle. Most of the wonks who gave him briefings were no more than speculators who reminded him of weather forecasters — if they made enough predictions, sooner or later they'd be right. His gut impression was that Herman Coyle was different. Coyle *knew* where this storm was headed. Townsend said, "All right. What should we do?"

"There is a precedent," Coyle said. "In the last few years, a number of hurricanes have struck the central Gulf Coast. In 2008, Gustav and Ike sequentially shut down fifteen and nineteen percent of our refinery output. Of course, these facilities were only lost for a matter of weeks. Still, gas prices rose significantly and spot shortages existed, particularly in the Southeast."

"I remember Atlanta being hit hard," said Spector, a native Georgian.

"And in charting our course," Coyle contended, "there is more to consider. Much has been made of the fact that no new refineries have been built in our country since 1976. In fact, the number of active refineries has been cut in half in that time. The remaining facilities are, of course, far more efficient than before. The downside is that these refineries operate near maximum capacity. We have little option of 'ramping up' production."

"It's all because of too much environmental regulation," Chief of Staff Spector chided.

"Actually," Coyle argued, "the cumbersome oversight process is only a minor nuisance. Like the rest of our economy, the market for petrochemicals has globalized. Simply put, it is cheaper for us to buy foreign refined products, incrementally, than to produce them ourselves." Coyle turned to Townsend. "With these factors in mind, Mr. President, there are four steps we must take immediately."

Coyle waited for a cue from his commander-in-chief.

Townsend nodded.

"First, we must protect our remaining facilities against further attack."

General Banks piped in, "I've already been in touch with the National Guard Bureau. I think they're in the best position to handle it, but if we need to augment with active duty forces, I'll see to it."

The president had only one addition. "All right. But I want every refinery locked down tight *by tonight*."

Coyle nodded approvingly. He said, "Second, we must fast-track all repair work. Corporations must not be hogtied with toxic cleanup plans from the EPA or safety audits from OSHA."

There was no dissent around the conference table. There wasn't a politician in Washington who, at least at some point in his or her career, hadn't relished the chance to tell EPA and OSHA to go jump in a toxic lake without a safety line.

"Third, we must procure every barrel of foreign excess capacity we can get our hands on. This must take place at both the governmental and corporate levels."

Again Coyle's directive went unchallenged. The room remained silent for his final decree.

"My last suggestion," he said, "requires an understanding of the term 'forward cover.' Simply put, it is the amount of time that the refined petroleum in our system will stretch given standard rates of usage. Yesterday, we had a forward cover of twenty-one days."

The president wanted to be sure he understood. "You're saying the gasoline already in the pipeline will last us twenty-one days?"

"Essentially, yes. Since we still have significant production in place, and with the purchase of additional stores on the global market, the effect on supply should be manageable. However—" Coyle parked at the podium again and his voice rose for emphasis, "*this all makes one assumption.* Mr. President, you must appeal for calm. Americans will be inundated for weeks with images of these attacks, images of lines at gas pumps. As I said, there will be spot shortages due to kinks in our distribution network. Any panic, any mass hoarding of gasoline or other refined products will exacerbate the problem. It could quickly wipe out our safety margin and induce a catastrophic shortage."

President Townsend said, "So you want me to make an appeal for calm."

"It is vital, sir." Coyle then made eye contact with the rest of the table and his thin lips puckered as if he had encountered something distasteful. "Any missteps, ladies and gentlemen, will result in a most dire crisis."

Townsend had the distinct feeling that Herman Coyle was telling them not to screw this up. It was probably good advice.

CHAPTER SEVENTEEN

The meeting at Building Sixty-two was one Davis did not want to miss. The initial play of the cockpit voice recorder, or CVR, was scheduled to take place. Together with the flight data recorder, it was among the investigators' most critical evidence. These were the infamous black boxes — a sensational misnomer since they were actually life vest orange — the digital record keepers that stored detailed logs of what occurred in an aircraft's final minutes.

Typically, it was the data recorder that garnered the greatest interest from investigators. It tracked hundreds of parameters — control inputs, instrument readings, switch activations. It was a series of technical snapshots — three per second — that when strung together could identify virtually any anomaly. Unfortunately, in the case of World Express 801, the data recorder information had already been declared useless, although the technicians were not ready to give up. Given this lack of flight and performance information, the voice recorder took on even greater importance.

Davis arrived early, and with time to kill, he went to the hangar where pieces of wreckage were slowly accumulating. He spotted Thierry Bastien meandering amid the debris, sipping from a china cup — tea, Davis guessed. Probably some kind of pointless decaf chamomile. As he watched Bastien go about his work, his opinion of the investigator-in-charge dropped yet another notch. When Davis walked through a pile of rubble, he could never resist the urge to dig, poke, and smell. Bastien was simply strolling. He might have been window shopping on Rodeo Drive. Surely any vital clues would jump out at him.

Bastien looked up and saw him coming. "Ah, Monsieur Davis. You have been in the field, no?"

Davis looked down at his boots. He had knocked off the worst on a stone wall outside, but they were still caked in mud. He gave Bastien a dry look that said, *Brilliant deduction, Sherlock.*

Bastien pursed his lips. "Please, my friend. You and I have gotten off — how do they say — on the wrong leg."

"Foot."

"Yes." Bastien sipped from his cup. "I think you did not agree with my initial assessment yesterday."

"You mean when you publicly accused the captain of committing suicide?"

In the midst of his sip, the Frenchman pulled away looking like he'd just sucked a lemon. "I only said that we consider these possibilities. There are many similarities to the SilkAir tragedy, you must agree. I have seen the circuit breaker panel behind the captain's seat, and indeed the data recorder breaker has been deactivated. To suggest such a thing could happen by random chance in the very moments before this disaster — an overvoltage at that precise point in time? The odds against it are insurmountable. You try, sir, to put the square peg in the round hole."

Davis thought, *I'd like to put my square fist in your round mouth.* He said nothing, but was looking forward to his own inspection of the circuit breaker panel.

Bastien said, "I told you earlier that we spoke to the bartender at the hotel where Captain Moore stayed. Has your Human Factors Group followed up on this?"

"No. But let me guess — you have?"

"In fact, yes. There are many witnesses. Captain Moore was indeed drinking the evening before the incident."

"How long before the flight?"

Bastien's eyes went skyward in thought. "Roughly twelve hours."

"Eight makes him legal. How much did he drink?"

"His bill was for four beers."

"Was he alone?"

Bastien hesitated. "He was with a woman."

"His first officer."

"This has not yet been verified. But possibly, yes."

Davis felt his ire rising. He wanted to talk about bent elevons and fire damage, but Investigator-in-Charge Bastien couldn't get past bar tabs. "So he and his first officer each had two beers — twelve hours before the flight. And he picked up the tab like a good captain. From experience, Terry," he said, again Anglicizing the name, "I can't think of any more normal behavior for a couple of pilots."

Bastien bristled. "I can only say, Mr. Davis, that we will continue to examine this evidence as a contributing causal factor."

Davis thought about that. Last week Earl Moore had been a veteran, a dad who took his kid to ballgames. Now he was a "causal factor." When Davis had been in the Air Force there was an unwritten rule about dead pilots. Around the squadron, you never said somebody had been a drunk, a philanderer, or a buffoon in the cockpit. You never said it — even if it was true. But accident investigations were different. No one here had known the crewmembers. They were just names, numbers on pilot certificates, and so expediency and a reckless search for the facts overcame any quaint semblance of honor. Davis knew it would always be that way. But he didn't have to like it.

A young woman rushed up and passed a message to Bastien. The investigator-in-charge frowned sourly. "*Mon Dieu!*"

"What now?" Davis asked.

"So much important work to be done," he waved the paper, "and I am pulled down by the weight of dead horses."

"Dead horses?"

"A horse was victim to the crash and the owner is now demanding compensation."

Davis prodded, "A champion Thoroughbred, no doubt."

"The man is outside complaining to the press." Bastien straightened his tie and began to walk away. His gait was stylish, confident. In parting, he glanced over his shoulder, a look that said, *We will resume our discussion later.*

Davis nodded in return, his eyes sharp. *Yes, we will.*

Davis continued his walk through the hangar. The investigators were gathering amid rising mounds of debris. He counted four regionalized conversations where the working groups had divided into packs. The building's tall, rectangular frame was an acoustic nightmare, and so the competing words mixed in a chattering waterfall, the aggregate indistinguishable to Davis' ears. In three of the pods, the participants were bantering—loud, animated discussions, the usual give-and-take over early findings and theories. The fourth group, however, was different.

Dr. Ibrahim Jaber presided, giving muted directions to two colleagues. He talked, they listened. He moved his hands in slow chopping motions and his colorless face was compressed as he emphasized a point. On their first encounter, Davis remembered Jaber as being subdued, almost listless. Now he looked like a mime on Valium. From a distance, even his eyes appeared changed, lacking the intensity Davis had seen earlier. Now they were dim, like a light that was neither on nor off, but something in between.

Sorensen hadn't come up with anything yet on Jaber's background, but Davis had asked around among the other investigators. He'd found out that the guy was Egyptian, just as he'd guessed, and had a Ph.D. from Cairo University in systems engineering. After a short stint writing computer code for an Italian avionics supplier, he had hooked up with Aerostar, a nascent Russian airframe manufacturer. Neither job was management, but rather technical in nature. Apparently the guy was some sort of expert in software integration, made his living by renting out his skills to whoever was buying. A hired gun. Not bad work, but hardly the résumé of a chief project engineer for a new civil aircraft program.

Davis edged over.

When Jaber saw him coming he ended his one-sided conversation. The two men he'd been lecturing faded away.

"Hello, Mr. Davis."

Davis nodded. "Dr. Jaber."

"Are you looking forward to hearing the cockpit voice tapes?"

"Looking forward to it? Not really. But we might learn a few things."

"Yes, indeed."

Davis said, "I understand that you're something of an expert in the design of flight control software."

Jaber waved the compliment away, that false air of coyness so imbued in people who thought highly of themselves. "I would more precisely describe my work as systems integration — it is my duty to bring conformity to the various aircraft computers and data inputs."

"Then I should ask your opinion. Whose concept do you prefer — Boeing or Airbus?"

Jaber cocked his head to one side, the way people did when they were perplexed, as if a new angle of perspective might bring enlightenment. "I am an engineer, so Airbus, of course."

In the decades since Airbus had come into existence, two essential theories had evolved concerning the design of flight control systems. Airbus had pioneered fly-by-wire technology for commercial aircraft, a method where the pilot controlled what was basically a joystick, and a series of computers then provided inputs to hydraulically actuated flight controls. Boeing, on the other hand, had long kept a more traditional method, retaining mechanical links between the pilot and the flight control surfaces. Over the years, the two manufacturers had gravitated to something of a middle ground, but these divergent design philosophies gave rise to yet another division — pilots favored more direct input, while engineers liked to give their computers ultimate say. Davis knew, from a neutral investigator's standpoint, that each camp could point to spectacular failures of the other.

Jaber continued with what sounded like a well-rehearsed sales pitch. "At CargoAir we have embraced technology, Mr. Davis. The C-

500 functions on a triple redundant system. The calculated chance of three concurrent failures — if that is what you allude to — is one in six billion over the life of the program."

Davis never liked numbers like that. The guy who designed the Hindenberg probably had great numbers. Lethargy aside, Jaber was beginning to remind him of Hurricane Sparky. He said, "Okay, so let's say the flight control system was working as advertised. Would it have allowed such a steep dive? Wouldn't it have limited the angle of descent or the airspeed?"

"These questions are yet to be answered. But, of course, everything must be measured with respect to the control inputs made by the pilot."

Careful words, Davis thought. Throw it all back on the pilot. "So you give credence to Dr. Bastien's theory regarding the accident? You think it may have been an intentional act?"

The Egyptian shrugged. "It is not for me to say, Mr. Davis. My expertise lies not in the human condition, but the far more predictable arena of software interfaces. I understand logic, sir, not emotion."

Davis nodded politely. Then he tried a new tack. "Bastien suggests that the data recorder contains no useful information because the circuit breaker was pulled just before the dive began."

Jaber nodded as he followed the thought.

"Well, I've been wondering — just for the sake of argument, you see — if there was any other way the data recorder could have failed."

Jaber's movements turned glacial. Again Davis noticed the eyes, filled with — what? Acceptance? Resignation?

"Another failure mode?" Jaber queried. "The data recorder is one of many systems on the aircraft, Mr. Davis. None are perfect, and so it could have been a routine failure, of course. But I believe that to certify a data recorder, your own FAA requires a demonstrated time-between-failure rate of no more than one in every twenty thousand hours of flight time."

Davis thought, *More numbers*. He said nothing.

"Therefore," Jaber extrapolated, "could this have happened? Yes. But I ask you, what are the odds?"

Davis didn't stop to calculate. "But you are an expert in systems integration. What if another system failed, something tied in with the data recorder? Maybe a component connected to a common electrical bus?"

Jaber shrugged. "There are remote possibilities. I am told there was a brief power interruption on the ground as the crew was preparing for flight. As a pilot, you know such events can play havoc on individual systems."

"Queertrons," Davis said.

Jaber cocked an ear. "I beg your pardon?"

"Queertrons. That's what pilots call them. Those little stray elements of matter that gum up everything with a circuit board. When an instrument goes haywire, you remove power for a few seconds, turn it back on, and the problem is usually solved. Usually."

"Yes, from an operator's perspective you are essentially correct. And I will tell you that the same difficulties can occur when various aircraft systems interact. But this power interruption on the ground we are speaking of — it took place fully half an hour before the data recorder ceased functioning. Any relationship between the two would seem highly unlikely."

"Highly," Davis repeated.

Someone shouted a five minute warning for the briefing.

"Clearly you have more questions," Jaber said. "Perhaps we can discuss this at a later time."

Davis nodded. More discussion. His day-planner was filling up fast.

Jaber headed for the briefing.

Davis stood right where he was. In front of him was a section of wreckage. He recognized it as the remains of a cockpit windscreen, the thing twisted in its frame, inch-thick layers of clear laminate shattered beyond recognition. He was glad Jaber had at least given him hope — there was a remote chance that the power interruption could have some relationship to the data recorder failure. Davis had one tiny straw to grab for, something beyond the possibility that Earl Moore had pulled the circuit breaker himself, rolled inverted, and pulled toward the earth.

There was, however, one certainty in it all. One thing that Bastien was actually right about. The fact that the data recorder had failed only seconds before the airplane started its final dive — that was too much of a coincidence. Davis didn't know the method. Not yet. But some-one had *made* it happen.

Someone trying to hide what really caused the crash of World Express 801.

CHAPTER EIGHTEEN

Sorensen took off her New Balances before she entered her room. They were caked in mud, and she figured housekeeping would appreciate it if she didn't track it all over the carpet. She had just tossed them in the tub when her phone rang.

It was a government-issued device — big, heavy, and power-hungry, with a battery symbol that always seemed to be pressing the last bar. The thing was supposedly secure, another satellite gadget, but these days you could never be sure. She walked to the window with the phone in hand, allowing two more rings to shift her mental gears. Sorensen glanced outside. Her room had a reaching view of an open field bordered by brown, dormant hedgerows. In another three months it would be nice to look at. She turned away and hit the green button.

"Sorensen here."

"We need a status report."

She rolled her eyes. No, *Hey, how are you?* Not even a name to the voice. Just some mid-level guy on the European desk who'd been tasked to keep a distant eye on her. The hard truth came to Sorensen's mind that in five more years it would probably be her on the other end of the line. It made her think about Jammer Davis and his distaste for big, faceless bureaucracies. Maybe he had a point.

Her reply came with an edge. "My status is that I just spent my entire morning with Davis crawling through mud at the crash site. I learned a lot. It'll give me some credibility."

"So he's cooperating?"

She hesitated. "He said he'd help. The guy knows his stuff. He has some good ideas about what brought the airplane down."

"We don't give a rat's ass about what brought the airplane down," countered the terse voice of Langley. "We want Caliph, and you've been inserted into this investigation to take a thorough look at CargoAir."

"Give me a chance, I've only been on the job for two days. We have to go through a few motions here."

"Screw the motions — there's no time! You know what's been happening. Caliph has attacked us directly. This investigation crap will take months. We need results now!"

Sorensen gripped the phone tighter. She really had a way with men these days. "What have you got for me?" she said, turning the tables. "I need that information on Ibrahim Jaber."

After a long pause, the man in Langley began dictating. It didn't take long.

"That's not much," Sorensen said.

"We're still working on it. We dug up what we could. You just didn't give us enough —" the voice faded.

Time, she thought with a grin.

"Look, Sorensen, this is highest priority. You and Davis need to work fast."

"I realize that. And as far as Davis goes — he's a lot of things, but patient isn't one of them. He'll make headway."

"Check in tomorrow at the usual time." The connection cut off abruptly.

"And you have a great day too," she said mockingly to the steady tone that buzzed from her handset.

Sorensen turned off the phone and threw it onto the couch where it clattered against a spent room service tray. A metal cover plate hid the remainder of her half-eaten midnight sandwich. It had been dreadful.

Sorensen went to the bathroom and forced her eyes to the mirror. She knew it wouldn't be good. Her eyes were bloodshot under a dirt-smudged forehead, and damp hair was matted to the sides of her neck. She looked like she felt — tired. She could use a day at a spa, maybe a massage. Fat chance. Her reality was surly phone calls and bad hotel food. Sorensen wasn't normally one for self-pity. Not for the first time, though, she questioned her career choice. It was an argument she'd been having with herself for six months now.

Her sister had married well — or at least rich. At thirty-six, Vicky was three years older, but looked five years younger. Missing were the worry lines drawn by too many all-night surveillance shifts and the stress of endless travel. Vicky Sorensen had her Waspy husband, her über-house, her twins in preschool. Anna Sorensen had turned it all down.

His name had been Greg. Greg Van Essen. B.S. from NYU. Then an MBA. Landed at UBS. All the uppercase letters you needed in life. He was good looking, in a preppy kind of way. Considerate, in a roses on Valentines Day kind of way. She'd known him and liked him for two years. They were easy together, comfortable. So there was no reason for her to say no when, last summer, he had asked her to marry him.

And she hadn't said no. She'd asked for time. But wasn't that the same thing? When a great guy gets down on a knee and says, "Spend the rest of your life with me," you're not supposed to say you'll give it due and proper consideration. You're supposed to gush, "Yes! Yes!" But that never happened. Maybe it would someday. Maybe she'd spend twenty years at the Company and then find that one great guy who had somehow slipped through to middle age unscathed and without baggage. The one who wouldn't worry about crow's feet or a few gray hairs. Sure she would.

Sorensen turned to the tub and began to run water. The hot side wasn't working. So, under an arctic spray, she went to work scraping mud from her tennis shoes with a hotel toothbrush.

The conference room was a standard affair, institutional chairs and three tables mated end-to-end. Over a dozen people associated with the investigation were present, including the head of each working group. Bastien kicked things off with a reminder for everyone that what they were about to hear was privileged information, not for public release. Davis found the warning laughable given what the investigator-in-charge had done yesterday.

"As you all know," Bastien said, "the flight data recorder has so far given no usable information from the moment the dive began. Our technicians, of course, will continue their work. It has been determined, however, that up to the moment when the data stopped streaming, everything was consistent with a normal flight profile."

Bastien introduced the lead engineer from the manufacturer of the voice recorder, Doral Systems. The guy passed around a stack of business cards and everybody took one. Davis saw a cell phone number scrawled on the back and thought, *He'll be sorry*. He tucked the card into the Rolodex that was his jacket pocket, not bothering to alphabetize.

The Doral man explained that his technical team had been over the recording a half-dozen times, and had transcribed a rough text of the dialogue as well as all readily identifiable sounds. These secondary noises could be every bit as vital as the crew's words. Levers raised, switches actuated — all of it registered.

This nonvoice data would eventually be replicated, switch and mechanical sounds mimicked in a real cockpit, extraneous noise filtered out. Voice recorders were notoriously hard to decipher given the degree of background clutter — wind stream, instrumentation, ventilation ducts, mechanical actuators and automated voices and warnings. The cockpit of a big airplane was a virtual ocean of chatter that could mask and mislead. All of it would be processed, simulated, filtered again and again until everyone agreed on each action that had been performed by the crew. It wasn't the same as having solid information from the flight data recorder — that loss tied one hand behind their collective backs — but much could be learned.

The Doral man passed out a four-page transcript to everyone. The information Davis began to scan was preliminary, but in time the

technicians would nail everything down, save for the occasional garbled, unintelligible word.

"We will begin," the Doral man said, "at power-up, roughly forty-
two minutes before impact."

The audio began. It was rather scratchy, but the voices of Captain
Earl Moore and First Officer Melinda Hendricks were clear. The dialogue was also projected on a screen at the head of the room, a Pow-
erPoint mirror of the printed copy everyone had in front of them. A
clock in one corner of the screen tracked time to the nearest one-
tenth of a second.

The crew could be heard running through the Before Starting
Engines checklist, standard challenge and response items to ensure that
every lever, switch, and instrument was prepared for flight. The use of
checklists was standard procedure at all airlines. While most pilots
could climb into a familiar airplane on any given day and fly without
issue, it took only one distraction, one ill-timed sneeze-and-
gesundheit, to keep the flaps from being set for takeoff. Virtually every
item on the checklist, Davis knew, was written in blood — at some
point in the past a mistake had been made, an airplane crashed, and the
checklist grew another step. Some of the crosschecks went back to the
very dawn of aviation, while others were more contemporary. Altogether it made for a good system, helped aviators not repeat the errors
that those before them had made. But as airplanes became more advanced, more complex, each new step in technology brought a matching stride of uncertainty — there were always new hazards to uncover.

Midway through the checklist, the audio hiccupped. The Doral
engineer explained, "Here, we have an electrical interruption. We believe the ship was on ground power, and it has already been confirmed
that the portable power unit they were using had been giving the
ground crews trouble for weeks. Everything comes back up in roughly
ten seconds — not enough time to lose any navigation alignments."

This had to be the glitch Jaber was referring to, Davis thought, his
far-fetched secondary theory on how the flight data recorder might
have failed. Indeed, the voice recording soon picked back up and the

crew could be heard finishing their checks. The only other anomaly before takeoff was a mention by the first officer that her clock had lost the correct time. Just like at home, Davis mused. The power goes out, and you have to reset every damned clock in the house.

Takeoff and climb were normal. With the aircraft established at 38,000 feet and flying nicely on autopilot, things started to go very wrong.

CHAPTER NINETEEN

Davis listened to the words, but he also registered the tenor of the voices. Not for the first time, he put himself in Earl Moore's place.

The recorder had four channels of input: CA1 was the captain's microphone, the voice of Earl Moore; FO2 was the first officer, Melinda Hendricks; CAM was the cockpit area microphone, picking up everything, including extraneous sounds on the flight deck; ATC was air traffic control on the number 1 VHF radio. The local time for each entry was also listed.

0600:15 *CAM: Warning horn*

Davis recognized it as the autopilot disengage warning.

0600:18 *FO2: Did you do that?*

0600:20 *CA1: No.*

0600:25 *FO2: Watch your altitude, Earl.*

The airplane had begun its descent, and from the edge in the voices, Davis decided it was not a gentle maneuver.

0600:27 *CA1: I'm trying. What's that light?*

0600:40 *FO2: Altitude! Pitch!*

0600:46 *ATC: WorldEx 801, check altitude.*

0600:49 *FO2: Earl!*

0600:51 *CA1: I know! There! FCC1 . . . no 2 . . . checklist!*

0600:58 *CAM: Airspeed clacker (continues to impact).*

FCC1 was Flight Control Computer 1. Davis circled this entire line on his copy of the transcript. The airspeed warning was referred to as a clacker — it sounded like a pair of castanets in rapid fire — and the meaning was clear enough. The craft was headed down in a severe dive, exceeding its maximum allowable speed.

0601:02 *ATC: WorldEx 801, Marseille Center, over.*

0601:12 *FO1: FCC1 . . . no action required . . . the FCCs are triple redundant and . . . there's nothing in here!*

The first officer was reading from the aircraft's emergency procedures checklist. It gave no help, just told them there wasn't a problem. Told them that what was happening couldn't happen.

0601:16 *ATC: WorldEx 801, Marseille Control! Are you experiencing difficulty?*

0601:18 *CA1: Look at all these lights! There has to be something!*

0601:21 *ATC: WorldEx 8-0-1 this is Marseille, do you read?*

0601:24 *CAM: click-click (Actuation of unidentified switches)*

The Doral engineer stopped the recording. He said, "At this point, ladies and gentlemen, we have a problem. It seems that the voice recorder's power was somehow interrupted. There is no more data until roughly ten seconds before impact, at which point, everything returns."

0601:41 *FO1: Marseille . . . WorldEx 801 . . . Mayday! May . . . (unintelligible) Pull! Harder!*

0601:46 *ATC: WorldEx 801, you are clear of all traffic. What is the nature of your difficulty?*

0601:48 *CAM: (Unidentified mechanical sound)*

0601:50 *CA1: (Grunting)*

0601:54 *CA1: I love you, Luke!*

0601:56 *CAM: (Sound of impact)*

0601:58 *End*

The recording fell silent.

The room did the same. In the middle of this massive, clinical examination of the demise of World Express Flight 801, all were clearly struck by the humanity of what they had just heard. The tape would be gone over again and again, and each time the silence would grow shorter, propriety giving way to the relentless drive for facts. As the pause extended, those in the room began to look at one another guardedly, like a congregation waiting for the minister to issue his "amen."

The technician from Doral, already running the show, finally said, "Dr. Bastien?"

Bastien, having slumped over the table, sat more erect in his chair. "Yes, very well. Your thoughts, ladies and gentlemen?"

Nobody ever wanted to be first at such a moment, even in a room of Type As like this. Davis let the silence sit as long as he could. Then, just as a Japanese air traffic control guy was about to open his mouth, he lobbed his mortar. "We have to issue an emergency directive — ground the entire fleet right now."

"*What?*" Bastien sputtered. "For what possible reason?"

There were other reactions around the room. Davis watched one in particular. Then he said, "The number of catastrophic events that will bring an airplane down in this manner is very limited. In my mind, I've already eliminated a fair number of them, and it leaves me with one overriding concern." Davis got up and walked to the screen at the front of the room. He said to the Doral technician, "0600:51, please."

The screen flashed and Davis pointed to what he wanted. "Here." The line referenced was:

0600:51 *CA1: I know! There! FCC1 . . . no 2 . . . checklist!*

Davis looked over the crowd and locked eyes with Jaber before he spoke. "The captain says 'FCC1 . . . no 2.' I think it is very possible that we are dealing with multiple flight control computer failures."

The Egyptian stiffened, maybe flinched, but he said nothing.

Another guy with a CargoAir ID spoke defiantly, "No! There are many possible explanations for an FCC warning light. And even if there were two failures, the third channel would have taken over. What you suggest is simply not possible!"

Bastien said, "And we still have the issue of Captain Moore. It is clear from the recording that he was the pilot flying during the mishap sequence. If his intent was as we suspect, he might say anything — he knew the voice recorder was active and would be reviewed. I suspect he also knew that the data recorder was disabled. Moore even says goodbye to his loved ones at the end, knowing we will be here today listening to his words. This, I tell you, is evidence of what I have been suggesting all along."

Davis said, "Saying goodbye simply means he knew he was done for. You just said it yourself — all pilots know their words are recorded. What Moore said is the second most common thing to hear at the end of a tape. The first being, 'Aw, shit!' "

"No!" Bastien insisted. "No! We cannot possibly recommend grounding the fleet."

Davis went back to his spot. He didn't take his seat just yet, but he eased up. "All right," he said. "The voting members of our investigation team are all here. Maybe it's time for us to tally things up."

Bastien bristled openly. He scanned a room awash in undercurrents. Davis figured he was calculating his odds. The idea of grounding an entire fleet of airliners worldwide was extreme, but not unprecedented.

Bastien finally said, "I suggest the following course. We will not recommend grounding the fleet. However, Mr. Davis, since you feel so strongly about this possible mode of failure, I will instruct Dr. Jaber to commit his team at CargoAir. They will address specifically this avenue of our investigation. Should Dr. Jaber find any firm — I repeat firm — evidence of flight control anomalies, we will then revisit the possibility of an emergency grounding directive."

Davis thought it was ridiculous to put a company rep in charge of a branch analysis, even if the guy was an expert. The conflict of interest couldn't be more obvious. He decided to let it go for now.

Bastien said, "A show of hands, please — those in favor of the course I suggest."

Three hands shot right up, including Bastien's. Two others followed slowly.

"And against?" Bastien said, now looking rather pleased with his little display of democracy.

Davis raised his hand. Behind a grave expression, however, he too was pleased — and not quite done with his own touch of showmanship. He got up brusquely and stormed from the room.

Jammer Davis careened out the front entrance of Building Sixty-two, a bowling ball just looking for a few pins. He found them idling by a news van. With no further briefings scheduled today, the press pool had thinned down — two bored camera crews. Davis only needed one.

He paused, made sure his board member ID was prominently displayed. He waited for the reporter to hold out his microphone, waited for the red light on the camera. Then Davis made his statement in clear French.

"We continue our investigation into the crash of World Express Flight 801. With respect to possible causes, we have identified a new theory to explore, a technical issue not related to the headlines of yesterday."

And he stopped right there. Left it at that.

"Can you give any further details of this new theory?" the reporter asked.

"No." Davis began to walk away.

The reporter held out his microphone like a fencing foil. "But, sir. Surely there must be more —"

"Go to hell!" Davis yelled in English.

The reporter's hand dropped, the microphone dangling by his knee. "Idiot American!" he muttered under his breath.

CHAPTER TWENTY

Ibrahim Jaber stood near the window of his fourth-floor flat. His arms were crossed over his chest and a cigarette dangled loosely in two fingers. The ashes were long.

The world outside was subdued and gray, fading in the waning evening light. The steep roofs of the buildings along the place des Terreaux were uniformly topped with tiles inspired by the colors of the sun, those pink and orange hues that adorned virtually all architecture on this side of the Mediterranean. Today, however, it was a lie — there was no sun to be seen. Jaber did not like French weather, especially in the winter. The wet, the cold. He dreamed idly of an Egyptian sun, a hard heat that could be taken in and absorbed by the body.

He turned away from the window and drifted into the realm of his modest quarters. It was a one-bedroom suite, reasonably clean, on rue d'Algérie in central Lyon. The lease had been arranged hastily in another's name, and Jaber circulated the story that he was to endure the investigation as a houseguest of his maternal aunt. No one in the CargoAir delegation seemed to mind — Jaber had never strived to be social or well liked. He decided that the others would probably hold a secret celebration, cheer that their demanding boss had sequestered himself with an old spinster. A woman who existed only on paper.

Arms still crossed, Jaber paced in a tight two-step pattern. *How had it come to this?* he wondered. The lies, the deception. Until recently he had made his way with honest work, getting by on the strength of his intellect and diligence. Indeed, Jaber never doubted that he would have been an unqualified success, a leader in his field, had it not been for the curse of his nationality.

Deep down, he wanted to be proud of his Egyptian heritage, proud to have risen from the ancient cradle of civilization. Yet, in his line of work, the lineage gave nothing but misery and unwarranted shame. Engineers who specialized in aeronautical systems integration did not find work in Egypt. Jaber had fallen to become a gypsy, an overeducated whore selling his technical services across the world.

For years he had bounced from here to there, each employer using him for a time, then, when a particular project was complete, casting him aside. No longer needed, no longer useful. The Russians, the French, the Americans, the Japanese. All had taken his help, but in the end offered nothing more than cash, modest severances to help him find the door. His only other earnings were suspicion and doubt, a capital of mistrust borne from the simple fact that his passport had been issued by a predominantly Muslim country.

Many times, Jaber had tried to convince his supervisors that he did not even practice the religion, that his was a life steeped in science, not theology. To no avail. The Americans were the worst — most could not distinguish a Muslim from a Hindu. Anyone from "that part of the world" was simply trawled into the widest of nets and labeled as undesirable. So it was, when the executives of CargoAir had given him this opportunity, a chance to lead, he could not have said no. The effect on his psyche had been almost pharmaceutical in nature — an antidepressant for a depressed career. After toiling for so long, clawing his way up, Jaber had finally been recognized, finally reached the pinnacle. Only to face yet another curse.

Jaber winced as a sharp pain shot through his ribs. He went to his suitcase, fished out a bottle, and extracted two large pills. A glass of water was already there, half empty, and he used it to wash them down. The pain he could deal with. What troubled him more was the tiredness, the utter depletion he had begun to feel recently. Jaber had found out about the cancer just after taking the job with CargoAir. The specialists had given him hope at first, and he'd undergone the terrible treatments. They seemed to work for a time, and his emotions vacillated wildly, each new doctor's visit a reason to either buy a case of champagne or jump from a bridge.

Then, just over a year ago, the inevitability of his condition finally settled in. It was at this same time that Jaber was approached with regard to a uniquely challenging project. Indeed, a uniquely dangerous project, one that would strain his technical skills to the limit. For a time, he had wondered why they'd chosen him. Had they known he was a man with nothing to lose? Today he no longer cared.

Gently, Jaber sat in his best chair, allowing his bones to settle. To one side, on an artfully crafted end table, was a framed picture of his family, his good wife and two young sons. The picture was three years old. He had seen them only twice in that time, yet another trial of his rueful existence. They might as well have been taken away and held hostage. In essence, they were. And for Ibrahim Jaber, the only ransom could be his life.

He pulled a phone from his pocket. It was a simple device he had purchased with cash some weeks ago at an anonymous store. Yesterday he had pried and sliced it from its hard plastic shell, run the activation procedure. Now Jaber would use the thing once, then toss it in the trash. Discarded before its time, like so much these days.

The number to dial was engraved firmly in his memory, yet a number he had never before called. Jaber idly touched the keypad on the bulky handset, felt the plastic numbers beneath his fingertips. It was the same keypad, the same ten digits that billions of people might feel under their fingers. But few others knew the combination, the code that would bring Caliph to bear. Jaber had been told that the number was for emergency use only, and his mind began to sift through data, functioning not unlike the operating systems he so diligently designed. Had things really gone that far?

The investigation was stuck at a crawl. But the American was impatient, asking the right questions, arguing the right points. Still, Jaber was confident in his work. In the traditional sense, he was not an artful man, no use with a paint brush or a piano. But he *was* creative, math and logic being his chosen medium. Jaber weighed it all, then decided the call was necessary. His fingers moved.

He heard only two rings before a familiar voice picked up. There were no salutations.

"Have you changed the timetable?"

The question threw Jaber's well-organized thoughts into disarray. "Yes," he stumbled, "of course. But there can be no further alterations. Nothing can be stopped." He looked at his watch. "Thirty hours remain."

"So why have you called?"

Ibrahim Jaber swallowed hard. "We have a problem—"

The passage from Italy was misery itself.

Fatima sat hunched, staring alternately at the pitching deck and the churning sea below. She could not decide which was less nauseating. The conditions on the northern Mediterranean tonight were horrid, a stiff wind and cold rain lashing the deck, and tremendous seas rolling the craft mercilessly.

Fatima remembered, back on the dock in Genoa, pausing for a moment to study the boat. In the fading light of late afternoon, the passenger ferry had seemed a relatively large ship, a thing of stout decks and heavy construction. Not that she would know. Fatima had been on airplanes before and a few trains, but never a boat. It had seemed like a good idea at the time.

At the beginning of the voyage she'd taken a seat on the roof, open to the elements. This proved another mistake, even if made with good intentions—Fatima knew it was always preferable to travel away from crowds, and at the outset of the trip all but two of the other passengers were ensconced below in the warmth of the protected main compartment. When Fatima vomited the first time, the young couple had been downwind. Soon she was alone.

That she now had privacy was small consolation. Sharp gusts snapped at her flimsy jacket and rain pelted her cheeks. Fatima's stomach churned and convulsed to no end. She was leaning over the rail and heaving when a steward came up to check on her—the man had most likely been alerted by the deserters. Keeping his distance, he suggested something in Italian.

Fatima replied with a blank stare. He would reason she knew nothing of the language. The man pointed downward with a rapid motion that could only mean, *You will feel better below.*

Fatima puked.

The putrid stream splashed over the deck, and nearly splattered onto the steward's work shoes. When she got her breath back, she cursed both him and his wretched boat. The words were in Arabic, but the sputtering cadence and harsh consonants crossed any linguistic divide. As a visual exclamation point, a strand of green spittle dangled from her lower lip, fluttering in the breeze. The steward, who had certainly seen this kind of thing before, seemed genuinely repulsed. He left her alone.

Once again she had privacy. But once again it seemed an empty victory. Such was Fatima's state that she soon reconsidered. Ready to try anything to ease her agony, she went below and found a seat nearer the center of gravity of the tumbling ship. Back among the crowd, Fatima muttered her frustrations, one expletive, one demon at a time. She cursed Italy and France. She cursed the sea, the wind and the steward. Cursed anyone who looked at her.

Few did.

Ten minutes after going below, the combination of Fatima's stench and demeanor created a five-meter buffer that lasted all the way to France.

The four hours seemed like a lifetime. When she finally stepped off the ferry in Marseille, Fatima's legs wobbled. She paused for a moment, steadied herself, and made a quiet vow to never leave dry land again.

Finally having something firm beneath her feet, she trundled ahead unsteadily with the crowd, aiming in a general way for the immigration desk labeled NON-EU. There were two lines — on the left a man and on the right a woman. Both were middle aged, both disinterested.

For Fatima Adara, the choice was easy.

Two minutes later, the Frenchman asked for her passport. The document was an extremely good forgery, a Jordanian item with smudged

entry stamps from seven countries — mostly EU, but with a smattering of the less controversial non-EU federations. Fatima handed over
the passport, having already wiped it on her shirt where a ripe streak
of vomit held fast.

In what had to be his natural rhythm, the man eyed her passport
first. Then he pinned his gaze on Fatima. She watched his face sink
into a mask of revulsion, as if he'd just watched someone get doused
with a chamber pot. Then the scent of the passport hit his nose. The
immigration man's arm locked out as if a bolt of lightning had struck
his nervous system. He held the document at the greatest possible distance, probably wishing his arm was longer.

"*Quelle désastre!*" he said.

Fatima took on a puzzled look, played it for just a moment. Then
a lightbulb seemed to go off over her head. She gave him a wink and
replied in rough English, "Pleasure."

The man huffed and snorted, shrugged his shoulders in a classically
Gallic fit. He kept the passport at rigid arm's length and used the eraser
of a pencil to flick through a few pages. Two more standard questions,
two more incomprehensible answers, then a stamp. The man grimaced
through it all. Finally, the immigration officer handed back her passport and gave Fatima a sharp wave through.

She began to amble away. Fatima was three steps past the podium
when the man suddenly barked, "Mademoiselle!"

She froze.

Very slowly, Fatima turned and met the immigration officer's eyes.
They were stern, accusing. He lifted an arm and pointed stridently to
something in the distance. She followed his gesture and saw stenciled
letters, thick and black, over an open passageway. It was labeled
TOILETTES.

Fatima Adara took a deep breath and headed for the ladies' room.

He was on the balcony, twenty feet up.

Wilson Whittemore IV twirled the cold tail of a latte in a paper
cup and thought, *This is not what I signed up for when I joined the CIA.*
The arrivals from the Genoa boat were streaming in, another decrepit

mass of Mediterranean humanity. Grandmothers, laborers, tourists, immigrants—some legal, some certainly not. Whittemore had been watching this stinking terminal since noon. Eight hours. And he still had four to go.

His eyes settled on a young Italian woman as she strode away from the EU passport stand. She *had* to be Italian. Her long dress was cut to accentuate tan legs and high heels. She knew how to walk in heels, Whittemore decided. Not all women did. A jacket was slung over one shoulder on a finger, the chin was set high, and her boobs bounced freely under her dress. She had the look down. *What a firebrand,* he thought. Whittemore saw her wave to a young man in the distance, and the two closed the gap. When they were ten paces apart, she started reading him the riot act.

Whittemore couldn't hear a word—didn't need to. Her chopping hand motions made it clear she was upset. That's how Italians talked. An expressive people. The guy gave back as good as he got, and soon they disappeared around a corner, a whirlwind of flailing hands and Armani and gnashing white teeth. Whittemore figured that inside thirty minutes their designer clothes would be scattered on the floor of some nice hotel room, and they'd be having frantic sex. A passionate people, the Italians.

The show over, he turned back to the arrivals gate and thought, *One lover's spat. The highlight of my day.* The boat from Genoa was the third he had monitored. Each group of passengers took roughly thirty minutes to debark, get filtered by immigration, and connect with luggage and relatives and taxis. The whole thing was damned tedious. If there was anything more boring than having to stand in line, it was watching other people stand in line.

Whittemore was fed up, ready to move on. He had his sights set on a posting to an embassy staff. Still "in the field," but civilized. Mingle at cocktail parties, maybe rub ankles with a baroness under the table at a State Department dinner. Martinis and proper clothes. Not cold lattes in filthy ferry terminals.

He'd been with the CIA for ten years. They had nabbed him in his sixth year at Dartmouth, graduation unavoidably imminent. He hadn't really needed the job to begin with — he had his trust fund. But with his family already frowning on his extended bachelor's degree, Whittemore decided he had to do something to make himself appear useful.

The visiting CIA recruiter had told him he was just what they were looking for — Ivy League with two years of Arabic language under his belt. Grades didn't matter, thank God. Whittemore had enjoyed college and his transcript proved it. The recruiter had been slick. He'd made it sound exciting — not by telling vivid stories, but just the opposite. What will I be doing? *I really can't say.* Where might I get posted? *Could be anywhere.* Career path? *You fill in the blanks.* Mystery and intrigue. Now there was a sales pitch. Whittemore had taken the bait and run.

He swirled the end of his latte again, the settled remnants thick, cold, and chocolate brown. He tilted his head back to drain the cup, and as soon as it came back down he spotted her. Whittemore didn't need a double take — he had seen three pictures. Side face, frontal face, and full body. There was no mistaking Fatima Adara.

She had just cleared the immigration desk. In front of her, an old guy in a knit fisherman's cap was walking away. Behind, still at the podium and waiting his turn, was a teenager with an iPod. Fatima just stood there with a nylon bag in one hand, frozen while the clerk gave her a hard time about — something. It didn't look like he was detaining her. The guy was actually pointing off in the distance, a disgusted look creased onto his swarthy face. It was as if he was trying to get rid of her but she wasn't moving fast enough. *What the heck?* Whittemore wondered.

The standoff ended when Fatima bundled off in the direction of his gesture. It was then that Whittemore realized his problem — from his present vantage point, he was going to lose sight of Fatima as she moved toward the exit. But then he relaxed, and his confidence returned. There was only one way out of the terminal, a single passage to the streets of Marseille. If Whittemore took up a nice position, he couldn't possibly miss her there.

He pulled out his phone, flipped it open. But then he hesitated.

Fatima Adara was public enemy number two. He began to scan the terminal frantically. Could Caliph be in the crowd as well? That face was also one he'd memorized. The guy in the fisherman's hat was far too old. The kid behind Fatima too young. Nobody that had come off the boat looked remotely like the terrorist.

Whittemore considered his options. Considered his career.

In ten years, he'd never had a score like this — Langley was frantic to find Caliph, and Fatima was the next best thing. If Whittemore called it in now, there would be six more agents circling within the hour. Twenty by midnight. They'd let Fatima run, see where she led. Somebody senior would take charge of the operation, and a month from now Whittemore would get a pat on the back. Maybe even a plaque of commendation for meritorious service — some six-by-ten-inch, imitation mahogany, brass-engraved attaboy.

But if he *didn't* make the call just yet, Fatima might lead him straight to her boss. And if Whittemore called in with a spot on Caliph, he could write his ticket. He flipped his phone shut.

It was time for a little tradecraft.

CHAPTER TWENTY-ONE

Jammer Davis was nursing a tall beer at a tall table and staring at a soccer jersey.

The bar at L'Hotel Continental Lyon was the usual sports theme, pictures of famous athletes and lightly used equipment tacked all around. Of course, everything had a decidedly European twist. Baseball and American football were nowhere to be seen. Soccer and rugby dominated the photos. There were cricket bats and oars, tennis and squash rackets — all just the right size and flavor for nailing to a wall. The uniform Davis was looking at had been pinned up in a glass case along with a plaque explaining the significance of the game in which it was worn. He saw a distinct grass stain on the tail, implying it hadn't been washed after the match. *Good thing it's in a glass case*, Davis thought.

He checked his phone. There were no new messages from Jen. He had left her up in the air about the dance. His finger went to the green button and paused idly on top. He still wasn't sure what he was going to say. *No, you can't go this time. You can never go. You can go with me when I get back.* None seemed completely right.

Davis needed something more uplifting. He had a fleeting thought about calling Hurricane Sparky. She must have seen the news clip by now, his brief engagement with the French camera crew. Rita McCracken wasn't his boss any more, but it might be fun to call, just to yank her chain. *I've alienated the entire board, Sparky, and they want a replacement. I gave them your name. Don't worry, it shouldn't take more than a year. I'll look after your plants.*

Davis snapped his phone shut and shoved it into his bomber jacket that was hanging on the back of the chair. He sipped his beer, wiped a trace of foam from his lips with the back of a wrist. The brew was something local that looked and moved in his glass like 40-weight motor oil. He scooped a handful of snack mix from a bowl on the table. It was nice and salty. This made him take another sip. He was enjoying the cycle.

Davis thought hard about what he'd heard on the voice recorder tape. He had caught something in it, something that likely escaped the others in the room. It was there in Earl Moore's voice. Calmness, confidence — even at the last moment. Davis recognized it for what it was.

To the uninitiated, the concept of flight can seem intimidating. Those without training and experience often find pause at the risks involved. One-off mechanical disasters, the perils of turbulence or storms in an unpredictable sky. When such misfortunes actually rear up — fire and meteorological brimstone — those outside the fraternity might pray to God for deliverance, or even succumb to an aura of serendipity, resigned to let fortune settle things. No aviator worth his salt ever sees it that way. A technical malfunction is taken in stride, even seen as an opportunity to display one's firm hand and steel will. Bad weather need only be circumnavigated or endured, for in the true aviator's psyche there is that inescapable maxim — the surety that one is better than God and his elements.

It is, of course, all an illusion. That much is certain. Davis had seen the sky claim fine pilots, and more than a few fools. But equally certain rests the advantage of perceived invincibility in the face of crisis. Soldiers in combat often found it. Bulletproof status. To some degree, every sure-handed pilot Davis had ever met possessed it. And Earl Moore had it in spades. He'd heard it on the tape. The man was screaming toward the ground at nearly Mach 1, well in excess of the aircraft's placarded Vne — velocity, never exceed. But Moore was still aviating. Still thinking clearly.

Davis tapped the side of his cold mug with a fingernail. Twice. *Click-click.*

Of all he had heard today, of all the drama on the voice tape, that was what stuck in his mind. Right before the voice recorder had gone briefly off line — not one click, but two. Clear and close together, like a three-position switch being pushed fast through two detents.

Click-click.

He remembered back to his first look at the radar data in Sparky's office. It had gone blank at roughly the same point in the descent as the voice recorder, maybe 10,000 feet. At the time, Davis had wondered if the airplane might have suffered a structural failure, broken up under the extreme speed. But now that he'd seen the crash site, he knew all the big pieces were accounted for. That theory didn't fit. And Davis was only happy when things fit.

He was lost in thought, staring at the floor, when a stylish pair of shoes and an even more stylish pair of legs came into view. He looked up and saw Sorensen. She was wearing a dress, mid-length but with a slit up one side that showed some thigh. They had agreed to meet at six. She was two beers late.

"Hi, Jammer. Sorry to keep you waiting."

"No problem, Honeywell. Been busy?"

"Not as busy as you — I saw the news clip of you leaving that meeting. You really caused a ruckus."

"Thanks. It's my signature move."

"I especially liked the end, when you told the reporter to go to hell."

"They played that part?" He feigned surprise. "Oh, well. It could have been worse. I was going to call Bastien a manipulative shitmouse — just couldn't think of the right French translation."

Sorensen stared him down and was about to say something when a waitress scooted up and looked at her expectantly.

Davis advised, "Go with the imported beer, Budweiser. It's only eight bucks a bottle."

She ordered a martini, then reached for the snack mix and took a handful. "So is there really a new angle in the investigation?"

"Maybe. We listened to the voice tapes. I heard some things I didn't like. I think we should be looking deep into the flight control software."

"You think there's a glitch in it?"

"It has happened before. The designers can't imagine every corner of the flight envelope. I've seen accidents where computers and pilots have gotten into a fight for control. It's not pretty. So I gave the board a recommendation."

"What was that?"

"I said we should ground all C-500s."

"You can't be serious — will they?"

"No, not a chance. But it'll give them something to think about. Something besides Bastien's spectacular suicide theory."

She said, "I understand that Bastien has called another press conference for tomorrow."

"I heard. He asked me to come. Probably so we could hold hands and show unity."

"And?"

Davis popped a pretzel into his mouth. "I told him he didn't need another press conference. I told him he needed a piece of rebar shoved up his undulating spine."

He saw Sorensen stifle a grin, but then her expression turned serious. "You're kidding, right?"

Davis shrugged, left it open.

"Jammer, do you think this is smart? Antagonizing him?"

"I don't like how things are going, and I'm not one for half measures." He sipped his beer and reflected, "You know, it's probably just as well I didn't stay in the Air Force. Can you imagine me as chairman of the Joint Chiefs of Staff? I'd just advise the president to go nuclear for everything. And none of that gradual response crap. Massive retaliation, that'd be my style."

Sorensen's martini arrived. It came in a curved-stem glass that looked very unstable. She took a long draw. "So why do you think Bastien wants to hang this whole thing on Earl Moore?"

"Hard to say. Maybe because it's easy. Earl Moore isn't around to defend himself. Or maybe because it's more dramatic than a line of bad computer code or a faulty mix of composite resin."

"Did you ever consider that he might be right?"

Davis paused. "It's not out of the question. But I really doubt it."

"Why?"

"I visited his wife back in Houston. After I saw her, I made a side trip to Moore's apartment. In truth, I found a few things I hadn't wanted to find. An empty Jack Daniel's bottle in the recycle bin. A few beers in the fridge. But that was it. And thank God, no 'goodbye cruel world' note sitting like a headstone on the dining room table."

"So he *had* been drinking," she said.

"Apparently. Just like at the hotel the night before the flight. But I found some other things in his apartment. There was a schedule for his son's soccer team with the scores filled out to mid-season. An e-mail confirmation for a pair of shoes he'd ordered online the day before he left. He just wrote a check to fund his IRA account. And Moore TiVo'd two ballgames on TV."

Davis drained the last of his beer and looked squarely at Sorensen. "I can't say what was on his mind the day of the crash. But when Earl Moore left home, he had every intention of coming back."

Two hours after spotting Fatima, Whittemore was sipping ginger ale in a dark corner of a cheap bar. He would have preferred something more substantial — disciple of the grain that he was — yet the idea that Caliph might be nearby demanded absolute sobriety.

Fatima had taken a cab from the ferry terminal and checked into a cheap hotel, a place that might get two stars if the rating inspector came on just the right day. She had taken a key from the front desk, given her bag to a bellman, and gone straight to the bar. That was over an hour ago. Since then, she'd done nothing but drink — rum and soda, if he wasn't mistaken. The more plowed she got, the more Whittemore was sure that Caliph's arrival was not imminent. Who would meet their boss in the shape she was getting into? Especially when your boss was the world's most ruthless terrorist.

It was a dreary establishment. The old wood floors had been worn smooth by generations of hard boots and dragged chairs, and patterns of dirt and dust denoted the spots where there had been no recent meeting between spilled beer and a mop. A brass rail, dull and dented, ran along the foot of a hardwood bar. The elbow-high bar itself had probably been stout fifty years ago, but now was riddled with tiny holes — termites or worms. Above it all, the wall trim sported a coat of fresh red paint that accented the rest like lipstick on an aging drag queen.

It was just after nine in the evening and the place was half full, a typical mix of transients and regulars, Whittemore figured. Groups of men and women interacted casually, and a few couples nuzzled in dark corner booths. A handful of men were perched at the bar on high wooden stools. They were spaced evenly between empty seats, hunched and immovable, the type who hold drinking among life's more solemn pursuits.

Fatima was largely ignored.

Whittemore decided that the pictures he'd seen had not done her justice. She was even uglier in real life. The dim light, mostly red and green hues cast from neon beer signs, gave her dark, pitted complexion an unearthly aura. She still had on the same clothes she'd worn on the ferry, and if Whittemore had read the immigration guy correctly, she probably smelled like puke. Even from thirty feet away in a dark room, her hair looked like she'd just rinsed it in the crankcase of an old truck. She was overweight, maybe a hundred extra pounds on a five-five frame. Not obese by American standards, but her clothes were inappropriately tight and highlighted the fact that all her acreage was down the wrong roads. Big thighs, big belly, no chest — Fatima was the penultimate loser in life's genetic game of roulette. Whittemore's regard for Caliph slipped a few notches. *If I was the world's most wanted terrorist, I'd at least have a hot messenger.*

His attention ratcheted up when Fatima stood. Looking marginally steady, she stretched like an overweight cat, scratched her crotch, and moved to the bar.

"I wan' another drink!" she demanded in English. Her voice was throaty, the words slurred like she had a mouthful of glue.

The bartender was a short, heavyset guy wearing an apron. He frowned. The room was relatively quiet, so Whittemore heard his response. "One more," he said, "then you must go."

Fatima smiled and looked the guy over like he was hanging on a hook in a butcher's shop. "You married?" she asked.

He held up his hand to show a ring.

"Ah, hell, that don't matter! You kinda cute."

He slid her cutoff drink across the bar, along with the tab.

"What time you finish work?"

The man ignored her and went to the far end of the bar to engage one of his regulars — a guy who was snickering.

Whittemore gauged the scene. He knew a lot about drinking. Knew people handled it differently. Some giggled. Some got nasty. Some fell asleep. From the look of it, Fatima Adara got horny. One of God's little jokes, he decided. He hoped none of the men at the bar was that desperate. The last thing he needed was for some free-range drunk to stumble in and confuse things. Ever so briefly, Whittemore considered sending Fatima a drink himself, maybe engaging in some alcoholic nuptials. A little amorous pillow talk might give him Caliph. Then again, it might give him erectile dysfunction. Whittemore wanted a promotion, but he had his limits.

Fatima downed her last drink, snapping her head back to get every last drop. Then she fished into her pocket, dropped a wad of euros on the bar, and headed out.

Whittemore had settled in advance. He was increasingly disappointed. Short of spotting Caliph, he hadn't known exactly what he was looking for, what to expect. But so far, Fatima had gone to a hotel, gotten drunk, and now she was probably headed to her room to pass out. Once that happened, there wouldn't be anything to do until morning. If that was how it went, Whittemore didn't have much choice. He would have to call in the contact. Take his commendation plaque.

He followed Fatima into the hotel lobby. Whittemore looked discreetly toward the elevator, expecting to see her there. Nothing. His head whipped around and he spotted her, just a flash, as she cleared the main entrance and headed down the street.

CHAPTER TWENTY-TWO

The bar menu had a decidedly European tilt. Davis and Sorensen both skipped the special of the day, seaweed and oyster tartare, and neither gave a thought to ordering snails. He went with the salmon bagel, while she settled on onion soup.

"So that file you have on me," Davis asked, "what's in it?"

Sorensen dipped a crusty piece of bread into her soup. "It said you put your fist through a wall at an officer's club."

"That was in there?" He shrugged it off.

Sorensen gave him a look that asked for more. Perhaps a reasonable explanation.

"I was at a dining in," he said.

"A dining in?"

"It's a formal military banquet where the whole fighter wing gets dressed up in our best uniforms. We do guy stuff—eat meat, drink bourbon, smoke cigars. On the night in question, some of my squadron buddies and I were having a stud-finding contest. I lost."

Sorensen took the bait. "Okay—and what does the winner get in this event?"

"A broken hand."

She paused, but then moved on without comment. "The file said you spent three years in the Marines, then got an appointment to the Air Force Academy. Why did you switch services?"

"The Marine Corps is a great organization, but I wanted to fly jets. The Air Force seemed the most likely place. Plus I was a little tired of living in dusty tents and eating MREs."

"And you shot down a MiG in the first Gulf War?"

"Yeah, I was flying F-15s at the time. My wingman and I tracked down a MiG-23 that was headed for Iran. Saddam thought his jets would be safer there."

"I guess you proved him wrong."

"I guess."

"So it was a dogfight? Just like in the old movies?"

"You mean like with the wind snapping at my scarf, maybe shaking my fist at the other guy? No. The real thing is very clinical, very quick. And usually very one-sided. The Iraqi pilot had been ordered up on what was basically a suicide mission — his commander told him to fly a jet to Iran before we blew it out of its bunker. He got airborne and was running away at six hundred knots. I chased him down doing six-eighty, put a heater up the poor bastard's tailpipe. Bottom line, we both had jobs to do and gave it our best — but my airplane, missiles, and information were a lot better. So I killed a guy in a fight that wasn't fair."

"In combat I suppose that's how you want all your fights," she said.

He shrugged.

She said, "I remember reading a report a few years back — it said a lot of those Iraqi pilots who actually made it across the border were never heard from again."

"Which means what? That I gave his family a little . . . closure or something?"

Sorensen said nothing.

Davis spread mustard on his bagel. He had an urge to change the subject. "So tell me what you found out about our Egyptian friend."

"Dr. Jaber? Nothing troublesome. At least not yet. He's a career engineer, sort of a vagabond. He's worked for a number of the big aerospace companies. There's no evidence of any fringe politics, no family members in the Islamic Brotherhood. Jaber has a wife and two kids back in Cairo."

After a pause, Davis said, "And that's it?"

"Langley says they're still working on it."

Davis was putting the finishing touches on a clever reply when the phone in his pocket buzzed. "Excuse me." He wedged it open with a thumb and saw a message from Jen: AUNT L CAN CHAPERONE AT DANCE. PLEASE! PLEASE! KISSES, J.

Davis weighed a reply, maybe something like: GO DO YOUR HOMEWORK. Sure. That would score points. Davis put the phone away and frowned. He rubbed a hand over his face, top to bottom, and let out a long, controlled sigh.

"Your daughter?"

He nodded.

"Can I help?"

"You don't even know her."

"I'm a girl."

Davis gave her a hard look that said, *No shit*. He turned his beer mug by the handle. "Jen is fifteen years old. It'll get easier, right?"

"My mom used to say that kids are the reverse of anchors — the more they weigh, the less they hold you down."

He didn't reply.

"Jammer . . . what happened to your wife?"

The question caught him off guard. He replied in a smartass tone, "Wasn't that in the file?"

This time Sorensen went silent.

"Sorry," he said, "you didn't deserve that."

Davis had told the story more times than he could count. But not lately. Family and friends all knew what had happened, which meant he only had to deal with fresh acquaintances now. People like Sorensen, Jen's teachers every year, the occasional new neighbor moving in. Someday, he figured, time would do its thing. People would stop asking altogether. Davis wasn't sure if he'd like that or not.

"Diane was killed in a car crash. It was almost two years ago now. She was on her way home from a night class, some kind of healthy-living nutrition class. A big delivery truck — not a semi, but the next size down — blasted right through a stop sign and hit her Honda square in the driver's-side door."

"God, how awful. For you *and* your daughter. I can't imagine dealing with something like that."

"I'll tell you what really made it hard. It was just an accident. The truck driver was an old Guatemalan guy, barely spoke English. But he was here legally. He'd been working a thirteen-hour shift. That's legal too."

After a pause, Sorensen said, "So there was nobody to blame."

"Exactly. If he'd been drunk, I could have kicked his ass. Maybe I'd have stopped drinking myself and joined MADD, or DADD, or whatever the hell. Or if she'd died from colon cancer I could run a race, wear the right color ribbon, eat cruciferous vegetables the rest of my life. But the way it is —"

"No reason," she said, finishing the thought. "Just random chance."

"But doing what I do, Honeywell, investigating accidents — if it's taught me anything, it's that there's never just one single cause for any disaster. There's always a chain, a series of things that go wrong."

"Even with what happened to your wife? One guy running a stop sign?"

"That night I had thought about calling her on her cell. If I'd gotten through when she was walking out of class it would have slowed her down. Maybe she wouldn't have been at the intersection at that one precise moment. Maybe the truck would have just clipped her. And when she bought that car I tried to talk her into something bigger, something with a little more iron. But Diane insisted on doing the right thing for the goddamn environment. And —" Davis stopped abruptly.

She eyed him with concern. "Jammer — you can't blame yourself."

He stretched, trying to force the tension from his shoulders. "That's what I do for a living, isn't it? Find blame. Sometimes I don't like the answers, don't like what I find. But it's there all the same."

She thought about this, then said, "My job can be a challenge sometimes too. You know — the evasion, the lies."

"Like you did to me?"

"Yes," she said squarely. "Like I did to you."

Davis nodded, took it as an apology. He worked some more on his bagel, then asked, "What about you, Honeywell? Husband, kids, tragedy, scars?"

She looked skyward in mock contemplation. "Almost but no, no, yes, and—" she lifted the sleeve of her dress to reveal a three-inch scar on one shoulder.

"Rotator cuff?" he asked.

"And then some."

"What was the tragedy?"

"Not a big deal, but you'll have to get me much drunker to hear about it."

He nodded. "It's a date."

Davis grabbed the bill and stood. "But in the meantime, confessional's over. I spent some time in the hangar this afternoon—a good part of the wreckage has made its way there. Let's head over, there's something I want to show you."

Seared scallops and mushrooms in a basil reduction. Or braised veal cheek served with semolina gnocchi. For Dr. Hans Sprecht, it had been an exquisite dilemma.

The place was called Il Lago, a transcendent sliver of Italy that had found its way to central Geneva. The décor was sublime, the walls a sweeping array of hand-painted murals in a room divided by gilt French doors. Accenting brocades and crystal chandeliers gave the place a positively palatial feel.

Sprecht chased the last scallop around his plate, allowing it to baste fully in the superb sauce. He had surely made the right choice. The waiter appeared, prompt and efficient—as all good waiters were—and took away Sprecht's empty plate. The man was immediately replaced by a wine steward who had already been most attentive. Sprecht hesitated, but then signaled the fellow one last time, curling three fingers. His glass came full.

The dinner flow was at its peak, and he watched the diners as they changed shift, early birds leaving and late comers finding seats. Waiters and busboys circulated at speed, maintaining the establishment's epicurean lifeblood. On top of the wine, it all made Sprecht's head spin.

An elegantly dressed man roughly Sprecht's age was walking

smoothly up the main aisle, an attractive woman on his arm. She was not young, not old. Her dress was expensive, and there was jewelry around her wrist and neck — only a few pieces, but there again, quality. When the man whispered into her ear she laughed on cue. Hans Sprecht sighed.

Earlier, a striking woman had passed his own table and glanced, a fleeting attachment of the eyes. As a young man, Sprecht would have taken it as a sign of interest. Now, the first thought that had come to his head was that he might have a blob of butter on his chin. It was curious, he mused, how age crept up on you. You didn't just wake up one morning old and spent. It was gradual thing — tapping on your shoulder, closing in from behind. It came with greater frequency each day, a coarse accretion of aching hips and holding menus at arm's length and turning your head to favor the good ear. Any part, on exclusive merits, no more than a nuisance. But collectively it gave one a certain sense of . . . urgency.

Sprecht tipped the wine to his lips. A life companion was the one thing he had never found — not really — and he wanted very much to rectify this, to live his remaining years well and in the company of a woman who exhibited quality and refinement. But Sprecht knew what the good life required.

He had spent the greater part of the day working in his rented office, organizing and making preparations. Much of what he would need was already there, but at least two of the procedures were beyond the normal scope of his landlord's practice. For these, accepted professional standards would normally dictate the use of a fully sterile operating room. Sprecht, of course, had no time for such nonsense. And in any event, as viewed by the prism of his dubious circumstances, the specter of postoperative infection was far down on his list of worries. He already had more serious complications.

The upcoming job made him nervous, never a good thing for a surgeon. The other jobs had been relatively simple. Risks well taken. At first Sprecht had been encouraged — happy being too strong a word — to have acquired this new patient. But in the weeks since accepting the contract, he'd had second thoughts. He had been watching the news, reading the papers. Caliph was attacking the West. Caliph was attacking the world. Everyone wanted his head. And Hans Sprecht — perhaps only Hans Sprecht — knew exactly where to find it.

He finished his wine and settled his bill, the latter causing him to think more positively — his Cayman account was flush, and would be more so in a few day's time. At the entrance, Sprecht donned his overcoat and dipped a hand briefly into the right front pocket. His insurance policy was still there, cool and smooth and round. He wasn't sure why he'd even brought the thing. It had been reckless, in a sense. But the comfort was undeniable, because in some way — Sprecht wasn't sure how — he knew it would be his salvation.

Sprecht headed out into the crisp night air. He breathed deeply to clear his head. The crowds on the sidewalks were light, as was the traffic in the streets. Geneva didn't hold the bustle of some big cities. Even during rush hour, things flowed smoothly here, as precise and predictable as the clocks on every corner. The buildings were square and efficient, the streets freshly paved, and the sidewalks clean. It was all so very — Swiss. A Berliner by birth, this was where Sprecht felt most at home, where he belonged. His visions of setting up a practice in some sunny, faraway paradise were exactly that — daydreams, idle thoughts never to be realized.

He turned into an alley. It was a shortcut to the room he had let for two months, a modest but well-appointed base of operations that Sprecht would abandon as soon as this last job was complete. And this *would* be his last job. He left the crowds behind on the quai des Bergues and quickened his pace. Fifty steps into the alley, however, Sprecht had a strange sensation. He stopped, fell completely still, then heard it distinctly. Footsteps behind him.

Fighting an urge to turn and look, he began moving quickly. His apartment was still two blocks away, so he made a right turn into another alley that he hoped would lead to a busier street. As he turned the corner, Sprecht cast a glance back and spotted his follower twenty paces behind — a man moving with equal speed, his outline large but ill-defined in a heavy, shapeless overcoat. Sprecht dashed ahead momentarily, but then skidded to a stop as he realized his error. The alley was a dead end.

Sprecht panicked.

He saw two doors at the top of the pathway, but one was blocked by trash and the other secured by a metal bar and padlock. He spun to face the mouth of the alley — just in time to see the large man stop and stare directly at him. Sprecht tensed and his hands began to shake. The face he saw was covered in a dark beard, and two eyes, coal black in the dim light, locked on him intensely. Sprecht could try to fight, but what good would it do? He knew nothing about such things, and the other man was far bigger, far younger.

The stranger stepped closer. Sprecht was at least proud that he stood his ground, no shrinking to a corner to delay the inevitable. Two paces away, the man stopped and put a hand in his pocket.

Sprecht went rigid, immobile. Then he heard, "Can you tell me where this club is?"

The words had come in German. More oddly, they'd come in a high-pitched, almost feminine voice. The man held out a business card, turned it at an angle to catch a stray shaft of light. Sprecht saw the name *Club Bleu* on the card. He had heard of the place, and knew it was a club for homosexuals. Sprecht had no earthly idea where to find it.

"Back to the river," he said quickly. "Turn left and go two blocks to quai du Mont Blanc. You'll find it just off to the right."

The man smiled, withdrew the card. He turned and began to amble back toward the river. But then he paused. "Hey, you want to come?"

Sprecht stood taller, lifted his chin. He wanted to say something derogatory. What came out was, "No, thank you. Not tonight."

The man shrugged and walked off.

Sprecht entered his flat ten minutes later.

He locked the door and leaned into it with a shoulder, his chest heaving as if he'd just run a marathon. Underneath his clothing he was drenched in sweat, notwithstanding the cold, dry night air. Then and there, Hans Sprecht decided he could not go on. He was a man of order and precision, yet the path he had chosen seemed more perilous at every turn, fraught with disarray and uncertainty.

But what could he do?

Sprecht put a hand into his pocket and withdrew the vial of blood. Rolling it gently between two fingers, he studied the dark purple color. Hans Sprecht went to a writing desk and put down the glass tube. He sat, pulled out a pen and paper, and began to compose a letter.

CHAPTER TWENTY-THREE

Sorensen offered to drive, but the hangar was only a mile from the hotel and the weather had moderated. No rain or sleet, just a cool breeze.

They both dressed appropriately, Davis wearing his throwback bomber jacket, Sorensen more contemporary in a ski parka, stylish blue and thick. It left Davis to conclude that, unlike the military, the CIA didn't issue uniforms — no standard issue trench coat or wide-brimmed hat.

When they got to the hangar there were only six people left in the place. Four were on their way out. Davis nodded as they passed, feeling like a salmon swimming upstream — an image that slotted nicely with his whole investigation. Even though they were miles removed from the crash site, the bitter stench of fire was etched into the air, unavoidably imported with the accumulating wreckage. At nine o'clock in the evening, the workday was long done, yet the place was still bathed in light so intense it would have blotted out the sun. It reminded Davis of a stadium where every light was kept on for hours after the big game. Self-important and wasteful.

He led Sorensen to the desired section of wreckage. Their footsteps echoed on a concrete floor that was cold and naked, no one having thought to add paint or lacquer to dampen the effect. The only other sound came from a pair of Asian men at the far end of the building who were chatting quietly near a main landing gear truck. Chances were, it was their product — and accordingly, their duty to convince everyone that a burst tire or hot brake assembly hadn't been the culprit to bring down World Express 801.

Davis drew to a stop at a piece of metal the size of a refrigerator.

It was upright, enough of the supporting structure still in place to hold everything in a more or less natural alignment.

"This is the rear flight deck bulkhead," he explained, "or at least part of it. This particular section was behind the captain's seat. There's a matching bulkhead on the starboard side, behind the first officer — that one's not as intact."

"So it's basically a wall," she suggested. "To separate the cockpit from the rest of the airplane."

"Right."

Sorensen looked more closely and asked, "What are those?"

"That's what I wanted to show you."

All along the surface of the bulkhead was an array of what looked like small buttons. They were black circles, each a quarter inch in diameter, and protruding from the bulkhead roughly the same amount.

"This is one of the main circuit breaker panels," he said.

"And those are all circuit breakers? There must be hundreds of them."

"I've never counted, but yeah, there's a lot. The panel behind the first officer is about the same, and a there's a bunch more down in what we call the E and E bay."

"E and E?"

"Electronics and Equipment. It's a compartment in the belly where all the avionics are stashed. There are thousands of electronic gadgets, relays, and buses on an airplane like this, and each one has a breaker. The idea is, if there's an electrical problem like an overvoltage or a spike in the current, the breaker pops and removes power from that particular instrument. That way a box doesn't just sit there and fry until it catches on fire. It's a protective measure."

"Like a fuse in a house."

"Exactly."

"So which one controls the data recorder? That's the one everybody is interested in — especially Bastien."

Davis pointed to a breaker that stood out like a lone whitecap on a calm ocean. The black cap jutted out, and at its base was a half-inch cylinder of white. "This one has popped," he said.

"Boy, it'd be hard to miss. Between the black wall and the cap —
the contrast is eye-catching."

"That's the whole idea."

Sorensen looked closer. Each breaker was labeled, and she read out
loud from the one that was popped. "FDR. Flight data recorder?"

He nodded.

"So that's the one."

"Yep."

"And it's right behind the captain's seat."

"Yep."

"So Bastien was right?"

Davis caught her eye, shook his head. "One big problem."

"What's that?"

He swept two fingers across the panel. "Do you see any other
breakers out?"

She scanned the black rows. "Yeah, I see six or seven. But they're
different. They have some kind of colored plastic things holding them
out."

"Those are collars," he said. "Sometimes maintenance deactivates
certain circuits, disables equipment. A red collar might signify permanent disabling, blue temporary — that kind of thing."

"Okay, but what's that got to do with the data recorder?"

Davis pulled a pen flashlight from his pocket. The vertical panel
was resting at a slight angle, so even in the harsh fluorescent glare the
circuit breakers were dimmed by shadow. He shone the light on one
of the collared breakers. It was labeled VHF3.

"This is for an extra radio that's not installed," he explained. "New
airplanes are just like new cars — buyers don't necessarily want every
option. Now, take a close look. Tell me exactly what you see."

Sorensen leaned in. She clearly hadn't hit the middle-aged road-
block of degraded near vision. She said, "The breaker is out, and it has
a red collar."

"Describe the collar."

"It covers the white part, but not all the way around. There's a gap,
maybe forty five degrees. That's how you get it on and off, right?"

"Yes. And in that gap you see part of the white breaker cylinder."

"Okay."

"Now —" Davis reached down and pulled the collar from the breaker labeled VHF3.

Sorensen saw it right away. "The part that was under the collar is a lot whiter, cleaner."

"The smaller portion in the gap was exposed to soot and smoke in the crash. Together with the heat, it makes for a permanent change. Any breaker that had been out when the airplane hit the ground would show the same degree of discoloration."

Sorensen stood back, looked at the sparkling white FDR circuit breaker. "You're saying this breaker wasn't out when the airplane hit? You mean —" her voice caught on the realization, snagged like a dragging anchor hitting a rock.

"Yep. Someone has been tampering with our evidence."

Whittemore had no trouble keeping Fatima in sight. Her pace was quick for someone her size, but he decided the cold might have something to do with it.

The wind was sharp, so it was easy for Whittemore to keep his collar high and his face turned down under his hat — it would have looked unnatural to do otherwise. He had followed a lot of people in the last ten years. Some were clumsy. Some were rather clever. None had ever shaken him. Whittemore was built for following. He wasn't tall nor short, fat nor thin. He wasn't much of anything. His hair was medium length and dark brown, his skin tone nondescript. A Scandinavian who'd seen some sun. Or a man of Mediterranean extraction who had not. Whittemore was built for blending in.

Fatima Adara was not.

Presently, she was moving like she had somewhere to go. The drinks had clearly had their effect, but sudden exposure to the elements had a way of sobering people up. From the hotel, she'd headed straight for the old harbor. The ancient cradle of Marseille's seafaring heritage, the harbor had succumbed to the contemporary, woefully reinvented as a mooring station for a thousand pleasure boats of all sizes and varieties. A few token older ships were lashed to the docks, barquentine relics that had been restored to well-lacquered semblances of their original glory for the sake of the tourists. On any summer evening, the sidewalks would have been shoulder-to-shoulder with pleasure seekers and bored teens and counterfeit mariners. But tonight, both the season and weather were against it.

Which gave Whittemore little crowd to work with.

Fatima ignored the waterfront as she pressed onward along the quai du Port, passing rows of souvenir shops that were shut down tight. She eventually paused at a corner, near an espresso shop. An outdoor seating area was completely deserted, empty chairs and tables looking cold and lifeless. Inside, however, there was still a warm glow, and a narrow ray of light sprayed out over the sidewalk like sunshine through a broken cloud. Even at this late hour, caffeine was being served.

Fatima stood immovable. She looked obviously over her shoulder. Lousy tradecraft? Whittemore wondered. Or was she lost? He slowed his closure and coasted into a shadow.

Fatima pulled out a pack of cigarettes. She turned to put her face leeward to the wind and fired one up. It might be a signal, a message to Caliph. More likely, it was just another bad habit. Whittemore knew smoking was endemic in the Middle East — Phillip Morris and Lorillard had probably killed more bad guys than the United States Army and Marine Corps combined.

Fatima began to move again. She fell in behind two nuns whose robes flowed and fluttered in the wind, giving the appearance that she was following two black ghosts. The whole curious entourage went out of sight, onto the side street. Whittemore hurried to the corner. As he closed in, he had yet another nagging thought about calling in his spot on Fatima. If he lost her now — and anyone ever found out — he'd be in deep trouble.

He reached the espresso shop and slowed to a crawl, looked in the window as if considering a stop. Down the side street, he spotted the nuns as they turned into the first building on the right. Fatima was nowhere in sight.

"Dammit!" he cursed under his breath.

He trotted ahead, discarding any illusion of stealth. Whittemore *couldn't* lose her now. He was sure Fatima hadn't gone into the espresso bar—the entrance had been in clear view. It only took a few steps to discern that the big building the nuns had disappeared into was a church, a big stone statement that looked like it had been there a thousand years. It was set back from the road, its placement slightly out of line with the rest of the buildings along the street.

Whittemore passed an alley that was also askew, a fitting separation of church and capitalism. He paused for a good look. On one side of the passageway were piles of empty boxes. They all looked the same from where Whittemore stood, but he reckoned you could probably tell which shops were in front by the smells—stale tobacco, old coffee grounds, rotten vegetables. On the other side of the alley he saw overflowing trash cans, spent building materials, and a shattered old lectern with the sign of the cross. Even God had his refuse.

Amid it all, Whittemore saw no movement. No sign of Fatima. A pair of undersized bulbs cast twin shafts of light into the alley, spilling as if from doors in a dark hallway. There were any number of alcoves and obstructions. Fatima could be there—somewhere. Or she could be in the church. Whittemore flipped a mental coin.

He headed for the church.

He walked quickly and climbed an ancient set of stone steps. At the crest was a massive door, the wood scarred and bent. The door swung open freely, belying its size and aged appearance. Soft light bathed the space inside, and when Whittemore closed the door behind him the biting wind was cut off. He instantly felt warmer. Stretching out before him was a church like any other, a long central aisle that delivered the faithful to rows of wooden pews. An ornate runner covered the cold stone aisle all the way to the front, and at the head a series of steps gave rise to the place of holy issuances. Above it all was Jesus on the cross, his enduring figure mounted over stained glass that sat muted for lack of light.

Whittemore spotted the two nuns for an instant as they disappeared into a vestibule at one side of the stage. A line of candles were arrayed at the steps in front, and two people kneeled in prayer — women probably, though it was hard to tell in their layered coverings. Neither could have been Fatima Adara. Whittemore eyed the path the nuns had taken and cursed under his breath.

He went back outside.

CHAPTER TWENTY-FOUR

Whittemore heard it first, even before he had reached the mouth of the alley. Sound traveled well in cold air, and the hard, scraping noise was clear, undeniable. It reminded him of two smooth stones being rubbed together. Whittemore edged closer to the alley, peered around the corner and spotted Fatima. She was a hundred feet back, bent at the waist and leaning into the church wall. His view was blocked by the old lectern, but Fatima was definitely busy, her hands working on — something.

While she was distracted, Whittemore crossed the opening and set up watch from a better angle near the espresso shop. A tree of street signs — warnings to not trespass, drive through, or dump trash — gave good cover. Fatima seemed to finish whatever she was doing, and she pulled a wobbly chair from a pile of rubble and sat down.

What the hell?

Then Whittemore heard a new sound. Retching. Coughing. He couldn't see her face, but she was doubled over on the chair. Fatima Adara was puking her guts out. *Jesus,* he thought, *this woman is a piece of work.*

It went on for ten minutes. She would blow and hack, sit slumped on the chair for a time, then do it all over again. Whittemore considered his options. Fatima had definitely been busy, digging into the wall. He figured it for a dead drop, a makeshift post office box for messages either to or from Caliph. With this realization, Whittemore's spirits soared. He had just hit sevens. As soon as Fatima got her legs back, she'd come up the alley, walk to the hotel, and pass out.

Which made everything simple. When Fatima emerged, he would

duck into the espresso bar, wait for her to pass, then head down the alley fast and find the dead drop. If there was a message, he'd read it, maybe take a picture with his phone. Or even call it in if he thought Caliph's arrival was imminent — Whittemore was ambitious, but he wasn't a fool. If the drop was empty, he'd catch back up with the lumbering Fatima. Then he'd have more decisions to make. But so far, Whittemore was sure he'd made all the right calls.

He took a look around the corner. Fatima was still saddled miserably in the chair. Whittemore eased out of sight and his attention drifted to the church. A woman, tall and slim, was making her way up the sidewalk. She wore a long jacket, but the sway in her hips told Whittemore she was wearing heels, while the jaunty angle of her head and flow of dark hair in the breeze told him she was young. A streetlight cast over her face at the alley entrance. She was a goddess — fiery eyes, high cheekbones, pouty lips. He looked at her openly, and as she passed her eyes flicked to his for just a moment. She entered the espresso shop. Whittemore turned back to the alley with a smile.

A smile that evaporated instantly when he saw the empty chair. Fatima was nowhere in sight.

Dammit! Not again!

Whittemore took in everything. He saw no movement, heard no sound to indicate where she'd gone. He eased to his left, hoping to find her leaning against the wall behind an obstruction. Nothing. Squinting, he tried to make out the other end of the alley. Did it open to a different street? Or was it a dead end? He couldn't tell.

He moved into the alley, slow and alert. He eyed every shadow, every dead spot. Whittemore stepped as lightly as he could, but gravel crunched under his feet, each step sounding like a snap burst from a rock crusher. He reached the chair she'd been sitting on. It was crooked, the high back broken. Whittemore looked to the far end of the alley. There had to be a second way out, he decided, another access. His nerves began to settle, and Plan A fell right back into place.

You're still in control. You know where she's going. Check the dead drop, old boy, then follow her if you need to.

Whittemore knew exactly where to look — waist high, in front of the chair. It turned out to be an old window frame embedded in the church's stone wall, the opening having been mortared and plastered over by some ancient clerical administration. He ran his hand along the base, felt for a loose section. As he did, something registered in the back of Whittemore's mind, a vague discomfort he couldn't quite specify. The impulse was discarded when he found what he was looking for — a dull red brick the size of a man's shoe. Whittemore pulled, the brick moved. It was tight, but began to slide out with the same scraping noise he'd heard earlier. Stone on stone. Working it free, he saw a recess behind, a fist-sized hole. He dropped the brick, twisted his hand inside and hit a home run.

Whittemore pulled out a folded note.

His training kicked in — this was evidence. He handled it by the edges, patiently unfolding. Once. Twice. Again something seemed wrong, and finally Whittemore realized what it was. He was standing right where Fatima had been puking, yet he saw and smelled no sign of it. Whittemore turned the note right side up and read. Felt his blood go cold.

DO NOT MOVE
HANDS AT YOUR SIDES

Whittemore heard quiet footsteps behind him. Then he heard an even more disconcerting sound. *Chink-chink.* Absolutely unmistakable. He'd heard it a thousand times before on the firing range. The sound of a slide being racked on a handgun. But it made no sense. *Who carries a gun without a round in the chamber? An idiot. Or . . . someone who was trying to instill fear.*

The voice came as a whisper, colder than the midwinter wind rushing down the alley. "Turn slowly."

Whittemore did, and he saw the one thing he had hoped to never see. A gun sight from the wrong end — front post ahead of the U-notch. Perfectly in line, perfectly steady. Then he saw the sharp eyes behind.

"You seek Caliph?" the voice hissed.

Frozen with fear, Whittemore could not respond. The gun lowered to his chest and his eyes went wide.

A lifeless smile, then, "You have found him."

The first explosion sent him reeling. It seemed to tear his chest apart and he fell against the wall in blinding pain. Two more blasts and a fog descended. He slumped to one side, his face compressed on the gravel-strewn dirt. He saw heavy shoes receding, trotting briskly away.

Whittemore tried not to panic. Tried to ignore the searing pain. His left side was useless, immobile, so he went to work with his right, putting every effort into his only chance. He clawed into a pocket and found his phone. It fell to the gravel, and Whittemore groped and pawed and scooped it closer.

God the pain!

His fingers fumbled on the keys as he tried to focus. It seemed he could barely breathe — liquid in his chest, in his mouth. He was drowning.

A stern, beautiful female voice burst from the phone. "Authenticate."

Whittemore croaked, "Help. Ca —" the word was lost in a gurgle. He tried one last time, "Caliph is —"

And then his world went black.

Davis and Sorenson were about to leave the hangar when his phone rang. He saw that it was Larry Green.

"It's my boss," he said.

"I didn't think you had one." She gave him a shrewd look, then, "But maybe you should take the call." Sorensen excused herself, claiming she needed a bottle of water.

He picked up the call. "Hi, Larry."

"Hello, Jammer. How are you?"

Davis thought, *Pretty damned lousy. The CIA is trying to recruit me as a spy.* He said, "I'm just great."

"How about the investigation — running smoothly?"

"Nothing a little napalm wouldn't fix." Davis thought he heard a slight chuckle beam across the Atlantic. He gave Green a rundown on Bastien, followed by his take on the voice recorder tapes. He didn't mention his suspicion that somebody was tampering with evidence.

A no-nonsense retired general like Larry Green might react badly to that, raise a fuss from the top. The resulting intergovernmental fallout could get in the way of Davis' preferred method of assault — start low, in the trenches, and fight your way up.

"Jammer, I've got that info you were asking for, about the skipper getting in trouble last week."

"Okay."

"It turns out there *was* a traffic stop, but it wasn't Moore. He was leaving a bar with one of his buddies, another pilot. The other guy was going to do the driving. They got stopped in the parking lot and an HPD officer made him walk a line."

"Did he pass?"

"That part's a little murky."

Davis suggested, "Maybe he didn't, and that's why Moore went to see his flight doc. Advice for a friend. Black is as much a lawyer as he is a doctor."

"Could be. But the point is that Earl Moore wasn't in any trouble here."

"All right — that's a good thing. But keep checking for me, will you, Larry? Find out exactly what happened."

"You've got it."

"Oh, and there's one other thing."

"Shoot."

"You said I got this assignment straight from the director, right?"

"Collins gave me your name personally, told me to accept no substitutes."

"Any idea why?"

"Sorry, Jammer. Not my bailiwick. You think something is screwy?"

Davis thought, *Everything is screwy*. He said, "Nah, don't worry about it."

They agreed to talk again soon, and Davis ended the call.

He was sure Green was being straight with him, that he knew nothing about an interagency loan to the CIA. Part of him seethed at the lies involved, the backroom dealing. Another part said, *To hell with them, just do what needs to be done.* His internal strife didn't last long. It rarely did.

Davis pocketed his phone and went to find Sorensen.

He found her sitting at a table in the break room. She'd gotten two bottles of water and held one out.

"Thanks," he said, picking it up.

"That was quick," she commented.

"Neither of us are the chatty type."

The water had a fancy name and claimed to be from a hidden spring in the South Pacific — water from halfway around the world. Davis twisted off a very unfancy plastic cap and took a long swig. It tasted like any other water.

"What did he want?" she asked.

"He wanted to know how the investigation is going."

"And?"

"I told him it made that whole Amelia Earhart thing look pretty straightforward."

"Right."

"But he did have some useful information. Larry checked with the Houston Police and found that Earl Moore and a buddy actually were out drinking last week. But it was his buddy who was doing the driving and had a little run-in with the law."

"What happened to him?"

"That part's not clear, but the important thing is that Moore wasn't in any trouble. The whole thing might have scared him. Maybe his buddy was in the same sad boat, a pilot who'd already been to rehab. I don't know. But the situation wasn't something that was going to put Moore's career on the line."

Sorensen finished her water and tossed the empty neatly into a trash can ten feet away. She said, "So who do you think is messing with our evidence?"

Davis shrugged. "Hard to say. There are a lot of reasons why somebody might pull that circuit breaker. I don't like any of them."

"Bastien?" she suggested.

"He and I won't be exchanging Christmas cards, and I don't think he's much of an investigator. But manipulating evidence like that— it'd be crazy."

"His accusations about Earl Moore are bound to have a lot of people talking, considering the suicide angle."

"Yep," Davis agreed. "That popped circuit breaker helps prove Bastien's case. But besides him, who benefits?"

Sorensen thought about it. "Practically everybody. The contractors, CargoAir, World Express, air traffic control. If Earl Moore pleads nolo contendre from the grave, they're all in the clear. Everybody wins."

"Exactly. Everybody but Luke."

"Who?"

"Luke Moore. Earl's son. He's probably the only person on earth in his dad's corner right now."

"Aside from you."

Davis tipped back his water bottle, drained it, and took aim at the same trash can. He missed badly, the hollow plastic bottle bouncing off a window before clattering to the linoleum.

Sorensen looked straight at him and smiled. She was starting to give as good as she got. Davis liked that.

He got up, retrieved his miss, and said, "Come on, Honeywell. Let's head back."

CHAPTER TWENTY-FIVE

It was nearly eleven o'clock when Davis and Sorensen left the hangar.

Winter was taking its grip on the night. The temperature had fallen precipitously and a frigid wind was misery itself. The streetlights overhead blazed bright and a cold drizzle danced in the halos, cyclonic swirls that seemed to spin without ever reaching the ground.

They kept a brisk pace to generate heat, kept their jackets fully zipped to hold it. Davis liked being out in the elements, and so he was glad they hadn't driven. The street they used as a guide ran through a quiet residential district, and Davis was struck by the flow of the place — or lack thereof. It was a spaghetti layout, a thousand-year stitch-work of trails, shops, and homes. Some of it had probably endured Napoleon and the Revolution. Much of it had seen two World Wars. But on this day in history's timeline it was just another neighborhood, patient and still, waiting to witness whatever chaos people thought of next.

Sorensen said, "So tell me, are you going to make a career out of the NTSB?"

He thought about it, but confessed, "I don't really plan that far ahead. I tried to quit a few days ago, but it didn't work out."

She smiled.

"But it's just a matter of time. I'll get fired long before I qualify for any kind of pension."

"Yeah. I bet you will."

"Thanks, Honeywell. I appreciate your confidence."

"And then what?" she asked.

"I'll move on to something else."

"Another temporary job?"

"Like I said, I try not to plan too far ahead. Today, I'm in the field making things a little better. I'm a happy guy. But in my experience, if you stick around any place too long, somebody will try to put you behind a desk. That's the day I move on."

"You'll never get promoted that way."

"That's my advantage. I don't want to get promoted. I've got plenty of friends who are still in the Air Force — lieutenant colonels, full birds, even some one-stars. Most of them are parked on their butts in the Pentagon, writing mission statements and sitting in conferences."

"It can't be all that bad."

"Are you kidding? It's a military officer's gulag. On your performance report they call it 'career broadening.' For me it'd be more like career waterboarding. Nope. I'm right where I want to be — out here in the cold getting things done. But Jen is my wild card. She comes before any of it. With Diane gone, I'm all she's got."

Sorensen nodded. "Your daughter is a lucky girl."

"I don't know. Our home life isn't exactly something Norman Rockwell would have painted."

"Not many are these days."

"Look at me right now. I should be home reading her the riot act about — something." Davis looked skyward. "Or maybe shooting a few hoops in the driveway."

"A good parent has to do both."

He pulled up the collar on his jacket. "Yeah."

They walked in silence for a time. An ancient building of indeterminate use butted up against the road. It looked abandoned, dark, and empty, and its chipped walls rose high, topped at the crest by carvings of leering gargoyles. Farther on, the lane doglegged right and came to be bordered by an amalgam of fences and gates and a stone wall that had to be four feet thick, great slabs of Alpine granite. In any big city in the States it would all have been plastered with graffiti and topped by razor wire. Here, unadorned by blight, the borders engaged an Old World feel, a reminder that virtually everything predated those walking past.

Davis finally said, "That file you have on me, Honeywell — it probably didn't explain how I met Diane, did it?"

"No."

"It was during my first assignment after pilot training. One day I was out flying with a new guy in the squadron, Rick Foster. I was a brand new flight lead, Ricky was a lieutenant. Just two kids out having the time of their lives in a couple of F-16s. We were doing a few practice bomb passes — just dry, not releasing anything. I said something on the radio and got no reply. When I looked over my shoulder I saw a smoking hole. No warning. One second he was there. The next he was gone. Just like that."

"What happened?"

"I hadn't gotten into the investigation business yet. The team that looked into it determined that Ricky had his head down, probably distracted by something in the cockpit. Maybe he dropped a pencil or was fiddling with a screwy gauge. He just flew into the ground. Chances are, he never knew until the last moment."

"That's awful."

"Yeah, it was. Unfortunately, it happens all too often." Davis stopped. A few steps on, so did Sorensen. "But the story doesn't quite end there. You see, Diane was Rick's wife."

Sorensen stared at him, clearly searching for something to say. "You married your buddy's widow?"

"Yes."

"That sounds incredibly . . . chivalrous or something."

"There were people who saw it that way. Others were sure the two of us already had something going on. But none of that was right. I guess I felt some degree of responsibility. Diane and I drank a lot of coffee, had some long talks. It took over a year, but we eventually fell pretty hard for each other. What she and I had was the real thing."

"Was this the reason you got interested in accident investigation?"

"I don't know. Maybe."

He started walking again. Sorensen fell in step. Both were quiet until Davis asked, "What about you, Honeywell? Career CIA?"

She hesitated. "I guess I don't have any other plans. Maybe a cabin in Colorado someday, deep in the woods. I've always had a vision of that."

Davis almost asked if she was alone in her vision. Instead he asked, "How long have you been posted here in France?"

"Almost a year. The assignment kind of surprised me at first, because my French isn't all that good."

"I think it sounds okay."

"I took it for three years in college — and four years at Mardi Gras."

"*Laisse le bon temps rouler!*"

She laughed. "Exactly."

"I wouldn't have figured you for a party girl."

"I wouldn't have figured you for a guy who quotes Shakespeare."

"Touché."

They were halfway back to the hotel when the neighborhood gave way to a sector dominated by small businesses — garages, machine shops, a computer repair place. All were locked down tight for the night.

He noticed that Sorensen was walking awkwardly, the heels of her shoes digging into cracks in the rutted sidewalk. They weren't exactly stilettos, but the sleek two-inch lifts were clearly giving her trouble. Davis pointed at them accusingly. "You know, those aren't as sensible as the ones you had on in the field this morning."

"I'm a woman," she countered. "All shoes are sensible."

Davis grinned. Then he looked up and saw trouble.

CHAPTER TWENTY-SIX

They appeared out of nowhere, three men fifty feet ahead. Shoulder-to-shoulder, they stood facing Davis and Sorensen. No motion, no purpose. Just stood there. Any of them would have looked right at home in a police lineup. Together, they practically made one. There was no one else in sight.

"Jammer!" she whispered harshly.

"I know," he said, "keep going."

They moved closer. Thirty feet, twenty. The three men fanned out to block the sidewalk. Davis and Sorensen had to stop.

Davis checked all around. They were in front of a bakery, a commercial pâtisserie. No going left. To the right, across the street, was an auto parts store. It was shut down, the windows above dark. No help there. Then he sensed movement behind. He half-turned and saw a really big guy closing off the rear. Davis stood so as to keep everyone in sight.

"You guys want something?" he asked. Davis said it in English, playing the stupid tourist. Hoping they'd feel free to talk among themselves in French. Unfortunately, the group of three began babbling rapidly in a language that made no sense to him. Or maybe it wasn't rapid. Some languages just sounded that way. They looked North African — dark olive skin, curly black hair. There were a lot of North Africans in France — Algerians, Libyans, Moroccans. Right now Davis didn't care much about their heritage.

He saw a calm confidence in their posture, in their eyes. This wasn't just a random roust. These guys were here with a purpose. The oaf in back had to go six-six. He was heavy, but bigger in the waist than the shoulders. He'd have lots of momentum, a good thing if you knew how to use it. The one in the middle of the trio was skinny, a kid. He pulled out a knife, flicked it open like he'd seen *West Side Story* one too many times. The one on the right was hard-faced — flattened nose, cauliflower ears, a few missing teeth. A man imbued with the richness of life's experiences. He had a hand in the pocket of his jacket, gripping something big and bulky. Brass knuckles, a sock full of coins. Or maybe a gun.

It was the one on the left who took a step forward.

Not big, not small, he seemed to have a little more European blood than the others. His prominent eyes were unusually round and his ears pointed, one anchoring a big gold earring. His nose and cheeks were sharp, framing a wide-open stare. Davis figured, a few generations back, one of his relatives might have modeled for the gargoyles up the street.

He looked at Davis and said, "We take your money." Then a nasty grin for Sorensen. "From her, we take something else."

Davis glanced at Sorensen. She seemed steady enough.

He said, "That's not nice." Then he jabbed a thumb over his shoulder. "And Lurch here smells bad. One more strike and you're out."

The Americanism seemed to escape them. Which was fine with Davis. He looked at Sorensen, saw her gnashing through a decision. He hoped she would reach the same conclusion he had.

Davis watched their feet. You could tell a lot by the way a guy stood before a fight. Martial arts training, police or military experience. It was there if you looked. He saw little — some puffed out chests, stiff stances, itchy hands. They were comfortable with their numbers, expecting a tussle. Not ready for war. Of the group of three, Davis decided that the ugly guy fondling his pocket was the most pressing problem.

Jammer Davis had been a Marine. He'd boxed at the Air Force Academy and spent years training in the arts of hand-to-hand combat. But his move was pure rugby. With quickness that defied his size, he lowered a shoulder and ran straight at the rough-looking guy. The hand came from his pocket, but it wasn't fast enough. Davis crashed into him with a lowered shoulder, wrapped up and kept driving. Five feet later he planted the guy hard into a stone wall. There was a crunch, an expulsion of air, and he collapsed to the sidewalk.

Davis turned fast and looked for the knife. He saw it coming in an arc, a glint of steel that might have sliced his chest had he not blocked with a forearm. But he didn't just block — he held on, grabbed the weapon with one hand, then pulled the kid close and clamped down with his other arm. The kid was half Davis' weight, and short of chewing off his arm at the shoulder, there wasn't much he could do. So he flailed, screamed for help.

Davis took the moment to assess his tactical situation. The big guy had Sorensen by the arm. She didn't seem to be struggling much — he wished she'd raise a ruckus, at least go for a shin kick. But the gargoyle was lunging for something on the ground — Davis recognized it. It *had* been a gun in the ugly guy's pocket. He swept the kid's feet out and twisted his arm viciously. Between the opposing motions, something gave. The knife went flying and the kid fell down screaming, holding an arm that didn't look quite right. Davis launched himself toward the gun.

He hit the pavement just a little too late, didn't get the gun. So he did the next best thing. He rolled onto the guy, put him on his back. Davis let his weight do the work. He grabbed the gun hand and didn't let go, forcing it outward. The gun went off, a wild round flying across the street. Davis twisted, moved until he was lying full on top of the guy, face-to-face. With his free hand, he grabbed the earring to hold his head still. Then Davis raised up and smashed his forehead into the gargoyle's nose.

The scream came first. Then he gave up the gun. Blood poured from the guy's shattered nasal cavity and he began rolling on the ground, his hands covering his face.

Davis stood up. A gun in one hand, a bloody earring in the other.

He dropped the earring.

Lurch was standing behind Sorensen now, pressed against her back. A big arm was draped firmly over her shoulder and across her chest.

His other hand held a knife that was pointed at Sorensen's throat. Even so, the big lug looked more scared than she did.

Davis sized things up. He had a gun. He had a huge target — there was no way the oaf could hide behind the petit Sorensen. Davis had taken the gun face-to-face, so it was in his left hand. Not his preferred shooting hand, but at this range it didn't much matter. One shot was all he needed. The problem was the knife. It was up against Sorensen's throat, and he wasn't sure he could pull and shoot fast enough. Davis decided to ratchet down. He kept the gun where it was, hanging loosely at his side and pointed at the sidewalk.

"Keel!" the big guy grunted. He twisted the knife near Sorensen's neck for emphasis. "Keel!"

Great, Davis thought, *this imbecile doesn't speak a lick of English.*

He considered how to proceed with calm hand signals. From the corner of his eye, he saw the kid with the crooked arm hobbling away in a weaving stride. The ugly guy was still out cold by the wall, and the gargoyle was writhing on the sidewalk, clutching a bloody face and torn ear — not fully incapacitated, but not an immediate threat. Odds were, he didn't have a weapon of his own. Otherwise, Davis reasoned, why would he have moved for the gun? Sometimes you just had to trust in logic.

Davis slowly put out his empty hand, palm out, and gestured to the results of the melee. Then he held up one finger — what he hoped was the universal signal for *just a minute*. Very, very slowly, he bent down and put the gun on the ground.

The big guy eased up. As if he'd won a little victory of sorts.

Maybe he had.

Davis would be perfectly happy to let him run away down the street. To that end, he took a few steps sideways, away from the gun — though not too far. Then he made a shooing motion with his hands, like one might do to a kid who was driving you nuts.

It nearly worked. The big guy's eyes darted down the empty street. His fear drained away and the knife came down just a little. He almost seemed to smile.

Sorensen moved so fast Davis could barely see what happened. She twisted, seized the guy's weapon arm and bent him at the waist. Then a knee smashed into his temple, followed by a palm heel strike to the throat. The big lug stumbled, clutching his head. But he didn't drop the knife. Two more blows, quick and hard to the head, and the knife clattered to the ground. Lurch hovered for just a moment. Stunned, frozen. Then, with a blurring half spin, Sorensen whipped around and buried her sensible shoe into his crotch.

There was a grunt, loud and long. A slow bend at the waist. He didn't so much fall as capsize, his head going down slow, the rest following like a torpedoed battleship. He ended up curled on the ground with his hands on his privates, leaning against four feet of Alpine granite.

"Jesus!" Davis remarked.

Standing over Lurch, Sorensen was breathing heavily and looked a little disheveled. But she was still in a ready stance.

Davis walked over, waited for her to relax. When she did, he said, "You know, Honeywell, I'm amending my opinion of you."

He thought she might smile. Maybe give a high five. Instead, she said, "Let's get the hell out of here!"

CHAPTER TWENTY-SEVEN

Two blocks away they heard a siren. Four blocks away a police car whisked by. It took fifteen minutes to reach the hotel.

They went to his room. It was chilly, the radiator not keeping up. He instructed Sorensen to take a seat on the bed. Two years back, Davis had played on a traveling rugby squad, and so there was a leftover first-aid kit with odd-sized bandages and some antiseptic in his suitcase. The cuts and contusions were easy enough. Davis had a knot over one eye from the head butt, possibly a broken middle finger on his right hand. The finger hurt, but there wasn't much he could do about it. So he used the age-old analgesic of imagining how the other guys must feel right now — there was a strange, pugilistic satisfaction in the thought. He got a bucket of ice, wrapped a few handfuls in a towel, and held it to his forehead.

Sorensen kicked off her shoes and they clattered to the wood floor at the foot of the bed. She had jammed her wrist. Davis made another icepack and helped her wrap it. He checked her over for other damage.

"I'm fine," she said. "I'll be a little sore tomorrow, that's all."

"So tell me," he said, "if we had hung around and waited for the cops to show, would the CIA have bailed us out of a mess like that?"

"Me? Yes. You? Eventually."

He nodded. "I guess I shouldn't expect much. I'm not even on the payroll."

"Not yet."

"Forget it," he said. "My life was better three days ago, all regulation and squared away. I don't need this James Bond crap." He stepped back and studied her, his eyes narrowing. "But you, Honeywell — you've had some training. Where did that come from?"

"Remember you asked me about tragedies?"

"Yes."

"Summer of 2000. I came in first at the U.S. Olympic Trials in judo, sixty-three kilograms. I was headed to Sydney. Then, the next week," she lifted her shoulder, the one with the scar, "I tore this up in training. Had to have surgery."

He nodded. "Now that *is* a tragedy. You must have worked damned hard to get that far."

"You can't imagine."

"Well, there's no gold medal tonight. But you were pretty useful."

"That wasn't even judo. That was . . . something else. But I'd say you've been in a few scrums before."

Davis shrugged, "I had some training in the military. Studied a few of the martial arts here and there. But I never got serious about it, not like you did. I just enjoyed the sparring — in the studio you can hit people and not get arrested."

"So what made you start that?"

"Start it? It was going to happen, Honeywell, I just picked the moment. In the military they call it leading by example."

"I'd call it suicidal by example. That guy had a gun."

"That's why he had to be first. The others didn't look comfortable, didn't have any proficiency."

"And you gave me the biggest one."

He grinned. "I thought you'd handle him. And you did, although not like I expected."

It took her a moment. She said, "You thought I was packing?"

"I was hoping. But as it turned out —" Davis let the compliment drift off. He checked her wrist. "You think we need an x-ray?"

"No, I just sprained it. What about you? Are you all right?"

"A few bumps. And my neck is a little sore." He rolled his head in a circle. "It feels like a Slinky that's got one of those kinks you can't get out." He pulled the icepack away from his forehead, wrapped it around his finger, then blew out a long breath. "It's been a hell of a day."

Sorensen nodded. "Yeah, it has. I could use a good night's sleep, but right now I'm wound a little tight."

"A little?" He grinned a crooked grin. "Truth is, I could use a nightcap. Care to join me downstairs?"

"Sure." She did a quick self-assessment and held up a torn sleeve. "But I should probably go to my room and freshen up."

"Meet you in the lounge in ten minutes."

When Sorensen left, Davis laid back on the bed. He closed his eyes, breathed deeply, and tried to make sense of what had happened. He tried to convince himself that the four guys had been a chance encounter. A bad coincidence.

It didn't work.

Opening his eyes, Davis checked his watch. It was six o'clock in Virginia. Dinner time. He sighed, and thought, *What the hell am I doing here?* He should have been home, waiting on the doorstep to greet Bobby Taylor. Instead he was an ocean away, getting in fights, playing secret agent. About to go meet a pretty blonde in a bar.

Christ!

Davis picked up his phone and dialed. His sister-in-law answered on the second ring.

"Hey, Laura. It's Jammer."

"Well, there you are. How's France? Have you got it all figured out?"

"Not yet." Laura was a good sort, down-to-earth — just like her sister had been. Davis wasn't in the mood to chat. He said, "Is she there?"

"No, Jammer. It's Wednesday."

"Ah, dammit. Swim practice."

"Yeah. She'll be home in an hour."

"How's she doing?"

"Jen is a teenager. Other than that, she's fine."

"Tell me about it. Is school going all right? Is she still all fired up over this dance Friday? What about —"

"Jammer," Laura broke in, "she's *okay.*"

There was a long pause. "Yeah."

"What about you? You haven't been away from Jen since — since it happened. Are you all right?"

Davis didn't know what to say. That his investigation was stuck in a ditch and he'd probably be here for weeks, maybe months? That he and his attractive CIA sidekick had just beat the crap out of four guys? "I'm good, Laura. I'm fine."

"Right." Another pause. "Listen, Jammer, she'll be back soon. I'll have her call you."

"Great," he said, then added, "oh, and Laura —"

"What?"

"Thanks for being there. You and Mike both. You guys always come through for us."

"That's what family's for, Jammer."

Davis hung up and took the ice pack off his head. He went to the bathroom and looked in the mirror. Big mistake. There was a goose egg over one eye, scrapes on his cheek, blood in his hair. His or somebody else's? No telling. Either way, he looked like hell.

He ran water over the back of his neck, massaged his kink. Again, Davis thought about the four men who had rousted him and Sorensen. The thoughts were not good.

The attacks were nearly simultaneous and occurred in no fewer than twelve time zones. From Venezuela to Singapore, from Kuwait to South Korea.

The general scheme of assault paralleled the previous day's work in America — suicide bombers acting alone, with the exception of two bigger operations in India and Belgium, where the attackers came in pairs. The mechanics varied slightly. Automobiles or trucks were used for the initial perimeter breach only on targets where the access to service roads was good. Other attackers used more direct methods of cutting, scaling, and even blasting their way through the primary barriers.

From there, it was again off to the races, determined individuals sprinting toward crude oil furnaces with all the explosives they could carry. A handful of the more security conscious facilities — particularly those under national control, with military forces deployed around the perimeters — were able to derail the attacks, or at least mitigate the damage.

Due to the timing, late night in western Europe and early evening in New York, it was the financial markets of the Far East that reacted first. The broader stock indices took a massive hit in anticipation of a global economic slump, a magnification of the previous day's carnage in equities that had resulted from the wave of strikes in America. Commodities were a mixed bag, contracts for short-term deliveries of refined fuels skyrocketing, but long futures for crude stock losing ground on expected slack demand — an increasing percentage of the world's petroleum refineries were out of commission. Precious metals rose, while grain futures reacted wildly on differing opinions of the effect.

For those able to ignore this chaos at the margins, the cumulative reaction of the afternoon Hong Kong and Tokyo trading sessions was largely predictable — a heavy hit, but certain sectors finding distinct advantage. If there was any good news it was that, as with the attacks in America, the facilities put out of commission were all midsized in terms of output. The world's fifty largest oil refineries all remained unscathed. Speculation in the media and investment houses ran a uniform theory — that the largest refineries were simply too well guarded to fall victim to such rudimentary methods of assault. Within hours, governments and corporations around the world sprang into action to ensure that this continued to be the case, putting every refinery, no matter the size, under maximum security lockdown.

It was during the first minutes of these new attacks that two extremist Muslim Web sites took responsibility for the strikes. Both offered supporting evidence that left no doubt as to their authenticity. They reveled in the victory of their martyrs, exalted in Islam, and gave praise to their glorious leader.

The terrorist known as Caliph.

CHAPTER TWENTY-EIGHT

The hotel bar was still open, but last call was near. Sorensen hadn't arrived yet.

The lights seemed dimmer than they'd been earlier, probably a good thing for Davis given the way he looked. He had always operated under the theory that the lights in bars were purposely dimmed as nights wore on — an accelerant for romantic associations, or maybe a plot to throw confusion on currency denominations when tabs were settled. It had to be some kind of conspiracy.

Davis slid onto a stool at the end of the bar and ordered — a beer for him, and a glass of pinot noir that would breathe as it waited for Sorensen. The bartender went through a well-practiced sequence of motions — without the glasses it would have looked like a Tai Chi routine — before sliding the round in front of Davis.

The guy started muttering under his breath, glaring at the television above the bar. Davis saw a soccer highlight show. The bartender found a remote control and began flipping through channels. Either he wasn't a soccer fan, or the team he supported had lost badly. The guy spun through the stations at warp speed — an annoying thing when other people did it — and settled on a newscast. The volume was low, but judging by the graphics and film clip it had to be about the price of gas. The picture showed a long line of cars at a gas station, and overhead the price was posted in euros per liter. The conversion to dollars per gallon was more math than Davis wanted to tackle right now. He just knew it was high. Really high.

The barkeep turned up the volume enough for Davis to catch a few details. There had been a series of coordinated attacks against oil refineries, and Caliph was the primary suspect. Davis took a long draw from his mug. Caliph was the reason Sorensen was here in France. The reason he was on loan to the CIA. Davis wondered if one guy could really have a hand in so much. He remembered that Osama bin Laden had been held responsible for a lot of bad things, including some disasters he certainly had nothing to do with. But point a finger at a terrorist for any kind of trouble, Davis reckoned, and he was usually happy to take credit. He took another long pull and when his mug hit the bar he spotted Sorensen.

She looked good, better than she should have after sparring with a guy twice her size. She had on a pair of jeans and a tight sweater with the sleeves rolled up. A recent line of thought came back to Davis. Returning to the hotel from their rumble, Sorensen had fallen into her trade. He'd seen her checking six a lot, scanning for anyone following or watching them. It was probably something all CIA officers had to learn, but it must have been a doubly tough lesson for Sorensen. She was a nice-looking woman, the kind who naturally turned heads. He wondered how she could distinguish which stares were from enemy spies and which were from philandering husbands.

"Hi," she said, sliding onto the adjacent stool.

He pushed the wine glass by its base until it was in front of her. "It's a pinot noir from a little vineyard in New Zealand, Villa Maria. Really nice stuff."

She gave him a curious look.

Davis shrugged. "Not that I would know."

She picked up the wine with her good hand. "Thanks for the drink."

"Sure. How's the wrist?"

"It's all right." She nipped distractedly at her drink, and when the glass came down she held it just above the bar. Davis noticed a tiny wavepool of concentric rings inside.

"You okay?"

"Sure." She took another sip, this time seeming to almost kiss the glass. "But it's not the kind of thing I'm used to."

"That's a good thing." He saw her lower lip starting to puff up.

Davis reached out and touched it gently with the back of his thumb. "Looks like you caught one there too."

"Puffy lips are sexy, right?"

"Yeah, but it's supposed to be symmetrical — top and bottom."

One corner of her mouth broke into a grin.

Davis mused, "You know, there was a time when I'd have been fired up about a scrap like that. I'd be sitting here drinking whiskey instead of beer with my chest all puffed out. But it's different when you're a parent — especially when you're the only parent." He took a drink himself.

"So who were those guys?" Sorensen wondered aloud.

"I've been giving that some thought myself. Do you think Langley could give us any answers?"

"If the police got involved, or if any of them turned up in a hospital — probably. But it'll take some time. Things like this aren't a real priority for headquarters right now."

"Maybe they should be."

"It could just have been some thugs looking for a wallet."

The pause was long as they both let that hopeful thought die.

She said, "They were definitely North African or Middle Eastern. I couldn't make out the exact language, but France has a major immigrant population from those parts."

"All the big cities in Europe have a Muslim quarter these days." Davis sat stoically with both hands on his mug. "So are you thinking what I'm thinking?"

She sighed. "That somebody wanted us roughed up? Maybe called in help?"

"Yep — except for the 'us' part. You've been pretty quiet in your time here, Honeywell. I'm the one raising a stink in the investigation. I think they were after me. And I have a feeling they wanted me more than roughed up."

"As in dead? I don't think so, Jammer."

He looked at her, his expression saying, *Yes you do.*

Sorensen said nothing.

Davis' phone chirped. He picked up and got the highlight of his day.

"Hi Daddy!"

Sorensen excused herself to the ladies' room.

Davis talked to Jen for ten minutes. She mostly gushed about Bobby Taylor, but then he made her say that school and swim practice had been fine. Davis pictured her sitting on his sister-in-law's couch, legs tucked under, and wearing something warm and cottony. It was a cozy scene, probably not far off target. He let her talk, just wanting to listen. In the end, she brought up the dance again. And Davis put her off again, saying they'd talk about it when he got home. Which would have to be in less than a week. *What were the chances of that?* he wondered.

Jen ended the call abruptly, probably to answer a text from that malingering Taylor kid. Davis didn't take it personally. He pocketed his phone. The bartender was screwing with the remote again. Davis ignored the television, but found himself mesmerized by the remote control. He needed one for his life. Fast forward. Rewind. Maybe a mute or closed caption button for Thierry Bastien. Yes. That was exactly what he needed.

When Sorensen came back she looked a little more steady. He imagined she'd spent a few minutes in front of a mirror dabbing cool, water-soaked towels in all the right places.

"How's Jen?" she asked.

"All I heard about were boys and movies. She's great." Davis drained his mug and frowned.

"That was supposed to cheer you up, Jammer. Look, it could have been worse — at least it wasn't bring-your-daughter-to-work day."

His expression turned even more sour.

"Sorry. How about I buy the next round?" she offered.

He spun his empty back and forth in a half circle. "No thanks, I'm good."

"You don't sound like it. Let me guess — you'd rather be home."

"Yeah. And I'm still not sure I like being used by the CIA."

"Recruited is a better word."

He shook his head. "The army recruits."

"Okay, call it a draft."

"Let's call it a mistake and leave it at that. You should tell your boss that if I stay on this little project, I'm going to drive him or her nuts."

Sorensen finished her wine. She said, "Maybe you *should* go home, Jammer. I wouldn't think any less of you."

"Yes you would."

The television went back to Caliph's picture. It was a head shot, his crown wrapped in a pristine white cloth. They both stared.

She said, "Do you think it's really possible?"

He gave her a sideways glance. "That those idiots we ran into tonight were linked to Caliph? No, no way. He gets too much credit."

"You said yourself that we were rousted because of the investigation. That all your poking and prodding must have hit a nerve with somebody. And *I'm* here because CargoAir is somehow linked to Caliph."

They both distilled the idea.

She asked idly, "The name Caliph—do you know what it translates to in English?"

He shrugged. "Shitwad?"

Sorensen smiled. It was still a nice smile, fat lip and all. "It means 'spiritual leader.' Maybe he really believes it."

"Yeah. He's a real messiah."

Davis leaned back, clasped his hands behind the bent Slinky that was his neck. Everything here was wrong. Bastien, Caliph, pulled circuit breakers—and now four thugs had come after him. It probably meant he was on the right track, turning over the right rocks. It all screamed for him to stop, to bail out and go home. But he knew he wouldn't. Knew he couldn't. And once Davis had settled that, he wasn't going to sit around and wait for the next fight to come to him.

He said, "Want to take a road trip tomorrow?"

"Sure. Where?"

Davis liked how the first word had come right out. No hesitation. "Marseille. I want to get a firsthand look at a C-500 — a tail number that's still in one piece."

"Will they let us?"

"They'd better." He slid a wad of euros onto the bar and pushed his stool back. "And in the meantime, there's something I'd like you to look into — you know, with your connections and all."

"What's that?"

"I want to know how the Bureau Enquêtes-Accidents appoints these boards. I want to know how Thierry Bastien got in charge of this fiasco."

"You think somebody is messing with the investigation? Trying to manipulate the outcome?"

"No. That can't happen. There are a lot of competent people here — they'll figure out what happened to that airplane. But we have Bastien going after the captain and somebody tampering with evidence. And now you and I get roughed up. It's like — I don't know, it's like somebody is trying to delay the inevitable. Buy time."

"Buy time for what?"

Davis paused, said nothing. He reached out and took her elbow, inspected her wrist again. "This is swelling a lot."

"It's fine."

Davis kept holding her arm. Her wrist had a faint ring of white where a watch had been, the rest of her skin holding the subtle vestige of a distant, late-summer tan. The skin was smooth, all the way to her rolled up sleeve, and traces of faint blonde hair made it seem that much softer. When Davis looked up their faces were close. Probably closer than they'd ever been. Sorensen was looking at his hand, the one touching her. She was staring at his wedding ring.

Davis was struck by the odd realization that he and Sorensen were investigating each other. Searching for feelings and attachments, tying to make conclusions using all available evidence.

He pulled away.

Neither spoke for a moment.

"I guess we should get some sleep," she said.

"Yeah. But I really think we should wrap that wrist."

She looked at it and sighed. "I guess so."

Davis sat on his bed, the unused Ace bandage he'd dug out of his suitcase lying next to him on the blanket. His room was dark, the only light coming from the bathroom, a frail, indirect glow that left most of the room in shadows.

He'd been there for ten minutes. Sitting, thinking about Sorensen. Or more precisely, thinking about her wrist. It shouldn't have been such a complicated thing, yet Davis found no end to the tangents pinging through his head. Had she been wearing a watch earlier? He couldn't remember. Why didn't she wear one now? Maybe she had just started using her phone to keep the time like so many people. Or maybe the watch had been a gift from Mr. Almost, discarded when he was.

And why the hell are you sitting here worrying about it, Jammer?

Davis looked down and realized he was twisting his wedding ring, spinning the gold band in circles on his finger. He reached down and gave a slight tug. It moved.

For the first time in fifteen years.

Five minutes later Davis knocked on Sorensen's door. She opened it and then pulled back a stride, leaving plenty of room. She had changed into a nightshirt. It was nothing flimsy, just long and white and cottony.

Davis held out the bandage in his left hand.

Sorensen didn't take it.

He said, "Do you need this?" Because he couldn't just stand there and say nothing.

She stared at his hand for a moment, then took him by the shoulders and pulled him into the room. Sorensen took the Ace wrap. She dropped it on the floor. Then she stood on her tiptoes and put two very soft lips to his ear.

"Yes," she whispered.

Davis crooked his leg and shut the door with a heel. He leaned into her and they kissed. It was long and electric. Sorensen broke, stepped back a few paces. She looked him in the eye as she pulled her nightshirt over her head. There was nothing underneath, nothing except the hourglass shape of her hips and breasts silhouetted perfectly in pale light that cast through the window.

She smiled — slow, like a breaking sunrise — and said, "You're a visual guy, right?"

"Right."

CHAPTER TWENTY-NINE

At nine o'clock that evening, Herman Coyle was busy crunching numbers in a small office in the White House basement. Darlene Graham had given him the working space on his request. There was a cot in one corner — Coyle had not wanted to waste time commuting on the Beltway — and a dinner tray sat untouched by the door.

He had realized the magnitude of his miscalculations early this afternoon. The initial damage reports, security camera footage, and forensic analysis all confirmed his initial take — that the attacks on America's refineries had been very, very clinical. All but one had targeted the primary crude furnaces. Try as he might, Coyle could not think of a more incapacitating blow. But then, just minutes ago, he'd had his palm-to-the-forehead moment.

It came in the middle of a thick pile, a stack of corporate estimates regarding how long certain refineries would be out of service. Coyle had missed it completely, but at least one corporate planner was right on the ball. Two days ago, Colson Industries, the only domestic maker of crude oil furnaces, had seen their sole manufacturing plant burn to the ground in a suspicious fire. Coyle had been apoplectic. He knew that the production of such hardware was highly specialized — there would never be a widespread need for industrial-grade crude oil heaters when properly maintained units lasted more than a decade.

He quickly discovered that two other manufacturers existed. Or *had* existed. Russia's Petrov I.A. had been annihilated in a suspicious fire on the very same day Colson Industries had burned. The only survivor, a unit of the Dutch conglomerate DSR, was presently in the middle of a three-month shutdown for retooling. On this day, according to the corporate estimate he had read, there were no more than six replacement crude oil heaters inventoried anywhere in the world.

He continued to enter numbers into his calculator with the eraser of a pencil, the symbology of which did not escape him. New variables entered his mind faster than he could type. How long would it take to refit the Dutch plant? How would the energy markets react? What effect would extreme prices have on demand? The sheer number of variables made any answers he derived useless. Coyle stopped his guesswork.

He slammed the pencil onto his desk and walked quickly to Darlene Graham's office.

Coyle didn't knock, he just barged in.

He found more people than he'd expected. No one had gone home tonight, the administration clearly functioning in crisis mode. Graham was talking on the phone. She looked surprised to see Coyle, but waved for him to take a seat. Coyle took a chair and tried to sit still, but his feet bounced nervously. The director of national intelligence watched him guardedly as she sat with the phone glued to her ear. It was a one-way conversation and she was definitely on the receiving end. When she finally hung up, her face was grim.

Graham got up quickly from her desk, gathering a few files. "What is it, Dr. Coyle?"

"I was a fool for not seeing it," he began. He told her what he'd found, that a shortage of crude oil heaters was going to aggravate their entire problem. When he started spouting numbers, she cut him off.

"I'm afraid it's even worse, Herman. I just got off the phone with the FBI's Joint Terrorism Task Force Command Center. There's been another round of refinery attacks, even bigger than the first."

Coyle was dumbstruck. "But how? Our security was —"

"They weren't *ours*. It happened overseas this time. Europe, Asia, the Middle East. At least thirty more strikes." Graham dashed from behind her desk with an armload of manila. As she rushed for the door, she said, "Well come on, Coyle. Oval Office, now!"

Herman Coyle bolted upright and moved.

Truett Townsend was showing his temper again. Coyle watched the president pace in front of the tall bulletproof windows that overlooked the Rose Garden.

"Dammit! Didn't these companies — didn't these *governments* see what happened to us? They should have stepped up security!"

"A few did," Graham said. "Four, maybe five of the attacks were neutralized, or at least the damage kept to a minimum."

"Four or five out of what — thirty?"

"Thirty-two is the latest," Martin Spector said.

Spector had just arrived, along with Graham and Coyle. Other key members would be trickling in soon, but the president was clearly not in the mood to wait.

"So our plan to buy refined fuel on the open market is shot to hell!" Townsend looked directly at Coyle, waiting for a response.

"It would seem so," Coyle said weakly. He then told the president about his findings regarding the scarcity of crude heaters, and went over his latest calculations. The news was bad, but as he spoke Coyle thought he sensed a settling, as if his words, or maybe his numbers, had a kind of opiate effect on the others. When he finished, everyone deferred to the president.

"All right, Dr. Coyle. So what do you recommend? More pleas for calm?"

In another setting, it might have sounded sarcastic. Coyle, in fact, had spent much of his day analyzing this very question. "Calm? Certainly, Mr. President. But we must face reality. By midday tomorrow there will be cars lined up a hundred deep at every gas station in the country — at least, those stations that don't already have plastic bags over all their pump handles. We must immediately implement a rationing program."

"Rationing!" Spector shouted. "You want to tell Americans that they can only have one tank of gas a week?"

"One tank is probably excessive," Coyle said.

The president turned away and stared out across the South Lawn. He stood motionless, hands on his hips, his eyes seeming to look right through the necklace of headlights that churned over E Street in the distance.

Coyle said, "I am not ignorant of the political ramifications, Mr. President. I think you should stress that this is only a temporary inconvenience. A few months at the outside."

Spector argued, "We are talking about people's livelihoods. How will they get to work, get groceries, go to the doctor? Travel and the kids' hockey games will go right out the window! No, we can't do this!"

"Mr. Spector," Coyle said, "I understand the sacrifices involved in what I am suggesting. But there is no *choice* here. It is going to happen. All that we in this room can do is manage the discomfort."

Nobody spoke as Coyle's words settled in.

President Townsend seemed to break from his trance, and he turned to face his advisors. "Dr. Coyle is right. Let's get the Departments of Energy and Homeland Security together on this. I want a realistic rationing plan on my desk first thing tomorrow morning." He pointed at Spector. "Crude oil furnaces — our government is now in the manufacturing business. Spend whatever it takes to fast-track these repairs."

The president kept talking. Each new department head that came into the room was given an assignment. At that moment, Herman Coyle was proud of his president, glad he'd voted for the man. As he sat and watched the scene, however, something bothered him. It was triggered when the president started hounding Darlene Graham for new information on Caliph. She had little to give, and somewhere deep in the recesses of his mind Coyle found that he was not surprised.

Someone brought in the latest update and Coyle reached out to take a copy. He saw that it was a partial list of the latest targets. Singapore, Iran, China, Italy. Caliph wasn't playing any favorites. Then something else about the list struck him, the same thing he'd noticed about the domestic attacks — these were not the biggest facilities. They were

large, but second tier. Like everyone else, Coyle had reasoned that this
was because security would be easier to circumvent. Now he began to
revisit the conclusion.

Herman Coyle was not an expert on terrorism or national security. But he *was* a man of logic. As he considered the attacks, he put
them together as a whole and ruminated on the symmetry, the almost
mathematical pattern to the sequence of events. And in a moment of
clarity that bordered on the divine, there it was — *sequence*.

He sat very still and an odd corollary flowed to his mind. As a boy,
Coyle's hero had been Albert Einstein. He had read everything he
could get his hands on about the world's greatest scientist. Einstein's
work ethic was legendary, but by his own admission, his fame had been
cemented on a few moments of genius. Inspiration sometimes came
at four in the morning after spending a long night slugging through
equations, and sometimes it came in the shower. Clarity. Herman
Coyle had finally had his own moment, and it had come in the Oval
Office as the president was barking orders to his director of national
intelligence.

Coyle jumped abruptly to his feet and shouted, "It's not Caliph!"

Townsend stopped in mid-sentence. The room fell still, except for
the two Secret Service men by the door whose hands were unex-
pectedly poised at the fronts of their jackets. Coyle relaxed.

"I beg your pardon?" the president said.

"It's not Caliph behind this. At least, not in the way we think."

The president walked across the room, slowly and deliberately,
until he stood directly in front of Coyle. He was a good head taller.
"Then who *should* we be looking for?" he asked.

Coyle drew a blank. He had proven one solution wrong, yet not
come up with an alternative. "I'm not sure, sir. But I think I can find
out."

The president of the United States stared at him hard, like he
might divine more detail by some kind of telepathy.

"I'll need a lot of help," Coyle said. "FBI, Secret Service —"

"Secret Service?" Darlene Graham interjected.

"Maybe the SEC. I need full access, everything, and the highest priority. We have to be fast."

Townsend's eyes became slits. "Fast? Why?"

"Because we have less than twenty-four hours."

"Twenty-four hours until what?" the president queried impatiently.

"I don't know. But look at the pattern. On each of the last three days there has been a strike of some sort. It might not be further suicide attacks — but if something else occurs it will likely be on the same schedule. You see, I fear we've totally misread the motivation for these attacks. And if I'm right, I might be able to reverse engineer to discover who is really responsible."

The president kept staring. Then, very slowly, his head began a series of nods that gradually increased in amplitude. On the fifth, he said, "All right, Coyle. Whatever you need, you've got it."

CHAPTER THIRTY

Smoke swirled around Ibrahim Jaber as he worked on his laptop, a thin blue haze that drifted by the room's subtle currents. An empty soup can served as his ashtray, and next to that a cup of hot cereal gone cold stood waiting. As he pecked at the keyboard, Jaber thought the apartment seemed cool. He had already turned up the heat twice, but wind whistled through cracks at the fourth-floor window. It was an urban breeze, the air outside having accelerated to squeeze through the narrow passage between buildings. Bernoulli's Principle, he mused. The same concept that gave his airplanes flight.

When Jaber finished his work, he began composing an e-mail to his wife. Contemplating the words, he sampled the cereal. It was decidedly bland, but he kept spooning it to his mouth, knowing it was one of the few things he could keep down. The medicine was helping less now. It no longer touched the pain. Yet Jaber resisted the urge to up his dosage. To do so would dull his mind at a time when he needed all his wits about him.

Just a little longer.

Jaber stared at the flashing cursor as he arranged his thoughts, the hard reality setting in that these could be his last words to his wife. He began:

Dearest Yasmin,

I am about to begin my final journey home. I cannot say when, or even if, I will complete this voyage, so it is time for you to know more. My work for the last two years has been the most challenging of my career, and also the most rewarding. Soon, you will be told many things regarding what I have done. You may be confronted by many people. Some of what they will say is true. Other parts, less so. I ask only that you trust in this — all I have done is for the benefit of you and our sons.

My condition has not improved, and thus you shall soon be alone to care for Asim and Malik. Others may intervene, offer to help you. From them, take what you will, but always trust in the arrangements we have already discussed. Above all, tell no one of the existence of this account.

As for you, Yasmin . . .

Jaber's fingers hovered over the keyboard, motionless, like a concert pianist about to address a demanding passage. So much came to mind he did not know where to start.

A knock on the door startled him.

Jaber instantly looked at the window. He had pulled the curtains back to allow the rising sun to enter, hoping for a little added warmth. It had been a mistake. He could be seen from outside, and so now he had no option of ignoring the caller. Jaber quickly tabled the cereal and folded his computer without even shutting it down. He went to the curtains and closed them. With no time to stow the laptop under the hidden floor panel in his bedroom, he shoved it into a bookcase behind a tall row of scientific reference books.

He went to the door and opened it cautiously. His gaze sharpened when he saw her. "What are you doing here?" Jaber asked in a harsh whisper.

She tromped in without invitation, wheezing as she passed. "That's a lot of stairs you got out there."

Jaber shut the door and watched her collapse into his best chair, the springs pinging under her weight. He went over and drew the curtains shut. "Why are you here? We cannot jeopardize things now. Less than a day remains." Jaber had more to say, but his words were interrupted by a coughing spell. Retching and struggling for air, he dropped to the couch for support.

"You don't sound so good," Fatima said. "You taking your medicine?"

Jaber nodded as he recovered.

She pointed to an old television. "You been watching the news? Caliph's martyrs, they doing a good job."

"Yes, I know." It had long perplexed Jaber that so many young men and women could throw their lives under the bus that was militant Islam. But then he considered the economy of Egypt and her neighbors. A man who was well fed, prosperous enough to care for his family, would never consider martyrdom. But a man who was hungry and desperate — he might go to any extreme. This Jaber knew only too well.

"What about you?" she asked, disturbing his thought. "You finish that update thing, huh? Caliph, he wanted me to ask."

"Of course, yesterday." Jaber looked at his watch — it was now seven in the morning. "Seventeen hours remain."

"So how you do that? By computer or something?"

"Yes, my personal laptop has the software codes. But as I warned, we are now at the point of no return. The navigation updates are uploaded every two weeks. By the time the next one comes —" Jaber's voice trailed off. He pulled a pack of cigarettes from his pocket and tapped until one showed. Feigning hospitality, he turned it toward Fatima.

She cackled. "No. Those things will kill you."

He found some amusement in the fact that Fatima's answer had come in a raspy voice. Jaber recognized it as the kind of resonance a woman acquired, one cured by a lifetime of harsh tobacco and shot-grade whiskey. He lit up, then tensed as she reached for the framed photograph next to his chair.

"Pretty wife," Fatima said. "Good looking boys, too." She held it up high in one hand, like a lawyer displaying evidence to a jury. "Caliph, he's gonna take good care of them."

Jaber said nothing. He willed her to put it back down. "What about this bothersome American, Mr. Davis?" he asked. "Caliph was supposed to do something about him."

"Yeah, I know. He got some guys to do that, but they screwed it up. That's Algerians for you." Fatima chortled again.

Jaber was left to wonder if she was speaking of the same men who had been at his own side three days ago. If so, the fact that they failed did not surprise him.

Fatima got up and went to the window. She pulled aside one of the curtains Jaber had just closed and studied the street outside. "This a pretty good view," she said.

Jaber wanted to tell her to keep it closed, but he clenched his teeth tightly. Again he felt the cold, and he could not stop his thoughts from drifting a thousand miles away to the resilient warmth of Egypt.

Fatima began to wander the room. "You got that computer here?" she asked. "In this place?"

Jaber was very tired. So tired he nearly told the truth. But then something else came out, from where he had no idea. "No, I keep it in the safe at my headquarters office in Marseille. It must be kept secure at all times."

Fatima nodded, kept moving. "That's smart." Her great figure swayed under layers of cloth. Thankfully, she ended up by the door. "Okay. I'll tell Caliph everything is ready. That will make him happy."

Jaber watched as she let herself out.

As soon as she was gone, he went to the door and threw the bolt. He walked slowly to his chair, eased down, and took a long draw on his cigarette. If there was any consolation to his condition, it was that he would never again have to endure Fatima Adara.

Jaber had always considered himself above Caliph and his lot. Blinded by rage, they were such simple people. Not stupid, or even un-educated. Just simple. Fatima, of course, was a heathen. But the rest were so predictably pious — ruled by religion, and thus inseparable from the currencies of faith, hope, and prayer. A man of science, Jaber had never bothered with such delusions. He had been drawn into this unclean affair by a faith in other currencies, the denominations far more practical.

Caliph had offered assurances regarding the long-term security of his family — yet here Jaber had taken matters into his own hands. He would trust no one else when it came to Asim and Malik. He had found some distaste, of course, in what they'd asked him to do. But he also could not deny the excitement, even the pleasure he derived from it all. There was a distinct sense of satisfaction when one outsmarted the world.

Jaber looked at the picture next to his chair before closing his eyes. Soon it would all come to an end. And then he would find peace.

CHAPTER THIRTY-ONE

They woke up early, entangled in the sheets. Entangled in each other. Davis wasn't sure who was the first to stir. There was only gentle movement, an arm under a shoulder, a foot under a calf. Here and there, give and take, until light began to register at the window's edge. They didn't make breakfast for another hour.

At the restaurant, they lingered. Both hungry, both unrushed. They talked about the Air Force Academy and the 2000 Olympic trials. Daughters in Virginia and cabins in Colorado. Not a word was said about the investigation. It was a magnificent diversion from their work, a continuation of what had started last night. When the check eventually came it landed with a thud, like some kind of grim subpoena demanding their appearance before the real world.

They headed south to Marseille on the A7, passing through the region known as Provence. Davis knew the area well, and so he knew there was no specific federation or administrative boundary to claim the name. It was more of a culture, really. A mind-set. The geography of Provence was varied, gentle hills and abrupt massifs, all ceding eventually to the Mediterranean at the southern limit. Life here was slow, adaptive. The marks of man fell into flow with the mistral, the cold, dry wind that whipped down the Rhone valley with such fierce regularity that most farmhouses faced south to keep their backs to the maelstrom. Davis noted that the mistral was active today, the trees showing a stronger than usual southward tilt. He concluded, summing the cold and distinct lack of sun, that the Provence of mid-winter was not the Provence of tourist brochures.

The road was wet from an overnight rain, and the tires of their

Fiat 600 hissed over wet asphalt, punctuated by the occasional splatter of puddles into the wheel well. Reflecting the greater European way, driving in France was one part mode of transportation, one part sport. Sorensen held her own, negotiating the manual transmission smoothly as she maneuvered through the mid-morning rush.

Davis found himself watching her. She looked better than ever, fat lip and all. Or maybe his perspective had just changed.

She caught his stare and smiled. "What?"

"I was thinking you handle the car pretty well."

"The car."

Davis grinned.

She went back to the road.

He went back to her.

"Roundabout," she announced.

A distracted Davis looked up and saw a traffic circle closing in. Acting navigator, he referenced the map. "Straight through, the A7. No, wait—"

The signs at the intersection came fast, and thin wisps of fog had begun to bring the visibility down. They missed their turn.

"Sorry," he said, giving her the correct road.

"No problem. I'll bet even Lindberg got lost once or twice."

"Once or twice."

Sorensen kept in the circle and found their road on the second pass.

Davis' mood descended. A relationship with Sorensen was only going to complicate things. But then, how much more complicated could they get? A vision came to mind of the Fiat going round and round in the traffic circle, stuck in an eternal left turn and going nowhere. Just like his investigation.

He said, "So did you find out how Bastien got in charge of this fiasco?"

"Sort of. The Bureau Enquêtes-Accidents assigns all the spots on the board. Their original choice to head up the team was another guy—I think his name was Fontaine. Anyway, he pulled out and recommended Bastien."

"This all had to happen pretty fast," Davis said. "The airplane only crashed a few days ago."

"Yes. The word is, nobody thought very highly of Bastien."

"I don't think very highly of him either."

"You think they'll figure out why this airplane crashed?"

"Oh, they will. Like I said, there are plenty of good people here. Just not enough direction at the moment."

"Langley did mention one other thing of interest," she said.

"What's that?"

"It seems that last night one of our officers was gunned down in an alleyway. Before he died, he got a call through and was able to spit out one word — Caliph."

"So Caliph took out one of your agents?"

"Apparently."

"Where did this happen?"

She hesitated before saying it. "Marseille."

The two exchanged a look.

"So maybe you have good instincts," she offered.

"Maybe I need my head examined."

Silence fell for a long moment. Davis sensed Sorensen glancing back and forth between him and the road. He changed tack. "I spent a little time yesterday getting smarter on flight control software."

"Sounds scintillating."

"You can't imagine. Network protocols, information domains. Heavy stuff."

"So what did you find out?"

"The certification process is very, very thorough. Lots of review, lots of what they call beta testing on the programs. The whole airplane runs on code, just like any computer. When the pilot moves the joystick, he or she is essentially making a request for the airplane to do something — like say, turn right. That input commands the computer to look at air loads and performance data, then cross-check against gains and limits. Of course, this all happens in the blink of an eye. Once everything is sorted, the computer sends signals to move the flight controls. That's fly by wire. It's all buried deep in three independent flight control computers. They run in parallel and cross-check each other continuously. If one fails, the others rule."

"And the airplane can fly on one?"

"Supposedly."

"You said gains and limits. What's that about?"

"Think of them as restrictions — the software won't let the airplane go too fast or accelerate too hard, won't let it command any maneuver that would be dangerous or abrupt."

"Like pointing straight down from seven miles up?"

"Exactly. I asked Jaber that very thing — how would the computers have allowed what this airplane did?"

"And?"

"He threw it back on Earl Moore. Suggested that there are modes in which the pilot can override the computer."

"And are there?"

"Sometimes. It depends on what the designers build into the system."

Sorensen blew out a long breath as she worked through traffic.

"And I found out something else," Davis said. "Once this software is installed in the airplane, you can't get at it. When regulatory agencies like the FAA certify these systems, they make sure the flight control software is shielded, segregated to maintain its integrity. The big concern relates to passenger airplanes — you don't want somebody in row six hacking into the aircraft's systems using an airborne WiFi port."

"Okay, that makes sense. So it's secure."

Davis looked at the map, then outside. "That's what they tell me."

The guard at the gate of the U.S. Consulate in Geneva saw the young man coming. He was probably seventeen or eighteen, but looked ten years older. The Marine sergeant had seen the type before. Switzerland, for all its prosperity and orderliness, had a firm underclass of the homeless and drug addicted. They were kids mostly, swept aside into little-used corners of parks and public buildings. Hidden and unacknowledged.

The sergeant watched the kid come straight at the gate. Straight at him. He was carrying an envelope. Having served tours in Iraq and Afghanistan, the Marine was suspicious. In either of those places, he'd already have a hand on his sidearm. But then, in either of those places he'd be packing something more intimidating than a holstered 9mm.

The kid stopped right in front of him and held out the envelope. "Here," he said. "Take it, please."

The guard put on his I-eat-nails-for-breakfast face, and asked, "What is it?"

The kid raised the palm of his empty hand to the sky, like he'd just been asked to explain quantum theory. The Marine took a good look at the envelope. It seemed harmless enough. He looked over his shoulder at his partner, a corporal standing behind a concrete blast barrier. His buddy shrugged. The guard took the envelope and the young man scurried off.

There were procedures to be followed now. It was a regular thing to be handed trinkets and missives. Most of the letters were appeals for visas or political asylum, along with a few hostile rants against American foreign policy. Last week they'd gotten a scathing review of Leonardo DiCaprio's newest movie, somebody figuring that the U.S. Consulate in Geneva was the best way to get word to Sony Pictures. Still, when the sergeant read what was carefully typed on the front of the envelope, it did get his attention: INFORMATION ON CALIPH.

They'd had a few Caliph tips lately. Diplomatic stations all over the world were getting them. Put ten million bucks on a guy's head, the sergeant figured, and you'd get lots of tips. The two guards couldn't leave their post, so the man with the envelope in his hand called inside. Another Marine, the captain in charge of the detachment, came out and took the offering.

Inside the consulate, the captain's first task was to run the envelope through a scanner at the entrance. The machine was normally used for luggage and coats and briefcases — pretty much everything that came through the front door. He didn't like what he saw on the display monitor. Inside the simple white envelope was a vial containing some kind of liquid. This complicated things greatly.

It took another thirty minutes of scanning and careful manipulation to reveal the envelope's complete contents. A letter of demands, a printed record of a laboratory workup, and a test tube full of— something. The vial could not be dealt with here, so it was locked down. The rest was commandeered by the station CIA man, scanned into a computer, and forwarded by a secure line to Langley.

Within the hour, three men and a woman — a contingent no one at the consulate had ever seen — rushed into the building. Guided by the in-house CIA man, the original documents and glass tube were collected and whisked to a waiting car.

The tires began squealing before the back door had even closed.

CHAPTER THIRTY-TWO

They weren't exactly welcomed. Admitted without prejudice was more like it.

Davis had arranged the visit to CargoAir's production facility on short notice. He and Sorensen were escorted from the visitor's area by a serious guy — crew cut, square suit, shiny shoes. He reminded Davis of a JAG he'd once known, a military lawyer. Or at least the French version. Their guide explained that a full-scale factory tour was available, but Davis figured it was the one that tourists got. He said they weren't interested. He made it clear that he and Sorensen wanted only one thing — to get inside a C-500.

The hangar where they ended up looked a lot like the one attached to Building Sixty-two in Lyon. It had the same bright lights, but everything here was cleaner, more antiseptic. The floor sparkled, and massive banners on the wall exhorted everyone, in both French and English, to BE SAFE. A wide net to cast, Davis thought. He considered all the unfortunate things he'd seen happen in aircraft factories — people falling off scaffoldings, stray screwdrivers getting left behind in newly assembled jet engines. Once he'd seen a work crew forget to put chocks under the wheels of a half-million-pound airplane, watched as it rolled free and crashed into a hangar door. In one bold stroke, CargoAir had made it all expressly against company policy, writ large. BE SAFE.

Davis had seen a lot of hangars in his time. This one reminded him of a showroom at a new car dealership. Everything was neat and tidy, ready for sales pitches and public relations tours. There had to be a production hangar elsewhere on the property, bigger and dirtier, a place where wrenches turned and machinists cussed. But at the moment, Davis was happy to be right here — because in the middle of it all was what he wanted. A C-500.

Their guide stopped. He didn't say anything, and Davis figured he was letting them have a look from a distance, letting them experience the airplane in all its glory. The guy must have thought they'd be impressed.

Davis was.

"Wow," Sorensen exclaimed. "It's bigger than I expected."

"Yeah," Davis agreed, "it's a monster, all right."

He decided the impression of size was likely due to the aircraft's unconventional shape. Davis was familiar with the B-2 bomber, and in terms of general layout, it was the closest thing he'd seen. The C-500 was shaped liked a fat boomerang, or a flat V if viewed from the top. Its four engines were integral, built into the fuselage instead of hanging out like some afterthought appendages. It was wide, at least two hundred feet from wingtip to wingtip, Davis guessed. The center portion was all business, thick and spacious for swallowing cargo, but the body of the craft tapered and blended into sleek wings. It was a nice design, simple and clean — the kind of design that made engineers proud. This particular airplane was tagged in the colors of a Japanese cargo carrier, a white fuselage under red accents and a logo.

"So this thing really flies," Sorensen mused. "It's such a strange shape."

"It does look different. Gets good gas mileage, though."

"The Toyota Prius of airplanes?"

"Something like that."

The JAG led them closer to the airplane and stopped near a ramp that rose on an incline up into the belly of the beast. The ramp had to be twelve feet wide and was hinged at the forward edge, integral to the structure of the C-500. Davis figured it was a feature that would make loading and unloading a cinch, another advantage over any kind of recycled passenger airframe where the cargo containers had to be lifted twenty feet in the air and shoved through doors.

Their guide spoke again, a tricky thing where his lips moved but the rest of his face seemed set in stone. He said, "Wait here, please." And that was it.

The guy marched away, and no sooner had he gone than a woman came bounding down the loading ramp with a clipboard under one arm. She smiled broadly, and her free arm stretched open in welcome — a severe contrast in hospitality to the brick who'd brought them this far.

"Hello, I am Rene Scharner." She spoke English with a stiff German accent.

Davis and Sorensen introduced themselves.

"I'm here to provide any assistance you might need," Scharner said cheerily. "I am the vice president for operations here at CargoAir."

Davis was surprised. "The VP for operations? Giving tours?"

Scharner cocked her head. "I would hardly call this a tour, Mr. Davis. We have had a very serious event. CargoAir is committed to finding the reasons for this tragedy. When I heard you were coming, I decided to personally offer any and all assistance."

Davis had the impression she meant it. "I appreciate that," he said. "I need all the help I can get. If you don't mind my asking, Miss Scharner, how long have you served in your present position?"

"I've been with CargoAir for roughly a year now. I was previously in a parallel position at Dornier."

"I see." Davis pointed to her clipboard and said, "So is there something in particular you wanted to show us?"

"Oh, this? No. Only a few last minute checks. I try to get out of my office each day and spend time on the factory floor. This particular airplane is scheduled for acceptance and delivery tomorrow."

Sorensen was peering into the cavernous opening above, and Scharner said, "Feel free to step inside. I'll join you in just a moment." She scurried off.

Sorensen and Davis exchanged a glance.

"So," he said, "let's have a look."

Davis led the way up. The incline was mild, and he envisioned a stream of pallets and cargo containers motoring up the ramp in a constant flow. When they arrived in the main hold, he stopped and studied things. The cargo area was massive, at least a hundred feet in width, maybe forty in depth. It had to out volume any conventional freighter design he'd ever seen.

Sorensen took it all in. "You could play football in here."

"Even rugby. But the tries would be hell." He stomped hard on the metal floor.

"I have to say, though, the décor is kind of basic."

Davis saw her gaze locked on the sidewalls where green primer was sprayed over metal stringers and composite siding.

He said, "It's prettier on the outside, I have to admit. But remember, Honeywell, this is a freighter. They're not going to waste any weight on carpet or plastic fittings. Nothing rides back here but boxes, and they don't care about the temperature or color schemes or how many bathrooms there are."

Scharner came bounding back up the ramp. "Impressive isn't it?"

"Very," Sorensen agreed.

Davis moved forward to a short set of metal stairs. It led up to a second, mid-level tier. "Is this the flight deck?" he asked.

"Yes," said Scharner.

He noticed a door nearby on the forward bulkhead. It was marked ELECTRONICS BAY. "Is this where the avionics are racked?"

"Yes," she said, "most of them. There is a secondary bay, but it can only be accessed on the ground from an exterior door near the nose-wheel well."

Davis stood staring at the door, eyeing it like he might want a look. Instead, he said, "Dr. Ibrahim Jaber is the chief CargoAir representative for our investigation. Does he work directly for you, Miss Scharner?"

"Yes, he does. Dr. Jaber heads the C-500 design team."

"Do you know him well?"

Scharner hesitated. "I'm not sure any of us here at headquarters would go that far. Dr. Jaber is an intensely private man. He keeps himself to himself. But I can certainly vouch for his work — it is first rate."

"That's good," Davis said. Then a vision came to mind, Jaber with his tired posture and skin the color of clay. "Can you tell me one thing — is he ill?"

"Ill?"

Davis said nothing more, only pinned his eyes to Scharner's.

"Yes," she relented, "I have had the same thoughts. Dr. Jaber has told me he's been feeling unwell for some time, but that it is nothing serious. It seems not to affect his work, so I take him at his word."

Davis caught a subtle shrug from Sorensen that echoed his own instinct. *Let it go.*

Scharner moved toward the short metal ladder at the forward edge of the cargo area. She said, "Would you like a tour of the flight deck?"

Davis grabbed the metal handhold and smiled broadly. "Yeah, I think we would."

Five steps later they found themselves on the flight deck.

It was spacious compared to some Davis had seen. Two comfortable-looking seats for the pilots, wide with a downy covering, and behind each an equally plush jumpseat mounted in tandem for observers. The forward panel was a sea of color, glass panel multifunction displays and instruments glowing with the essentials of flight — lines, symbols, a spray of alphanumeric gibberish. Every inch of space above, below, and to the sides of the crew stations had been used, plugged with control heads and switches. To a layperson it would seem overwhelming, almost haphazard. But to Davis' eye it was something else — at first glance, well organized and purposeful.

The empty captain's seat called to him. He pointed and said, "Do you mind?"

Scharner said, "Not at all. Perhaps your partner will take the first officer's seat."

Sorensen shot him a glance. Was she wondering if she should? Or had it been that word? *Partner.*

Davis said, "Go ahead."

Sorensen took the right-hand crew station. Davis got comfortable in the left seat. It was roomy compared to an F-16. And also like an

F-16, there was a joystick, but in the wrong hand, his left. A look at the instrument panel put him on more familiar ground. Basic attitude, airspeed, altitude, and compass. The usual information. It wasn't presented in the traditional *T* arrangement of round dials, but a more modern variant of vertical tape scales. Accurate and easier to comprehend — at least that's what the human factors Ph.D.s would tell you. To Davis it was all just one big video game.

Sorensen said, "It smells like a new car."

"This is a cargo airplane, Honeywell, so it can't be from the rows of leather seats. More likely toxic fumes from some kind of adhesive they've used."

She looked at him sourly. "Are you always such a positive person?"

"Without fail." He turned to Scharner and asked, "Is everything powered up?"

"Yes. The navigation platforms are aligned. Start the engines and she would be ready to fly."

"Assuming someone opened the hangar door," Davis quipped.

Scharner laughed. "Yes, that would be required."

Davis looked overhead. He saw switches involving flight controls, electrics, and hydraulics. He asked, "Would you do me a favor?"

"Of course," Scharner said.

"Let's turn down all the lights — the overheads, the worklight. I want it to look just like it would in flight, at night."

The technician turned a half-dozen knobs and the cockpit got darker. But there was still one problem. Davis gave a sideways nod out the front window where the hangar lights still blazed.

"The hangar lights?" Scharner queried, the first tinge of annoyance coloring her tone.

"All of them. Please."

"I'll have to do it myself."

Davis smiled.

Scharner relented.

"All right," she said, pointing out the window. "I will be on that scaffolding, near the exit door. Flash the dome light when you want me to turn everything back on."

She left Davis and Sorensen alone.

"What are you up to?" Sorensen asked.

It had been in the back of his mind ever since he'd heard it on the voice tape. *Click, click.* "I'm trying to simulate the last two hundred fifty milliseconds before we lost the voice recorder."

"Two hundred fifty milliseconds?"

"In the middle of the dive, right before we lost the recorder, there was a very distinct sound. I think it was two switches being actuated. You see, the voice recorder has a built-in capacitor that functions like a tiny battery. When it loses power, the recorder will still operate for a quarter of a second."

"And that's significant?"

"Very. I think it recorded the sound of the very switches that were used to shut it down."

Sorensen seemed to get it. She tilted her head back and scanned the overhead panel. "Now if we only knew which ones. There must be a hundred buttons and knobs."

"Sure. But only a few would have the desired effect."

The lights in the hangar suddenly went dark, and the instruments in front of them dimmed, adapting automatically to the lower level of light outside. Even so, the glowing displays seemed bright in contrast to the newfound darkness all around. Davis put his head back and closed his eyes. He put himself in an airplane that was diving severely, headed for an uncomfortable meeting with some picturesque French countryside.

What did you do, Earl? What would I do?

The solution that came to mind was fundamental. Every type of airplane had slight variances in design, but there were certain absolutes. Davis opened his eyes, looked up — and there they were. It all made perfect sense. Just as Earl Moore would have done, Davis reached up fast, slapped back two plastic safety guards and actuated the switches.

Click-click.

Everything went black.

CHAPTER THIRTY-THREE

"Jammer!"

Sorensen's voice came sharp through the pitch darkness. The tone didn't carry fear. It asked, *What the hell are you doing?*

"Hang on," he said, "I'm counting." His fingers were still on the two switches. They had to be or he might not find them again in the dark — probably just what Earl Moore had done. *Seven, eight, nine* —

"Now!" Davis said.

Two more clicks and the lights came back on. He looked over the displays in front of him. The primary flight instruments came right back. Elsewhere there were a few flags, some amber warnings, but these systems soon righted themselves. After twenty seconds, the only thing amiss was the ship's clock in one corner, flashing 12:00 like a cheap alarm clock after a thunderstorm.

He said, "That's it! That's what happened!"

Sorensen blinked as her eyes adjusted. She looked at the labels on the switches, trying to understand. "B-A-T? You turned off the batteries?"

"I turned off everything. On the C-500 these two battery switches control electrical power to all the busses. Turn them off, and virtually everything shuts down."

Sorensen remarked, "And you're saying the captain did that?"

"Yes. Only he did it while they were screaming at the ground at nearly the speed of sound."

"Jeez. That would have taken some pretty big — well, you know."

"Yeah. But I don't think he was finding a lot of alternatives at the time." Davis cycled the overhead dome light on and off twice. The fluorescent hangar lights outside staggered back to life. "And if you ask me, there's only one reason he'd do something so drastic."

"I can't imagine."

"I think Earl Moore was holding a joystick in his hand that wasn't responding. I don't think he had any control whatsoever over that airplane."

The drive back to Lyon passed quickly. Davis thought out loud, bouncing ideas off Sorensen while she drove.

Before leaving the factory, he had asked Scharner for an aircraft systems manual. In the Air Force, they called it a Dash-1, and the C-500's was a four-inch-thick doorstop. It described, from an operator's viewpoint, every system on the aircraft. Electric, hydraulic, fuel, air conditioning. While Sorensen drove, Davis pored over the sections labeled "Flight Controls" and "Automatic Flight." He studied diagrams and control law and flow charts. He was sure that Earl Moore had cut off all power because he'd lost control of World Express 801. And the shallow dive angle at impact proved that he had almost figured things out in time to save the airplane.

Almost.

By the time they turned into the parking lot at Building Sixty-two, Davis was in a slow burn. He closed the flight manual as Sorensen pulled into a parking spot. The sun had set, and darkness blotted the nearby buildings to mere silhouettes. With the Fiat's engine off, cold began to seep in. He felt it pulling from the window, drifting over his feet. Davis made no attempt to move. He knew he had to be calm, had to think about his approach.

He had already called ahead. Bastien was here, working late. He hadn't sounded thrilled about a meeting and was even more reluctant when Davis told him to make it alone. So Davis had insisted. And the investigator-in-charge had agreed.

Sorensen said, "Refresh me, Jammer. Why are we here?"

"To have a word with Monsieur Bastien."

"So you're convinced that we're dealing with a problem in the flight control software?"

"It's the only thing that makes sense."

"And you're going to tell him what you discovered at the factory about turning off the battery switches?"

"I'm going to tell him a lot of things."

Davis fell silent. He watched the headlights on a nearby street flow in steady circulation. He watched airplanes take off and land from the runway in the distance, their blinking beacons and intense landing lights guiding them through darkness. In his mind, Davis added things up. It was a lot of math, and in the middle of it all he felt a hand on his arm. He looked over and saw Sorensen trying to read him.

"Are you okay?" she asked.

"No."

"Don't do anything silly, Jammer. Can you imagine what would happen if you got kicked off this investigation?"

"I'd go home and see my daughter. That's what would happen." He saw the seriousness of her expression. "Look, Honeywell, don't worry. Bastien is due some pain, and I'm looking forward to delivering it. But I won't do anything that will involve his dentist, if that's what you're thinking."

She looked relieved. "Can I?"

He grinned. Which was probably what she was after.

"So am I invited to this meeting?"

He almost said no. Davis hadn't been counting on it. But then he had second thoughts. "Yes. I *would* like you to come."

"Because?"

"When your weapons are dull, Honeywell, strike thine enemy with greater force and repetition."

She took a stab. "Sun Tzu? *The Art of War*?"

He shook his head. "Jammer Davis. The game of rugby."

Darlene Graham walked into the Oval Office as a shell-shocked director of Homeland Security was walking out.

President Townsend was standing, looking beleaguered himself.

"We've found something, Mr. President."

Townsend seemed not to hear. He said, "The lines at gas stations are getting huge. People are panicking, filling up milk jugs and water bottles. What the hell good is a ration plan if there's nothing left to ration?"

"Dr. Coyle said to expect a short period of widespread unavailability. The supply system will gradually catch up once rationing has begun."

"Twenty gallons a week," the president said, "for each licensed driver. That's what the secretary of energy has come up with. But it's only preliminary. I think it might go lower. We'll need to make adjustments for people who use their cars for work. Taxi drivers, Meals-on-Wheels. How the hell—"

"*Mr. President*," Graham interrupted loudly.

Townsend's attention came full. "Sorry, Darlene. This is a little overwhelming. Thank God I've got three and a half years until re-election. What is it?"

"We have something on Caliph, sir."

This got his attention. "Something?"

"Early this morning a package was dropped at our embassy in Geneva. It was sent by someone who claims to know Caliph's whereabouts."

"I'd reckon a lot of people *say* they know where he is. We've slapped a pretty hefty reward on his head."

"Yes, and that was clearly the motivation in this case."

The president bit. "Okay. What makes you think this one is on the up-and-up?"

Graham said, "You've been briefed on our DNA identification program, right? The one for high-value targets?"

The politician in Townsend winced at the word "targets." But he was aware of it. "I believe it's a CIA program."

"Yes, for big-name terrorists. We try to track down family members, the closer in the bloodline the better, and take samples for analysis. Clans in the Middle East tend to be big, so we can usually find somebody who will either take a bribe for a mouth swab or just plain doesn't like their violent uncle. Once we have a sample, we keep it on file. That way, if we ever get a bead on the target and strike, we have a quick and sure way to identify remains and confirm the kill."

"Okay," the president said, "so you're saying we have a sample on Caliph?"

Graham nodded.

"And what happened in Geneva? Did somebody send a piece of him to our Swiss Embassy?"

"Maybe."

Townsend's eyes narrowed. He'd meant it as a joke. "You can't be serious."

"We got a vial of blood that we're currently analyzing. It takes time. But there was also a copy of a report from a very reputable German laboratory. It showed the DNA profile of a second sample. This test was performed over a year ago, and we've already confirmed its authenticity with the lab. The data matches their records precisely."

"And?"

"The test results from last year are almost certainly Caliph. We should have results on the new blood sample in a day or so — like I said, it takes time."

"But what you have *today* is a lab report that matches Caliph and a random blood sample. That's a little thin to get excited about, Darlene."

"I know, I know. It could just be a lab tech trying to make a quick buck. But we haven't had many breaks in our search for Caliph. We're following it up."

"All right," the president agreed. "And what does that involve?"

"Whoever gave us this sample has asked for a meeting in Geneva."

"When?"

Graham looked at her watch. "In about six minutes."

CHAPTER THIRTY-FOUR

Hans Sprecht was not nervous. In truth, the idea of meeting clandestinely with someone from the CIA had grown on him. It was exciting, even dramatic. And in any event, he felt far more comfortable dealing with American intelligence agents than his increasingly nefarious patients.

He walked along the quai Gustave Ador, a busy thoroughfare that snaked through the central city and fronted Lake Geneva. Cars whisked by as cars did in Switzerland, in an organized, quick flow. As he neared the rendezvous point, Sprecht's attention was drawn to a small bird darting in and out of the street. The creature was trying to get hold of something in the road, perhaps a small insect. Yet each passing car proved a foil, the bird forced to flutter away at the last second. He thought, *You risk a lot for a meal, my friend.* Sprecht kept going, not wanting to know the outcome.

It was a terrifically cold day, soon to become an even colder evening. The air retained a dry, almost brittle quality, and the other people Sprecht saw were not near the park, but rather across the street, well-wrapped and scooting toward the warmth of cars, homes, and shops. That being the case, he had no trouble finding his contact.

As instructed, he was waiting near a quaint river ferry that was stilled for the season on a solidly frozen Rhone River. Also as instructed, he wore a brown scarf, a theatrical touch Sprecht had not been able to resist at the time, but something he now regretted as amateurish. The man was rather short and heavyset, which seemed a disappointment. But then Sprecht chided himself for such a meandering thought. It was crucial that he stay focused on the only thing that mattered — the deal, reaching acceptable terms and conditions.

Sprecht had, at least, resisted the temptation to require any code words or silly phrases. He simply walked straight up to the man, on schedule, and said in strongly accented English, "Hello, I am Dr. Hans Sprecht."

The CIA man forced a smile that looked vaguely familiar. This puzzled Sprecht momentarily, for he had certainly never met the man. Then he realized it was merely the expression he recognized. It had been present on certain men and women who'd set upon his practice in the old days, the more hardened sellers of medical equipment and pharmaceuticals. It was the empty smile of a hustler, a practiced liar.

"Hello, Dr. Sprecht. My name is Edwards." The reply was in effortless German, the man's breath going to vapor in the cold. The name was certainly an alias, and Sprecht gave the man a knowing look.

"Edwards" held out a guiding arm and they began to walk, the CIA man steering toward the park. The walking paths were covered in a mix of fresh snow and old slush, and Sprecht's brand-new friend gave a turn to his brand-new brown scarf to repel the cold. He said, "We have not yet completed our work of analyzing the sample you've given us."

Sprecht had anticipated this. "But you have verified the laboratory report. You know I hold valuable information regarding Caliph."

"We know you have access to a lab report that probably involves him."

They came to the Promenade du Lac and turned to follow the shore of the frigid Rhone. Sprecht lost his footing momentarily on the icy sidewalk, and the CIA man caught his elbow, helped him right himself. They exchanged a look, but neither spoke. Sprecht immediately started walking again, feeling foolish. His eager anticipation of this meeting was slipping as well. Sprecht had no desire to joust with the man. He suddenly wanted only to get their business done. Arrange his payment and disappear.

"I can tell you where to find him. This will entitle me to receive the full reward, no?"

Sprecht saw a qualified nod. "Yes . . ." the man hesitated, "but the source of your information, it puzzles us. How does a — how shall I put it — a retired Swiss plastic surgeon know the whereabouts of the world's most wanted terrorist?"

It did not surprise Sprecht that the CIA had moved quickly to discover his identity, what he did for a living. It had likely come when they'd researched and authenticated the lab report. He was ready. "Is that not a question," he said coyly, "which tends to answer itself?"

The man stopped and stared at Sprecht. "Tell us where you think he is, Doctor. If your information is accurate, we will be pleased to pay the entire amount."

This was most of what Sprecht wanted to hear. However, he too had done his homework. Sprecht was familiar with the gray means of moving black money. He dictated his terms and handed over a card with account numbers carefully typed. He watched as the man studied them, and reasoned from the look on his face that the CIA was indeed serious. Sprecht's terms were solid.

The American nodded.

The deal struck, Sprecht could now only pray that his information would hold true. If not, he had more to sell, but the price would be something less.

He said, "Caliph is in Mosul, Iraq."

The man whose name was anything but Edwards asked, "Where in Mosul?"

Sprecht told him. Then he told him *how* he knew.

"You want what?" The clerk stared at the huge woman, trying to be polite as they fenced in broken English.

"Screen — you know, for bugs." She made a wiggling, flying motion with the fingers on one hand. Her other hand was occupied with a store basket that held an assortment of items from at least three other aisles — a hammer, a screwdriver, tacks, spray lubricant, and a utility knife.

"*Insecte?*" He was about to tell the wench that they didn't sell insecticide when he realized what she meant. "*Moustiquaire!*"

He led her away and turned down the aisle where the window frames and moldings were stocked. Halfway down, a six-foot roll of window screening was shoved back into a shelf. He pulled it out and wiped off the dust — the stuff hadn't caught on yet in France.

"How much do you want?" he asked, reverting to French.

She looked confused, so the clerk made a snipping motion with two fingers. Then he held out his arms at varying widths to suggest measurement.

She grabbed roughly and took the whole thing under one arm. Her face was curled and sour. Without so much as a "*merci*," she waddled away, dragging the filthy roll of screen behind her. There was probably enough material to cover a dozen windows, the clerk thought.

Stupid immigrants.

They found Bastien in his makeshift office.

The room was on the second floor, a suite with large plate glass windows that overlooked the hangar bay. There, wreckage was accumulating fast, and dour workers in orange jumpsuits crawled over everything, examining and recording — pressing ahead to the inevitable truth of what had brought down World Express 801.

When Davis and Sorensen came in, Bastien was seated behind his desk studying a file. He looked tired, like he hadn't slept well. Or maybe he'd just missed his evening espresso. He didn't rise to greet them, but acknowledged their presence by saying, "I hope this is truly important. I am very busy right now." The words were taut, edgy.

Davis answered by closing the door very slowly. When the latch fell into place it did so with finality — *clunk*, loud and solid. Lockdown. This got Bastien's attention. He closed the file in front of him and tapped at its sides deliberately with two sets of fingers. Straightening, organizing. Davis hadn't seen what was in the manila folder, but it was very thin. Could have been empty. He guessed it held one page.

There was already a chair facing Bastien, and another was pushed against the far wall. Davis dragged over the spare to make a pair, and he and Sorensen sat. Sorensen kept silent — that had been their arrangement, although Davis hadn't told her why. He began in a calm, level voice.

"Miss Sorensen and I spent this morning in Marseille. We looked over the CargoAir factory and sat in a C-500. Have you ever seen one?" Davis jerked a thumb toward the big window. "Besides that one?"

Bastien ignored this and asked, "Surely you did not go all the way to Marseille for a factory tour. What were you looking for?"

"I wanted to check on something that's really been bothering me. You see, in the last few seconds of this crash, shortly before the airplane hit, we lost the voice recorder. And the air traffic controllers lost their transponder data at the same time. Exactly the same time. I figure the whole airplane lost power, had some kind of electrical interruption. Wouldn't that make sense?"

Bastien was silent.

"So I decided to look into it. Miss Sorensen and I went down and sat in a real airplane. That's always a good thing to do, Terry. Try to replicate things as they were at the time of the crash. And you know what? I discovered that the power *did* go out. Can you imagine how?"

Bastien made a quixotic stab. "The ship was traveling at an extreme speed — some kind of structural damage could easily have brought about an interruption of electrical power, perhaps tripped a generator off line."

Davis continued in a steady, unwavering tone. "The power went off because the captain turned it off." There was a glimmer of hope in Bastien's eyes. Davis removed it. "But this wasn't something sinister. In fact, it was pretty valiant, given the circumstances of the moment. And it almost worked. If Earl Moore had shut down power ten seconds sooner, I think they would have made it."

"They were running an emergency checklist. Are you saying that he was performing some part of it?"

"No, quite the opposite. It was pure intuition on the captain's part. A hunch, the kind of thing that is at the foundation of putting—" Davis paused, "experienced people in positions of importance."

Bastien stood abruptly and walked to the window. He stood silhouetted by the ever-intense hangar lights and dug his hands deep into the pockets of his neatly pressed trousers. His shirt looked the same—starched and stiff. Almost like that's what was holding him up. Davis gestured to the file on Bastien's desk.

He said, "The toxicology report on the crew was due today. Is that it?"

Bastien nodded, still facing the open hangar.

"And it's negative. Alcohol, drugs, carbon monoxide. Everything negative. There was no chemical impairment on the part of either pilot, no loss of cabin pressure."

Bastien turned immediately and opened his mouth to speak.

"Human factors," Davis said, cutting him off.

"I beg your pardon?"

"You were going to ask me how I could know all that. Human factors. That's the term you guys use, right? You see, Terry, I know you have a Ph.D. in clinical psychology and all, but this isn't a clinic. It's the real world, with real people. And I understand people. Which is strange, because I don't always get along with them—you know, in a social way. But I know what makes them tick. I'm pretty sure I understand Earl Moore. I understand exactly what he did and why he did it. So now I'm trying to understand you."

Davis let that settle.

"This toxicology report is only preliminary," Bastien argued. "Far from conclusive."

Davis ignored the comment. "Some of the things you've done, professor, they don't measure up."

"What are you talking about?"

"I'm talking about hotel bar tabs, press conferences, dead horses, popped circuit breakers. Being a man of science, I'll let you pick the metric."

Bastien glared, but Davis saw no fire behind it. This was not a man about to corkscrew himself into the ceiling and toss them from his office. Which he could have done. Thierry Bastien was a man getting washed away, his thoughts channeled into that deep groove dug by fact after inescapable fact.

With a nod toward his partner, Davis said, "Do you know what happened to me and Miss Sorensen last night? We were accosted. A group of four thugs tried to hurt us. Maybe worse." Davis saw something in Bastien's gaze. He'd scored a hit.

"There are dangerous sections in every town," Bastien said weakly. "Living in America, surely you know this."

"It might have been that, just a random bad experience. But I'm going to find out. And you know what else, Terry? I'm going to find out why this airplane crashed. It might take some time, but the cause *will* become clear. You see, I'm going to take this whole investigation and dump it into a big sifter. And then I'm going to start shaking. Bit by bit, little pieces of mud and filth are going to get rinsed out, and in the end I'll be standing there with a few shiny nuggets of truth. Right there in broad day —"

"All right, Mr. Davis! All right!" Bastien roared. "You have made your point. I admit that my theory about a possible suicide involving the captain — it was premature." He slapped the file on his desk. "This evidence does not support it. I can understand that you are upset."

Davis did not raise his voice. He stayed firm in his chair and, if anything, his words fell more quiet. "You don't read me right, Terry. I'm not upset. I'm actually very content." Davis turned his palms inward. "This is me when I'm content. You see, I'm sure that everything is going to become very clear. Very soon. Which brings me to Miss Sorensen."

Davis saw Sorensen stiffen in her chair. He hadn't told her what was coming — hadn't asked because she might have said no. He addressed a motionless Bastien. "Have you noticed Miss Sorensen? I mean, I know she's cute and all, but have you *really* noticed her?"

This got Bastien's attention. He looked at her suspiciously.

"She doesn't have a lot of input into our investigation, does she? She listens, but doesn't say much. That's because she's not really an accident investigator. In fact, she doesn't even work for Honeywell."

Sorensen shot him a look that asked, *Do you know what you're doing?* Davis gave her a subtle raised finger.

Bastien said, "I hope you will not tell me that she is some kind of reporter."

"Oh, no. For you, far worse. She works for the CIA."

Bastien's eyes went wide.

"Yes. *That* CIA," Davis said.

"Why would American intelligence be interested in our proceedings? This is wholly unacceptable!" Bastien sank into his chair and addressed Sorensen. "We cannot have someone such as yourself involved in this inquiry. I will see to it that your credentials are revoked immediately!"

Davis said, "I'm not sure you want to do that. You see, her presence here has nothing to do with airplanes or safety reports. There are some very suspicious people connected to this inquiry, the kind of people the CIA watches. The kind of people who confront others on sidewalks with knives and guns."

That did it. Bastien cracked.

He slumped forward on the desk, two hands concealing his face until they rubbed back along the sides of his head. The man that was then revealed looked instantly older, haggard.

Davis stood and leaned forward over the desk. But it wasn't with menace. He looked Bastien squarely in the eyes, and for the first time pronounced his name correctly. "Thierry . . . tell me what the hell is going on."

Bastien nodded, looked at Davis, then Sorensen. He seemed close to tears.

"Yes. Yes, I must tell someone."

CHAPTER THIRTY-FIVE

Fatima dragged her purchases up the service stairs. The wooden steps creaked, challenged under her weight. Her load was not particularly taxing, yet the long roll of screen was awkward and she struggled, especially at the narrow switchback landings. The elevator would have been far easier, but most of the residents used it. Having arranged her lease only days ago, Fatima had no desire to meet her new neighbors.

She reached the fifth floor completely winded. Fatima let herself into the apartment, dropped her purchases, and leaned on a table to catch her breath. The place wasn't much to look at. Then again, given that she had been raised in a mud-brick shanty with dirt floors, it was a step higher in the world than she might once have imagined. And soon she would go higher yet.

Once she'd caught her breath, she laid everything on the floor. Fatima took the screwdriver in hand and dragged a chair to the closet. Standing on the chair, she began to pull screws from the shelf bracket at the top. The shelf was heavy wood, five feet long and over an inch thick. She struggled mightily, yet even with all the screws removed she could not get the thing loose. Fatima retrieved the utility knife and began carving around the edges of the board, slicing through countless layers of paint that had accumulated over the years to bond the shelf to the walls. Slowly, she wiggled it free.

In the middle of the room, she shoved aside a chair to make a clear area big enough for her next job. On hands and knees, Fatima rolled out the screen and gauged the window, knowing she could err on the large side. She started cutting with the utility knife, and right away realized she should have bought scissors. The knife cut the screen well enough, but it also carved a rut in the wood floor, and became awkward when the rug underneath came into play. She kept going, though, slicing a neat path that nearly split the old rug in two.

Once the screen was shaped, she stood and evaluated the rest. Moving the furniture would be the trickiest part — doing so without getting complaints from whoever lived below. She decided that if anyone knocked, she would simply not answer. Once everything was ready, there could be no plausible explanation for the appearance of the room.

Fatima took the hammer and, as an experiment, tapped gently along the window casing. The wood was old and brittle. She realized that if she got too close to the edge the frame would crack and splinter. Fatima went to her little pile and retrieved the can of spray lubricant. Back at the window, she went to work.

"Can you protect me?" Bastien pleaded.

He was looking at Sorensen as he said it, so Davis figured he was referring to the CIA. Davis traded a glance with her, and said, "Protect you against who?"

Bastien rubbed his hands together. "It began on the night I was put in charge. You see, this was the first time I had ever been chosen to oversee an investigation. I was quite pleased with the honor, and so to celebrate I went to dinner in Paris with two of my colleagues from the university. It was nearly midnight when I returned home. Three men were waiting for me."

"They had broken into your house?" Davis asked.

Bastien nodded vigorously. "I told them to leave, to get out. I threatened to call the police. They only ignored me. I did not know what to do."

Davis said, "Do you know who they were?"

"Two were immigrants, North African, I think. Dark skin and hair. One of them was very big, very tall. The other I cannot describe. Perhaps he seemed more European than the others."

Davis traded a glance with Sorensen. She was thinking the same thing.

"And the third man?"

Bastien hesitated mightily. "It was Jaber."

"*Our* Dr. Jaber?" Davis exclaimed.

Bastien nodded. "I had never met the man before, but knew him by reputation and had seen his picture in a trade magazine. I could not imagine what CargoAir's chief engineer was doing trespassing in my home . . ." he hesitated mightily, "carrying a suitcase full of cash."

"Cash?" said Sorensen.

"A hundred thousand euros, perhaps more. I don't know. I have not even looked at it."

Davis realized what this implied—that the suitcase was still at Bastien's house. The investigator-in-charge was in some serious trouble. He said, "What did Jaber want?"

"It was very strange. He wanted me to delay the investigation, go through all the procedural movements, but get nothing done for a time. He said CargoAir needed a few days to prepare for certain matters. If I could only delay things briefly, the money would be mine."

Sorensen asked, "You're saying CargoAir needed time to get ready for this investigation?"

"I assumed they had shortcomings, perhaps involving records or questionable data. Jaber said he would let me know when everything was in order. At that time, I would be free to proceed as I wished with the investigation. He made it sound so very—" Bastien paused again and crossed his arms tightly, "simple."

"And you agreed," Davis said flatly.

"No!" Bastien insisted. "I protested. But then the other man, the smaller one, he threatened me."

"How?" Sorensen asked.

"I . . . I don't know!" an agitated Bastien said. "He was not specific. He only said that if I went to the authorities or failed to heed Jaber's instructions, they would be back." Bastien was crumbling fast. He was pale, his gaze unfocused.

Davis looked at Sorensen. She gave her head a subtle shake. They both knew he was done.

The Frenchman addressed Sorensen with pleading blue eyes. "Can you please help me, mademoiselle? I have now violated their directives. Surely you can give me some kind of protection."

"Yes," she said, "I'll arrange something. Probably the local police. But I'll have to go through proper channels."

If the thought of police involvement bothered Bastien, it didn't show. He actually looked relieved, like Atlas free of his burden. Davis didn't like the vagueness of it all. He kept wondering what Jaber was trying to accomplish. Whatever it was, the money and intimidation proved he was serious.

Davis prompted Sorensen by spinning a finger — *let's move*. She nodded.

They gave Bastien firm instructions to stay in his office and promised to have the security man downstairs stand at his door until something better was arranged. When they left, Thierry Bastien was catatonic in his chair, staring blankly at the walls.

They rushed down the hallway, Sorensen slightly behind. Halfway to the front of the building, she grabbed Davis by the arm and whipped him around. "Don't you ever do that again, mister!"

Davis stood dumbstruck. "Do what?"

"Blow my cover. If you want to use my job title for theatrical reasons, you tell me first!"

Davis said, "It worked, didn't it?" He turned away. "Come on, we don't have time for —"

"Jammer!" she yelled.

Davis stopped, stared at her impatiently. Then he gave it some thought. "Okay, you're right. I'm sorry."

She met his gaze on equal, hard terms.

"I *swear*, Anna . . . never again." It was the first time he had used her real name. It did the trick.

"All right," Sorensen said, seeming satisfied.

They started walking again.

"Other than that," she said, "I thought you handled Bastien pretty well."

"You sound surprised."

"I guess I expected a little more volume, maybe some bad words."

"Bad words? No way. That's Navy stuff. I never worked there."

She asked, "How much of Bastien's story do you buy?"

"Most of it. The part about CargoAir needing extra time is rubbish, though. If an airplane manufacturer makes a design mistake or has lousy recordkeeping, they don't fix it with suitcases full of cash."

"I don't know, Jammer. Remember, CargoAir is flush with oil money from the Middle East, Russia. In those parts of the world that's how business is done." Then she said, "What about the two guys Jaber had with him? Do you think they were the same ones we met last night?"

"Probably. So tell me, can you really get Bastien any kind of protection?"

"I have no idea."

Davis glanced at her and Sorensen shrugged defensively. "What was I supposed to say?" She was nearly running to keep up with his strides. "But why would CargoAir do something like this? What could be the point of bogging down the investigation?"

"CargoAir has orders booked for hundreds of airplanes. If they suspect there's a glitch in the flight control software, they might want time to try and isolate the problem."

"Or," she suggested, "maybe they already know exactly what the problem is. Maybe they want a chance to erase it, put a fix in the code before anyone finds out."

"Good point. But for us, either case results in the same endgame."

"Which is?"

"Just what I suggested yesterday — ground the entire fleet."

"Oh, sure. And how do we do that?"

"We get details, specifics. And I know just who has them."

He led to the receptionist's desk at the front of the building. A new woman was parked there, a dour young creature with questioning brown eyes behind tortoise-shell glasses.

"Dr. Jaber!" Davis barked as he closed in.

"Pardon?" she said.

"Dr. Jaber — is he in the building?"

"I believe he left, perhaps an hour ago."

Davis turned to Sorensen. "He's not staying at the hotel, is he?"

She shrugged. "I've never seen him there."

Davis turned back to the receptionist. "Where does he stay?"

"I cannot give out such information, sir. Even to a member of—"

Davis moved. She had said she couldn't *give* information—not that she didn't *have* it. He circled around to the business side of her desk and opened the biggest file drawer.

"Sir! You cannot do this!"

Davis did it anyway. He found the personnel files, everyone with investigation credentials arranged in nice alphabetical order. He flicked through the tabs and found JABER, opened it and began scanning for a local address.

"Laurent!" the receptionist cried.

The lone security guard got up from his chair and started over. "Monsieur!"

Ignoring the guard, Davis found the address and memorized it. He saw a note that suggested Jaber was staying with his aunt. He put the file back, between T and U, and said, "Thanks," adding a smile for the receptionist.

The guard closed in.

He was roughly Sorensen's height. Roughly Sorensen's weight. Which meant that he tipped the scales at about Jammer Davis, divided by two. And chances were, unlike Sorensen, he wasn't an Olympic-class practitioner of any martial art. Still, he had the confidence a guy gets from an embroidered security company badge and striped epaulets on his shoulders. He also had a thick belt full of accessories. A flashlight, a radio, and a couple of pouches that probably held keys and flex cuffs and maybe some pepper spray. Most conspicuously, there was no sidearm.

The guy came to within an arm's length of Davis and put a finger in his chest. "Sir, if you persist I will have your credentials!"

Davis looked at the guy's finger. Then he leaned forward slowly on the balls of his feet. It wasn't good posture for a fight. Wasn't good in terms of center of gravity or room to maneuver. But if they had happened to be outside, particularly any time near the middle of a day, Davis' profile would have blocked out the sun.

Total eclipse.

He delivered his words in his most persuasive manner — slow and low. "And if *you* persist, I will put your nuts in that drawer and slam it closed so hard you'll need a crowbar to get them out."

The guard took a step back. Then another. He pulled his weapon of choice from his belt — the radio. Laurent was calling for backup. Davis didn't feel like waiting. He turned to Sorensen and said, "Let's go."

The receptionist actually snorted. The guard stood tall, but not as tall as Davis, who strode past with Sorensen in tow. On the way out, he called over his shoulder, "You both need to go up and report to the investigator-in-charge. He needs you immediately!"

Outside, Sorensen said, "You really know how to make an impression on people."

Davis said nothing.

"Jammer, are you sure this is wise? We can't just go to Jaber and accuse him of shaking down the investigation. We have to get the BEA involved now, the French authorities."

"No time."

"But Jammer —"

"Car!"

They found the Fiat and climbed in. She looked at him plaintively. "Why not —"

"Go!"

She put the key in the ignition. "You really have that nickname because you talk too much?"

"Yes."

CHAPTER THIRTY-SIX

The raid took four hours to coordinate. It was carried out by the Iraqi Army, which had taken full responsibility for such matters. The home in question had already been subject to some scrutiny in recent months, and for a short time had even been quietly monitored. In the course of that surveillance, there had never been anything suspicious, any cause for a physical breach.

Tonight there was.

The woman who owned the house was a second cousin to Caliph, a spinster who spent her days selling dates and figs behind a pushcart at the market. They knew going in that she was a widow, a result of the Iran-Iraq war, and that she lived with her mother, a woman of nearly ninety.

It was almost ten in the evening when a squad of Iraqi Army regulars arrived at the front door. They didn't bother to knock. A rifle butt did the trick for entry, and six men swept from room to room, clearing as they went — not much of a feat since there were only four rooms to deal with. The two women were rousted from their beds. Once the place had been declared secure, the captain in charge ordered a more thorough search. Soldiers began to turn over beds and shove furniture aside.

It was a junior man who spotted the giveaway glance from the younger of the two women huddled in the corner. He saw her eyes dart toward a large bin of dates at the back of the kitchen. The bin looked heavy, but the soldier saw tracks where dust on the floor nearby had been disturbed. He gave the bin a shove and, much to his surprise, found that it moved easily. He yelled for his commander.

The captain came at a trot. "What is it?"

The young soldier showed him the bin, showed him how freely it moved. "It must be on wheels," he said.

The captain called the rest of the squad over. Everyone kept their weapons trained loosely on the foot of the bin. On the officer's order, the container was pulled clear, indeed sliding easily across the hardpan floor. And there it was. They had found their spider hole.

The entrance was three feet square, and a wooden ladder dropped down into the earth. The soldiers peered cautiously below. On closer inspection, they saw that the space was more than just a simple nook for hiding. It was a basement of sorts. At the bottom, there was little distinguishable beyond a dirt floor, but bright electric light streamed up from the passageway. The men stood stockstill, the business ends of their weapons addressed without compromise on the narrow opening. The captain listened intently but, aside from the rapid breathing of his men and a muffled wail from one of the women, he heard nothing. There was, however, a distinct smell wafting up from the pit. The rank signature of human feces.

The captain gave his orders, pointing to one of the men. "Guard those two wenches. If either moves, shoot them both." Then another, "Husam, go outside and get Seven Squad."

The second unit involved in the raid had formed a perimeter outside, but the commander wanted all his firepower now that a frontal assault seemed inevitable. He knew all too well what had happened the last time, when the Americans had tangled with Caliph. The soldier ran out of the room, and minutes later came back with six more men. To explain the situation, the captain simply pointed to the gaping, silent hole.

"I need two volunteers," the captain said. He immediately regretted it — no one spoke up. Taking a deep breath, he checked that his weapon was on full automatic and put a foot on the ladder. "Husam, come!" he whispered sharply.

The captain's first inclination was to go down the ladder slowly, but the tactical repercussions of that seemed negative. His eyes were locked below, yet he could still see nothing beyond a dirt floor pock-marked with footprints. Four feet from the bottom, the captain cleared the area below and jumped. He landed awkwardly and promptly fell on his butt, an incident he would later recount as a tactical rolling ma-neuver. Rising quickly to one knee, he scanned the room, his weapon trained and ready. It was much larger than he'd expected, perhaps eight meters square. He saw no immediate threat, but there was a single passageway, and at the end of that a closed door. *Another room?* he wondered.

He waved Husam down. When he arrived, the two men stood to-gether and tried to comprehend their surroundings. They saw furni-ture and boxes of supplies. One corner was overrun with medical equipment—a hospital gurney, a heart monitor, an IV pole, the whole lot covered with dust. Stranger still, in another corner was a collection of video equipment, including a large white screen that hung vertically from the ceiling—a photographer's backdrop. It was a peculiar col-lection, the captain thought, but better that than crates full of guns or rocket-propelled grenades.

The remaining room to be cleared loomed large. The captain called down two more men, then he approached the passageway slowly with Husam at his side, their rifles trained on the door. Using a visual signal, the captain commanded that Husam would be first this time. He saw the young man swallow hard as they set themselves.

The captain kicked and the door flew open. Husam rushed into the opening. The captain watched his man turn ninety degrees to the right and freeze.

Husam shouted, "Don't move! Don't move! Don't move!"

The captain expected a barrage of gunfire at any second. He could actually see Husam's finger shaking on the trigger of his weapon.

But nothing happened.

The captain burst into the room, twisted right with his own weapon poised. And then he saw it for himself. A man sitting on a bed, propped up by pillows. He was motionless, his eyes fixed to a television on the far side of the room that glowed with glittering static. The audio speaker on the television had been ripped out and a pair of wires dangled limply from the vacant compartment in the plastic frame. As for the man, there could be no doubt. It was Caliph.

The two soldiers let the muzzles of their weapons drop.

The captain said, "Blessed is Allah."

Caliph did not respond. Caliph only sat still — his eyes as dull and blank as a clouded night sky.

Herman Coyle's task was not an easy one, but he had a godsend.

Her name was Marta Ventrovsky. She was an Estonian transplant with an advanced degree in applied mathematics. Her obscure corner of expertise involved using computers to whittle massive amounts of data into smaller, more chewable bits. Not yet naturalized, she worked for the FBI on a contract basis. Yet when Coyle had explained to the director the specific talent he needed, there was no second choice. Marta Ventrovsky was made available.

Ventrovsky used a finger to guide Coyle's eyes over her latest sort. Still on the kind side of forty, she was blonde, statuesque, and legitimately excited about the practical applications of her arcane work. "Here. You see? More heets."

Hits, Coyle had learned, were a good thing. Hits backed up Coyle's revelation. It was the timing of the refinery attacks that had fueled his curiosity. Why two separate events? Why not just attack the whole world at once? Then he had found out about Colson Industries. Another strike, another day. Evenly spaced. And now Marta Ventrovsky was shaping it all into a nice tidy package.

"Shorts, longs — all depending on industry," she said, the consonants thick under her still heavy eastern European accent. "Drilling and raw production stocks, down. Will be big decline in raw crude demand — many months. Spot prices for spring delivery, already crashed. And see here? This hedge? Is already worth nearly one billion dollars."

The laptop was smudged with prints from her index finger.

The last hour had been constant "heets" for Marta. Her computer was simply relaying information from a bank of mainframes at FBI Headquarters a few blocks away. There were literally billions of financial transactions over the period they were searching. Indeed, the period itself was only a guess. Without the help of massive computing power it would have been absolutely impossible. Fortunately, the FBI had done this before.

"Have we got any identities yet?" Coyle asked over his shoulder, addressing a young man seated at a desk. He was planted behind a computer of his own, the keyboard nearly indistinguishable amid data discs, cables, soda cans, and empty junk-food wrappers — the detritus of a life spent behind a hard drive. The kid shook his head gently so as not to dislodge the phone that was pinched between his ear and shoulder. Coyle wasn't even sure what agency he worked for, but he seemed very bright.

A new page came up on Marta's laptop screen. "Heets!" she squealed.

Coyle had to smile at the speed of his success. He knew there would be no single piece of damning evidence, no lone smoking gun. It would instead come as a matter of weight and volume — massive amounts of circumstantial data, building and accumulating, until the truth came crashing down.

He was proud that he had so accurately focused the search. Marta had needed parameters to help narrow things. Coyle had first thought of Colson Industries, and so the computers segregated the COLI ticker and searched for telltale trading patterns. A certain Swiss brokerage had been unusually active. Coyle then instructed Marta to cross reference two other stocks — Petrov I.A. and the Dutch conglomerate DSR. Both traded on the London exchange, but this didn't stop the FBI. Finally, Coyle had added a fourth company — CargoAir. That's when Marta had started screaming "heets."

They had established a concrete pattern of trades going back three years, involving a global array of markets and industries. Surely more would be uncovered as the data was filtered and digested, probably much more when commodities and margin were cross matched. But what they had already was mind-numbing in scale. It had to be worth a hundred billion dollars, Coyle thought.

The man on the phone spoke up. "Here we are!" He scribbled on a notepad, then hung up his phone. He held out a list to Coyle. "We have three names."

Coyle took the list. None of the three meant anything to him. He went to his own laptop, called up Google, and typed in one of the names. Then, on a whim, he typed a second name from the list. The search engine came up with a number of hits displaying both names. Coyle clicked on the first option and a news article from a European daily filled the screen. There was a photograph of six men, and in the text beneath they were identified. Three matched his list exactly.

Then Coyle saw their collective title. He saw *why* they were in the picture.

"Good Lord!"

CHAPTER THIRTY-SEVEN

Coyle burst down the hall to the Oval Office, but came to an abrupt halt at the entrance. Two Secret Service men blocked a door shut tight. A woman at a nearby desk controlled access, and Coyle pleaded his case. She knew who he was, so she got on the phone. The door opened thirty seconds later.

Coyle found a strange scene inside. President Townsend, Martin Spector, General Banks, and Darlene Graham were all in the room. And they all had stunned looks on their faces.

"What's happened?" Coyle asked guardedly.

Graham was the first to leave her stupor. "The Iraqis found Caliph."

"That's wonderful news!"

No one reacted.

"Isn't it?" he prodded weakly.

"He was taken alive," Graham said, "but there's a problem."

"A problem?"

"Remember, Dr. Coyle, I told you that we tried to take him out about two years ago?"

Coyle nodded.

"Well, General Banks was right about the soldier who took that shot—he *didn't* miss. Caliph took a bullet in the head. He wears a wrap around his skull now—that's how he has appeared in every recent picture."

Banks said ruefully, "I can't believe I didn't pick up on it. And he always had that damned vacant look in his eyes."

Coyle thought about this. It was true. Caliph always wore something on his head.

Graham continued, "The damage doesn't appear all that bad, at least not on the outside. Caliph has had some work done. In fact, it was his plastic surgeon who gave us the location. But the man has suffered severe brain damage. He can't speak, barely walks. And he doesn't seem to understand a thing that's said to him."

The president said, "So all those Web postings, they really *were* a PR campaign. That's why there was never any video or audio. His image has been kept alive to retain support, to keep his networks strong—with the distinct advantage that Caliph himself, such as he is, could be hidden indefinitely in a dirt cellar in Mosul." Townsend leveled his eyes on Coyle. "Dr. Coyle, didn't you say something about Caliph not being responsible for all that's been happening?"

Coyle had almost forgotten why he'd come. "Yes, I did. And now I can back it up."

He laid out the financial patterns he and Marta Ventrovsky had uncovered. He told how a group of men had been making huge financial plays on markets all over the world and explained that they had spent years putting themselves in position to benefit from the refinery strikes.

It jolted the room back to life.

Townsend said, "So you think this entire series of attacks was done for profit—not ideology?"

"Not completely," Coyle cautioned. "Those men and women who dressed in explosives and threw themselves at crude oil furnaces—they were clearly after religious martyrdom. They were the soldiers. But after hours of research, I think my team and I have identified the creators of this entire disaster."

"Who the hell are they?" General Banks demanded.

"There are six," Coyle said. "The names would mean little to you, but their titles are much more relevant. As you all know, certain oil-rich countries have been amassing tremendous wealth in recent years. However, realizing that there will someday be an end to this sole means of support, they've begun to diversify, investing in natural resources, corporations, universities. Even building entire cities from scratch."

Spector said, "But what does that have to do with wrecking refineries? No oil-rich country would do that."

"Mind you," Coyle said, "I am not talking about countries. The tool of choice for investing oil-derived dollars is the sovereign wealth fund. These funds hold incredible reserves of capital and are essentially unregulated, allowed by their respective states to be run by any committee or individual who can show a good return on investment." Coyle looked at the president, saw that his attention was full. "We have identified a network of six individuals who are in line to benefit from these attacks, by a very conservative estimate, to the tune of one hundred billion U.S. dollars."

"A hundred—"

"*Billion*," Coyle repeated. "These individuals are the principle actors of sovereign wealth funds involving five countries—Russia, Dubai, Saudi Arabia, Singapore, and Abu Dhabi."

"I thought you said six," the president remarked.

"The sixth is a Swiss national. I would place his skill more in the category of obfuscation. He is a lawyer, an expert with shell companies, offshore banking, wire transfers. For anything dirty, he creates institutional rinse cycles."

"Not expert enough," the president said. "You found him."

"But I knew where to look. Once we spotted one of these fellows, the others came easily. You see, aside from managing vast amounts of wealth, these six individuals have one very significant thing in common." Coyle paused. "They are the board of directors of CargoAir."

"You can't be serious!" Spector cried out.

The others only stared in shock.

Darlene Graham was the first to apply the knowledge. "You're saying that this entire series of disasters was instigated by . . . by a handful of billionaires looking to get richer? We're talking about the board of directors of a major multinational corporation. You expect us to believe this, Dr. Coyle?"

"I am only delivering the facts as I know them, miss. I will leave it to you to decide what they mean."

Graham said, "There's no way men of such stature could have operational control over a terrorist organization. They wouldn't get their hands that dirty. And on the other side of it, no suicide bomber is going to sacrifice himself for a bunch of financiers."

President Townsend said, "I agree, Darlene. But . . . could there be somebody in the middle who's joining the two? Bringing them together in such a way that they don't even realize it?"

General Banks said, "It would have to be somebody very, very clever."

"And if it's not Caliph," Graham added, "then who?"

Fatima Adara stood admiring her work.

In a technique she had devised years ago, two layers of screen now covered the room's only window. It would make her nearly invisible from the outside. The telltale muzzle flashes would be muted, nothing more than what might come from a flickering television in a dark room. Yet she could see outside with just enough clarity, just enough precision to complete her objective.

She had used nails along the inside frame, small gauge to keep the pounding to a minimum. The tattered old window curtains were pulled aside. As for the window itself, Fatima had lubricated the ancient metal hinges and exercised its swing mechanism until the action was smooth — probably better than it had been in forty years. Presently, the window was closed to hold the heat, but soon Fatima would open it. When the time was right.

She checked her watch and saw that slightly over an hour remained. This was her final errand, the last act of her commission. Yet there was also a degree of self-interest. The man whose life she was about to end could give her trouble, one of two who might piece together the measure of her duplicity. The other was the Swiss doctor, a man too smart for his own good. *You are the terrorist, Caliph*, he'd said. Those words had sealed his fate.

Many others knew half the puzzle, saw bits of reality, but could have no way of discerning the entire truth. To misdirect the elders in Damascus had been simple. Indeed, they were simple men. Their awkward affiliation reminded Fatima of a movie she'd seen in which a group of Italian Mafiosi had met — preening crooks, brimming with false confidence, joined for a dubious cause. The atmosphere in Damascus had been useful. Civility on the surface, but swift undercurrents of distrust. So worried about one another, the men had never bothered to notice Fatima. And on the other end were the financiers, men not accustomed to dealing with ruffians. Men who simply paid for results, not caring how things were done. Or by whom.

Minutes earlier, Fatima had taken a call from Mosul. She now knew that the mystery of Caliph had been solved, though this had been inevitable. Today it no longer mattered. Fatima had no further use for her brother, and his captors would find only a shattered mind. Caliph could give them nothing. Her plan was working more smoothly than she had hoped. Events were running — she tried to remember the American phrase — "on autopilot" now. Fatima Adara, née Fatima Taim, had to smile. She cared little if this insane plot succeeded. Deep in the vaults of a half-dozen banks across the globe, Fatima had what she wanted. What she deserved.

She edged to the window and looked out. There were still no lights in the flat across the street. Fatima trundled across the room and ended up in front of a full-length mirror that was mounted on the bathroom door. The lights were set low, a condition she had always preferred. But soon this would change. She had seen the doctor's results, seen his work on Caliph. He was good. Fatima put a hand to her gut, then let it run up over her breasts, shoulder, neck, and finally to her face. She stroked her flabby jawline, pulled a trestle of coarse black hair behind one ear. She fantasized briefly about buying designer clothing, custom-tailored garments of the highest quality. Perhaps she would have her hair done properly by a high-end coiffeur. So many possibilities.

She had been thinking about it more and more, ever since visiting the Geneva office where her transformation would take place.

Dreaming about what the surgeon could do. He had emphasized the magnitude of change possible, told her how different everything might be. And even if things were not perfect this time, there were other doctors. All Fatima had ever needed was the means, and now she would have it, enough to begin life anew. As if reborn. In the tall mirror she stared deeply into her own eyes, black pools in the dim light, and tried to divine if she really believed it.

Fatima turned away from her reflection and went again to the window. The room across the street was still dark. Her gaze dropped and she searched the street for her target. She saw only late night revelers, men and women heading for the nightclub district two blocks away. She spotted a skinny young woman in a thin dress strutting along. Without a coat, she must have been freezing. But the men looked at her openly. This Fatima had never known. She had never been one of the pretty girls. When Fatima turned heads on the sidewalk there were never leers or brazen invitations — instead, she took snickers and filthy comments.

She moved to the middle of the room where a pile of furniture sat neatly stacked. A solid desk would serve as her seat, and next to it she had placed the heavy closet shelf between two big chairs. It was a sturdy arrangement, but she checked again for stability. There could be no movement, no wobbling of a leg when she distributed the weight of her arms and the weapon. The rifle was her preferred Dragunov SVDSN, a compact variant of the base Russian weapon with a ten-round magazine, night sight, and custom sound suppressor. The load was a standard 7.62mm steel jacket projectile, lead core for maximum effect. At a range of ninety meters, the target would be unusually close. But Fatima never took chances.

In Iraq, Caliph had always been at her shoulder, though he wasn't any better a spotter than he was a marksman. Still, he had always been there — watching, preparing his firsthand account so that he could later take credit for her work. In spite of being good at the shooting, Fatima had never particularly liked it. Her first kill was from a mosque tower in Mosul, an American soldier. She'd taken the young man as he stood in the street talking to a child. It was in her thoughts for a time — what the child must have seen — but in the end Fatima decided this was the nature of things. With each new kill her thoughts drifted less. And with each new kill her brother's legend had grown.

"*Caliph the marksman,*" she spat under her breath.

That her brother was now damaged gave Fatima no grief. In the end, he had become insufferable, awash in his own legend as a sniper, even if he could not hit the broadside of a camel from twenty paces. For all his ineptitude behind the trigger, however, the great Caliph was not without strengths. He was handsome, and exuded power and authority. It was, of course, all a swashbuckling façade. At base, he was a coward. It had been that way since they were children, Caliph taking credit for Fatima's accomplishments. There was really no other way in a society where women were granted so little respect — and even more so for women who were physically unattractive. Caliph was seen as the leader, while she was simply not seen.

Fatima the Invisible.

It was a terrible way to go through life. But a distinct advantage for certain applications. She looked out the window and saw night coming full. It was then that she first noticed a single, very faint light coming from the flat across the street. Fatima picked up the gun and trained it on the source. What she saw through the scope was dim and rectangular.

A computer screen.

CHAPTER THIRTY-EIGHT

Davis and Sorensen approached the address carefully.

Thick, broad snowflakes drifted overhead through the spray of streetlights, their reflections telltale indicators of otherwise unseen currents and eddies. The street was like a hundred others in Lyon, a muddled mix of businesses, homes, and apartments. Near the place des Terreaux, many of the buildings had been in place for centuries, while others were newer, or at least updated. It all blended to afford the district a patchwork, almost cluttered appearance.

Number 27, rue d'Algérie, was five levels, a burnt-brick façade that was in need of some work. There was little to distinguish it from the surrounding structures. Maybe a lack of anything ornate — no columns or arches, no carved lion's heads or coils of rope. It was just there, plain and square.

And somewhere inside was Dr. Ibrahim Jaber.

"What was the apartment number?" Sorensen asked as they weighed the place from across the street.

"Nineteen," Davis replied.

"I see twelve windows in front. There must be more on the backside. Third floor?" she guessed.

"Maybe." Of the three windows on that floor, only one was lit. "Let's go have a look."

They crossed the street to the building entrance and found twenty mail boxes in an alcove. Some had names. Number 19 did not.

Davis said, "Jaber was supposed to be staying with a relative, an older woman."

After a silence, Sorensen said, "Okay. So let's go meet her."

At the building entrance there was no indicator of which rooms were on which floor. To the positive, the entryway wasn't locked — just an old door that opened freely against a tired spring, and behind that a stairwell. Davis and Sorensen headed up. The door labeled "19" turned out to be on the fourth floor, higher than predicted. There was no light coming from the crack at the base of the door. Davis checked his watch. 10:52.

"Do you think he's in bed?" he whispered.

"I wouldn't be surprised — you know, with the way he looks and all."

"Great. So now what?"

Sorensen stepped up to the door and knocked, the sound echoing down the long hallway. Davis sensed nothing from inside the apartment, no stirring sounds, no change to the bland darkness at the bottom of the door. He gave the second knock, quick and sharp like a chain gun. More insistent. Still nothing.

"What now?" she said. "We don't have any authority for a search. I wonder how hard it would be to get approval from the French."

"Are you kidding? At this time of night? We took the word 'bureaucracy' from French, Honeywell."

"Okay. Any other ideas?"

Davis smiled.

Sorensen frowned.

"All right," she said. "But let me do it." She moved back a step and took a firm stance.

Davis put an arm in front of her. "I don't think so."

"I've done this before," she argued.

"Sorry, Honeywell, but you're built to have doors opened for you. I'm the one made for knocking them off their hinges."

Davis studied the door, looked up and down for locks and striker plates. He saw only two, both at hip height. Davis quarter-turned to one side and raised a leg.

She whispered harshly, "Jammer, are you sure about this?"

"No."

He kicked hard, his flat heel slamming into the door right where locks met wood. With a crash, the old jamb splintered and the door flew open, smacking back hard against the inside wall. They stood completely still, watching the dark interior of the apartment. Alert for any movement, any sound. There was nothing.

They stepped inside over splinters and plaster chips that had sprayed across a worn rug. The door was hanging crookedly on one hinge, the other two having pulled away from the wall. Sorensen looked at the door. Then at him.

He shrugged it off. "So I got a little carried away."

The room was chilly, clammy, like it had been closed up all day. Davis found a light switch and snapped it on. The room that came into view wasn't much to look at. The walls were covered with a mix of faded paint and peeling wallpaper. The wood floor and trim were at the stage where dirt, mold, and dry rot had to be declared the winner. If there could be a label for the room's décor it would be "minimalist"—just a few sorry pieces of worn furniture and the basic accessories of life. There was no sign of Ibrahim Jaber.

Davis looked around for confirmation that they had the right apartment. He found it on a table near the door—Jaber's investigation credentials, nested by a lanyard to his CargoAir ID. He held it up for Sorensen to see and said, "This is definitely the place."

Davis saw one adjoining room. He eased over and looked inside, saw a single bed, empty and neatly made. There was a suitcase on the dresser, packed to the brim, its flap lying open like a shucked oyster. One fresh suit hung in the closet amid a lineup of empty hangers. In the adjacent bathroom Davis found a toothbrush, a razor, and two pill bottles. Nothing else.

He went back to the main room. Sorensen was on the far side going through the small kitchen. It was separated by a laminate counter, watermelon red, and on the back wall two stacks of worn wood cabinets were divided by a stove and a naked section of wall that had been splashed years ago with lime green paint, somebody's crude attempt to spruce the place up.

"What do you think?" he asked.

They both looked around. There was a teapot on the stove, a box of breakfast cereal on the table, a few dishes in the sink.

"There's not much here," she said

"I'm more struck by what's *not* here. No books, no pictures, no artwork. Jaber was supposed to be rooming with a relative, an older woman. If it's true, then she's led a really boring life."

"And if it's not?"

Davis scanned the room and wondered the same thing. His eyes settled on a laptop computer on the kitchen counter. It was already powered up, the lights on the keyboard shining, but a screensaver — a cute little progressive design of children's blocks snapping together — had kicked in to indicate standby mode. Davis went closer and saw a scattering of papers and printouts on the counter next to the computer. Most if it was indecipherable, page after page of equations and instructions.

"What do you think this is?" he asked.

Sorensen took a look. "I'm pretty sure it's computer code. You know, lines of instruction. He's a software guy, right?"

Rifling though the stack, Davis found a few pages that looked less daunting. They were flow charts of some kind, groups of rectangular boxes connected by lines. All the boxes were labeled with acronyms and he recognized a few. FCC for flight control computer, ADS for air data system, and FDR — flight data recorder. At the top was a title: C-500 Standby Three Architecture. Davis sifted through the rest of the papers and found another that pulled his attention. It was titled: Coordinate List.

He drew it from the pile. "Look at this."

"What is it?"

After a good look, he said, "These are all lat-longs."

Sorensen eyed the paper with suspicion, but didn't seem bowled over. "Latitude and longitude coordinates. So what? It's an airplane. You pilot types use that stuff all the time, right?"

Davis shook his head. "I dunno. There's something weird about this." He looked again at the flow diagrams referencing aircraft systems, the pages of computer code. He thought aloud. "Fly by wire. Flight control software, integration. That's Jaber's specialty, isn't it?"

She nodded.

"Remember I told you I had looked into that? I explained how the software that controls this airplane is supposed to be shielded from intrusion."

"Okay."

"But that means protected from *hackers*. What about somebody on the inside? What about an imbedded malware program that comes right from the factory? Commercial aircraft manufacturers don't sell airplanes, they sell safety. Who would ever think to scrub millions of lines of computer code that are sourced straight from the design bureau?"

"You're saying that Jaber *programmed* World Express 801 to crash?"

Davis reached into his mind and strove for an alternate explanation. There wasn't one. As if trying to convince himself, he said, "I can't see it any other way."

Davis turned to the laptop and poked a random key. The machine began to spin through its wake-up call.

Fatima cursed under her breath. Her support arm was going numb.

The man and woman had been in her sights for nearly ten minutes, easy prey from this range. She decided it had to be the two irksome American investigators. She had never seen either, but the descriptions given by her useless Algerians matched perfectly — the woman a petit blonde, the man a big rough-looking type. She tracked them alternately, watched as they rifled through Jaber's papers and tinkered with his computer. She wondered about that — was it the computer that held the critical instructions? The one Jaber had told her was in a safe in his office in Marseille?

She decided it probably was.

Fatima kept shifting her sight. First the man, then the woman. She could take them both in seconds, but that wasn't why she was here. She needed Jaber first. For Fatima, *he* was the true threat. If she killed the

Americans now there would be two muffled shots, a pair of bloody bodies lying near an open door. Any passerby could spot them. Or if Jaber returned to such a scene, he would know immediately what had happened. He would flee, not give Fatima a second chance. In either case, the alarm would be raised, and the police would come swarming in a matter of minutes.

She put her crosshairs on the head of the big man. Fatima ignored the bullet drop and wind compensation references built into her sight. They were little help at such close range. She sensed her finger putting slight pressure on the trigger. Fatima took a long, deep breath. The pressure eased.

She could not allow herself to lose a shooter's most important weapon — patience.

Sorensen asked, "But why would Jaber sabotage these airplanes? To bring down the CargoAir corporation?"

Davis cupped his chin as he tried to figure that one himself. "I can't believe he'd have a grudge against the company. This whole design, the whole project was under his watch."

"There's no way the chief engineer would sabotage his crowning achievement."

Davis was distracted by a beep. The computer was up and running. He saw a security screen asking for a password. "Great."

She sighed, "Too bad this isn't a movie — we could just guess his password."

"Yeah, right." He shoved the machine aside. "This is a waste of time."

Davis went back to the printouts and scanned over the latitude-longitude pairs until he found an eerily familiar set. N45.6 E004.8. He shook his head uncertainly. "That's got to be close, but —"

"What's close?"

He rapped on the paper with an index finger and showed her. "This lat–long combination. I think it might be our crash site."

"World Express 801? The crash site is on that list? Jammer, this is crazy."

"Yeah, it is. We —"

"What are you doing here?" a strident voice interrupted.

Davis and Sorensen both turned to see Dr. Ibrahim Jaber standing in his shattered doorway.

CHAPTER THIRTY-NINE

Jaber looked terrible. He was slumped and his face sagged behind skin the color of putty. He was holding onto the shattered doorframe with one hand in a precarious stance, listing like a palm tree that had just come through a hurricane. The other hand gripped a small plastic bag emblazoned with a red cross — part of a logo Davis recognized as being from a French pharmacy chain. Yet as weak as Jaber looked, there was fury in his yellow eyes. He took a step into the room, raised a finger to lodge his protest.

And then he fell.

Davis watched him go down, pivoting back like a tipped domino. It seemed to happen in slow motion, and when Jaber hit the floor he was slack weight, smacking down hard like a sack full of grain. Some long-dormant instinct kicked in. In a fraction of a second Davis made the connection, recognized the sound — a sharp, barely audible crack that had been nearly simultaneous with Jaber's drop. It brought a re-action he'd not had since his days as a Marine. Sorensen was standing five feet away. Davis flew across the room, arm outstretched, and knocked her to the ground. He heard the second crack before they hit the floor.

"Gun!" he yelled.

They crashed in a heap and Davis scrambled to right himself. He kept moving toward a wall, dragging a scrambling Sorensen with him. He glanced toward the window and could just make out a subtle flash across the street as a third round splintered into the wood floor next to his head.

Sorensen moved with him now, and they backed up to a wall near a heavy desk. Davis checked the angle. He no longer had line of sight to the window across the street where he'd seen the flash. Which meant the shooter no longer had line of sight to him.

"Honeywell—"

A fourth round slammed in. The laptop on the counter kicked into the air and then crashed to the floor. It came to rest in a wisp of smoke, the keyboard a shattered cluster of alphanumeric characters. Then another pause from the incoming fire. It grew longer and longer. Sorensen pulled a gun from her jacket, held it muzzle up with a cocked elbow.

Davis asked, "Where the hell did that come from?"

"After last night I thought it might be wise," she said tensely. "So who the hell is shooting at us?"

"Hard to say. But I'm pretty sure I saw a muzzle flash across the street, fifth-floor window. I think we're good here. As long as there's only one shooter."

"I heard the bullets come through the glass, but I didn't hear any shots."

"The gun must be sound suppressed," he said.

Davis took stock of Jaber. He was lying motionless in the doorway. There was a black hole centered perfectly on his forehead, a crimson pool blossoming under his skull. "We can't do anything for him."

Sorensen stared at the window. "I'd say somebody across the street is a decent shot."

They exchanged a look.

"Caliph?" she wondered aloud.

"Could be."

"But he didn't stop with Jaber, did he? He tried for us too. Not to mention that—" she pointed toward the devastated laptop.

"Whoever it is," Davis reasoned, "he's probably been over there for quite a while, waiting for Jaber. Chances are, he was watching us tinker with that computer and go through the papers."

Sorensen had her cell phone out. "I'm calling the police."

He nodded, and said, "I think that'd be a good idea."

Everything was still while she made the call. No new bullets came crashing through the window. Sorensen gave the address and situation, but didn't give her name. She hung up. "Okay, now what? Do we just sit here until the police come?"

"I've got better things to do. It'll take five minutes for them to get here. Maybe ten." Davis thought about this. "Caliph, or whoever is across the street, might still be waiting for us to show. But he'll bolt when the police show up."

"Probably. Right now I'm more interested in how *we* get out of here."

"Good question."

The silence grew longer. So long it was overwhelming.

Davis ended it. "Whoever's over there is using a sound-suppressed weapon. The only reason to do that is to escape attention. Aside from us, nobody around here knows what's going on. I don't hear anybody outside screaming frantically about guns or bodies. I figure there are two possibilities at the moment. Either the shooter is gone because he just wanted Jaber, or the guy is still there, looking straight through that window with his scope."

They both studied the window, saw four tightly shattered holes.

"So how do we tell?"

"If I'd worn my Stetson I could put it on an umbrella and waved it in the window."

She frowned. Then, "Jammer, how about we make him go away?"

"And how, pray tell, do we do that?"

"What kind of scope do you think he's using?"

"Scope?" he asked.

"Some kind of low-light optical number. And right now he's looking into a brightly lit apartment."

"Yeah . . . so?"

Sorensen hugged the wall and crawled closer to the window. She stopped just aside the frame and looked at him. "When I give the word, I want you to pull the plugs on those two lamps."

She pointed to a pair of cords plugged into the wall. Davis realized it would kill the majority of the light in the room. There was still a small overhead fixture in the kitchen, on the other side, but it was less intense than the two main lamps.

"But what good is that —"

"Just do it, Jammer!"

"All right." Davis scooted to the plugs and said, "Ready when you are, Honeywell. But I hope you know what you're doing."

She raised an index finger high, then chopped it down. He pulled the plugs and the room fell dark. An instant later, Sorensen extended her gun into the window opening and tilted it down, aiming at the baseboard across the room.

Three shots burst through the night.

Fatima blinked. The sudden darkness had surprised her. She pulled away from the scope and locked her naked eyes on the window across the street. Then came three flashes, followed by three cracks.

Fatima instinctively ducked. What were those fools doing? Could they have seen her muzzle flashes? Even so, what idiot returns fire at such a range with a handgun against a rifle? Anger overcame her. She cursed and looked through the sight, scanned every part of the flat. Nothing. Fatima cursed again.

She had wanted to take the two Americans earlier, but Jaber had been the priority. Yet as she waited, she had watched them go through his papers. Now Fatima wondered what they'd found. Could they understand what was about to happen? Had that idiot Jaber left too much lying around? At least she had taken care of the computer.

A police siren wailed in the distance. Fatima saw a man on the street pointing up toward Jaber's window. A woman next to him had her phone out. Fatima looked at her watch. It was too late to stop the final blow. Yet there was a possibility, ever so slim, that the Americans could minimize the damage.

The damned Americans!

In a fit of rage Fatima pushed over her shooting stand, the lumber and chairs clattering to the floor. She dropped the Dragunov on the couch and picked up a Glock semiautomatic from a nearby table. She racked the slide to chamber a round, then ejected the magazine and jammed in an extra bullet to bring it full. Reloading the magazine, she tucked the gun into the waistband of her pants.

Fatima shrugged a jacket over her shoulders and headed for the door.

CHAPTER FORTY

They walked quickly along the rue Terme. Sorensen was leading, weaving among groups of late night revelers. One side of the street was bright with faux gas lamps, the other side dark. Sorensen chose the light. Davis used it to scrutinize everyone on the busy sidewalk. He knew she was doing the same, looking for Caliph, the face that had been on the front page of every newspaper in the world for the past three days.

The night had turned messy and snow was coming down. It wasn't a fluffy Christmas mix, but frozen granules that gave the sidewalk a gritty feel and crunched under their feet. Turning into the place des Terreaux, Sorensen found what they needed.

"There it is, Jammer. I knew I'd seen one."

It was an Internet café, the standard all-hours marriage of caffeine and WiFi. Viewed from the street, the place oozed a warm, inviting light. Davis and Sorensen went in to find rows of glowing screens, soft chairs, and the thick aroma of the *café du jour.*

Or *noir*, Davis figured.

The café was busy, but Sorensen found an open machine and went to work on access. Davis stood behind her impatiently. Before leaving Jaber's he had dashed to the kitchen counter and swiped up a pile of papers, including the one he reckoned was the most important — the page with the matrix of coordinates. He had rolled them up and stuffed the wad into his jacket pocket. Davis pulled them out now, un-rolled and shuffled until the one he wanted was on top. Latitudes and longitudes. Something about it bothered him. Really bothered him.

Davis racked his brain, made approximations. The coordinates were scattershot, sprayed all over the world, but a preponderance were in places he was familiar with, places he'd flown before — Texas, Louisiana, the Middle East. He tried to add it all up. Jaber's papers, World Express 801, a terrorist taking potshots at them. The events seemed incredibly disjointed, each disturbing in its own right, but collectively unrelated. Davis stumbled to find a relationship, some link to make it all fit.

His eyes were drawn to a discarded newspaper at a nearby workstation. The entire front page was engulfed with articles about oil refinery attacks, spiraling fuel prices, and turmoil in the financial markets. It wasn't just his investigation coming undone — the whole world was fracturing.

And that was when it hit him.

His head spun. The vacuum of ideas was replaced by its antithesis — everything came at once. He alternated between the newspaper and Jaber's printouts. He stared at words and numbers. *Flight control software. Architecture. Integration.* Then a picture filled his mind, an image he had first seen three days ago in Sparky's office. The overhead satellite view of the crash site. He remembered what had been off to one side, barely in view — an image that brought cohesion to everything.

"Christ almighty!" he spat.

"What is it?" Sorensen asked, still typing.

"Just keep going!"

"We're online," she announced, sliding her credit card back into her wallet.

Sorensen got up and gave Davis the seat. He called up a commercial mapping program, selected satellite view, and typed in a set of coordinates from the list, the ones he thought approximated the crash site. Davis had to be sure. He needed one precise picture. Seconds later he had it.

Davis adjusted the view to zoom in. "There!"

"What?" said Sorensen, looking over his shoulder.

He tapped the picture on the screen. It was an overhead view of an oil refinery — piping, stacks, holding tanks. "Does this look familiar?"

"No."

Davis used arrows on the screen to shift the view less than a mile. A pristine meadow came into view. "There's our crash site," he said. Davis looked at the date on the satellite image. "Or at least that's what it looked like six weeks ago." He tapped Jaber's page of coordinates with a finger. "This is not a list of simple lat-longs. It's a *target* list!"

"That refinery near the crash site was a — a target?"

"Straight from this page. And the only thing that kept World Express 801 from hitting it was Earl Moore. He rebooted the damned airplane." Davis typed in a second set of coordinates from the list. An overhead shot of a Japanese oil refinery came into view. "It'll take some typing to prove, but I'd guess that every latitude-longitude pairing on this list is the geographic center of an oil refinery."

"Jammer — this is scary."

Davis looked at the list. He remembered his bombing missions from the Gulf War — he had always been given a primary and a secondary target. The page in front of him held at least two hundred. This wasn't just a target list, it was an Air Tasking Order, a tactical war plan.

"Every one of these airplanes must have the same code," he said, "with this coordinate list embedded. These jets have to be grounded right now."

"How can we do that?"

He thought aloud, "Bastien is worthless. And I'm sure the BEA won't be answering any phones until the start of business hours tomorrow morning."

After a lengthy pause, Sorensen said, "I could do it."

"How?"

"I'll get through to the very top, the director of the CIA if I have to. If I can convince Langley this is for real — I mean, really convince them — they can patch me through to somebody with enough clout to ground these jets."

"Okay, Honeywell. Give it a try."

She pulled out a fancy phone and he watched her dial. Sorensen began talking to somebody, but right away got put on hold.

Davis went back to the computer and typed more coordinates from the list. Just as he'd guessed, each set gave him an overhead view of yet another oil refinery.

With the phone to her ear, she said, "I gave it the highest priority. They're running a connection to Langley." She stared at the screen as she waited, her face taut with concentration. "Jammer—"

He broke away from the computer and gave her his full attention.

"There's one thing I don't understand," she said, her thumb pressed to a set of pursed lips.

"What's that?"

"If Jaber planted a virus in the system, then all those airplanes are affected, right?"

"Probably."

"Well—World Express 801. Why did that particular airplane go down?"

He shrugged. "I don't know. I guess the whole program must have some kind of trigger, some instruction to—" Davis stopped in mid-sentence. He looked back at the computer and stared at the tiny clock in the bottom right corner of the screen.

Clock. Computer.

"That's it!" he said.

"What?"

Davis didn't answer. He rifled through his jacket and found the wad of business cards still jammed into one pocket. He threw them aside one by one until he found the card he wanted. With his own phone he dialed the number scribbled on the back.

CHAPTER FORTY-ONE

The first call went unanswered. Davis got a voice mail.

Not good. It was eleven o'clock and the Doral tech was probably asleep. Davis ended the call and redialed. On the fourth ring he got a drowsy answer.

"Hullo—"

"Is this—" Davis flipped the business card over, "is this Carl Wright?"

"Yeah."

"Carl, this is Jammer Davis from the investigation."

"Wha—oh, yeah. Um, do you know what time it is, man?"

"Where are you right now?"

"I'm in my room—in bed."

"Carl, listen very closely. We have a serious situation. There is no time to explain, just trust me that this is life or death. I need you to do something for me."

There was a long pause on the line. Davis had a vision of the tech sitting up in bed, trying to decide if this was really something important or just a crank call from a drunken associate. "This is *really* an emergency!" he added.

"Okay, okay. What do you need?" The software guy still seemed skeptical. Davis figured that in his line of work the word "emergency" was normally used for things like power outages or hard drive crashes.

"Do you have a copy of the voice recording there?"

"Yeah, sure. It's digital, so we all download a copy onto our laptops in case we want to work after hours."

"Great," Davis said. "Call it up and go to the preflight portion, the spot where they lost power and the clocks got screwed up."

"Hang on —"

Davis heard the tech's phone rattle onto a table. The wait seemed interminable.

Finally, Wright said, "Okay, here it is. The first officer is having clock problems. That's life or death?"

"Can you play it so I can hear?" Davis heard a sigh.

"All right, here goes. I'll put my phone down by the speaker."

The audio was clear, even over the phone line — the Doral boys had been busy with their filtering programs.

The first voice was female, Melinda Hendricks, the first officer: *This clock is all screwed up, boss. The time is way off.*

Earl Moore answers: *Ah, just leave it. The maintenance boys in Houston will figure it out. Maybe we'll get paid for the extra flight hours.*

Both laugh.

Moore: *How much is it off by?*

Hendricks: *It's six hours slow. Crap, the date is off too — four days fast.*

Davis dropped the phone to his lap. He looked at his watch, did the math. Then he did it again. He remembered seeing Jaber's suitcase packed and ready to go.

"Honeywell —"

Still on hold, Sorensen raised her eyebrows inquiringly.

"I hope you're making some headway."

"Why?"

"Because every C-500 in the world that's airborne is going to crash in forty-one minutes."

President Townsend was still hunkered down with his staff.

Coyle's information on who'd instigated the disaster had been a revelation. They now knew who and what they were up against. Every refinery in the world was under lockdown — those in the United States by emergency presidential directive, and those abroad by a combination of prodding and common sense. If nothing else, there was unanimous agreement among the members of the intelligence staff that the situation had at least peaked. Going forward, the only issues were damage control and recovery.

The president was deep in a session with Herman Coyle when Darlene Graham's phone buzzed. She flipped it open and moved discreetly toward a wall — there were no corners in the Oval Office.

"Hello."

She heard the distinctive baritone of Thomas Drexler, head of the CIA. "Darlene, I've got someone on the phone you really need to talk to."

"Who is it?"

"I told you we had people working on that CargoAir accident investigation, remember?"

"Yes."

"Well, my agent is on the line from France. She insists that in half an hour over a hundred of these C-500 aircraft are going to dive down and crash into oil refineries all over the world."

For the first time in all her years in the intelligence business, Darlene Graham felt a pang of helplessness. On top of everything that had already happened, it seemed perfectly insane. Perfectly outlandish. And so, by some immaculately twisted logic, she sensed it was perfectly true.

"But Thomas, how could we allow this to —" Graham felt herself losing control. She had to do something — anything. So with an open hand she slapped the wall hard. This had two results. First, the Oval Office fell silent. Second, Graham got her focus.

"Do you still have her on the line, Thomas?"

"Yes."

"All right. Patch her through to the blue line."

Thirty seconds later, Darlene Graham had repeated to everyone in the room what she'd just been told. Anna Sorensen's voice came across the speakerphone for everyone to hear.

"Miss Sorensen, this is the director of national intelligence, Darlene Graham, from the Oval Office. I'm here with the president and most of the National Security Council."

Sorensen's voice replied with a slight delay, "Yes, ma'am."

"How sure are you of this information?" Graham asked.

"Well, we haven't really had much chance to cross-check, but I felt I had to call immediately since we believe time is so critical."

"But what has brought you to this conclusion?"

"We discovered that Dr. Ibrahim Jaber—" Sorensen's voice cut off. Suddenly, another voice blasted over the speaker, so loud that Martin Spector covered his ears. "God dammit! This is Jammer Davis! Who the hell am I talking to?"

"This is the director of national intelligence, Darlene Graham."

"Well, Director Graham, we have thirty-four minutes until Armageddon! Here's what you are going to do. First, find out where every C-500 in the world is—there are over a hundred and fifty out there. Contact every air traffic control agency across the globe and get those airplanes on the ground—battle speed! Second, establish a way to communicate with every airplane. Air traffic control will work, but all airlines have company data or voice communication links. Get those set up in stone. Some of these airplanes are over the ocean and will not be able to land for hours. I think I can trick the system into not going haywire." The connection seemed to fade and there was a pause. Then, "This phone I'm using is going dead. You need to call me back in ten minutes on another phone." Davis gave his own number and said, "Are you getting all this, Director?"

Graham looked around the room. Three people were writing. "Yes, but I don't see how—"

"*You are not listening to me! People are going to die in a matter of minutes if you do not do your job!* Use the FAA, Homeland Security, the State Department! Nobody in this government can be sitting on their—"

"Stand down, mister!" President Townsend broke in.

Davis lashed right back, "No! You stand down!"

"Do you know who you're talking—"

Davis' voice exploded from the speaker, *"I am talking to a goddamn paper pusher who needs to go piss up a rope! Now get those comm links established and call me back in ten minutes! Go! Go! Go!"* There was a distinct click and the line went dead.

Silence befell the room.

Everyone looked at the president, probably expecting him to ask, *And who the hell is Jammer Davis?* In fact, Truett Townsend didn't hesitate. Not even for a moment. "I want the FAA on line one! Homeland Security on two! Get the State Department to call every—"

Davis sat sulking. Sorensen was right next to him, having leaned closer to hear the conversation. She sat back in her chair, and Davis handed over her dead phone. She was grinning.

"What?"

She couldn't seem to contain her humor.

"What the hell could be funny right now, Honeywell?"

"Jammer, do you know who that was on the phone? The guy?"

He shrugged to say he didn't.

"You just told the president of the United States to go piss up a rope."

Sorensen started giggling uncontrollably, her eyes alight with life and amusement.

His gaze narrowed and he looked at her hard, trying to gauge if she was serious. And then his mind went adrift. The visions of doom and catastrophe — crashing airplanes and burning refineries — all disappeared. At this very moment he could only see how beautiful she was. Davis had an irresistible urge to reach out and take her in his arms, to hold her and never let go. He lunged forward.

In that same instant, the computer monitor next to his head exploded.

CHAPTER FORTY-TWO

Glass sprayed everywhere.

Davis dove to the floor as the shot echoed through the room. He caught a glimpse of Sorensen disappearing behind a table. She called his name, but then he heard screams from the other direction. Davis looked up and saw a big woman struggling with a man in an overcoat, their arms intertwined. He couldn't get a look at the guy, but decided it had to be Caliph. Without hesitation, he clambered to his feet and lunged into the melee.

Shoulder down, he made big contact. All three went sprawling. Davis landed near the front entrance. He got to one knee and was about to coldcock the guy when he got his first look. Mid-twenties, well dressed, blond hair — it was definitely not Caliph. Confused, he then saw the woman. She was ten paces away, lying in a heap under a table. It only took one look for Davis to understand — it was the woman from Sorensen's picture. Fatima Adara. The shooter. And Davis had probably just taken out an off-duty cop who was trying to save his ass.

Great move, Jammer.

Davis had taken one step toward her when Fatima rolled and locked eyes with him. She was grimacing, snarling like a rabid dog. She wrestled an arm from under her hip and Davis saw the gun. He changed direction fast and lunged for the door.

He crashed through just as bullets smacked into wood and glass all around. Then he felt pain, like his leg had been struck by lightning. More glass shattered. Davis rolled into the street and scrambled to his feet. He looked at his thigh and saw blood. He'd been hit, but everything seemed to be working.

Davis hesitated, looked back for Sorensen. He didn't see her anywhere. But he saw Fatima Adara. She was sweeping the gun across the place, keeping the rest of the clientele at bay as she moved for the door Davis had just flown through. He searched desperately for Sorensen one last time. Nothing. He was on his own.

Davis ran.

The crowds were thick. He bolted down the sidewalk, running through the pain. Davis weaved between people, his feet slipping constantly on the slick sidewalk. At the first corner, he looked back and saw Fatima trundling after him. She stood out like a Hummer in a sea of Volkswagens. Her gun hand was tucked against her side, and judging from the lack of panic around her, Davis decided she must have buried the weapon in her pocket.

He turned onto a side street that looked even more crowded, lined by nightclubs and theaters. The street was washed in an ethereal glow from banks of colored neon, an illusionist's scene that sparkled in gust-driven swirls of ice and snow. Davis kept moving. One block, then two. Even with his handicap he was making good time. He knew he could outrun Fatima — and that was all he had to do. As he ran he dug down into his jacket pocket. An instant later, Davis skidded to a stop on the frozen sidewalk.

His cell phone was gone.

The White House Situation Room was madness. Truett Townsend counted at least a dozen people on phones, all jabbering and yelling. He hated chaos, but right now it was the only way.

Darlene Graham announced, "The latest count is one hundred and six C-500s in the air. Over half are domestic, here in the States."

Someone yelled, "Does anybody speak Chinese?"

There was actually a "yes" from the crowd, and two staffers linked up on one handset.

If there could be a lone symbol of the sense of desperation, it was Herman Coyle. As the leaders of the world's technology superpower governed their crisis, the most accomplished scientist in the room was rushing around with a legal pad and number two pencil striking tally marks as he kept count of aircraft. Supercomputers were no longer any help.

Martin Spector said, "The Secret Service wants you to evacuate the White House, sir. They're afraid these airplanes might be aimed at political targets."

"Mr. Davis says the jets are headed for oil refineries," Townsend argued.

"But, sir——"

"No, Martin! I'll take responsibility."

Townsend took a seat behind his desk. He had learned a lot in the last five minutes. He had learned about a system called ACARS, or Aircraft Communication Addressing and Reporting System. It was the communications data link used by most airlines to track their airplanes, download maintenance and operational information, and— most important right now— to send messages to the crews. He had also learned about cargo hubs. At this moment, most of the C-500s in the world were airborne, either on their way to a late-night sorting facility in Europe or America, or headed for a second-day sort in the Far East. Whoever had planned this unnatural disaster had done a damned good job of maximizing the potential.

"We have a map," someone shouted. A large screen at one end of the room came to life and a Mercator projection of the world was presented. "It's a hybrid view," the same voice said, "combined data from our own FAA, European Control, and two commercial flight tracking Web sites."

"Are they all displayed?" Townsend asked.

"Yes, all that we know about."

Townsend didn't like the caveat. But what could he do? He watched one hundred and six tiny crosses floating across the globe. The representation seemed feeble, inadequate given the threat that was posed.

"One hundred and two," Graham said. "Four more have landed."

"How many can we communicate with?" the president inquired.

"All except—" Herman Coyle tapped out a count on his legal pad, "seventeen."

Townsend checked the clocks on the wall that registered both Eastern time and Zulu. They had nine minutes. "All right," he said, "keep working it—those are the top priority. We have to transmit instructions somehow. Let's get Davis back on the line."

His leg felt like it was on fire.

Davis was limping mightily as he navigated back to the Internet café—his phone *had* to be there. As he walked, he kept searching for Fatima. He suspected he'd lost her, figured she would give up the chase knowing she could never keep pace. That's what they called it in rugby —pace. Davis had always had it for a guy his size. Right now he was clocking in at far less than full speed, but he was still covering ground.

He checked his watch.

How long did he have until the president returned his call? Two minutes? Three? He hoped like hell he could find his phone. His stride quickened when he saw the café in the distance. But then he spotted an unmistakable shape on the sidewalk ahead.

Davis whipped his head left and right, desperate to get out of sight. Taking what had to be a page from Sorensen's book, he shot left and ducked into the nearest alcove. He peered through the corner of the shop window and found her. Fatima was fifty feet ahead, walking briskly. Closing fast. She had both hands in her pockets—to have only one hidden might look threatening. Her head was tilted down, but her eyes were quick and alert. The eyes of a hunter.

Her quarry suddenly realized his mistake—there was no way out of the recessed entryway. He should have just turned and run. Even with his bad leg he could outdistance Fatima Adara. But now he was trapped—glass on three sides, and soon a killer with a gun at the fourth. A killer who was looking for him.

Davis took a closer look at the store. It was an old music shop, at this hour locked down tight with a FERMÉ sign posted in the window.

Inside, row after row of ancient vinyl relics sat waiting for some au-
diophile purist to come rescue them. A rescue that would almost certainly never come.

I know just how it is, he thought.

Davis backed against the side window. It would buy him an extra
second, maybe two. Nothing more. All Fatima had to do was look —
and he knew she would. An old newspaper swirled in an eddy at his
feet. If she would only pass by, he could still get to the café and find
his phone in time. Or find Sorensen and get the headquarters number, use another phone. Davis would make it work. He just had to
stay alive for the next thirty seconds. And to do that, he needed to
become invisible.

He took a step back and heard a hollow clink.

Fatima cursed the pain in her hip.

The American had been lucky, moving at the very moment she'd
taken her first shot. And even luckier that some idiot had tried to wrestle her gun away, keeping her from taking a follow-up shot. But then
the American had been stupid, misidentifying his threat. Not for the
first time, Fatima had been saved by her appearance. Still, it had hurt
when she'd crashed against the big table. Grimacing, she scanned the
frozen street, looking for the bastard. He was big — but the size that
had sent her flying minutes earlier might soon be his downfall.

She kept her hands in the pockets of her jacket, the right having
a firm grip on the Glock. Handguns were not Fatima's preferred
weapon, but if she could find the American again she would not miss.
As she walked, she didn't bother to look at faces. Fatima would find
him by his shape, just as he would attempt to find her. Yet she had to
be careful. She'd noticed blood outside the café entrance, and Fatima
reasoned she must have struck home with at least one round. He
might still be close, and a wounded animal was always a dangerous
one. She only had to see him first, not get too close.

She looked across the street and eyed every group for a man who
didn't belong, a large figure trying to look small. To her right was a line
of shops, but most were closed. She approached the recessed entry

of a record store, a tattered poster in the window depicting an old black man wailing on a trumpet. Fatima edged away from the entrance, sensing a presence there. Then she saw him, curled into a ball — a drunk passed out on the cold concrete. The miserable wretch was using a newspaper for a blanket, and an empty bottle lay tipped on its side, near where his head had to be. Then a glimmer of motion came from above. The hand in her pocket tensed and Fatima's eyes were drawn higher.

For a moment she thought she had seen movement inside the store. But then Fatima realized it was only her reflection in the window, her profile taking the light at just the right angle. She stood still for an instant and looked at herself. The image transformed as Fatima again imagined what the surgeon might accomplish. The shape, the textures. She might be able to affect some changes herself, adjustments to her carriage and posture. She stood more erect, straighter, and taller.

Then Fatima chided herself.

She pushed the thought away. Now was not the time. Again she began to move up the sidewalk, her eyes studying an intersection ahead. She was nearly to the side street when she felt a vibration. It came to her knuckles, the same hand that was curled around the weapon in her pocket.

She had found the cell phone right where the big American had fallen, and so she'd picked it up. Fatima suspected it was the one he had been using as she'd maneuvered into position. Just before she'd missed the most simple of shots. *Why had he moved at that moment?* Fatima let go of the gun and pulled the phone from her pocket. It buzzed again. She stood still, staring at the thing, wondering if she should answer.

Curiosity got the better of her. She used her masculine voice, the one she had mimicked so many times before to become Caliph. "Hello."

The reply came in a squealing pitch, "Daddy, I have to talk to you!"

Fatima stood dumbstruck. Her thoughts stumbled. She muttered, "No, not now."

"Daddy! This is so, so important —"

CHAPTER FORTY-THREE

Davis was almost in the clear.

Fatima had gone for his ruse, taking him for a drunk. When she was ten steps past the alcove, he silently edged to his feet, ready to make a move for the café. Everything outside seemed fuzzy now, the thickening snowfall churning and spinning like a million tiny mirrors in the floodlit street. Davis checked the sidewalk, hoping for a group to blend into. Hoping for a nice rugby squad, drunk and loud, headed for the next bar. He saw no one within a hundred feet. A couple were shuffling arm-in-arm across the street, and in front of Fatima a cabbie was getting in his taxi. No help.

When Davis stepped out on the sidewalk his boots crunched over the icy mix. It sounded like thunder. Might as well have been an alarm going off. He looked over his shoulder and saw Fatima stop abruptly, saw her digging into her jacket pocket.

Davis froze.

He was caught in the open, twenty feet away. Fatima's hand came smoothly out of her pocket. He expected to see the gun, expected her to whip around and take shooter's choice — head shot or center of mass. But then he saw it wasn't a gun at all. Fatima was standing on the sidewalk staring at a cell phone. Staring at *his* cell phone. Probably because it was ringing. Probably because the president of the United States was calling.

Just what else could freaking go wrong?

Fatima put the phone to her ear and began talking. She half turned. For Davis, there was no one else nearby, no cover except for a dead-end alcove. He might as well have been standing there naked.

Fatima stood facing him, not twenty feet away, yet by some minor miracle she didn't *see* him. She was lost in a cellular fog, that hazy mental limbo where people engaged distant callers as they drove their cars over embankments. Fatima's eyes were locked straight on him, but they were a blank. No alarm, no recognition.

Davis considered his options. It didn't take long — there weren't any. The gun was in her pocket. She was twenty feet away. He needed that phone right now and there was only one way.

Davis broke into a run, his first two steps skidding on the slick sidewalk. It hadn't been bad when he was just walking, but now that he was trying to move fast, Davis felt like he was ice skating, or maybe ice dancing, two hundred forty pounds of unconserved momentum in boat shoes. It didn't matter. He was committed now, no turning back — because his quick movement had drawn Fatima's attention.

Her focus came sharp as she recognized Davis. She dropped the phone, dug into her pocket. Davis kept moving, legs pumping, gaining speed. His bad thigh felt like it was shredding. Halfway there she had the gun swinging level, slow and controlled. Or maybe it just seemed that way, the world slowing down. She had it pointed right at him, and Davis heard an animalistic scream. He wasn't going to make it.

He raised his hands to cover his face, hoping his headway would carry him through the first shot. The first two. He lunged, threw himself airborne in a desperation tackle. He waited for the bullet, ready to keep fighting. Then the shot came, a deafening blast at close range. Davis screamed as he flew through the air. He heard another shot, and another, all in what seemed like an instant. Then he made contact. But not firm contact — a glancing hit. Fatima had somehow slipped beneath him. She'd ducked low at the last moment, and Davis had gone right over the top.

He came down hard, sprawling across the cement. Davis never stopped moving. He was slipping and sliding again. As he moved he questioned his body, searched for the hits. Everything seemed strangely intact, still functional. He whirled his head and spotted Fatima on the ground. Davis blindly launched himself again, his feet spinning out from under him on the ice rink that was the sidewalk. But he kept going, kept moving.

Get the gun — go for the gun!

"Jammer!"

It came out of nowhere. Sorensen's voice.

Davis stopped, fell still. He allowed his gaze to settle, tried to make sense of what he saw. Fatima was lying in a heap on the sidewalk. She was completely motionless. Sorensen closed in, both arms extended with her gun trained fast. She hovered over Fatima for a moment, then kicked away a gun lying on the sidewalk. Sorensen bent down cautiously and checked for signs of life. Apparently there were none. She pointed her weapon toward the sky and backed closer to Davis.

"Are you okay?" she asked.

Davis had ended up on his knees. He eased back, grimaced as the pressure came off his ravaged thigh. "Yeah, Honeywell," he said, his breath coming in massive gulps. "Yeah, I'm just great."

Then Davis heard a faint sound, distant but undeniably familiar. It seemed like something from a dream and brought a thousand emotions at once. He spotted the source — his phone lying on the ground next to Fatima's body, half buried in a grainy footprint of slush.

Davis scrambled over and swiped it up. "Jen? Is that you?"

"Dad! What's going on? What's all that noise?"

The voice of his daughter hit him like a train, dragged his head to another place. A place he couldn't be right now. *Noise? Nothing, sweetheart. Just a friend shooting the terrorist who was about to kill me. How was school today?* The phone beeped. He had another call waiting. *Sorry, the president of the United States is on line two. He's waiting for me to save a hundred airplanes from crashing.* Davis forced himself back.

Jen was saying, "I have to talk to you about Bobby—"

"Sweetheart . . ." he stammered, "not now! I'm in the middle of something really important. I will call you back as soon as I can." He was about to hang up when he added, "But I'm glad you called, Jen. Really glad."

"Dad—"

He cut her off and picked up the other call. "Davis here."

"Where the hell have you been?"

He recognized the voice. "Sorry, Mr. President." There was a very brief pause as decorum and apologies ran their course. Davis ended it by saying, "Have you got those communication links established?"

"Yes. There are —" the president paused and Davis heard chatter in the background, "ninety-six airplanes still in the air. I think we have some kind of channel to all of them."

"*Think* isn't good enough, sir. If you fail to connect to one aircraft, we've lost two lives and probably more on the ground."

"I know, I know. We're doing our best, Davis."

"Okay, here's how I believe this works. At the top of the hour, in five minutes, every one of those airplanes is going to have its flight control computers take over, like an autopilot you can't disengage. The aircraft will run a course to the nearest target — that is, the nearest oil refinery — then go into a dive and strike it."

Davis saw a police car pull up. Bystanders were pointing at him and Sorensen. He pulled away from the phone and said to her, "Quick! Go run some interference. I can't be interrupted."

She nodded and hustled off.

Townsend's worried voice dueled with the approaching sirens. "Davis? Are you still there?"

"Yes. Now write this part down. Tell the crew of every airplane that the sequence is initiated by the airplane clock. They can defeat the takeover by resetting it. Move it back a few hours, even a day — whatever it takes to get on the ground. If they can't get that done before the top of the hour, the software is going to take over. But control can still be regained — all the crew has to do is turn off both battery switches on the overhead panel. Have you got that?"

"Battery switches — yes."

"Turn them off for ten seconds, then back on. The airplane should still be flyable in the down time and come back up clean. The clock is the key — that's what cues the entire sequence."

"We've got it," Townsend said. "We're sending it now."

"Good. I'll keep the line open." Davis looked at his very accurate watch. Four minutes.

Townsend's voice came back, "All right, we've sent the word. So now we just wait?"

"Hell, no — I mean, no Mr. President. Now we get to work. Keep double-checking that the word has gone through. Have all the air-planes contact you once they're under positive control. Some of these planes will take hours to get on the ground. Have NORAD launch their air defense fighters. Get them to escort as many as possible — but no shooting. They can help identify airplanes that are having trouble. Send out these same instructions to every country that can help. C-500s are flying all over the world and we have to track them all until the last one is safely on the ground."

Davis heard more chatter over the line. He looked for Sorensen and spotted her engaging the police. Her gun was on the ground and she was showing an ID. He wondered which company — CIA or Honeywell? She was going to have some explaining to do.

A woman in EMT gear came trotting toward him. She had a med-ical kit in her hand and said in French, "I am told you have a wound."

Davis didn't fight it. He kept the phone to his ear, but stretched out his injured leg and pointed to the spot. The woman went to work, cutting away his trouser leg. He thought, *My best pair of Dockers, shot to hell.*

"You must lie back," she ordered.

The woman put a blanket over his shoulders, and Davis leaned back gingerly. He could no longer see Sorensen amid the gathering storm of authorities and onlookers. Bystanders were circling around Fatima's body as well, while a pair of policemen tried to push them back.

The phone on the White House end had gone to speaker. Davis heard the president still giving orders. He heard information coming from a half-dozen voices, an accounting of airplanes safely on the ground. The numbers were rising rapidly. And there were no shouts of imminent disaster. Not even one. He checked his watch. Twenty sec-onds to spare.

He felt a twinge of pain from something the woman was doing to his wound.

"Keep still, please," she said.

Davis tried, and with his head resting on frozen concrete, he took a deep breath and closed his eyes.

He pictured the cockpit of a C-500 and imagined the flash messages crews were getting at this very moment, imagined them resetting clocks. Others — those who didn't read the message right away, or who spent too much time deciding if the crazy instructions were some kind of twisted joke sent by a flight dispatcher — would get the scare of a lifetime. They'd be riding in an airplane that no longer responded to their commands. At that point, they'd realize the situation was dead serious and start powering down electrical busses in a frenzy to save their airplanes.

Davis hoped that's how it was all happening.

He racked his brain for anything else, any uncovered angle. Nothing came to mind. When he opened his eyes again, he was staring straight up at the night sky. There were still clouds above, but the ceiling had gone to a broken layer, the moon and stars filtering down through vague, misty gaps. It was heavenly. Davis spotted a glimmer up high, a tiny set of sequenced flashing lights — an airplane soaring miles overhead. There was a chance it was a C-500, the crew fighting for their lives. But more likely it was something better.

Still, he couldn't pull his eyes away as he watched the blinking beacons. They carried on true, no turns or swerves or dives. Just kept going, steady and serene. At that moment, Jammer Davis very much wished he was up there, slipping smooth and quick through the cold winter air.

EPILOGUE

The terminal meeting had been prearranged, the purpose being to conclude affairs after the last decimating attack. It was held, by Dubai's arrangement, in a region referred to as the Empty Quarter, a name that had been coined a thousand years ago but stood as accurate today as it had then. Deep in the ungoverned desert of northern Yemen, Rub al-Khali was as barren as the moon, an endless ocean of sand dunes that flowed to the Saudi border and beyond.

The night was clear and cold, a deep burgundy sun having surrendered hours ago to the full moon that now cast its silver veneer over the desolate terrain. A single large tent was the sole convenience, and acted as focal point for the heaviest security effort to date. Three dozen armed men patrolled a perimeter that was defined by a convoy of six Chevy Suburbans. The trucks were parked in a rough circle, although large gaps gave the image of a wagon train come short. Two helicopters also lay in wait, their anxious pilots chain-smoking, ready to launch on a moment's notice. It helped no one's nerves that the men inside the tent were arguing vociferously.

All six members of the CargoAir board of directors were present — Saudi Arabia, Dubai, Russia, Singapore, Abu Dhabi, and Switzerland. Their bellowing voices competed for attention, competed for air. It would have been worse had the sound not been muted by the heavy fabric of the large tent.

"Enough!" Luca Medved screamed, having had enough. "We are

wasting time! There is no use speculating with regard to how our plan failed. We cannot go back. Our only option now is to disband. It is time for each of us to pull his ripcord and escape the entire affair."

"I would like nothing better," Singapore shouted, "but with what means? My accounts have been frozen, every single one!"

Five sets of eyes went to Switzerland.

"As have mine," he said defensively. "I tell you, I have operated from these tax havens my entire professional life, but never have I seen such a level of government involvement. Switzerland, the Bahamas, Lichtenstein — all of them. Banking laws that have been on the books for five hundred years are being ignored, thrown away only for us. We have bitten off too much."

"You were supposed to be the expert," Saudi Arabia accused. "Now is not the time to realize this could happen."

There was finally a break, a moment of stillness.

It was Medved, the Russian, who filled the void. "But what bothers me most, gentlemen, is what has *not* happened. Why are we not sought individually? Our personal finances have been shut down, and we can no longer access the wealth of our nations. Clearly, they know who we are. Yet our names are not in the newspapers, nor our pictures on television. And here we sit, united as ever. *Why?*"

Quiet fell again, for none could answer that question.

Ten miles to the west, a U.S. Air Force B-2 bomber was gliding smoothly at twenty-four thousand feet. It was, like the C-500, a flying wing design. Indeed, from an aerodynamic standpoint, there were great similarities between the two aircraft. The glaring difference involved payload. On this night, the jet designated *Spirit of Texas* was carrying twelve GBU-31 JDAMs — two thousand pound bombs that were guided by an intensely accurate marriage of inertial and satellite inputs.

The weapons operator in the right seat monitored his display. They had been watching the site for two hours, long before the target set had become complete. Under magnification, the right seater momentarily amused himself by distinguishing which of the guards were smoking and which were not. He confirmed his coordinates before announcing, "Target locked, weapons master arm shows a green light."

The pilot in command keyed his secure radio. "PORTAL, Plank 21 is inbound hot, standing by authorization."

The transmission traveled by satellite link, and settled in a bunker seven thousand miles west and four miles down. "Roger, Plank 21. PORTAL, here. Confirm no change in target status."

"Plank 21, negative. No vehicle movement, and all choppers still cold." The aircraft commander adjusted his course ever so slightly. He didn't have to wait long for a response.

"Plank 21, PORTAL. You have authorization Golf Oscar. You are cleared hot."

"Plank 21 copy, Golf Oscar."

Eight seconds later the bomb bay doors snapped opened and six JDAMs fell sequentially from their rotary launchers. Another clutch of six weapons was reserved for the second pass — assuming there was anything identifiable left to hit. The pilot announced that his bombs were away.

Halfway around the world in a Pentagon bunker, chairman of the Joint Chiefs of Staff, General Robert Banks, answered. "Plank 21, PORTAL. We copy. Standby for possible reattack."

Banks stood watching a satellite monitor. The picture of the tent in the Empty Quarter was quite clear — until the first two-thousand pounder hit. The next five bombs were certainly overkill, all right on target. "Shack!" he said on the radio. "Nice work, Plank."

Banks, a native of Austin, couldn't resist muttering under his breath, "There's a little Spirit of Texas for you, you bastards."

Fredericksburg, Virginia

"Okay, Dad, I'm ready!"

Davis was fiddling with the coffeepot in the kitchen. "All right, hang on! I'm coming!" he called. The thing finally started chugging and he went to the living room. Jen wasn't there. He looked up the stairs and saw her standing at the top. Davis had not been prepared. The view took his breath away.

She was posed on the top landing. Her evening dress was stunning, her hair shimmered in the light. And then there was the smile — the one he'd seen a thousand times before. Jen was the image of her mother.

Her smile suddenly sagged. "What's wrong?" she asked. "Don't you like the dress? Aunt Laura and I spent a whole day shopping for it."

Davis wiped the stupefied look off his face. "It's beautiful, baby. You can't imagine how beautiful."

The glow returned, a smile that could light the world. She came down the stairs carefully, awkwardly in mid-rise heels. She stopped two steps from the bottom and stood along the banister. He wondered when she'd become a woman. Soon Jen would be driving, graduating, heading off to college. Navigating life's waypoints all on her own.

Davis went closer, engaged his daughter eye-to-eye. "You're a vision, sweetheart."

She checked the clock on the wall. "Bobby's going to be here any minute!"

Don't remind me, Davis thought. He said, "Great."

"Dad, do you really have to stay the whole time? Can't you just drop us off and then —"

"Jen!" he said. "No more! We have been over this. I talked to Bobby's mom and we agreed I'd chaperone. I drive you there, I stay. Period."

"You don't trust me!"

"I trust *you*."

"So you don't trust Bobby?"

"I don't even know Bobby."

He watched her face, saw the cracks begin to form. *Here it comes,* he thought. *Great going, Jammer.* When he'd first gotten home from France, there had been hugs and kisses. They lasted ten minutes. Then it was back to the usual parent-teen roller coaster — one minute they were best friends, the next inmate and warden.

Davis was saved by the doorbell.

"Oh my God!" she cried. "He's here!"

Davis made a move for the door.

"No!" Jen whispered, horrified.

Davis stopped in his tracks. Facing away from his daughter, his eyes went to the heavens. "All right," he said, "all right. Give Bobby the full treatment. I'll be in the kitchen."

Davis strode away, forced himself to close the connecting door. The coffeemaker was in top gear, making a throaty gurgling noise like it was choking on whatever he'd put in the filter. So he didn't hear the front door open. Didn't hear anything until Jen called out, "*Daddy!*"

Something in her tone made his blood go cold.

He bolted to the living room and saw Jen backing away from the door. Davis rushed to put himself in between the two. It wasn't Bobby Taylor. On the left and right of his doorstep were two clean-cut men nearly as big as he was. Between them was the president of the United States.

The two bodyguards looked very alert, and Davis realized he was set in a strong stance. He eased up.

The president put out a hand. "Hello, Davis. Good to meet you."

Davis shook hands. "Hello, sir."

Truett Townsend looked past him into the living room. "I hope I haven't come at a bad time."

"No, no. Not at all."

Townsend looked at him expectantly.

"Oh, sorry," Davis said. "Would you like to come in?"

"If you can spare a few minutes."

The president stepped over the threshold, his two Secret Service men right behind. Davis looked outside and saw an armored convoy on the street in front of his house — three limos, four Suburbans, and a half-dozen black-and-whites. The vehicles were surrounded by a platoon of Secret Service and uniformed police. Mrs. Irving across the street was standing in her driveway wearing a housedress and a priceless expression of bewilderment.

Davis eased the door shut and saw Jen eyeing the president. She was positively starstruck.

"Oh," Davis said, "sorry. This is my daughter, Jennifer."

Townsend shook Jen's hand and said, "You look magnificent, dear. Are you going out with your father?"

"Uh — well, no. I don't dress for him — I mean — it's not for him. I'm going to a dance. You know. With a boy." She closed her eyes, bit her bottom lip.

Townsend smiled. The president was probably used to it.

"Have a seat," Davis said, sweeping the sports section up from the couch.

Townsend did.

"Can I offer you some coffee?"

"Yes, actually. Black would be great."

"Jen," Davis said, "would you mind?"

His daughter collected herself enough to take the cue. "Okay, Dad. Sure." She headed for the kitchen, but not without a few bobble-headed glances over her shoulder to make sure this was happening.

Townsend said, "I'm sorry you weren't able to make the ceremony yesterday, Davis. We —"

"Jammer."

"Sorry?"

"Everybody calls me Jammer."

"Oh, right. Well, Jammer, we quietly honored a handful of people who helped keep the damage from this disaster to a minimum."

"Please don't think I wasn't honored by the invitation. I had some important things to take care of here at home."

Townsend nodded. "I can see that. You made the right choice. But you really saved our butts. If those airplanes had done what they were programmed to do, a lot of people would have died. Not to mention the economic impact — it would have been a disaster all around."

"If you ask me, Earl Moore was the real hero. And I wouldn't be standing here today if it wasn't for Miss Sorensen."

"Yes, Miss Sorensen. She's still over in France, tying up loose ends. I'm going to make a point of seeing her when she gets back."

"So am I," said Davis.

The president's eyes narrowed and the hint of a smile creased his lips.

Jen came in with a tray holding two cups of Davis' special brew. She gave one to the president and he immediately took a sip. Didn't spit it out. Davis took the second cup as one of the Secret Service men leaned over to Townsend and whispered something in his ear.

The president addressed Jen, "I think your escort has arrived. A young man by the name of Bobby Taylor?"

Jen nodded excitedly.

Davis had a vision — the Taylor kid outside getting frisked by the president's Secret Service detail. He kind of liked the idea. Maybe the kid would figure that's what you got when you made a move on Jammer Davis' daughter.

Townsend signaled to his man. The door opened and a wide-eyed Bobby Taylor came in under escort. He was dressed in an ill-fitting suit and had a plastic box with a corsage dangling forgotten at his side. To his credit, he seemed to recognize the president of the United States. Jen took social flight and issued proper introductions to her overwhelmed date — first the president, followed by her father. Davis didn't take offense.

Having given Jen her moment, Davis said, "Sweetheart, can you give the president and me a few minutes?" He gave a nod toward the stairs and Jen led Bobby up to her room. Davis checked to make sure the door was left open.

He turned to Townsend. "You have kids, right?"

"Two, both grown. But I can remember. Tough, isn't it?"

"Yep."

Townsend sipped again. "Anyway, Jammer, I just wanted to tell you in person how much I appreciate everything you did. Not a single airplane was lost. We've determined that they were set to strike the biggest refineries across the world."

"Jaber programmed it like I thought?"

"Yes, his software had the flight computers taking over at the exact time you said they would. It also instructed the flight data recorders to blank out when the clock kicked everything off."

"For insurance," Davis reckoned, "in case of a malfunction. Like World Express 801."

"Yes. Jaber was a clever man. I guess he wanted to prove it to the world before he died. The postmortem showed he had advanced stage cancer — the primary site couldn't even be determined, but he wouldn't have lasted more than a few weeks."

"Fatima got to him first. She was a real piece of work."

"That, she was," Townsend agreed. "She brought it all together. She took over Caliph's system, a potent network of suicide warriors. Then she sold their services to the highest bidder."

"Profiteering disguised as holy war."

"Yes. We believe the entire CargoAir consortium was created with this plot in mind. A handful of sovereign wealth fund managers put the company together — roughly five billion dollars that they hoped to turn into fifty times as much."

"So you know who they are," Davis surmised.

"Yes."

Nothing more came, and Davis had to ask, "Do you know *where* they are?"

The president took a long look at his watch. "I have a pretty good idea." Instead of expanding on this, he said, "In the end, CargoAir was to aviation what Chernobyl was to clean energy. Our intel people estimate that at least half of those airplanes would have made it to their targets. If you hadn't figured things out, we'd be facing a damned global economic catastrophe."

"I just paid six bucks a gallon for regular yesterday. I'd say there's been some damage done."

"Yes, no doubt. But I got briefed a few hours ago — the refinery repairs are running well ahead of schedule. Worldwide, we should be back to ninety percent production within three months. It's a big hit, but nothing like it could have been."

"And what about Caliph?"

"We messed up there. All those pictures of him on the Web — taunting, just daring us to find him. It was all misdirection, a ploy to throw us off."

"So he wasn't even involved?"

"No. But I *can* tell you that Caliph will never harm us again."

Davis wasn't sure what that meant, but he took it for fact.

Townsend smacked a palm on his thigh. "You know what? I forgot the medal. I brought a little token of our appreciation, but it's out in the limo." The president paused long enough to look around the room. Davis' own I-love-me wall hadn't made it out of the moving boxes yet—even though they'd been living here for three years. Townsend added, "But I know that kind of thing doesn't mean much to some people."

Davis caught his drift. "I'll find a spot for it, sir."

"So will you go back to the NTSB, Jammer?"

Davis shrugged. "Like I said, right now I've got some higher priorities."

"Fair enough. But if you ever do go back, you can go anywhere you want. I'll personally see to it."

"I appreciate that. But if I do go back, I'd probably just prefer to keep the same old job."

The two locked gazes for a moment. As a career politician, it probably surprised Townsend to see his largesse turned down. But then he nodded and seemed to understand.

A security man eased between them and tapped his watch. The president stood and Davis followed him to the door. They shook hands and Truett Townsend spoke in an earnest tone, "Jammer, if there's ever anything I can do for you, please let me know."

"Thanks," Davis said.

He watched the president and his detail recede down the front steps toward the motorcade. When they were halfway to the street, Davis shouted, "Actually, Mr. President, there is one thing—"

Ten minutes later Davis again stood on his front porch. This time he watched President Townsend walking arm-in-arm with his daughter toward an armored limo.

Jen was over the moon, about to arrive at her first high school dance in a presidential motorcade, a touch of style that would be talked about in the halls for a generation. Immediately behind her, Bobby Taylor was wedged in between two of the president's biggest men—

he looked like a toothpick between two oaks. Davis was surprised, though, when he actually rushed forward and pulled open the rear door for Jen. Maybe there was hope for the kid after all.

After hitting the school drop-off loop, the plan was for one armored limousine and the two burly agents to remain behind and stand watch at the dance. When it ended, the Secret Service would bring the two teenagers home. Safe and sound. Davis watched Jen, Bobby Taylor, and President Townsend climb into the back of the limo. They were all smiling.

Jammer Davis was smiling.

Lights began to flash, sirens blared, and a squad of police motorcycles led the way as the motorcade snaked into motion. Davis caught a glimpse of Mrs. Irving peering out her front window. He gave her the queen's wave, then went back to watching the procession as it drew away down the street.

It was a great visual.

Coffee cup still in hand, he took a long, hearty sip. Then spit it out on the lawn. "God that's bad!" he muttered. Truett Townsend was either very polite or his taste buds were shot. Davis dumped the remains on a dormant shrub by the front door. He watched the motorcade until the last car was gone, then went inside a satisfied man.

Moments later, the front porch light came on.

AUTHOR'S NOTE

A few words regarding the technical details of this book. The C-500 aircraft, of course, is a creation of my own, yet the idea of a flying wing cargo aircraft has been studied for many years, to include a number of NASA conceptual designs. The inherent aerodynamic efficiency of the flying wing configuration may well lead to the launch of such an aircraft within the decade.

With regard to certain aircraft systems — in particular, flight recorder backup power and electrical bus tie-ins — I have taken some liberties from standing architecture for the sake of simplification. The essence of interplay between these systems, however, I hold to be largely plausible. Any other technical errors or faulty assumptions are my own.

As to fly-by-wire flight control systems, they are a fact of life. Fly-by-wire technology has been with us for nearly forty years and, by and large, has been beneficial to the safety of flight. But as with any technology, designers and flight safety experts must make an effort to challenge new systems from every conceivable angle — something I hope to have done here.

ACKNOWLEDGMENTS

The assistance of certain people was invaluable in the creation of this novel. All thanks to the wonderful staff of Oceanview Publishing. In particular, Bob and Pat Gussin, and Susan Greger for their continued support and enthusiasm. Thanks also to Frank Doran, of L3 Communications, for his expertise on flight recorders. To Sam Yarish, former U.S. Secret Service countersniper, for his tactical wisdom, and also his enduring patience in helping me shoot straight. Thanks to my agent, Susan Gleason, for her steady encouragement. And as always, to my family for their unwavering patience and support.

Last but not least, thanks to the real Jammer Davis. The character is not you. But then, it never could be.